A Knight and a Spy 1410

Simon Fairfax

Other books by Simon Fairfax
Medieval series

A Knight and a Spy 1410

A Knight and a Spy 1411

A Knight and a Spy 1412

Deal series

A Deadly Deal

A Deal Too Far

A Deal With The Devil

A Deal On Ice

Published by Corinium Associates Ltd.

A CIP catalogue of this book is available from the British Library

ISBN: 978-1-999 6551-5-0
Info@simonfairfax.com
www.simonfairfax.com

For my son, the real Jamie, who rode Richard like a centaur and swung a polo stick as well as any sword.

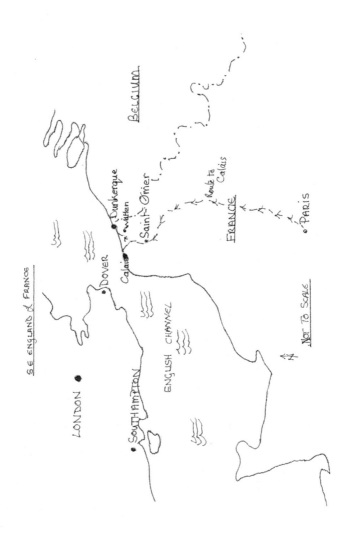

SE England and France

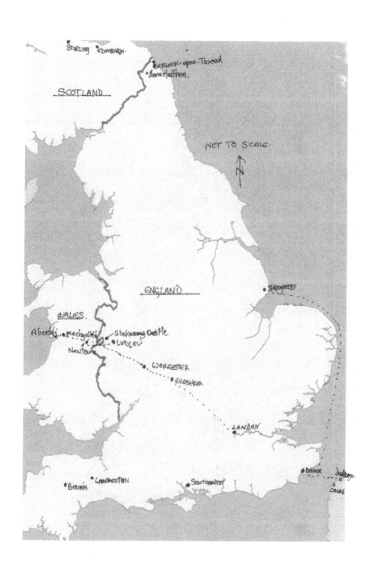

Map of Journey

Chapter One

Paris: January 1410

The figure padded through the cobbled streets, stepping lightly on the balls of his feet, the thin and lightly cushioned soles of his boots giving him the advantage of stealth despite the fact that the time for subterfuge and claims of innocence were long gone. His senses, honed through years of training, instinctively told him that he was being followed – and by more than one person, if his acute hearing did not deceive him.

The faint sounds of pursuit resonated from the two streets running parallel to his, and a third sound came from behind: they had him boxed in. Even in his peril the fugitive was puzzled: *Why no hue and cry? If his deed had been discovered, why not raise the Watch and run through the streets crying murder?*

The hooded figure, clad in dark grey, looked up at the night sky, cloudy and swollen with snow waiting to fall. It was bitterly cold and only the low temperature had kept the full force of the blizzard at bay. But already a light sprinkling had fallen and the fugitive was leaving a trail that even his light steps could not hide. He knew what he had to find, and he knew he had to find it quickly. They would be upon him soon enough. The timber frames of the shops and the wattle infill of the buildings offered no cover, no purchase for climbing. The shallow barred doorways gave no recess for hiding.

Up ahead in the gloom he saw what he wanted, on the corner of a narrow side street where the main boulevard curved to the left. A water trough, iced over now, sat beneath a metal sign that displayed the crest of the weavers' guild. The fugitive sprinted, leaping from the balls of his feet. He landed on the icy edge of the wooden trough, held his footing and sprang upwards, seeking a hold on the metal bar that supported the sign, praying that it would bear his weight. It did. He swung, arching his back to gain momentum, and swung again. On the second swing, he pulled himself upwards, landing with his stomach across the bar. Pushing himself up with his hands, he managed to stand with his feet and hands on the bar, then before gravity took him he leapt upwards, securing a handhold on a wooden dragon jetty that protruded over the street. He repeated the process again and found himself at roof level, in the lea of the eaves where two gables met and formed a shallow valley gutter, offering an escape route onto the roofscapes of Paris.

He crouched to prevent his silhouette from showing against the skyline and scurried quickly up the gutter, over a ridge and down a similar gutter overlooking the side alley. He paused, quieting his breathing, remaining immobile, waiting and listening. His ploy would soon be discovered. Footsteps in the snow didn't just stop, and people didn't suddenly take to the air. But it had bought him some time, and he knew he could no longer use the street with the snow giving him away. His senses were soon rewarded. A cloaked figure surged around the bend, looking down at the footprints and around at all potential hiding places for fear of ambush. The snow was falling faster now, filling in the fugitive's footsteps. The pursuer ran on, fearing the loss of his quarry. But then the fugitive heard his pursuer stop, clearly puzzled by the lack of tracks, and he knew he must act or be caught.

As the buildings rose, more wooden jetties protruded, cantilevered across the narrow lane, so close they almost touched. He spotted a window standing slightly ajar on the opposite building. There were no window dressings, there was no candlelight within. Servants' quarters this high up, he presumed, edging his way forward, feeling exposed as he was briefly outlined against the skyline. The gap between one building and the next was an easy transition and he fell once more into shadow. He took a knife from the sheath at his belt, and it was the act of a moment to push up the catch. He eased himself through the open window, into the safety of the gloom within, his movements lithe and almost soundless. He pulled the window in on silent hinges, leaving it in the position he had first seen it, as he heard voices below.

"*Merde*! Francois, to me," his main pursuer hissed as another figure joined the two men below. "Where has the murderous pig gone?" The hushed and determined voices cursed as the pursuers returned to the main street. He heard one say. "He must have gone up. Check the roof all along. He cannot get far."

Smiling to himself, the fugitive turned, adjusting his eyesight to the gloom and the vague shadows of sparse furniture. As he completed the turn, a sharp point pierced the skin below his eye, drawing a trickle of blood. The blade of the sword was barely evident in the gloom. A recumbent figure lay half raised on a trestle bed, the sword held by a steady arm at full stretch. A voice whispered in the darkness.

"Move and I take your eye, and then your life. Hands up above your head."

The intruder cursed himself for a fool. Pleased to escape his pursuers, he had forgotten his training, and only now did he hear the breathing of his interrogator.

"Drop to your knees," the voice commanded, and he complied. "Now on your face."

The sword point had followed him expertly all the way, and was now pointing down at his eye socket. The blade was abruptly removed, he heard a scratch of flint as a candle spluttered to life and the room was bathed in a gentle glow, illuminating his prostrate figure. All the intruder could see was the bare feet and leggings of the swordsman who now stood upright, a few steps away. With the candle lit, the sword was back on him, the point steady, offering no chance of retaliation. He calmed himself, biding his time.

"My lord Thomas! Come my lord, we've caught a gutter rat." The man shouted, presumably to a friend in the rooms below. He heard the sounds of doors opening and muffled steps. Three men appeared at the door of the garret. One, clearly a servant, was prepared with a long knife, ready to defend himself. Candlelight flickered from the blade. One of the men, the eldest of the three, took command.

"That will do. Let me through, I'm sure John has it all secured."

The two servants pulled back, parting to allow their master to pass between them into the small room. His hair was awry and he wore a warm padded night coat, belted tightly around his thickening figure. His deep-set eyes were bleary with sleep, yet wary.

"What has occurred, John? How did this villain find himself in your room?"

"He entered through my window. You know how I cannot

abide the closeness of a room, even in winter. He is good. I only sensed him as I'm a light sleeper." They had spoken in English, but now John reverted to French.

"Up, cur. On your feet – carefully, mind, or I'll gut you. Undo your cloak and move it aside."

Moving slowly, the fugitive complied, exposing the sheathed knife at his belt which John deftly removed, maintaining his grip on the sword. He pushed upwards onto his knees and in a seemingly innocent move, brushed his hands upwards past his boot tops. The move was fast, and with blinding speed his right hand swept up holding a slim bladed stiletto with which he lunged at the grizzled soldier holding the sword, who had relaxed his grip slightly, dropping his guard and moving his blade to one side. But John was an old soldier, and he used years of muscle memory in an apparently casual flick of the wrist, deflecting the stab and bringing his sword down through the cloth on his assailant's forearm as he did so, expecting to see blood drip from the resulting wound. He stepped forward and smashed his left elbow into the jaw of the assailant, who dropped to the floor, semi-conscious. An evil grin split the old soldier's face. He had enjoyed the brief exchange and stepped back to replace his elbow with a sword tip, carefully sweeping away the stiletto with his foot as he did so.

"Swallow your teeth, then get up," he ordered. "If you do anything like that again I will kill you."

The dazed figure rubbed his jaw and gently opened his mouth to see if it still worked as it should. The blow had been fast and very hard, delivered with a brutality born of long practice. With the cloak and hood removed and his hands exposed, the fugitive stood before the two men. His skin was olive and his eyes were dark grey in the dim light.

"Ho, a heathen Saracen, by the looks of him. That explains

the tricks. Any more knives on you, boy? Answer me or I'll cut your clothes and boots off to check."

"I am not a heathen *saraceni*!" The fugitive snapped, clearly angered at the assumption. He answered in French but with a strange accent. "I am a Christian, an Italian."

"An *assassinato*? Yes, don't look surprised, I've met your creed before in the Holy Land. Murdering devils. What's your name, boy?"

"Cristoforo Corio, at your service." The young man replied with a flourish and a slight bow.

A frown creased John's features. "Insolent dog, I'll have your ears off."

Also aware of the creed of assassins, Master Thomas put a hand on John's arm and fired off his own question. "Well you've certainly got the arrogance for it. Who do you serve and why are you here?"

Chapter Two

The questions hung in the air unanswered as Cristoforo Corio looked from one man to the other in the gathering silence. John seemed to have a permanent scowl upon his face, forged by a long scar that ran vertically across his left eye. The eyeball was marled, indicating partial blindness. The tousled hair and well-trimmed beard were streaked with grey, framing a tanned and weathered face that showed evidence of the man's time under foreign suns. Despite his middle years, his ability with the sword showed no sign slowing. He held the weapon almost negligently, but Cristoforo knew he'd be ready to use if any further aggression was shown.

The other man, Thomas, was completely different. He was of a similar age to John, but his jowls were heavier, his body was bulky with good living and he looked a good deal more unfit than his servant. But he bore a stamp of authority, and carried himself with the demeanour of one who was used to giving orders rather than taking them. He gesticulated impatiently at Cristoforo.

"Answer my questions or we hand you over to the Watch

and let them hang you for the murdering thief you doubtless are," he snapped. John's sword arm twitched and the weapon appeared in a guard position as if by magic, reinforcing his master's demand. Cristoforo sighed and answered.

"I was on an errand, the outcome of which caused me to be chased through the streets on a misunderstanding. The men would not listen to reason, so I ran, pursued by three armed guards. They wanted my life and were not prepared to listen, so I chose to escape, eluding them temporarily, I took to the rooftops, saw an opportunity in your open window and took it. And here you find me." He spread his arms apart and shrugged in a typically Italian way. "I meant no harm *signori*, I merely wanted to escape my pursuers and leave quietly when they had passed on." His attitude was that of someone giving a perfectly reasonable explanation.

Keeping a wary eye on the man, John moved to the window and glanced down, realising that Cristoforo must have leapt and climbed with great agility to achieve such a feat of acrobatics. Could he have mirrored such a feat in his youth? Probably not, he ceded grudgingly. The lad was obviously well trained and dangerous.

As a merchant and master weaver, Thomas de Grispere was used to travelling abroad, meeting people and summing them up quickly and accurately. In Cristoforo Corio he saw an intelligent young man, educated, with a good command of French. He probed further: "I can surmise what your errand was. Who did you murder, and on whose orders?"

Cristoforo made to protest, then caught the look in Thomas's eye.

"I had no paymaster on this occasion. He was a merchant, like yourself, and he committed a crime against my family," he finished quietly.

"And?"

"I was not paid to kill him for his misdeeds." Cristoforo's answer implied that his actions were intended to pass on a message.

"What did he do, this merchant, that demanded so harsh a penalty?"

"He raped a woman, a lady of gentle birth and good reputation." Cristoforo snapped, as if begrudging the continued interrogation. John and Master Thomas shared a knowing glance, sensing that they were finally getting to the truth.

"Who was this woman? Why did her family not go to the courts and seek justice there?"

Despite the cold, the Italian blushed, looking down, his eyes filling with hot tears that he kept unshed. Finally he said: "She was my sister, and she was so ashamed after the attack that she drowned herself, leaving a note telling all." He then smiled a wicked smile that held no mirth. "But I gelded the pig and took his tongue ere I killed him, and he died like a beached fish seeking oxygen, with no voice to cry out with. And I would do it again in an instant."

"But the courts would still act, more so if a young woman's life was forfeit."

"*Signor*, have you travelled to Italy?"

Thomas nodded. "Many times."

"Well then you know how religious the people are. Suicide, even a suspected suicide, is against God's law." Cristoforo crossed himself and muttered a quick prayer. "Also, the man involved was very rich and powerful, commanding the influence of the leading citizens of *Firenze*. My sister and I are not of noble birth, our family has little status. Money and influence are the ultimate power. Anything other than direct action would have been futile." He looked with pity at Thomas and his naivety.

Thomas's response was wordless, just a grunt in acceptance of what he knew to be true.

"We'll keep you here tonight and decide your fate in the morning. I'm returning to my cot. No more disturbing my sleep, or I'll turn you over to the watch or your vengeful friends below." He glared balefully at Cristoforo, who bowed his head in acquiescence, unaccountably happy until John killed his hopes dead.

"Right lad, I'll have the knife from your other boot – slow as you like." Cristoforo's surprise at being found out was etched on his face as he reached for the second knife he carried and presented it to John. "No. Drop it to the floor, I've seen that trick before," John said. "Now turn half around," Corio did so, scowling slightly. *Could he know?* Sure enough, John slapped his back with the flat of his sword, hearing a metallic clunk as it made contact with the weapon that was strapped between his shoulder blades.

"I'll have that toothpick too."

"How did you..."

"Never mind how. Draw it slowly." John's lips twitched in what might have been a smile. Cristoforo reached up between his shoulder blades, securing a grip on the slim hilt and slowly withdrawing the blade of a specially fashioned Falchion. It was double edged in the Italian style, with a smaller cross guard than normal and a blade of about 16 inches that glittered wickedly in the candlelight.

"Please let me present it to you, I have no wish to drop my *Falcione*," he pleaded. John's sword danced in front of his eyes as Cristoforo placed the blade onto his open palm, knowing that one false move would cost him an eye, or worse. John clearly knew all the tricks. He flicked it expertly up into the air and caught it by the handle.

"Out there." He gestured to the landing outside the room,

which led to a solid wooden door that was being guarded by a servant. Master Thomas pulled back the catch and motioned him to step inside. He saw by the dim light that it was a store cupboard, full of blankets and other household essentials, but offering no window to the outside world. Resigned to his fate, Cristoforo shrugged and entered, turning as the door was sealed shut with an external locking pin. He then heard the wooden wedge being hammered home.

"Thank you, John. You saved us again," Thomas's man-at-arms nodded, bade his master good night and returned to his trestle, rolling back up in his blankets and falling asleep within minutes. Like any good soldier he slept when he could and had learned to do so under any circumstances.

Chapter Three

The following morning Cristoforo was released by John, who was now fully dressed, a scabbard belted at his waist over a thick, padded gambeson bearing the crest of Thomas's guild and crest. The captive was grumpy.

"I need to piss." He grumbled.

John motioned to a chamber pot in the corner of the room. As Cristoforo noisily relieved himself, he questioned John over his shoulder. "So what happens now? Will Master Thomas release me, do you think?"

"Wait and see."

Tying his braise, he turned to face John, arms akimbo. "So lead on and take me to my fate."

John nodded towards the stairs, and Cristoforo responded with a shrug. He stepped down to the next level and finally to the parlour below. The room was well furnished, heated by a roaring log fire that dominated the room even at this early hour, throwing its benevolent warmth into the furthest corners. Master Thomas occupied a padded settle to one side of the parlour, reading papers in earnest concentration. He looked up at John and Cristoforo from under raised brows, pausing from his studies, and returned to what was occupying him. Cristoforo had been taught patience, and he moved to the fireplace and stood with his back to the blaze, warming his hands behind him and awaiting Master Thomas' satisfaction.

A servant entered the room from the street, stepped forward and whispered in his master's ear, offering furtive glances in Cristoforo's direction. Twice, Thomas glanced across at the figure before the fire. With a final nod he dismissed the servant and stood to address Cristoforo.

"It seems you are skilled in your profession. Monsignor Deauville is indeed dead, murdered in his bed I believe. You are the talk of the city. A mysterious assassin, a Saracen, a spirit, a sprite come to life. Mothers are telling their children that if they misbehave, the assassin's spirit will get them." Thomas widened his eyes in a mirthless parody of a conjurer.

"I have no regrets, as I explained. My spirit is pure, may God forgive me, but I deal in honour, not the law. If I go to my death then it is fate and the stars that decree it. My sister's honour is avenged." He shrugged, apparently careless of his fate.

"I have a more useful purpose for you. And one that will spare you from the death you may or may not deserve. Listen before you posture in such dramatic gestures!" Thomas told him as the assassin rolled his eyes. "Your life may be forfeit in your heart, but I am minded to extend it for my own benefit – and therefore your own. I have need of someone with abilities and skills such as yours to facilitate my endeavours. A broader explanation: I travel throughout the Continent, and while John here..." he gestured to the watchful man-at-arms, "...is my bodyguard, I need more subtle services on certain occasions – and no, this will not entail murdering my competitors."

Cristoforo Corio was surprised: "You mean to say that you

will not turn me over to the magistrate or the servants of the man I killed?"

"That's exactly what I mean. I loathe rapists, and all men who take advantage of the weaker sex. But there are conditions. You will accompany me to England, and once there you will prove your worth and loyalty. I will be watching you closely. One false step, one treacherous move and your life will be as forfeit as if you were hung by the gallows today."

"To England? But that means crossing the Channel. I hate the sea, I fear water. They say that devils lurk in England and that it is wet and cold, causing men to die from pestilence and plagues of ill humours brought on by the climate." Corio was genuinely alarmed, shrinking at the thought of a sea crossing and whatever lay beyond.

At this John guffawed. "What? This ails you, lad? The heartless killer is frightened of a short sea crossing and a little wind and rain? You are nought but a spineless knave." He rounded upon him, and Corio blushed at the insults, spitting out a harsh response in his native tongue before responding in French.

"What do you know of me? I do what I do and am not afraid of any man, but the devils of the sea and the demons of a foreign land where all manner of evil lurks? Yes, this scares me."

"I care not for the superstitions you have of our fair land, nor of a sea crossing that I have achieved more times than I can remember. The choice is before you: accept my terms or stay and face justice here with the magistrate. Well?" Thomas demanded as Corio fought his own fears.

"I accept your terms," he said finally. "I will accompany you to England. But when will I be free? Am I to be bound to you forever? When will I see my family and my homeland again?"

"You should have considered that before you embarked upon your murderous deed. But I am not an unreasonable man and I shall see how you serve me. I will pay you and offer lodgings if you do well. But know this," he moved to within a few inches of Cristoforo, until their faces were almost touching. "Papers will be lodged with my advocate here, and if you betray me – on the road or later – and if I do not return safely from wherever my travels take me, word will be sent to him, a warrant for your arrest will be issued, and for that of your father who was implicit in the assassination. Do I make myself clear?"

Once again Cristoforo's hopes were dashed. He had hoped to slip away on the road to Calais or at the port itself and make his way back to Florence. Now it seemed that his future was inescapably bound to that of his new master.

"I understand. Master de Grispere, I have a boon to ask."

"You demand favours?" John interceded. "Knave, you'll get a favour from the flat of my sword." He snarled. But Thomas was curious and seemed well-disposed towards the boy, who was about the same age as his own son.

"Tell me, but be quick. We leave within the hour."

"I can't be seen on the streets, but my lodgings are near here. Could one of your men seek them out and retrieve my leather satchel? It contains things that are dear to me."

Thomas nodded in assent and motioned for one of his servants to come forward and take details of the lodgings and where the satchel could be found.

"Take care, lad. All may not be well on the streets." The servant nodded and left. "Good. Now we must get you dressed in different garb, you look like an Italian peacock in those colours and boots."

Corio looked down aghast: "What is wrong with my attire?"

"You look foreign. If you are to pass as one of my servants, you must dress like them. You must look English. And while

17

you're about it, try to act with less arrogance. You are now in my employ as a servant. Remember that and abide by me!"

Three hours later, Thomas de Grispere led his baggage train of mules and his two waggons towards the city's western gate and the Calais road. There was already a queue of travellers leaving Paris, even at this early hour, and Thomas and John exchanged a mutual glance that summed up the unsaid thoughts that ran between them. The men at arms guarding the gate were stopping all travellers and checking everyone on the way out. Thomas had papers of trade and identity which he had ready for such eventualities. Only the captain of the guard could read, and this was slowing progress.

Finally they reached the head of the queue, where they were stopped. The guard showed more respect than he had to the previous peasant group when he saw the mark of rank on Thomas and his easy command of his retinue, but he was still thorough, demanding to know from where he had travelled and what his business was.

"I have been through here many times, sergeant. Do you not recognise me?" he stated in a commanding tone. "I am trading with the Parisian guilds in silk and wool. I am bound for Calais and London and have a cog to meet for the tide in six days' time." He pushed aside his heavy brocaded cloak, reached into an inner pocket of his padded doublet and produced papers of trade together with his passage on a ship bound for England. The sergeant scowled at the papers and turned as his captain arrived.

"What now Jean? Ah, 'tis you, monsieur de Grispere." He said, looking up and waving the papers away. In response, Thomas gave a broad smile and nodded his thanks.

"My gratitude Captain, we must needs be at Calais for the tide."

"Of course Monsieur, and a safe journey to you. Pass them through, sergeant."

The nod was given and the party passed through under the scrutiny of the guard, who noted all members of the baggage train, including a hunched figure seated next to the driver of the covered waggon. They passed under the gate and Cristoforo crossed himself, muttering a prayer to his namesake. He was more frightened of the English Channel than he was of the French authorities, and he still harboured thoughts of escaping before his new master forced him to embark upon a vessel that would transport him across the waters separating France from the mysteries of England that lay beyond.

When they broke their journey briefly to rest and water the animals, John dismounted first and shadowed the Italian closely, muttering in his ear: "Don't think about it, lad. I'll have your ears before you get two paces."

Cristoforo grimaced in response, hugging his drab cloak about him and wishing he had his thickly lined apparel, which had been substituted for the rough tunic of a servant. After six days on the road they reached Calais, entering the heavily fortified town on much easier terms as it was under English control. Thomas de Grispere was welcomed as a well-known figure by the English garrison. John traded gruff jokes and comments with the men-at-arms with whom he shared a common bond. These were men who had been tested in the shield wall of steel and death and not found wanting. All were scarred and calloused, testimony to their hard lives.

Cristoforo looked around him. Despite being in France, the town was different. He heard the strange English tongue and saw for the first time groups of men with the war bows, tall staves of wood bent in a double arc. Here were the archers he had heard so much about. His countrymen from Genoa had hated them, had loathed being pitched against their lethal bows. They appeared arrogant and stood aside for no man, pushing through the throng as people moved aside to let them pass.

Among the noise and bustle he smelled strange yet appetising smells emanating from the taverns, inns that bore names like the Sleeping Dog and the King's Arms. To his eyes it seemed like another world. The houses and buildings were styled similarly, yet the feeling was alien to him, far less cosmopolitan than Paris. But Calais was a fortress town, a bastion against the French in what was once their own country, a country with which the English were currently enjoying an uneasy truce in a long running war. The styles of dress were eclectic, each offering a clue as to the nationality of the wearer, and the English were easily distinguishable from the traditional French countrymen.

The baggage train forced its way through the throngs of people, making its familiar way to the quayside and locating the vessel that was to transport Thomas de Grispere and his party across the channel. Cristoforo smelled the salty tang of the sea, much stronger here than the Mediterranean seaports he was used to. The quayside was paved with stone, with wooden jetties stretching out to accommodate vessels of all shapes and sizes. Seagulls cawed and dived, fighting each other for scraps and dominance. Fishermen mended their nets and cast half interested glances at the newcomers. The harbour was buzzing with activity as men cursed and fought with ropes, rigging and cargo.

At a far pier the waggons, mules and horses halted before the dark hull of a cog that loomed above them, riding easily in the gentle swell of the harbour, her bow and stern lines creaking with the strain of the rising tide. Her name, *The Swan,* was painted on her prow, white against the black. Sailors and steeves ran up and down the gangplanks, nimble as monkeys, carrying cargo or trimming the vessel in readiness for departure. Cristoforo glanced down at the murky grey waters of the channel, looked out at the swells that broke gently against the harbour walls. He shuddered, crossing himself, praying again to his patron saint and the Madonna.

A rough, sea-worn man appeared at the forecastle, better dressed than his compatriots in long sea boots and a padded leather jerkin which was greasy and shiny with age. He carried a mantle of authority and glanced down at the newly arrived party. He nodded and hailed Thomas de Grispere in English.

"I'd nearly given you up, sir. You've cut it fine. We sail by late afternoon on the high tide."

"Aye captain, and well you might be afraid. We've had our share of adventure, but we're ready now for loading. My men will help as they can. Go to, Will, unload and be ready to assist the captain's men." He ordered his head man, who nodded in turn and set about organising the others. Then he muttered a quiet aside: "John, bring the newcomer, I'll not have him questioned or known about until we're at sea."

John grunted in assent and with a firm hand at his back, forced Cristoforo away from the quay before he could resist.

"Come, take some food and ale for the journey. It'll do you good, calm your stomach."

Cristoforo shot John a look of pure malice, showing that he did not agree with anything he had suggested. They went to an alehouse two streets back from the quay. The doorway leaned at a crooked angle and they had to duck to enter. Despite the shabby external appearance, the inside was well lit by tallow candles held in sconces along the walls. The floor was covered in fresh sawdust and the trestle tables were scrubbed clean. The room was dominated by a huge fireplace of rough-hewn stone, ablaze with large logs and throwing out heat into the open bar.

A cosy atmosphere pervaded the inn and a solid, portly man clad in an apron presided behind the wooden bar.

By habit of long practice, John paused just inside the entrance, allowing his eyes to grow accustomed to the dimmer light, assessing all the customers with a sweeping glance, deciding if there was any potential threat to his master. Apparently satisfied, he walked across to a table chosen by Thomas and seated himself on a high-backed trestle with his back to the wall, his eyes on the bar and the door. He noticed that Cristoforo did the same, secure in the knowledge that his back was protected and ready for trouble. John nodded to himself approvingly. They were warriors both in their own way.

The landlord himself came over, shooing off the serving maid who made to approach their table.

"Good day to you, master de Grispere, how do you do? Good trade I hope?" He greeted his regular customer with a mixture of friendliness and deference. The question was in French and Thomas responded in kind.

"Good day to you too, landlord. Yes, a successful trip and well finished. We are on our way home, and the ship sails with the tide. Can you serve us some food ere we depart?"

"Of course, what will be your pleasure?"

"We'll have three of your beef and ale pies and tankards of your best ale."

"Of course, my lord." The innkeeper responded, and bustled off to ensure the food arrived in good time.

Turning back to the other two men, he addressed Cristoforo: "Now to you, master Cristoforo. Have you come to terms with your fate, now that we are safely free of Paris and are on English soil?"

"English? But this is not England, unless by Madonna's mercy we have spread wings and flown the Channel?"

Thomas smiled at his confusion. "No, lad. But the realm of

the English throne reaches these shores and Calais is under English jurisdiction and governorship as much as if it were the heart of London, by good King Henry's power, God bless him." He explained. "Uneasy lies the truce, for certes, but until a new war comes, the crown of England owns this land and holds it."

"Aye, and the *crapauds* hate us for it, damn their eyes," John interjected vehemently. For him the French were the perpetual enemy, only good for alliances in holy wars. Even so, eyes were raised at the comment made by the old warrior for those in earshot. A seaside town, Calais was home to people of many races, not all loyal to the English crown.

Thomas smiled at his servant's comments.

"I am still frightened." Cristoforo answered Thomas's question. "But you saved me from the gallows and I am in your debt. When will you return my weapons? I feel naked without them."

"When we are on board and you can do no harm."

"What? You don't trust me?" Cristoforo smiled wickedly.

"I trust no one, signor Corio, no one, until they earn that trust." At this point the deep crusted pies arrived upon a trencher of thick bread together with the ale. "Now eat, these are the best pies in Calais, and they'll settle your stomach." Thomas urged.

Cristoforo looked down in disgust, sceptical of the strange food, but upon breaking open the crust, a rich brown gravy emerged, soaking into the trencher and producing a mouth-watering aroma of herbs and ale. He sniffed and set to with gusto, all thoughts of the crossing forgotten.

With the meal finished, the three men reclined, looking out through the smoky latticed window that was set high in the wall. "Come, the day is darkening. The weather's bringing it to a close sooner than it should," Thomas commented. The men rose, Thomas heading towards bar counter to pay the landlord, complimenting him on his pies and promising to return soon.

They made for the door, Thomas left first, leaving the gloom and warm fug, walking out into a darkening day and a rising onshore wind. As he stepped out, Thomas half turned to say something to Cristoforo, who was following him closely behind. Two figures who had been lying in wait either side of the door appeared each side of him, while a third blocked Thomas's movement from the front. Steel glinted in the light as a dagger swung low and fast for Thomas's belt as the front man swung a cudgel at his head. The second assailant tackled Cristoforo from his left, aiming a long dagger downwards at his chest, the blade held underhand in a killing strike.

Cristoforo did not have to think. It was all pure reaction, and he almost laughed at the incompetence of his attacker as time, to his eyes, stood still. With blinding speed he reached up, deflecting the blade with his left hand, catching the wrist and twisting it backwards, wrenching his attacker's arm and forcing his elbow in a direction it was not meant to go. At the same time he punched at the exposed throat, but not in a conventional manner. His fingers were extended, like a human blade, jabbing hard and crushing the larynx. Continuing the movement with his right hand, he slipped along the dislocated limb of his lifeless attacker, grasping the weapon and spinning to his right, dropping as he did so and driving the blade into the extended leg of the cutpurse who had just sliced Thomas' money bag from his belt. The strike was well aimed, seeking and finding the femoral artery on the inside of the leg. Blood spurted as he ripped the weapon back towards him. The attacker howled an inhuman cry of pain as his life blood sprayed out across the snow-covered cobbles. The third man, distracted by the action, had struck Thomas a glancing blow, but seeing the fate of his comrades he turned and ran for his freedom. Pulling the dagger free, Cristoforo flipped the weapon in the air, deftly catching the blade by its tip. His arm blurred and the dagger flew through the air. As if by magic, its hilt suddenly protruded from between the shoulder blades of the fleeing assailant, who cried out in shock and pain as he twisted an arm up to try to pluck the blade from his back. He staggered forward and was dead before he hit the ground, his body twitching in its death throes.

The action had taken only a few seconds from start to finish. John emerged fully from the doorway, having been stopped by a fourth man inside the tavern, whose purpose had been to delay him. He had caught most of the action and looked in wonderment at Cristoforo, who was kneeling at Thomas's side.

"Signor, signor Thomas. Are you all right?" he asked, cradling the stunned man as he lay semi-prostrate on the floor. Thomas was in pain, and rubbed his bruised shoulder tenderly.

"I believe so, yes," he responded weakly. He was obviously shocked by the assault, and made to rise amid the growing throng of people surrounding him who had witnessed the attempted robbery.

John recovered and helped his master to his feet. "By the rood, I am sorry master Thomas. I was waylaid inside. It was as clever an ambush as I have seen. I spotted the blackguard yonder," he nodded at the body with the dagger protruding from his back, "and suspected some villainy, but this surprised me. And you, by God's legs," he swore, looking with awe at Cristoforo, "you're passing quick. I know of only one other with your speed, but with a sword, not a dagger!" His brow creased in a frown. "How did you deflect that blade yet come to no harm? I caught you with my sword yesterday eve, yet you filed no complaint of pain. Are you made of steel? Show me your arm." He ordered, turning the arm Cristoforo offered to

25

reveal through the cut sleeve of his jerkin a leather vambrace, laced on the inner side and cunningly reinforced with strips of supple steel.

"Ha, I suspected some knavery. A clever guise, but one that we're grateful for. That was good work and bravely done."

"Amen to that," Thomas said. "I owe you my thanks. You saved my purse and a broken head, had that cudgel landed square."

Cristoforo shrugged as if it was the most natural thing in the world, and appeared a little embarrassed at the praise.

"E was clumsy," he indicated the man lying on his side, dead from a crushed larynx, "and slow. That one was good but careless." He motioned to the second man, who had tried to crawl away but was now lying in a pool of blood, having bled to death. The other two men looked at the prostrate bodies. Neither of them was bothered nor moved by violent death. John had seen far worse and Thomas was no stranger to violence: they lived in difficult and dangerous times.

The Landlord appeared, full of apologies, concerned that he might be associated with the attack. He offered to report the matter to the sergeant-at-arms and explain everything. Thomas was only too pleased to be free of the incident, and with his two servants' help he managed to reach the quayside. Here he stopped before boarding, deep in thought. Looking directly into his eyes, he addressed Cristoforo.

"Signor Corio, it seems that I owe you my life as well as my purse. I'm not an unjust man, I pay my debts, both of honour and of wealth. I will say this to you: if you wish, you are free to go. But hear me out. I will not detain you, but if you still seek service in my employ, I will pay you for your services. What say you?"

The surprise was etched across Cristoforo's face. He looked from Thomas to John and back again.

"Signor, what I did was nothing. You undoubtedly saved my life in Paris and for me a purse is not worth a life. I respect your offer, but I too have my honour and she is a terrible mistress. I will stay, signor, until you order me to leave or the saints direct me, please God. But I have a condition," here the two men looked puzzled.

"I pray that you do not let me drown, for I cannot swim!"

John and Thomas looked at each other and both men roared with laughter.

Chapter Four

Peebles, Scotland

The spruce and pine trees stood like sentinels guarding the hillside to the south of the town. Gilded with a thick covering of snow, they cast shadows dark enough to hide the waiting war party. The mail and the cuirasses of the knights were covered by linen surcoats of dark grey, shielding any glint against the patchy moonlit sky. They wore no armour about their arms or legs, relying on speed and silence over protection. The men-at-arms stood patiently, moving their arms against the bitter cold of the night, scarves wrapped around each man's mouth muffling speech and masking the plumes of their breath.

"Are the horses secured, Jamie? I don't want to walk my arse back to England when this night's work is done" Sir Robert de Umfraville rasped quietly to the companion at his side.

"Aye, Sir Robert, the lads are holding them above the hill. They'll be good and quiet up there," the younger man assured him, then spoke of his concerns. "Do you think they'll come, sir? We've been here an hour or more and no sign."

"Fret not, lad. They'll be here, so my spy assures me, and I'll have his ears if they aren't. You'll have your fight yet." He gently clapped the younger man on the shoulder and whispered to a man-at-arms clad in a dark gambeson and a woollen cowl that shielded his open-faced helm.

"Gil, go to the bridge. Speak to the men there and see if ought's afoot. But softly mind. Slow is fast, remember?"

"Yes my lord." The man melted off into the darkness.

"We'll see them soon, laddie. They'll come by the Ludgate from the West and drop down to the bridge, and once across we'll skewer them." Jamie nodded, the impatience of youth making him keen for the action to begin. Gil materialised again in the darkness. Only minutes had passed since his departure.

"My lord, I met with Ben at the narrows. They come; you can see the torches at the gate."

Squinting into the darkness, they saw the brands held high as the war party left the town through the Ludgate, moving like some fiery serpent, marching for the bridge to cross the Tweed. Some of the war band appeared to be on foot, others were mounted on the light highland palfreys the Scots favoured. Nimble and mountain bred, they were ideal for a raiding party.

"By the torches I'd say five score or more." Gil estimated, uncertainty in his voice. They might be outnumbered, but he trusted his lord.

"Fear not Gil, we have archers and surprise on our side. We shall prevail, by God we shall. Ready men, and not a move 'til my signal. We'll have 'em boxed for slaughter. Gil, signal now!"

Gil cupped his hands around his mouth and produced a perfect imitation of a snowy owl in two mournful notes. Within seconds a response came from the woods on the other side of the road, mimicking the sound.

"Good," Sir Robert whispered. "Now we wait with patience to spring our trap." He pulled his scarf closer around his face so no breath betrayed him and waited for the enemy to arrive. Privately, he prayed that his captain of archers, hidden at the base of the stone bridge, would follow their instructions and time it perfectly for the success of the ambush for all their lives depended on it. In the stillness of the night, the watchers heard the clip of steel-shod hooves as the horses struck the cobbles of the stone bridge, and they collectively held their breaths in case their comrades in arms should be discovered hiding beneath it.

The march of the torches proceeded, and the occasional words of the barbarous Celtic tongue floated through the darkness to those lying in wait. The war band felt safe and secure this close to home. It would only be as they neared Innerleithen and the border that they would adopt a stealthier approach. From there the Scots would raid and plunder the farms and smallholdings nearby, stealing and raping, killing all in their way.

The tension mounted among the ambushers as the last of the Scots cleared the bridge. The excitement was contagious, each man finding his own way to deal with the madness of battle that took hold in those moments before combat: the dry mouth, the surge of adrenalin and the overwhelming urge to cry insanely and charge before muscles became leaden with adrenalin. Closer came the raiders, until they seemed too close, and then they heard it: the collective twang of bow cords, followed by whispers of air as the deadly barbed missiles flew through the night. Some men at the rear heard the gentle hiss and too late realised its cause. Solid thuds and cries of pain rang out as the hail of arrows hit their targets. Screams punctured the night and the Scots looked around in vain for the source of the assault. Horses whinnied and reared as they were struck or reined sharply in, adding to the confusion. Their leader rallied them to face back the way they had come and form up with whatever shields and bucklers they had.

Judging his moment, Sir Robert erupted from his hiding place, running down the slope shouting "An Umfraville, an Umfraville, kill them!" He knew his name struck fear into the Scots and used it to good effect.

His men followed him, charging down on the Scots, each man bellowing the same war cry or just roaring as loudly as they could, the killing lust upon them. Half turning to face this new threat, the Scots heard another cry from the opposite bank as the second party launched their attack only seconds later. The archers stopped firing for fear of hitting their own men, dropped their bows and ran forward with war hammers, axes and swords ready for the slaughter. The attack was brutal, and no quarter was given. The ambushers knew that an unexpected night attack is always the most frightening. The two waves of English soldiers smashed into the Scots, cutting upon impact, driving down a man, stabbing or crushing by blunt force, tramping over him and facing the next foe.

Sir Robert was at the vanguard of the attack, slashing with his battle axe, driving a vee into the melee of Scots, who were in disarray. Jamie had chosen a sword, knowing that the war band would be only lightly armoured. It was always his weapon of choice, and with little or no plate armour to protect them he inflicted heavy casualties. Such was the ferocity of the two men that they found themselves distanced from the main body of their party, briefly isolated by a sea of brand wielding Scots.

Two men faced Jamie, one wielding a war hammer, which he swung down, hoping to crush his skull despite the helm Jamie wore. Jamie deflected the full force with his sword in a cross bar, holding the blade in his steel-gauntleted left hand, catching the handle of the hammer against his blade and snapping it in two, the head flying off into the air behind. He continued his forward movement, stamping down onto the leg of the Scot, who howled as his knee dislocated and he fell to the ground. Then the second man was upon him, raising his sword for a slashing strike. Jamie turned, and instead of parrying, he drove the raised point of his sword into the exposed neck of his second assailant, knowing that the point will always beat the edge. A spray of liquid, dark in the night, spurted from the ripped throat as the man fell to his knees, vainly clutching his neck in an effort to stem the tide of blood.

Jamie reversed his blade, slashing down at the man whose leg he had broken, retrieving his sword with a rotation of his wrist and bringing it once more to a guard position.

Looking around, he saw Sir Robert in dire straits. A man had thrust a flaming brand at his exposed eyes, the sparks and pitch temporarily blinding him. Another man slashed at him with a dirk, stabbing for an opening in his mail or armour. The distance was too far for a sword blow so Jamie leapt, screaming his war cry at the top of his lungs. It was enough. Both men hesitated at the sound as a demon appeared to them in mid-flight, burnished metal shining in the light of the brand. In that instant of hesitation Jamie closed the gap, timing the slashing stroke to contact the brand wielder just as his feet made contact with the ground, giving force and balance to the stroke. Jamie's blade cleaved the leather helmet in two. Striking through to the skull beneath. The man fell to the earth stone dead, but the blade was torn from Jamie's hand by his fall.

Jamie left it there, and stepping forward he drew his dagger from its scabbard at the right side of his belt. The Scotsman now ignored the flailing Sir Robert and concentrated on his new opponent. The dirk flickered in the light, flashing towards Jamie's eyes. He blocked it inches from his face, locking blade to blade. But instead of forcing the dirk away, he utilised its lack of hilt, sliding his blade down over the Scotsman's and past the insignificant guard provided by the handle. Suddenly realising his weakness, the Scot brought his left arm up, which Jamie sliced to the bone before ramming the point home into the man's belly, cutting through his poor leather armour. He turned, concerned for his liege lord.

"Sir Robert, are you hurt? Can you see?"

"Yes, man. Get your sword, we've not won yet." Jamie grinned at the half-hearted rebuke and turned as another man swung a war axe, He ducked, grabbing him around the waist and thrust his dagger into his bowels. He found his sword still wedged in the head of his earlier victim, and this time he freed it at first pluck. He bounced back upright, re-entering the fray, slashing, parrying and stabbing as he went, Sir Robert gathered his wits, and surrounded by faithful retainers, he marvelled at Jamie's skill and ferocity. *He has outgrown me*, he thought.

Then, as suddenly as it had started, it was over. The battle was won, swords thrown down and cries for mercy as men knelt in obeisance. The brands still burned, but they were now held aloft by Sir Robert's men, who stood over their captives, still raging with the battle madness that follows victory.

Jamie felt a heavy blow at his shoulder and spun around, then grinned and relaxed as he saw Sir Robert.

"Jamie lad, you're a bonny fighter, and I'd like to thank you for saving my life. It was bravely done, and I'm in your debt."

He smiled at the praise. "What sort of squire would I be to let my lord be skewered by a barbarian Scot?" The two men clapped arms, realising how close Sir Robert de Umfraville had come to being killed by the axe.

"Now men, we move," he called. "Peebles will wait. Gather all the arms you can and we go forth to Innerleithen. They'll not sally forth tonight on an unknown force, but we need to be away ere we're caught in a trap."

Chapter Five

Bodmin, Cornwall

The cold wind blew in from the moors and through the streets of the town of Bodmin, chilling the ranks of men and women that thronged around the grass square that was roped off for the combatants. Normally reserved for Spring or Summer celebrations, the ropes now marked out the arena for the winter games, to celebrate Wassailing and bringing in the New Year. They had already been delayed by a freak snowstorm – the sort of storm that hit the province from time to time. Now the grass was silver with a frost and the ground was like iron. It would be hard to fall upon.

Chestnuts were roasting on braziers, pie men hailed for custom, vendors shouted everything from needles to sales of ribbons for loved ones. There was a carnival atmosphere for everyone but the two wrestlers and their followers. This was a grudge match. The two families had been rivals down the ages, and the animosity it bred had not diminished with time.

The two men could not have been more different in type, colour or mentality. Both had the muscular, developed shoulders of their calling. Not for them the knightly discord between left and right, dependent upon arms favoured. These two were broad of chest and rounded with muscle on the upper arms, showing through their white canvas jackets, roped shut across the front. However, Al of St. Magwan was almost as broad as he was tall. He was no more than five and a half feet tall, but solid down to his thickened waist and chunky thighs, clad in the traditional wrestling trousers that finished just above the knee. His face showed his Celtic origins, his dark sallow skin topped by an unruly flowing mass of dark curls. His brow was heavy and jutted over deep set eyes.

Mark, the local wrestler from Bodmin, was fair skinned, with close-cropped blond hair framing a handsome face that looked more like that of a poet or an artist than a combatant in a violent and dangerous sport. His physique was lithe, tapering to a tightly muscled waist, hinting at great power in the wedge-shaped torso. He was uncommonly tall, well over six feet, and he looked to be as strong as the horses his family used to work their farmland.

The two camps eyed each other warily, each ready to tear the opposition apart at the slightest excuse. This was the highlight of the day's events, and before the situation got out of hand the Stickier strode forward to referee the match. He was a gnarled old man whose skin was the colour of oak, clothed in the dark cloth of his standing. He brandished a stout rowan stick as he shouted for the two men to come forward. His Cornish accent was strong as he encouraged the wrestlers: "This be fair for a game to be had this day. You wrassle to the old rules and abide by them, mind, or my stick you'll feel. Now face each other and repeat the oath."

He began to recite by rote the oath from time immemorial: "I, 'pon my honour and on the honour of my country, swear that I shall wrestle without treachery or brutality. This be a token of my sincerity, as I offer my hand to my opponent and speak the words of my forefathers: good play be fair play."

The two men repeated the words and both raised their right hands clasping the others to seal the pact. Both men knew that the words they said would not hold true for this contest, despite the pact. Too much was at stake, and the feud cut too deeply. The two wrestlers separated, awaiting the command.

"Wrassle!" the Stickier cried.

The men lunged forward, each seeking a strong grip of his opponent, clasping hand to shoulder, bicep or wrist, the strong canvas jackets taking the strain as both grunted with effort, seeking the advantage. Al sank even lower than his stature, using his low centre of gravity to his advantage, forcing Mark to bend forward. To counter this, Mark pushed his foot towards him, seeking to redress his balance. This is what Al wanted, and he hooked his right foot around Mark's ankle, aiming to trip him. Mark resisted, pushing his foot backwards. Al disengaged, and in a trice, exploiting the wider stance of his legs, swept his foot from the inside, shifting balance and toppling Mark to the hard ground in a flurry of limbs. The first point went to Al, whose followers cheered in encouragement. Both men regained their footing to more shouts from the crowd, egging them on to impossible endeavours.

Mark had learned his lesson. He took a high grip behind Al's neck, controlling him, pulling him forward and playing to the adage 'where the head goes the body must follow' before seeking a low grip around his hip. Mark pulled hard and as he did so, slid his lower hand to grab Al's leg. With the forward momentum he spun, driving his right hip inwards, throwing his opponent into the air. Both men left the ground, but Al landed first with Mark on top, his hip smashing him into the ground with a shock that made even the hard earth reverberate to the impact.

Mark was first to rise to the cheers of his supporters, while Al lay moaning, winded or worse.

"You like to break my hip with that. I cry foul." Al's face was creased with pain.

"No foul, fair throw." The Stickier cried, motioning for the two men to rise and return to the centre of the ring.

With a surly scowl on his face, Al of St. Magwan rose, glaring pure hatred at his opponent. He flexed his fingers, readying himself for the final bout.

"Wrassle!" the stickier cried, and Al hesitated for a second then charged, head down, concentrated aggression channelled into that one explosive movement. The move caught Mark unawares, but he lowered one arm to block the left shoulder, while the other grabbed at the back of his opponent's jacket. The impetus was too much for Mark to withstand the solid charge below his centre of gravity, and he felt himself being driven backwards. Instead of resisting, he went with the fall, clamping Al's neck and shoulders as he did so between his arms, raising his right knee up, hoping to spring his opponent over in an arc and land him flat on his back.

The move was partially successful. Using all his strength, Mark heaved with hip, knee and arms, pulling Al down as he flipped him up with his leg, his back crashing to the ground at the same time as Al's legs defined an arc in the air above him. All would have been fine and the match would probably have been declared a draw, but he twisted, attempting to release the hold and land on his knees. The strain was all on his neck, and as he levelled out there was an ominous 'crack' as his neck broke. The cheers of encouragement from the crowd were silenced almost instantly as everyone gazing at the prostrate figure of Al, whose chest heaved twice and then was still.

The Stickier ran forward to check for breathing or a pulse: there was no sign of either. He looked up at Al's supporters and shook his head. The friends and family cried in horror, running to fling themselves to the ground beside their fallen champion. His mother led the mourners in a wailing scream.

"Dead! My son is dead. He is murdered! Murderer!" she pointed at Mark, who shook his head in disbelief. The Stickier and stewards came between the two factions, men at arms appearing with their swords drawn, ready to prevent a brawl. Al's brother Tor looked up from his fallen sibling, a look of pure hatred upon his face, stabbing a finger at Mark.

"You'll pay. Upon my life, I swear by the saints you'll pay with your life."

"It was an accident, I swear. I meant a fair throw, nothing more." Mark responded.

"Aaargh" Tor cried, the sound wrenched from him as he charged, seeking to get Mark within striking distance. Succeeding, he launched a clumsy roundhouse punch which connected, driving Mark backwards. Mark took it and offered no resistance. Then the men at arms were there restraining Tor from making any further attacks.

"You lie, you lie!" he spat. "I'll see you dead, just you see if I don't."

The Stickier cried out, calling for calm. "It was a fair fight, I be sure. There was no foul, Tor of St Magwan. Your brother turned; no intent was there for a broken neck. Accept it. It was honourable." Then turning slightly and altering his gaze, he addressed Al's grief-stricken father who was looking balefully down at his fallen son. In a gentler tone he ordered: "Take your son, sir, and place him for burial. No good will come of this, but he will be honoured as a great wrassler and as a man who fought brave and true."

The old man knelt by his son. He nodded sightlessly, and bending he lifted the recumbent form with great effort, shrugging off attempts to help him as he carried his son to their cart.

Following, Tor turned one last time, hatred etched into his face. "Sleep with one eye open. I will have vengeance, I swear it." He spat.

Mark shook his head, dismayed at the turn of events. Then he felt a soft hand on his shoulder. "Come lad, let's away. Naught will be served here, and only trouble will result."

As if in a trance he nodded, allowing himself to be guided to a waiting waggon and a mule with a saddle strapped to its back. He walked stiffly to its side and mounted easily despite his size, settling lightly in the saddle. The Stickier came up for a final word.

"You did well lad, take no heed, but mind your back, eh? The Magwans are as rough as they're lawless." Mark clasped the man's hand, thanking him.

The journey back to their farm should have been a celebration for Mark's family and friends, but it was a dour affair, overcast by the events and thoughts of things to come. His father finally said the words he had not wanted to hear: "Lad, you know what the Magwans are like. They'll not rest until they see you dead, especially that Tor. He's a bastard, that one."

"I know, he'll lie in wait for me and it'll be an arrow or a blade in the back when I'm not expecting it. But I'll take my chances. It's my life, and he'll find it harder to take from me than he thinks," Mark replied.

"Yea, but I'll not have another life taken or ruined," his father continued, building up to where his thoughts had taken him. "Lad, I hate to say this, but I think you need to go away for a while." In the gathering gloom, Mark looked around, trying to make out the expression on his father's face, alarmed at what he had just heard.

"What d'you mean away, Father? Away from the farm, away from home? Where? Where would I go?"

"Somewhere safe," he hesitated again. "I mean leave Cornwall," he finished quietly.

"Leave Cornwall?" Mark exclaimed. "But...but go where? Stay where? I don' know anywhere but 'ere. I be not afeard of any man in a fair fight, but I'm afeard of leaving this land. Where will I go? How will I live?"

Mark's father sniffed and spat before answering. "I've an idea how it could be done. There's a roving friar, you know of old? Well he comes through here on his way to Lunnon every year at this time. You go with him, 'e'll not mind and no one'll attack you on the road if'n you be on a pilgrimage with a friar."

"A pilgrimage?"

"Aye. You'll say you're off to Lunnon to ask God's grace for your soul for killin' a man."

Mark turned away, the tears in his eyes at the thought of leaving home mirroring those in his Mother's eyes as she stared off into the evening.

Chapter Six

The Port of London

With a following wind, the crossing took around four hours. It was smoother than Cristoforo had imagined, but he had nonetheless been ill, hanging his head over the side for most of the voyage, to the amusement of John and the crew. He was relieved to enter the estuary of the Thames and see dry land again, marked by the winking of lights on the dark shoreline. In the darkness of the winter's night, they could hear noise from the shore as London woke up for its nocturnal activities. The occasional lighter swept by, moving closer to the shore towards the docks and quays, lamps winking as the oarsmen called out a warning to avoid collision.

The captain was skilled and knew every inch of his home port, and he eased the cog carefully upriver with the forward tide, heading to the Steelyard docks and Ironbridge Wharf. The beacon lights of the White Tower glowed brightly as they passed, then they slipped under London Bridge and entered the wharf that had been constructed by the Hanseatic League. The cog slowed almost to a standstill as the sailors threw ropes that were caught by the steves on the shore. With capstans and greased piles, they pulled the vessel to berth at the wharf.

English voices called to the ship, cries of familiarity hailing friends among the crew. Two gangplanks were raised onto the leeward side and the unloading began. Cristoforo watched, taking it all in despite speaking no English at all, while all around him voices were raised in that language.

"So this is London," he said to John in French.

"Aye lad it is – the docks at least. Master Thomas has lodgings, workshops and warehouses in the centre of the city. We'll be there soon enough." John gazed out into the starless night above the city, breathed in and exhaled with an air of deep satisfaction. "It's always good to be back on English soil."

"My pleasure is to be on dry land again, regardless of whom it belongs to. I am sick to my stomach, and I hate the sea."

John snorted with what might have been mirth and reached down to his travelling bag. "Here, before you go ashore, you'd best have these." He produced a sheet of waxed canvas in which Cristoforo's two daggers and Falchion were wrapped. Cristoforo accepted them gratefully, balancing first one then the other on his fingertips. He flipped them in the air, catching each one and returning them to the concealed sheaths in his boots. He gripped the smooth hilt of the falchion and flicked his wrist, whirring the blade in the torchlight, pleased with the feel of it in his hand and grinning at the familiar balance of the weapon.

"I have lived so long with her, she is part of me, no? I feel lost without her. Every day since I was a child I have trained in her use." He explained as he kissed the blade, "Please God she never leaves me again." With that he reached over his shoulder with his left hand, pulling the open end of the scabbard upwards and in a move which showed great practice, he slid the blade home and nestled it between his shoulders within easy reach. John looked on with interest at the Italian's affection for the weapon and the ease with which he handled it.

"A neat trick, I was wondering how you returned it home," he said

He shrugged, "Just practice, *signor* John, just practice. Now we go, yes?"

"Indeed, come home now and get yourself a taste of some proper English food."

Cristoforo hefted his large leather satchel, which had been retrieved for him by John's servant, and moved down the gangplank, immediately feeling better at the feel of solid ground beneath his feet. They left the quayside with Thomas promising to return in the morning to speak with the Import Authority to certify the cargo with the officers at the port. He paid the captain and led his retinue north from the docks, up Soper Lane to where Cheapside bisected the north-south streets and onwards, heading north-west to Lawrence Lane. All the time, Cristoforo's eyes stayed alert. Despite the company, everything felt very alien to him: raucous noise came from taverns in a language he could not understand, and the streets were paved with shiny cobbles with dark doorways to each side. He was only too aware that his new master was carrying vast wealth through a dimly lit city at night. Cristoforo was a creature trained to inhabit the darkness and make it work to his advantage. Despite John's presence he did not relax until they reached Thomas de Grispere's home.

Cristoforo looked up at a grand building that reflected the wealth and standing of his patron. Beneath the light cast by the torches, brick footings rose from the pavement, out of which sprung half-timbered frames and latticed windows, reaching a full three stories in height. A large, solid, round-topped door was set into an oak frame, a step up from street level. Knowing it would be barred against the night, Thomas rapped loudly with the iron knocker, rousing servants within. A servant called out to ascertain who was without and cried out a welcome when he heard his master's voice. They heard the bar being removed from within, and the huge door swung inwards.

"Master Thomas, by the saints, it is good to see you. We were not sure of your arrival upon the evening's tide or the morrow's."

"Thank you Will, 'tis good to be home. Is there food to eat?"

He beckoned John and Cristoforo inside while more servants bustled with the baggage train and took the mules to a stable at the rear of the house. The servants gazed at Cristoforo with undisguised curiosity

"Tonight, master Corio, you will sleep here in the attic rooms. Then come morning, we'll sort proper lodgings for you in the apprentices' quarters or maybe here," he gestured. "Of that I am not yet decided. But for now, come to the hearth and eat with us."

With that he moved forward through an archway to a large hall, stepping forward to warm his hands against the chill of the night at the blaze which burned in the stone fireplace

Cristoforo looked around, amazed at the extent of wealth on display. There were thick rugs on the wooden floor, tapestries on the walls and padded hangings gracing the window openings beside the wooden shutters that sealed out the darkness of the night. The colours were rich and he recognised some Florentine designs. His thoughts were disturbed by the sound of light footsteps descending the hidden stairs. He whirled and stepped back into the shadows, ready to face a stealthy foe with the advantage of surprise, but instead he was treated to the sight of a young woman who seemed to have been freshly roused from sleep. She flew forward, a vision of night skirts and unbraided blonde hair.

"Father, you are returned!" She cried in obvious joy at his arrival.

"As you see, child, as you see. God be praised." Then he cautioned, "However, Jeanette, we have company and you are undone."

"John has seen me without a veil, father, we are at home and..." At which point Cristoforo emerged from the shadows, tucking something back into the side of his boot. "Oh, my apologies sir, I had not considered that others might be present." She held her hand to her mouth in embarrassment at the sight of the handsome Italian.

"I beg your pardon *Signorina*, it is I who should apologise for my intrusion into your home." He bowed deeply, sweeping his arm to one side in the manner of foreign nobility.

"Signor Corio, may I present my daughter, demoiselle Jeanette. My dear, this is Signor Corio. He made himself known to me by breaking into my lodgings in Paris, but subsequently saved my life. On balance, I decided that I would sooner he work for me than against me, and here you find him," Thomas offered by way introduction, his obvious affection for his daughter showing in the sound of his voice and the twinkle in his eye. But Jeanette caught only some of his words with any meaning.

"Father, are you hurt? Tell me what happened. Is all well?" She scowled at Cristoforo.

"Calm yourself my dear, just a little bruising on my shoulder. I have sustained worse falling from my horse. Now, my child, to bed. I will see you on the morrow. All is well, never fear."

She pouted her full lips, casting down her dark lashes as her blond hair swung forward, and made a deep curtsey to the company before sweeping gracefully from the room, Cristoforo following her form and elegant demeanour with his eyes as she left. John and Thomas caught each other's eye, and John moved between her and Cristoforo, his expression murderous.

Jeanette turned just before she reached the stairs. "Oh Father, I almost forgot, Sir Richard has called on you these two days past. But I know not what he wishes, other than for you to call upon him as soon as you are returned."

Thomas frowned. "He called in person?"

"Indeed Father, as I say." She answered coolly, then was gone in a sweep of skirts and a downcast flutter of eyelids in Cristoforo's direction, her footsteps light on the stairs.

"Well, well. I know not if that bodes ill or good. Sir Richard calling in person for my attendance," he mused. Cristoforo was at a loss as the conversation had been in English, worried that something was afoot, given the expressions on their faces.

"Cose?"

"Ah, yes. Sorry lad." Thomas continued in French. "Sir Richard Whittington is a leading mercer of my guild. However, he is much more than that: former Sheriff and Mayor of London, financier, politician and adviser to the king and young Prince Hal. He is a very important citizen, and it behoves a man to dance when he plays the tune. We have known each other for many years and I would account him a good friend, but lofty now in his position of state. If he should come in person – twice now and clearly in haste – I surmise he is vexed and in need of assistance."

"Help with trade?" Cristoforo asked.

"No, I am sure it goes deeper. He is exceeding wealthy, and trades in silks, wool and cloth. I suspect the answer will lie in matters of state. He has much influence there and is as adept a politician both in and out of Parliament. He advised the old king and the new; and seamlessly managed the transition without default. Sir Richard does well for the poor, is good to his apprentices and popular with Londoners for returning to them their Liberties, which had been removed by the old King. That said, there is steel within the velvet gauntlet, and he is perhaps the puppet master who pulls more strings than we might see." The last was almost as an aside to himself, as Thomas mused upon what might be so urgent as to require his assistance.

"The old king?" Cristoforo asked. "Who is this man? I know little of your country's history."

"King Richard, God rest his soul. But 'tis best not to speak of him, for circumstances were difficult, both of his rule and departure." Thomas cautioned.

Cristoforo nodded his acquiescence. Servants brought food on wooden platters, steam rising from a stew of meat with a yellow pepper sauce.

"Ah, *poivre jonet*. No one cooks it like Mabel." Cristoforo looked at the food with suspicion at first, but after a mouthful he set to, and the three men attacked the food with gusto, wiping all the remaining sauce with dried bread. The meal finished, Thomas gave his orders as they shared a jug of wine.

"*Signor* Corio, we will retire. My servant will show you to your cot. It is in the top attic rooms. I hope you will be comfortable there, and I bid you goodnight." Corio bowed in response and thanked Master Thomas for bringing him to this strange land and offering him sanctuary. He followed the servant from the room, leaving Thomas and John with their heads bowed together at the table, deep in discussion.

Chapter Seven

Bodmin, Cornwall

Over a week had passed since the wrestling bout and Mark had stayed wary, ever alert for any possible revenge from the St. Magwans. The sheriff had been informed and everything had been legally settled, but everyone knew of the hatred and resentment the death had caused, and everyone knew about Al's brother's oath to seek revenge. As his father predicted, the mendicant Friar Vincent had arrived at their farm, passing through on his long journey back to London. He had been fed and offered a place to sleep in the warm barn for the night in the soft hay, and was ready for departure the next day, having offered a blessing to the family for their kindness. The friar heard their confessions and agreed to take Mark with him to the order's main friary in London.

It was a forlorn Mark who bade his parents farewell on that cold morning, his huge muscular frame appearing to shrink at the parting. He hugged his mother and bade his brothers goodbye. His father stepped forward, with an old sword and scabbard wrapped in a belt.

"This was mine, son. You take it now, it'll bring you luck and keep you safe," he said, offering the bundle to Mark. "'Tis old, but the blade is sharp and it served me well when I fought for the old lord. That were a long time ago, mind."

"I'm not much good with a blade," Mark said. "I prefer this." He raised his stout quarterstaff of old oak.

"Aye I know, but take it anyway, a blade will sometimes serve better."

With a nod to his father, Mark took the sword and buckled it about his waist, balancing the hunting knife that was settled on his right hip. The unfamiliar weight and feel seemed awkward to the wrestler. He shook hands with his father and the friar motioned to go.

"Come my son, we must be away. The day beckons and we have miles to cover before nightfall."

Mark gave one long farewell look back at his family as the friar strode away, then he followed, his heart aching. As they rounded the track and the farm disappeared from view he grew silent and plodded disconsolately abreast of the friar. Eventually he spoke. "This is my first time north from the valley. Friar Vincent, where do we make for today?"

"Take heart my son, and look upon this as an adventure. You shall, if God wills, return to your family in good order. For the present consider that you are under the Lord's protection and no harm will befall you. We travel the road to Launceston. There is a monastery at St. Stephen's a few miles beyond the town. We should arrive before nightfall, God willing. Now, come tell me, what would you do in London when we arrive?" The friar encouraged Mark to speak, and soon the miles from his home increased unnoticed, distracted as he was with talking to Friar Vincent, until by midday they arrived at Bolventor, a small hamlet on Bodmin Moor.

"We will stop here for food and I will attend my prayers at

the church." They sat outside the wall surrounding the church-yard and ate the food Mark's mother had prepared. When they had finished the friar rose, put a hand to the small of his back and stretched, and walked towards the gates of the church.

"These bones complain in the damp winter days," he said. "I will not be long, I need to pray to our Lord." A short time later he returned to find Mark standing by the door.

"Are you fit? Good, let us continue our journey." Mark nodded and Friar Vincent strode forth, his energy seemingly replenished through the power of prayer.

They left the hamlet and proceeded back out onto the moor and the main road to the northeast, which at points was intersected by roads and tracks cutting north and south. The moor was a mix of landscapes – sometimes open and bracken covered land, now brown and faded as the winter pervaded. Old snowdrifts still remained in the lee of rocks and walls, and the wind cut across the open moor, icy and lazy, driving through them rather than troubling to go around. Other times they would dip into hollows, where visibility was restricted but the shelter from the wind was a blessing.

As they dropped down to pass through one of the many copses, they crossed a wooden bridge spanning one of the wide streams that coursed the moor, growing to rivers as they flowed towards lower ground. The landscape was wild and alien to Mark, who had rarely left his home shire and had heard wild stories of those who travelled these strange lands upon which he now walked. They heard a brief drum of hooves behind them as a party crossed the same bridge, and looking back they saw three horsemen top the rise behind them.

They were riding hard, that was apparent, and they seemed sinister in their intent. The two men stepped aside to let them pass unhindered, but as the three horsemen drew closer they reined in their mounts, with little skill. One nearly toppled forward as his horse bucked and skittered in his rough hands. Gathering their mounts to hand, one of the three moved forward to confront Mark and Friar Vincent.

"So I caught 'ee, scuttlin' off like a cur in the night." The stranger rasped.

At that point Mark realised that it was Al's brother Tor and two rough looking men whom he did not know. He stood his ground unafraid, almost welcoming the conflict, no longer needing to fear an unseen attack. But before he could respond Tor continued. "Now I'll 'ave 'ee. I'll take my revenge for my brother's death."

Mark raised his quarterstaff ready for the assault, but before he could engage or speak Friar Vincent interceded. "There will be no violence done to this man," he said, "for he is under the protection of the church and we are on a pilgrimage to holy shrines in London." He spoke authoritatively and for a moment the hands of the three horsemen were still. Then Tor spat and slipped from his horse's saddle, followed by his two companions.

"Your words mean little to me, father. God didn't save my brother and 'e won't save this bastard now." He swore, heedless of the power of the church or the friar's sensibilities. At this, one of Tor's companions raised a club and the other an old sword that had seen better days. They were clearly intent upon killing Mark, who stood his ground, ready with his staff in a fighting stance.

"If you cross the church, by the saints and God's grace you will be excommunicated, and may the Lord have mercy upon your soul." Friar Vincent shouted, standing by Mark's side.

"Out of the way Father. I will have this man's life." Tor raised his sword with more aggression than skill.

A calmness seemed to descend over Friar Vincent. With a sigh that sounded like a mixture of deep sadness and regret he moved, but not in the way Tor imagined he would, thinking that he had bullied the friar into submission. Mark felt a lightening at his side and saw the friar draw his father's sword underhand from the scabbard at his hip. Once clear of the scabbard, Father Vincent switched his grip from down to up with the flick of the wrist. Mark realised that the elderly friar had taken a guard position facing the two ruffians. He looked far more competent than they were, braced in a fighting stance that spoke of long practice.

"I pray thee, do not test me. I may have forsworn weapons and violence as the good Lord knows, but I will defend the weak and those whom He has entrusted to my care. Now, ere you insist upon your murderous intent, I shall level the tally, and Mark shall be better able to defend himself with more favourable odds."

Mark was surprised, but smiled and charged the open mouthed Tor, whose sword wavered for a moment before he struck forward in a clumsy, angry blow. His two companions both attacked the friar, who merely batted the sword stroke away, disarming the man. He pricked the hand of the clubman, who squealed in pain, holding his bleeding hand. The friar ordered them to sit and put their weapons aside.

The three men turned their attention to the fight between Tor and Mark. It appeared to Friar Vincent's tutored eyes a one sided fight. Tor's aggression and anger were no match for Mark's skill with the quarterstaff, and he almost seemed to give Tor chances before turning up the pace. He crossed Tor's blade, driving it away to his right, crashing the staff down upon his collar bone, which broke with loud crack. He followed up with a cross handed blow to the ribs, dropping Tor to the ground, gasping in pain. Sliding the staff he made for a coup de grace, aiming for Tor's head.

"Enough!" Father Vincent cried. "You have settled it and

little harm has been done. Be charitable, my son, and show forgiveness to this miscreant knave." The words stopped Mark in mid strike, and he froze, aggression written across his face, blowing hard and sneering down at the fallen man.

"Get you gone, cur." He spat, as Tor's comrades rose to help him, gently lifting him to his feet. Tor cursed and swore again that he would still be avenged. Helping him to his horse, Friar Vincent halted them.

"Wait." He ordered, and moved forward to fashion a sling from a scarf. He eased Tor's arm into the support and held the arm fast. "It will ease the pain and aid correct healing."

All the thanks he got from the ailing man was grimace of pain, then he mounted his horse with a gasp and some help from his friends. They moved off back towards Bodmin at a walk, disappearing from sight over the rise as Friar Vincent and Mark watched. Once they had disappeared Mark exclaimed.

"Friar Vincent, I am indebted to you, yet I am also in awe. How did you learn to wield a sword in such a manner?"

In answer the friar returned Mark's sword to its scabbard and with sad eyes said: "I was not always a friar, and you see before you a shadow of the fighting man I once was – but for all that, I am much happier and content than ever I was before. Now," he changed the subject swiftly, "we must move forward, for we have dallied here too long and the journey beckons us onward." With that he stepped once more upon the road to Launceston, giving Mark no time for further questions.

Chapter Eight

Berwick Castle: February.

The walls echoed with the metallic clang of sword blades that rang harshly against the muted thuds of the men at arms practicing at the pells in the exercise yard before the huge keep. The master at arms called the strokes: "Upper strike left, lower strike right, guard, thrust." The commands continued as the men responded in unison, training as if their lives depended upon it – which one day they might.

Two armoured men stood facing each other in the bailey, their breath pluming in the cold morning air as they heaved with their exertions. They were in full harness but without visors, their faces exposed and red despite the cold. They puffed air through blown cheeks. The men at arms practicing at the pell stopped their exercise to regain their breath and watch as the two opponents circled each other warily. The younger man took the upper guard, both hands on the hilt of his long sword raised above his head, intimidating and ready for a lethal downward stroke, beckoning his opponent forward into his range.

Jamie wished that he had his true, sharp sword in his

hands instead of this sorry excuse for a weapon. His sword had been a present from his father on finishing his training as an esquire. Forged from Damascene steel by a master craftsman, the blade sang in his hands. The perfect balance point had been attained by the final insertion of a semi-precious stone that had been set into the metal claw clasp of the hilt. At just over two and a half pounds it was heavy, but the perfect balance enabled a speed of movement that was more like that of a dagger than a sword.

The sword in his hands was a blunted practice weapon and mirrored its mate that lay scabbarded against the wall. His opponent stood balanced in a classic stance, point forward, knowing that the point will always defeat the edge. He feinted with a strike to the right, then lunged to the left, and Jamie responded with a fast downward cut, ignoring the feint and meeting the point, crossing and deflecting the blade, rotating under and over; using the strength of his wrist and what little there was of the sword's balance. He whipped the opponent's blade over, twisting it from Sir Robert's grasp, and with delight saw the blade fall to the floor.

Jamie grinned, stepping forward to seize his moment of triumph. In that instant, his disarmed opponent stamped on the hilt of the fallen sword, causing the blade to rise. He flicked it into the air with his foot, catching the pommel deftly and presenting the tip to the underside of the chin of his mesmerised opponent. The younger man gaped in awe, knowing his life would have been forfeit if this were a real bout.

"The devil, but I've not seen the like." Jamie exclaimed.

His opponent laughed, clapping him on the shoulder. "Aye, Jamie lad, that's one trick I've not shown you, but in all else you are now the master. There is nought else I can teach you, and you're uncommonly quick, with a speed I was not as like to match even in my younger days."

Jamie grinned modestly, grateful for the praise: "Now show me how you achieved that trick." He said.

Sir Robert dropped the sword again near his feet and showed Jamie how by pressing on the pommel end the blade rose up sufficiently to give space to slip his other foot beneath it, flicking the sword upwards. It was, Jamie saw, all to do with timing as Sir Robert dropped at the perfect moment to catch the hilt in mid-air.

"Now you try." Sir Robert offered. Jamie made to copy his tutor's actions but was nowhere near as successful, fumbling the pickup. Twice more he tried and only on the third attempt did he manage to grasp the handle of his sword. He realised that it would take a lot more practice to perfect the trick.

At this point hooves rattled upon the drawbridge and a messenger cantered into the inner bailey riding a blown horse. He curbed his palfrey and slid from the saddle. Clad in travel-worn clothes he tethered the animal, allowing it to drink slowly from the trough, then came forward towards the two combatants. He cut a bow and addressed them.

"My lords, I bear a message and seek James de Grispere. I believe him to be within these walls."

"I am James de Grispere." Jamie responded. "Present your message."

The messenger retrieved a scroll sealed with wax. Jamie looked at it, immediately recognising the imprint of his father's ring.

"'Tis from my father," he addressed Sir Robert.

"Open it lad, see what news he brings. Messenger, seek food and ale from my steward. We will summon you when we have an answer."

"Thank you my lord," the messenger bowed and hurried towards the kitchens at the base of the Keep, leaving Jamie to break the seal and read the parchment.

"It is indeed from my father," Jamie said, "and he bids me to return to London forthwith. He assures me all is well, but says that he has need of my services on a matter of great importance. He sends his regards and felicitations to you Sir Robert, and apologises for bidding me leave your service so abruptly." Jamie finished with a puzzled frown upon his forehead. "What can this mean? Ill news? No, he assures me not – yet I am much puzzled."

"Well whatever the cause, I am sure that it warrants your father's demands, for he would not order such a thing lightly. In all credence Jamie, it is time for you to depart my service in any event. Your training here as a squire has reached its zenith. Thou needst seek new challenges and be presented at court, young man, though I shall be sorry to see you depart my company, for I value you as I would a son." The old warrior addressed Jamie with a new air of respect. "You have honed your skills to their finest, and will henceforth best most men. All that is needed now is experience, and that cannot be taught. Come, follow me into the keep and we'll see if aught else can be gleaned from the messenger."

But when they sat down to eat and drink with the man, they learned that he was the third in line of a relay system that had brought the message from London and knew no more than the parchment contained. Jamie scribbled a hasty note in response, sealed it and paid the messenger to return the reply to his father.

After the messenger had left on a fresh horse Jamie turned to the knight. "I will depart tomorrow with your leave, Sir Robert. I am wanted at my father's side, and although reassurances were stressed, I will not relax until I understand his need."

"Certes lad, it is as it should be. Your father is a good man and you must answer his call. But," and here Sir Robert hesitated, "I know no more than you, but I am wiser in matters of politics. So let me air a feeling. The kingdom is far from steady, and different forces vie for power. So I warn you, if this concerns matters of state, the court can be as dangerous as the battlefield. Politics holds more tricks than a heathen's smile, so beware, Jamie lad, beware. The new king, God bless him, is a friend, but he is not yet secure and many would wish to topple him. So walk softly and say little until you are sure of the loyalty of those to whom you speak."

As part of Jamie's training, Sir Robert had tutored him in courtly manners and matters of war, but never before on politics and diplomacy. Jamie frowned, not sure how to proceed. Seeing his uncertainty, Sir Robert continued.

"Just be aware that the court – and London for that matter – is a nest of vipers. Now go and make ready, lad."

Jamie weighed Sir Robert's words, storing them away for future reference. He went to his chamber to think and make preparations for the long journey ahead.

The following morning saw him up early, waiting in the bailey for Sir Robert to appear. His pack mule was laden with armour and other gear, while a sleek, dark bay palfrey stood saddled ready for mounting. She had been brought from Ireland with a batch of horses and Jamie had bought her straight off the boat, liking what he saw. Looking at her now, he wondered if he might have been better off with a stout warhorse without Sir Robert to advise him.

His reverie was broken as Sir Robert appeared, followed by a groom leading another horse that was all too familiar to Jamie: he was a destrier with a flaming chestnut coat that someone had christened Richard. He stood just over 15 hands 3 inches, with plenty of bone leading up to a huge head with a thin white blaze. The groom, aware of all his tricks, neatly avoided the snapping of the stallion's teeth as he led him forward. The horse's eyes rolled in disgust at the harness as he preferred to roam free. Only Jamie could handle him with impunity, having trained him since Sir Robert had bought him as a foal. The angry stallion calmed as Jamie approached him and rubbed his huge ears playfully. The horse dropped his head in response. The change in his attitude was remarkable and a marvel to all who did not know of the extraordinary bond between man and animal.

"You brought him to say goodbye. Goodbye, Richard, be kind to the grooms, don't eat them, eh?" His eyes glistened as he spoke, so close to the horse he was.

"You mistake me, lad," Sir Robert said, "the old goat is unmanageable without you. Cross-tempered, always fighting and flaming red hair: we named him well after the Lionheart, God rest him, though he resembles some of the local women-folk, to my view. But he is a warrior, and he knows no master but you," he finished, hiding his feelings with the gruff retort.

"Richard is for me?" He cried in joy.

"Aye, take him before I change my mind. Now be off with you and mind all I've taught you." Jamie was delighted and thanked the knight for his kindness, overwhelmed at the gift. He shook Sir Robert's hand in the Roman manner, embracing hand to elbow and crashing shoulders in the greatest display of emotion the two men had offered each other in all the years of Jamie's training – one final gesture of equal measure that told the younger man that his learning was complete.

Jamie mounted the palfrey with a nimble leap, saluted Sir Robert and walked the horse and mule forward. His halter rope now tied, Richard whinnied, tossed his head and trotted after his master into the grey light of the Scottish winter morning.

Chapter Nine

St. Stephen's Monastery, Launceston

The two men reached Launceston at dusk, and continued on through the town until they came to the gates of the old monastery. They were welcomed by the brothers, who offered them food and shelter for the night with good grace and genuine warmth.

After attending vespers, Mark and Friar Vincent were bade to eat with the brothers at a large refectory table that was well stocked with simple but hearty country fare. Lent would soon be upon them, and with it would come restrictions on what the church would allow them to eat. The Abbot sat the two travellers at each side of him, so that he might question them further and gain news of the outside world. Attacking his chicken breast with gusto, the portly Abbot paused and pressed a cloth to grease on his chin.

"Now be good enough to tell me your news," he said. "How came you to retire here for the night, and what brings you on your journey to London?"

"I am merely a mendicant friar, Father Abbot, tending my

flock wherever I find them. I press forth for London and my home in the city's Carmelite friary," Friar Vincent replied

"And this young soul?" He pointed at Mark, who was seated to his left. "Is he one of your flock?"

Before Mark could answer for himself, Friar Vincent explained in loose terms how Mark had come to be travelling with him to London. At which point Mark, who was not to be silenced, vouched for his saviour.

"Aye, and right glad I was for him to be along. We were set upon by the man's brother and two churls, who would have done for me had it not been for Friar Vincent."

The Abbot raised his eyebrows in surprise, studying the unassuming Friar in a different light. But before he could interject, Mark's enthusiasm continued. "How did you come to wield a sword so, Friar Vincent? Were you a warrior?"

The Abbot's interest was now piqued: "A sword?" he exclaimed.

Friar Vincent looked embarrassed and could cheerfully have clipped Mark about the head for his volubility. "I merely borrowed Mark's sword and persuaded the other two men to leave the lad alone. I am of course dedicated to protecting the weak as our good Lord desires."

"Amen." The Abbot intoned, crossing himself, although he was not to be dissuaded. "But as our young friend here asked, were you a warrior?"

Friar Vincent sighed. "Yes, and more. I was a knight, but I saw and did things that were abhorrent to me, and I chose a different path to forget my ways and ask for forgiveness in God's eyes. I served a good cause, or so I thought, fighting with Henry Bolingbroke in the northern wars in Europe and the Holy Land. But in time I found myself disturbed and chose a life of repentance. I forsook the violence of my youth and sought instead the path of God."

"I am sure the Lord will bless you and keep you, forgiving any sins as you now serve him on a new path to redemption." The Abbot intoned piously. Mark was in awe, questioning further.

"So you served with the king?"

"Well, lad, he was not a king then, just a noble and fierce knight. He was one of the bravest and most honourable men I have ever served with. But war and combat change a man, and I could no longer stomach the life." The finality of the comment sealed the conversation, and it was apparent even to Mark – who clearly wished to hear more – that the topic was at an end. The meal continued without any further interrogation of Friar Vincent, and the abbot turned his attention to Mark.

"So my son, you wish to try your wrestling skills in London?"

"Aye, Father Abbot, I am told that wrestlers are much sought after in London. Even the prince enjoys the sport and favours a match as one of his entertainments. I should like to set myself against all comers, although I want a fair finish and no repeat of what happened at home."

"From what I have heard I am sure that it was a fair contest, and that no stain is left upon you as a combatant. If the good Lord gives you a skill you should use it and rejoice in it, not hide it away. Just give praise to him and you will prosper I am sure."

"Thank you, Father Abbot. I will follow your advice and pray that I find success," Mark answered, brightening at the Abbot's words.

Chapter Ten

London

Ten days later, Jamie de Grispere entered the walled City of London through the Cripplegate. Weary and travel-worn, he made his way down Wood Street, heading south towards his father's house. He marvelled at the changes that had taken place during his time away. The streets seemed busier, and new buildings were being constructed off to the west as the city expanded outside the walls at Farringdon, Ludgate and Friar Street. Everywhere was bustle, noise and energy. Jamie felt naked without his sword. He had strapped it away, as only knights were allowed to carry a sword openly within the city walls. Richard drew comment, as the powerful war horse was a huge presence that wasn't simply a matter of size. Everyone stood aside as the squire made his way through the throngs of people crowding the streets.

After the castle and the smaller towns he was used to, it was the smells of the city which assailed him most strongly. The stench of concentrated human existence was repellent at first, and he wrinkled his nose in disgust until he gradually became used to it. The central valley of each street was a huge gutter that acted as an open sewer, running with every conceivable excrement. Some of the major streets had been modernised to accommodate new underground sewers but this was only in certain parts of the city, and raw sewage still seeped into the Thames. Only recently had new acts been passed banning tanning water from being drained directly into the river.

Fighting his way through the crowds, he finally arrived at his father's home in Lawrence Lane. He was delighted to see that here at least little had changed and everything was familiar to him. Jamie sat astride his palfrey, Killarney, breathing in the street scene and the sight of his home. Here was where Jamie had been born, where his mother had died, where he'd played as a child, where John had first taught him how to handle a sword.

Shaking himself out of his reverie, he turned his train around and moved towards the large wooden gates leading to the workshops, stables and yard area at the rear of the property. As he approached, the familiar smells of raw wool, cloth and the harsher acrid odour of dyes came wafting across to him. He was home. Passing under the archway he saw the familiar sights of the yard and the archery butt where John had first shown him how to draw and fire a bow – a child's bow made from hazel. The bustle of voices and the frenetic activity of the apprentices and servants was comforting.

"What's a scrawny little runt like you doing back here? This is for workers, not peacocks!" A gruff voice called from just inside a shadowed doorway. Jamie twisted his head at the familiar tones that had chastised and encouraged him so often over the years.

"John!" he cried, freeing his right foot from the stirrup and swinging his leg in a high arc over the horse's neck and wither to slide gracefully to the ground. The grizzled veteran strode over, his lips twitching in what passed for a smile. He clapped Jamie on both shoulders with battle hardened hands that still had the power to shake him. Jamie was pleased to see that he now stood a couple of inches taller than his old teacher at arms.

"Well you've put on some muscle, lad. They must've been working you properly." Like all men at arms, Jamie's shoulders had become overly developed, with rounded and bunched muscles from training with weapons. As was the norm, Jamie's right shoulder was more heavily muscled than the left. He clasped John at arm's length, seeing more grey in his beard and more lines on his weathered face, but he still looked well, as though made of old iron.

"So you're not in your dotage yet, supping gruel from spoon."

"Aye, we'll see who's master soon enough when we've swords in our hands, young pup. That is if you can remember which end to hold!" John added scornfully.

Before the conversation could continue, a more cultured voice hailed him. "James, by the good Lord, it is marvellous to see you." His father strode forward, seeming to shed years at the sight of his son. In a rare display of emotion, he embraced Jamie and stood him back at arm's length to gain his measure. It was strange to hear his christened name spoken again. His mother had been an impoverished Scottish noble's daughter, and the marriage of convenience had turned into a love match. Although she settled in England, she had referred to him as Jamie from the day of his birth. Only his father and household adhered to the traditional version. The north men had all called him Jamie.

His father caught his breath for second, for his son had the dark, red gold hair of his mother and her green eyes, dappled with flecks of red hazel. The strong nose and jaw were his, but the full, bow shaped mouth was his mother's, who had died in childbirth. "You remind me so much of your mother, God rest her soul. You look well, boy, and fair. By the saints, tis good to have you home." Putting an arm across Jamie's broad shoulders, his father led him towards the house. "Your sister is within; she will be excited to see you."

Jamie stopped in mid stride, "Father, ere I go I must see to my horses."

"Nay lad, the groom will do that."

"Do you wish to be without a groom? I shall see to him, for Richard would eat him, after stamping on his head."

It was then that Thomas noticed the splendid war horse that was part of his son's baggage train. On hearing his name, the stallion snorted and stamped as a groom approached him. Richard had walked a few hundred miles, but he had energy to spare and was frustrated with the constant halter. Jamie called a warning just in time, as vicious teeth snapped within an inch of where the groom's hand had been. Jamie laughed, walking over to ruffle Richard's ears. John looked the stallion up and down appreciatively. "There stands a fine animal," he declared. "How did you come by him?"

"He was a parting gift from Sir Robert. I've trained him since he was a foal."

"But Richard? 'Tis passing strange to name a horse so," He commented.

"He is named after the *Coeur de Lion*, for all his attributes." This drew a laugh even from John, who knew well the reputation of the famous crusader Richard the Lionheart and the qualities that had earned him his name

With the horses attended to, they entered the main hall. With a soft cry, he was greeted by the final member of his family as Jeanette swept forward to embrace him in a fierce hug.

"James, James, you're home, God bless. You've grown. You've become a man, by all that's holy. Just look at you!" She said, rejoicing at the return of her beloved brother.

"You too have grown, little sister. You have become passing fair. I'll be bound that lords have been casting their addresses at you," He teased her.

"And your manners have grown with your stature. You will do well at court, I foresee." She replied coquettishly, curtseying in mock gratitude. As a brother and sister, they had been close growing up with no mother, and the bond between them was strong.

At this moment Thomas's steward arrived with servants bearing trays of food. "Wash away the dust from your travel, lad, then sit and break bread. You must be hungry from your journey. I await all your news, especially that of Sir Robert."

"I will tell all, father, when I return."

Later, with the meal finished and all the news imparted, the conversation took on a more serious tone.

"Now father, tell me why I am summoned home so urgently. All seems well. Home, hearth and family prosper, praise be to God. I am right glad to be here, my training had all but finished and I need to be indentured for knighthood ere I find reason and cause for such honour."

Thomas de Grispere smiled at his son's forwardness and his need to move on with his life and ambitions. He had bred a wild, strong son of whom he was secretly delighted and proud.

"The reason for the fiat was none of my making. You will recall Sir Richard Whittington?"

"I do. He is my godfather. He has ever been keen to promote me, and indeed helped me obtain a squire's position with Sir Robert."

"As you may be aware, he has risen high, both in politics and the king's favour. I know not of his full position or the extent of his power, but notwithstanding he is now a very important citizen within the realms of London and the greater kingdom. He has the king's ear on many matters along with the

Bishop of Arundel, Sir John Tiptoft and Sir Thomas Beaufort. Those men hold the power of the crown in their hands."

"And what of Prince Hal? I hear he has formed a new Council."

His father looked at him, surprised. "You know of this?"

"We may be far away to the north, father, but Sir Robert is a good friend to the king and he has kept abreast of his actions and position. Rumours spread many wings in times such as these."

"Mmm. Well I too have heard the rumours, but you would be advised to be cautious of where you air them. Yes, the prince seeks the throne and the power that comes with it. The king has not been seen in public now for some time. He has retired to Kenilworth Castle or Eltham Palace, depending upon his mood – and I suspect upon how threatened he feels."

"Threatened? Have there been attempts upon his life? This I had not heard."

"There remains a constant threat. Contingents exist who reject his status as king – and more importantly, how he claimed the crown. Remember that with the usurping of the old king, the people – especially the people of London – learned that they had the power to dethrone a king, and such power is a heady brew."

Jamie nodded, deep in thought. "Just so, but what service would he have me render him? I am a junior squire, seeking a knighthood with little to recommend me save your influence, father," he continued. "So pray tell me, what it is that Sir Richard Whittington wants with me?"

"That I know not, and it puzzles me. My thoughts follow the same train as yours. I have sent a messenger to inform him that you are lately returned to London. No doubt we will receive a response, as he was most insistent to hear from me ere you returned. I trust we shall soon have the answer to that question. I can only suppose Sir Richard wishes you to act as retainer for him, mayhap, for he conducts much business abroad on behalf of the crown."

At that moment the discussion was disturbed as Cristoforo Corio returned, entering from the rear of the building. The young man was now dressed in his Italian style, more flamboyant than the clothes of a merchant's servant, with colourful hose, a cloak and hooded cowl. He sketched a bow to Thomas as he entered, then his eyes fixed on Jamie, who returned his glance in full as each man took the measure of the other.

"What news, Cristoforo?" Jamie's father asked, changing to French. Since his arrival in England, Cristoforo had picked up a few very basic English terms, but nowhere near enough for a proper conversation. Jamie had not yet been informed of Cristoforo's presence in this father's household, and looked at the foreigner suspiciously.

"I have a message here, *signor*." The Italian strode forward, proffering a sealed parchment. As his father took the scroll he realised his mistake in manners.

"I am forgetting myself. James, let me introduce *Signor* Cristoforo Corio, an Italian, late of Florence and now in my employ. Cristoforo, this is my son James de Grispere, recently returned from our northern borders." Jamie rose and nodded, and *signor* Corio bowed his head in acknowledgement, the atmosphere between them still chilly. To ease the tension, Thomas continued: "Cristoforo saved my life in Calais."

"He saved your life? Was John not present?" Jamie asked askance, looking towards John for verification, knowing that the man at arms had never been bested in a brawl.

John took up the story, following on from his master, realising Thomas's intent and understanding that he sought no discord between the two men who at the moment resembled a pair of fighting cocks entering a ring. "We were set upon outside an inn by four robbing varlets. I bested one but before I could deal with the rest Cristoforo had killed the other three in as many seconds as it took me to tell you the tale. I considered it most unfair of him."

For a second a look of scorn remained etched across Jamie's face, suspecting a jest. Then, realising that the two men were in earnest, his expression changed to amazement and then gratitude. "By God's grace, I am in your debt *signor* Corio, for my father is dear to me. By Hell's teeth, how did you achieve this? You must be passing quick with a sword."

"Nay lad," John smiled, "'Twas not a sword. He disarmed the first of them and killed all three with the dagger he took," he let the words sink in.

Cristoforo bowed and smiled with uncharacteristic modesty, sensing an olive branch. However the moment was curtailed as Thomas interrupted, waving the parchment on which Sir Richard's message had been written.

"It seems that Sir Richard wishes to meet with you on the morrow," he said

"That will do well. Does he say where? His house in College Lane, perhaps?"

"No, he asks that you attend him at the Privy Chambers in Westminster Palace."

"The Palace? He has risen high, has he not?"

"As I say, the king is not in attendance and Sir Richard and his companions now rule the roost."

Chapter Eleven

Jamie set off for the Palace the following morning mounted upon his palfrey, Killarney. Pushing through the crowded streets, he was beginning to regret his choice and wish that he had walked. Pedestrians cursed as he forced his way through the crowds, causing them to move or be driven into the central drainage ditch. Without the lordly power or retinue of a knight, he was just another traveller forcing his way through narrow and densely populated streets, and the Londoners found it hard to forgive such a show of arrogance. The cries of shopkeepers, hawkers and traders showed that the city was thriving.

He turned south on to Paternoster and rode to Ludgate. As he passed under the archway he was relieved to move out of the commercial district. The streets widened and he was able to make better headway along Flete Street and The Straunde. Here he saw that the houses had changed, becoming grander and more affluent. The major friaries were set back from the road, newly constructed Bishops' palaces gleamed in the pale winter sun that hung low in the sky, its light reflecting off glazed windows that were a sure sign of affluence. At the end of The

Straunde he entered Whitehall, a broad thoroughfare carving through to Whitehall Palace and the seat of power.

He was stopped at the guard house and asked to state his business within, and was given directions to the Privy Palace, which was attached to the Great Hall. His horse attended to, he passed through a substantial arched doorway guarded by a single man-at-arms who again demanded his reason for entry. He gave over his letter of introduction from Sir Richard. The guard was clearly of a superior quality as he was able to read the missive. He let Jamie through, giving him instructions on how to navigate the corridors of power to arrive at Sir Richard's chambers.

As he went he saw a constant flow of courtiers, richly dressed and walking in twos and threes, deep in discussion. The feeling of power was palpable, from the rich hangings to the confidence of the courtiers, knights and lords, moving purposefully on errands of state. At each passing he was subjected to looks of assessment, the better to decide if he was worthy of a greeting. He was dressed in his best doublet, hose and boots, which were all of good quality, but he felt very much the poor cousin compared to the latest court fashions, and made a mental note to consult his father upon how to improve his state of dress.

After navigating a maze of corridors, Jamie reached what he supposed was Sir Richard's chambers. When he knocked on the door, a servant bearing Sir Richard's livery answered, read the letter of appointment and bade him enter. The chambers were lavish, with woollen tapestries to rival his father's and carpets instead of the usual rushes upon the raised wooden floor. A spitting log fire burned in the iron grate. Another door opened from the ante-chamber and through it emerged a figure who, although it had been some years, Jamie still recognised as Sir Richard Whittington.

Jamie saw a man in his late fifties, hatless, his hair streaked with grey. He had worn a beard the last time they had met, but was now clean shaven. His face was rounded and slightly jowly, but his expression was animated. The eyes were what held him; they were deep-set and dark, shrewd and intelligent, missing nothing. In stature he seemed to have diminished slightly in Jamie's memory, but he appeared in good health. He was dressed against the recent fashions for short doublets, and wore instead a long robe edged with ermine, permitted by the Sumptuary Laws to denote his status. A chain of office was hung around his neck, although power and authority cloaked him naturally like a mist. His waist was cinched with a bejewelled belt bearing an ornate dagger.

He strode forward, his energy tempered with a grace of movement that belied his years. "James, you've grown! Is this really the same boy I used to bounce upon my knee? By God's grace you've become a man, yet you have the look of your mother about you. She was a beauty – I remember her well, may she rest in peace."

"Sir Richard, it is good to see you and in such good spirits." Jamie dropped a bow.

"Come now, none of that. We are old friends, no formality here," embracing him. Over his shoulder he called. "Bring wine for us if you please, Alfred."

The servant nodded and went to prepare refreshments. Sir Richard was charming and drew Jamie in, leading him through to the inner chamber, which was even more luxurious than the first. In the centre stood a large wooden table laden with papers, documents and quills. However, Sir Richard drew Jamie to the hearth, towards two high backed oak chairs that were set before the blaze. He bade Jamie sit on the cushioned seat, and with wine served he continued to question the young squire.

"A good deal has passed since we last conversed. Tell me

how does Sir Robert? Is he still as robust as ever? He was ever a force of nature and a goodly knight."

Jamie smiled at the comment, yet he remembered Sir Robert's parting words about not trusting anyone and remained a little guarded, knowing that the open charm of his inquisitor would lead soon enough to the real reason for his summons here.

"He is as you say hale in health, and seems not to heed the passing of the years. His efforts on the border are a Godsend to all who live in fear of raids by the Scots. His name alone is enough to strike fear into his enemies and in combat he is as inspiring a fighter as ever I have seen," he finished.

Sir Richard nodded in agreement. "'Twas ever the case. His reputation precedes him and he is loyal to the crown as any man I've known. I imagine you found him a worthy tutor in all matters of squiring, and had plenty of opportunity to hone your skills battling the Scots."

"Aye, that I did, and there were raids and ambushes aplenty. He is a most excellent campaigner and tactician."

"You are also schooled in matters of court, I assume. Sir Robert was ever at court, and served King Henry well when he attended him."

"As you say Sir Richard, he was very particular in all matters of my education and I am indebted to you for your sponsorship."

"It was the least I could do for my godson and the son of an old friend. I wonder if I might trespass upon such acquaintance and bring you into my confidence?"

The question was phrased as a statement and Jamie merely acceded to the request as he knew he was expected to do.

"Of course, Sir Richard, I would be honoured to aid you in any way I can."

"You are very gracious. My task here at court is to act as an aide to the king in many respects, as I am sure you will appreciate. Chief amongst these is the safety of the kingdom. I am confident that reports will have reached even our northern borders of unrest and perfidy within the realm. King Henry has ruled now for ten years, yet still there remain elements who wish him harm and seek to assist our enemies in toppling him from the throne." Jamie nodded gravely, allowing the statesman to continue. "At the king's behest, I have attended to matters of security within the realm, and have kept abreast of factions that pose a potential threat to the crown." Jamie began to realise where this might be leading, yet he was still greatly puzzled as to how it concerned him sufficiently to warrant his recall from the north. But even as these thoughts crossed his mind, Sir Richard arrived at the point of his summons.

"These factions who sow sedition and strife act for their own personal advancement, and do not limit their sway to England itself. To this end I would enlist your services James, if you would be willing to serve your king?"

"For certes, Sir Richard," Jamie replied. "Yet I am greatly puzzled. I am but a squire at arms, lately returned as you know from a far outpost, more skilled in culling Scots than seeking shadows. If it is my sword arm you require it yours for the asking, but by the saints, I know not how I may aid you in other endeavours."

Sir Richard smiled benevolently. "You have answered my question by your own naivety. Let me provide an insight into the court: it swirls with rumours of treason and plotting, rumours that are as hard to grasp as the early morning mist. Ambition is the currency here. It is sought by many, and those who seek power would use the coin of deceit as a means to obtain it. Everyone smiles and displays their loyalty to King Henry, yet even his own family have been tested and found wanting, men such as Harry Hotspur – a former friend, cousin and ally, turned traitor and rotting in his grave. Whom should one trust? There's the nub of it.

"And here you are, newly arrived and clean of allegiance. You are well known to me and as straight and true as your father – whose ambition lies in trade and commerce rather than matters of state or the crown. It is solid allies like you of which I have need."

"By all that is holy, my loyalty to the crown is uncontested. Yet that said, how may I be of use? I know aught of that which may help you and have no important connections that may avail your cause."

"That is indeed the case, but your lack of fame and your obscurity is to your advantage and mine. To give further explanation, the Scottish borders you are already familiar with. Yet consider the Welsh, ever in revolt under Owen ap Glyndower."

"Ah, the Magician, but I thought his force was spent?"

"Far from it. He remains a rebel with sway over his people, an ember ever ready to fan brightly to flame and re-ignite a rebellion. To such ends he has strong connexions with France and offers them a ready landing point and a friendly welcome on our very shores. Remember how close they came to conquering us? Recall that they were forestalled at Worcester by the king, who chose his ground well?" Jamie nodded, recalling the conflict that had been averted by good intelligence and readiness. "The Scots too are ever keen to ally against us," Sir Richard continued. "And the French are plotting anew – and at this juncture I must have your solemn oath that you will not pass forth what I am about to impart..."

"My father? Does he know of our proposed allegiance? He wonders at my recall and will be keen to know the nature of our discussions," Jamie asked.

"He is aware of my needs in general, but not in specific

terms. I trust your father with my life, James, but I would not have him over-burdened with worry."

The answer was a model of diplomacy, but Jamie agreed without further hesitation, and Sir Richard continued. "Are you aware of the new Parliament that was convened this January past?"

"Aye, Sir Richard, I discussed it with Sir Robert at some length.," Jamie replied.

"Well, notice was given to that body and the Council that the French plan a new assault on Calais. As a solider I need not explain to you the strategic importance of the town, from both trade and military standpoints. We keep intelligence in place in this regard for fear of a military assault.

"The Duke of Burgundy has grown more powerful since the murder of the Duke of Orleans, and we strongly suspect that Burgundy was aided by the followers of Glyndower in that enterprise. So you see how malign influence festers and insinuates itself across all our borders."

"I grasp all that you have told me, but am still at a loss as to the role I can play."

"Then let me be clear. You will be introduced at court as just another squire at arms seeking his way, yet you may also travel freely abroad – more particularly to France, where you will be what you are: a merchant's son, bartering, trading and mingling with all who gossip and share knowledge. You will be able to go anywhere with impunity. You speak Flemish, French and English. You have relatives and legitimate connexions in all areas, offering credibility wherever you go as your father's ambassador. And you are trained in arms and able to defend yourself. I will not deny that I have lost two *insidiores* in the last two months, both in France. Their whereabouts are still unaccounted for."

"So by God's grace, you wish me to spy for you?" Jamie

responded quietly, daunted yet excited at the prospect of new adventure.

"Aye lad, that would be my aim, for you to give service to the crown in the appreciation of your king. You would of course not go unrewarded financially, and you would effectively be in the crown's employ, with all the authority that I am able to bestow."

With the impetuosity of youth and the lust for adventure Jamie agreed readily. "Of course, Sir Richard. I shall be honoured to aid the king in whatever way I can."

"Excellent. Now, to details. We must remain as aloof of each other as possible. Few know that I am your godfather, but do not speak of our connexions or our relationship to anyone of our close relations. They may be assumed outside the court and in the Guilds, but confirm nothing."

"How shall I proceed? I mean, what would you have me do? Whom do I need to contact? I confess that the idea of adventure attracts me but the details are a bafflement."

"Worry not, all will become clear in due course. I will arrange for you to be presented at court in the service of one of the knights who is loyal to me – or better yet, perhaps you can be positioned to attend to represent Sir Robert's interests in his continuing absence?" Here he paused thinking out loud. "Yes, mayhap that will do well. I shall send a message to him arguing the case for you. I will of course ensure that he shall not be out of coin on our behalf. So leave now for the moment and return in one week, by which time all will be settled and you will become a fixture of the court. Seen, yet not seen. You are to do nothing to distinguish yourself amongst your peers. I want you to blend in and observe."

"As you wish, Sir Richard. I do however have another question."

"Of course, If it is in my power to provide you with an

answer I shall most certainly do so." Sir Richard's voice held a slightly wary note.

"Whilst you instruct me, and my loyalty to my country and the kingdom is undoubted, may I ask whom exactly I serve?" Sir Richard's expression changed to a frown, but Jamie was not to be dissuaded from his course. "I ask because of the dissention between king and prince and the newly formed Council."

"James, you would be well advised to curb such thoughts. The dangers that lie at court are many and devious. Even tomorrow we shall burn an insurrectionist: a Lollard heretic who defames God and the Church. He has been fomenting lies and smears against the true Church and will not repent.

"You must contain yourself with the knowledge that you serve the crown and the best interests of the kingdom. As your direct master, I will ensure that this is so." The response to Jamie's ears held a tone of rebuke, but he smiled easily, glossing over the awkward moment.

"As you wish, Sir Richard, but it behoved me to ask, as I am sure you will understand. I reiterate my loyalty to the crown and the kingdom – and to you yourself – of that you may have no doubt."

The easy expression was back on Sir Richard's face now the danger had been averted.

"Of course, of course. And you are right to be cautious. These are dangerous times, young James. Now if you will forgive me, I have many matters to attend to and do not wish to associate with you here too long, ere tongues wag and suspicions are roused."

"For certes, and thank you for the commission. I will await your orders."

With a brief bow Jamie turned for the door, his head whirring with thoughts and excitement.

Chapter Twelve

The court, as Sir Richard Whittington had described, had no secrets, and Jamie's visit and the identity of the person who had summoned him had been noted and would in due course be reported to interested parties. He was followed discreetly back to his home, the watcher finding it easy to keep up on foot through the crowded streets.

In his time at the Borders, where had been ever watchful for ambush by the Scots, Jamie had developed a sixth sense for unseen eyes upon him. It had saved his life before and had not deserted him now. He kept looking around sharply, hoping to spot a figure amidst the crowds who might appear familiar – someone whom he had seen before.

"'Tis no use, Killarney" he told his horse. "There are too many people. Give me the hills of the borders, at least I can see my enemies there! I swear it is easier to spot a man hiding behind trees than behind his fellow man. But I can't shake the feeling that we are followed. I'm sure of it."

The horse seemed to acknowledge Jamie's comment with a knowing shake of her head as she pushed on through the crowded streets, and Jamie found his way back at the front door of his father's house without incident. But instead of passing through the archway, he rode past and into a narrow side street, slipping from the horse and letting it walk alone, as he had trained it to do. The clip of its iron shod hooves could be heard against the backdrop of activity in the street. Jamie paused, then moved stealthily forward towards the corner of the side street and the main thoroughfare. He waited for a moment and was rewarded by the sight of a shadow, pale against a mound of dirty snow. He pulled his dagger from its sheath, ready to grab the form when it appeared. A man passed the entrance and peered into the alley as he continued to walk. The man was only alerted to Jamie's presence by his sudden movement.

"Hoy, what is your business here?" Jamie demanded.

The man, once he had gained his composure, sneered as only a courtier can. "Me? I mind my own business, and what of it?" He demanded, looking down his nose at Jamie and reaching for his own dagger.

"Why do you follow me? You have done so since the court. Answer me."

The arrogant bluster continued. "Watch your manners, churl. I do not follow you."

"Then mayhap you should. I could teach you some civility towards your betters." Jamie responded in kind, not to be outdone by this courtly peacock. With that he closed the distance faster than the courtier could have imagined. Trained in the hard battles of the north, he knew speed was everything and pressed down on the man's dagger arm, preventing him from drawing his weapon. A look of consternation passed across the courtier's face as he realised he was not dealing with a callow youth, but a man trained in arms.

With his dagger pointing at the man's chest Jamie

demanded: "Now answer my question. Why do you follow me?"

The man's cloak fell back, revealing a formal livery emblazoned on his surcoat. He pulled it back further to show the full crest and colours. "I serve Sir John Tiptoft and I am on an errand for his employ," he replied. "Unhand me and tell me your own business." he countered.

"Well, errand boy, I live here at my father's house and was returning home."

The man looked up in faint surprise. "A merchant or weaver's son? But I thought..." He cut himself short. "Unhand me then, for I am a messenger of the court," he demanded.

Jamie sneered at him, releasing his arm but keeping his dagger unsheathed. "An errand boy, as I surmised. Be on your way, then."

The courtier spat and returned to the street, striding away from Jamie with as much dignity as he could muster. Then a voice floated out from a shadowed portico on the other side of the street.

"He was following you, I followed him as he did you."

Jamie span around at the voice and saw *Signor* Corio appear as if by magic from the shadows.

"You! What do you do here?" Jamie asked, surprised that someone could keep themselves concealed from him so well.

"Your father asked that I watch your back, just in case. You have made an enemy there, I think, a servant of one who is not well disposed towards you." Cristoforo replied in French.

Jamie switched languages with practised ease. "You are right, courtiers such as that are a law unto themselves and usually group themselves together under the power and protection of their master. But thank you, I am pleased to be vindicated. For a moment I imagined myself jumping at shadows."

A thin smile appeared on Cristoforo's face. "But you were

right. Men who have known danger such as you and me should always listen to the voice at the back of their heads, *non*?"

Jamie broke into a smile, realising that they shared a common bond.

"I am beginning to see how you came to save my father. Now, I must retrieve my horse and you must tell me your story, I wish to hear in full how you came to my father's notice, and to know more about the skill at arms of which John boasted yesterday evening."

"I should be pleased to enlighten you, Master James."

"No, as I said yester eve. Prithee, just James or Jamie, as you wish."

"*Grazie*, Jamie," Cristoforo reverted to his native Italian.

Chapter Thirteen

Carmelite Friary, London: March

The days since the confrontation on Bodmin Moor and their departure from Launceston monastery had passed without incident, and Mark and Friar Vincent had at last arrived at the main Carmelite friary. The large and imposing walls loomed above them as they approached the entrance on Flete Street. Friar Vincent grabbed the metal rod that was attached to the wall and pulled hard. He was rewarded by the sounding of a bell within. A few moments later, a wicket gate set into the large double doors opened and a fellow friar appeared through the doorway.

At first the man was a little puzzled, then he exclaimed: "Friar Vincent! By the Good Lord it is a pleasure to see you again. How do you do?"

"Godfrey, praise God. I have returned safely."

They embraced, and the chorus of greetings continued as others joined them. Godfrey beckoned Mark and Friar Vincent forward into the sanctuary of the walls, and Friar Vincent breathed a sigh of relief to be back within the ecclesiastical confines of his home.

An elderly figure appeared eventually, exuding authority through his grave demeanour. His robes were of a better quality and he wore a specially braided cord about his girth inlaid with silver. A heavy gold cross hung from a chain around his neck, denoting his rank. The other monks fell quiet as he approached, and a warm smile grew on his face as he greeted Friar Vincent.

"You are returned to us in good health, Friar Vincent, I am delighted to see." The shrewd blue eyes then turned their attention to the imposing figure of Mark at his side. "And who do we have here, a new convert?" Although the question was in earnest, there was a twinkle in his eyes as he spoke, not for a moment believing that a simple explanation would suffice.

"Guardian, allow me to present Mark from Cornwall. He wished to come to London through palliating circumstances and I offered to act as his guide. We have been good companions, and he wishes to enter the lists of wrestlers, for that is his calling."

Sensing that there was a good deal more to Mark's story, the Guardian nodded in acceptance, knowing that he would learn the full account when the time was right.

"You are welcome, Mark of Cornwall, and we shall be pleased to aid you in any way we can," the Guardian responded graciously.

Mark, whose eyes had been out on stalks since reaching the outskirts of the capital, was overawed at both the grand nature of the Friary and the Guardian who was head of the order. He bowed low. "Thank you, your worship; I'm right grateful to you, especially Friar Vincent, who has been my saviour on the road here to Lunnon."

The Guardian looked again at Vincent, raising an inquisitive eyebrow.

"London, sir. His accent is strong," Vincent answered the Guardian's unasked question.

The Guardian nodded but demanded no more details, replying to Mark in a self-deprecating manner. "Please, my son, I am merely a Guardian, and no more than my fellow friars except in name. Friar Vincent, please take our young friend to a cell, then once you have washed the travel from yourself, be good enough to attend me in my quarters." The Guardian turned to the younger man. "Mark, you are free to wander the grounds and gardens as you wish. There are some diverting walks within our cloisters, please avail yourself of them and we will find you ere supper commences."

Mark nodded and offered his thanks, looking up at the huge steeple that rose from the main church ahead of him. Dressed stone arches and walls faced the courtyard, with many doors and passages leading off in different directions. Mark was amazed at the size and grandeur of the priory. Friar Godfrey came forward smiling, and placed a gentle hand on Mark's sleeve.

"Come Mark, I will show you to a guest cell where you will be comfortable and can wash away the stain of travel. When you are ready I will be pleased to escort you as your guide around the friary.

"Thank you Friar Godfrey, I should like that."

With that they walked away. For the first time in many weeks, Friar Vincent felt completely at peace as he took the familiar path to his old cell.

A little later, Godfrey gave Mark the promised tour of the buildings and grounds, taking in the extensive orchard and herb garden, which interested him greatly given his farming background. He bent to look closely at unfamiliar herbs.

"What is this?" He asked.

"That is henbane. Mixed with hemlock we use it for ailing joints and pains."

"This?"

"That is the arnica plant, which would be particularly useful for you, I should think. Did not Friar Vincent say that you were a wrestler? Well this is the best unguent for bruises and sprains and the like. I am sure that you receive such injuries in your calling."

"I do indeed, and would be grateful for anything to ease the aches after a match."

"Would you like to visit our infirmary?" Mark nodded enthusiastically. "There are brother friars there who specialise in all forms of medicine, and who can instruct you in their arts. Our order was formed in Palestine many years ago, as I am sure friar Vincent has told you. We adopted and use many medicines not indigenous to this country. The Holy Land is a source of many miraculous cures, and the order brought them here to England, along with the lore of healing." They walked along a cloister then entered through a wide door marked *Item Infirmariam.*

The inside was well lit and smelled of herbs, rosewater and incense. Bunks and trestles lined the walls. Fresh, clean rushes were spread across the floor, and they rustled under their feet as they moved forward. Mark was stunned by everything he saw and realised that it was a far cry from the local rural physic of his village, who could barely pull a tooth and relied upon charting the alignments of the planets to aid his patients as much as any medicines. A sedate figure emerged with a white surcoat over his habit.

"Friar Michael," Godfrey greeted, "I have a new pupil for you." He went on to explain the circumstances of Mark's arrival, then left him in the care of the head of the infirmary.

After Vespers that evening they settled down to eat the

main meal of the day in the refectory. It was here that Mark regaled Friar Vincent with details of his tour, including an enthusiastic description of the Infirmary and all the benefits it offered. When he was able, Vincent interjected and was able to impart some good news to Mark.

"I have spoken at length with the Guardian and he has agreed to help you, for he is well connected at court through the ecclesiastical See and will be able to facilitate introductions on your behalf. Although the king is not currently at court, his son the prince is keen on the sport of wrestling and encourages any new contestants. I will present you tomorrow with the Guardian as our sponsor."

"Thank you, Friar Vincent. I am much indebted to you and of course the Guardian. Praise be to God for my good fortune and your helping me."

"It is a pleasure, my son."

Chapter Fourteen

Burgundy Castle, Dijon, France.

The huge castle dominated the skyline of Dijon, lying to the southwest of the city centre and close to Notre Dame Cathedral. The gatehouse was forbidding, reflecting the personality of its owner, John the Fearless, Duke of Burgundy.

The rattle of steel-shod shoes could be heard along the road long before the rider appeared, echoing off the cobbled streets and reverberating from the walls of the buildings as the figure appeared out of the darkness. Armed guards barred the way as the horseman approached. By his travel stained garb and the look of his tired mount, he was a messenger who had travelled far. He dismounted before his horse collapsed under him, sliding from the saddle and landing with a stagger before catching his balance. Gently gathering the reins, he patted his horse's neck, speaking calming words, his hand coming away wet with foamy sweat.

The guard moved forward to interrogate him as the hour was late and the outer gates closed.

"What business do you have here at this hour? No visitors are expected or permitted to enter."

The messenger reached into his leather satchel and produced a rolled parchment, creased with use. His voice croaked as he spoke.

"I have a message from the Palace on his Majesty's service. Here are my *bona fides*." With that he passed over the letter. The guard scanned it briefly, moving back into the light of the burning torch supported by a metal sconce built into the castle wall. His expression changed from scorn to alarm as he saw that it vouched for the owner to be extended every courtesy and aid: it was signed by the King of France himself, and the parchment bore his Royal seal.

The guard shouted over his shoulder to his comrades: "Raise the portcullis and open the gates!"

The messenger retrieved his pass and moved forward, leading his blown and tired horse behind him, its head dropped and swinging in exhaustion as it walked forward. A courtier came forward followed by a groom, but the messenger shook off the hand that reached for the reins. "I will see to him myself before I'm announced. He has carried me well and saved my life. I will see to him first."

Staggering with exhaustion, man and horse followed the groom to the stables and here, under a lantern away from the combustible hay and straw, he began to wipe away the sweat with a clean wet cloth. Then with firm gentle strokes he brushed the animal's coat. He offered up a bucket of water, but only permitted the horse a few mouthfuls. Turning to the groom he rasped.

"Only a little more, no matter how much he wants, do you hear? If he gets colic I'll have your balls. Then walk him around the courtyard 'til he breathes right. Afterwards, just a small amount of hay, no oats until I return and see how he is." The groom nodded, scared by this soiled and fearsome figure come straight from the king's court.

"Good boy." The man flipped a coin in the lamplight which the groom deftly caught.

"Thank you monsieur." He called, pulling at his forelock as the messenger finally relinquished control of the animal. The messenger followed the courtier through a formal archway into the bailey, then up steps to the main hall and finally to the private chambers of the duke. The chamber was well lit and bore the trappings of luxury from the carved furniture to the ornate rugs and tapestries adorning the walls and floor. The floor was of wooden planks and warm under foot.

"Wait here, and my Lord will attend you in due course," he was ordered. "There is wine on the table and some food." The messenger nodded his thanks and with a goblet in his hand he chewed hungrily on a chicken leg before heading towards the warmth of the fire that was radiating heat into the duke's quarters. At length he heard footsteps and a clunk as the door catch was raised, and two men entered through the open door.

The first was clearly in charge. He had the natural arrogance and hauteur of the aristocracy. It seeped out of him from his elegant clothes to his widely spaced, pinpoint eyes hooded by large lids. He had a long aquiline nose and full red lips. He strode forward, a strong physical presence as he entered the room.

The man who followed him was also obviously of noble blood, judging by his arrogance and dress. His clothes had been thrown on hastily by his appearance, but he had taken the time to cinch around his waist a jewel-encrusted belt that sported a dagger, upon the hilt of which his hand rested. He was ever watchful, despite the hour, and the messenger knew that he would draw and cut with the weapon at the first sign of trouble.

"Well, do you have a message for me?" The first man demanded, holding out his hand.

"If you are his grace the Duke of Burgundy, I have a missive from his majesty the king to be delivered safely into your hand."

"I am he. What do I look like, his cook? Give me your letter."

The messenger decided that only a senior member of the French aristocracy could possibly treat him so rudely, and passed over the letter bearing the king's seal.

"As you wish, your Grace," he offered, bowing.

The Duke of Burgundy dismissed him. "Await my pleasure in the kitchens, there will be an answer."

The messenger turned and left, shaking his head at the curt dismissal once he left the chamber. When the door had closed the duke broke the seal and read the contents, his face expressing both surprise and glee the further he read. He slapped the back of his hand against the letter and cried: "Hah! I thought he was a milksop, a spineless popinjay. But it seems our esteemed king has some balls after all. Jean, we have the authority to retake Calais! The death of that Armagnac traitor has paved the way."

"Full authority?"

"*By whatever necessary means*," he read the words out loud. "We have carte blanche."

"By God's grace we will rid the loathsome English from our soil forever. God bless France!"

"We will send our response with the messenger and begin making plans on the morrow. We know how it will be prepared. Victory and power lie within our grasp, Jean. With this we will be the force behind the throne – Calais first, then Paris."

Chapter Fifteen

Lawrence Lane, London

The morning after his trip to the Palace saw Jamie rise in good spirits. He had been economical with the details of his discussion with Sir Richard, and whilst John and Thomas exchanged knowing glances at his explanation, nothing more was said. However, John was curious in another direction: he wished to see how his former protégé had progressed in the fighting arts.

They all stood in the yard behind the house: Jamie, his father and sister, John and Cristoforo.

"So, Lad, can you still draw a war bow, or have you grown soft fighting the Scots?" John chided as his lips parted in a gently mocking grin.

Jamie grinned back at the comment. He pulled the draw string, sliding it up the body, to push the loop over the horn nock of the powerful war bow. Like most Englishmen, he had been trained in the bow from infancy, but many knights or esquires abandoned their instruction before their training reached the point at which they were able to draw the full strength of a mighty one hundred and sixty pound war bow.

It was not just a matter of strength, as the French had found to their cost when they tried to train their own brigade of archers. It took years of training, muscle memory and technique. The untutored assumed a position with a straight left arm and tried to pull the mighty weight using the right hand alone. They failed, and Jamie now demonstrated why. He looked down towards the archery butt, set some 50 yards away at the far end of the yard. Jeanette held up an arrow bag and he selected five strong, straight ash shafts, fletched with goose feathers and pushed these into the ground at his feet. Cristoforo looked on in interest. He had of course heard stories of battles in which the legendary weapon had been used, but like all his countrymen, particularly the Genoese, he favoured the continental crossbow. He had never seen or experienced this weapon up close before, and was sure that its efficacy had been exaggerated.

Jamie nocked an arrow and held string and bow separately, then as Cristoforo watched, he stood into the bow, bracing both legs and drawing left and right arms simultaneously, pulling bow and cord apart, using his whole body as a vast retracting mechanism with long-remembered muscle memory. Then he surprised Cristoforo, who assumed that the draw would finish at the eye to sight the arrow. Instead, Jamie continued, drawing the bow string back to his ear and with every sinew and muscle straining, he held for a second then released. There was, to the English present, that magical sound that resonated with success in battle, the *whoosh* and whistle as the arrow flew, faster than the eye could follow at this close distance. A moment later a solid thud was heard as the arrow rammed straight into the butt, its point driven through to pierce to the far side, such was the power of the bow at this close range.

"*Dio mio...*" Cristoforo muttered, but stood mute as Jamie's arm flew down without thinking, plucked another arrow and sent it flying towards the butt. Three more times he repeated the process; and in less than thirty seconds all five arrows were protruding from the target, with the last still quivering in its mark. He looked down the range to see that of the five arrows, four were within the centre ring and only the first lay outside it.

"*Incroyable*," Cristoforo spoke in French this time, "if I hadn't seen it with my own eyes, I would not have believed it possible." He immediately understood the power and lethal capability of the weapon and why it was so feared. "But why do you draw to the ear? How do you sight your target?"

Jamie turned, smiling and pleased that he had acquitted himself so well, especially with John watching. "The extra draw adds a deal more power." He explained, "And the sighting is done by instinct borne of long practice. It cannot be explained – it just is." He finished. "Should you like to try?"

Cristoforo took the bow, tested the strength of the yew shaft and laughed, shaking his head. "No, that would be an exercise in futility, I can see now why it cannot be learned save from an early age."

Jamie accepted the response with a good grace and asked for an answer to a question that had been puzzling him since his first acquaintance with the Italian on the day of his return home. "Now as to skills, I wish to understand how you came to save my father. It was not with swords, so what, the knife at your belt?" He asked puzzled.

Cristoforo looked at Thomas who encouraged him to perform. "I can show you better than explain."

"Please," Jamie said, still puzzled.

With that, Cristoforo dropped nimbly and at great speed,

bending knees and waist, hands swooping briefly to his boots. He straightened, holding a dagger in each hand as if by magic. Jamie was amazed.

Jamie was then treated to a skilful display of juggling, as the silver blades whirled in the air, at once dropping by point, then handle. Each time it would seem that they would fall or pierce Cristoforo's skin, yet they were caught by the hands of a master. In a blur of incredible speed, the Italian used an overhand grip, spin to reverse, handle for lunge, blocking moves and finally both weapons were simultaneously caught by the tips of the blades, perfectly balanced for throwing. Jamie was about to praise his lethal dexterity when he saw Cristoforo's arms whip back and forward, sending the two daggers flying through the air each side of Jamie's head to end quivering in the lean-to post behind him.

However, Cristoforo too was surprised, for in the split second of movement Jamie had sensed attack and had instinctively reached for and drawn his own sword with a speed that had surprised the Italian. There was a frozen moment when neither man reacted, one holding a sword, the other empty-handed, having launched his deadly assault: then they both burst out laughing.

"I can see that my father was in good hands." Jamie offered.

"You too, Jamie. This was the other who was of similar speed to me whom you mentioned on the voyage here?" Cristoforo demanded of John.

"It is, and I intend to see if he is still as skilful." He grunted.

Jamie smiled at the familiar challenge of his old tutor in arms. John produced two blunted swords and both men donned thick gauntlets armoured on the outside with flexible mail to protect their hands. Then, assuming an *en-garde* position, they fought, as Jamie and Sir Robert had done in his castle. The blades flicked out searching for weakness: the older warrior's experience matched against the speed of youth.

First a cross then a parry, Jamie sought to test his opponent, who had taught him many tricks and forms. Points flicked out, seeking an opening. Then with a change of direction, a cross guard at the blade, John battered against Jamie's sword, but instead of resisting he retreated and seemed lost. He span away and circled, ramming the hilt of his pommel under John's guard and into his ribs. While the thick gambeson took the force out of the blow, it still hurt the older warrior, who winced and reacted by dropping his shoulder in pain. At this, Jamie reversed the blade; twisting his wrist and stepping backwards half a pace for more room, he presented the point inches from John's face in a backward strike.

Holding his side, John shook his head in disgust. "God's eyes, but you're fast and tricky as a snake. Where did you learn that last move? It was not one I taught you."

"Fighting the rabid Scots in the border country – and devil take it I nearly lost an eye to a similar move. Were it not for thrusting a dagger in the whoreson's ribs I should not be here now. I vowed then to learn the ploy and use it myself."

Cristoforo had looked on with interest. He realised that Jamie was not just a merchant's son, living off his position, but a warrior. He was impressed with his skills. Jamie then proceeded to show John the move in slow motion, and they practiced for a while, to the interest of the onlookers.

That noon at the midday meal, Thomas grew more inquisitive as to the role that Sir Richard had outlined for Jamie.

"I can only answer as I was instructed to by Sir Richard." Jamie responded "He is understandably worried by the events pertaining to the king, whose state of health is apparently a cause of great concern to the court. However, he fears enemies within as much as those abroad. With such thoughts in mind he has asked that I aid him where required to provide information that may prove of interest to the crown and the country's security. He has asked that I keep him appraised of any events and plans to which I may become privy, particularly should I travel abroad.

"To this end, he has assured me that Sir Robert would be grateful if I were to represent him at court, to look after his interests. So, I shall continue to esquire for him in London. He also asked, father, that if the need arose I should represent you abroad," Jamie looked to his father for support, "and aid him in his intelligence in any way I can."

"Huh," John snorted. "He couches his orders in diplomacy and fancy words, but he wants you to spy for him."

Jamie nodded. "Yes: to serve my king and keep the realm safe from traitors and invasion. It will be a chance for me to earn my spurs and rise to the king's attention at court. All is there to be gained, and it will be an adventure."

The young man's eyes were filled with the excitement of youth; he had chanced upon an opportunity to become a knight and seek fame and fortune fighting for his country. He was already more than a callow youth. He was battle hardened from the borders, and wished for a chance to prove himself further.

"Did Sir Richard mention the insurrection caused by the blasphemers? There is to be a burning today in the square."

"Aye he did that. The Lollards, a man named John Bady, I hear. Will he recant, think you?" Jamie asked.

Cristoforo was puzzled.

"*Cosa vuol dire* 'recant'?"

"Ah yes, you will not know. A new movement was founded by the cur Bady, who believes that the Holy sacrament is not so holy, and that blessing it does not mean that it becomes the body and blood of Christ."

At which all around the table crossed themselves, with Cristoforo taking a deep intake of breath at the shock of the blasphemy as he did so.

"*Madonna.* They burn him today at the stake?" The others nodded. "It is well done; such words are a crime against God. I shall go and watch this heretic burn." He declared.

Chapter Sixteen

The French Court, Paris.

A week later the Duke of Burgundy and his companion-at-arms, Jean de Grisson, rode through the streets of Paris, turning eventually into the rue Saint-Antoine, which led to the gates of the royal palace, the Hotel des Tournelles. As they approached the palace they noticed the series of small towers that gave the royal residence its name. The towers reflected a cluster of buildings built according to different architectural styles, from spires to turrets, sharp gabled chapels and huge stone zigzagged walls that came together to embrace a vast twenty-acre estate in the heart of Paris.

Although the street was wide, they still had to fight through crowds of milling pedestrians and vendors. Paris had grown rapidly, and was now home to a population of nearly 200,000, making it far larger than any other European city. The forbidding towers of the Bastille lay to the northeast, casting their daunting shadows across the streets. But it was here, in the pleasurable confines of the Hotel des Tournelles, that the royal chambers and residence lay. They passed through the outer arch of the gateway and presented their papers to the sergeant of the guard, who recognised the duke and passed them through with barely a glance at the royal warrant. The duke's reputation as a hot tempered and vicious aristocrat went before him, and he was not a man to be crossed.

They came to an inner gate, opening out into a courtyard, where they were met by an equerry dressed in the royal livery. The man nodded to the duke and his companion before summoning a groom, who took their horses by the reins and quietly led them away.

"Your Grace, I trust that you fare well and had a good journey?"

"We did, thank you," the duke responded.

"Would you like some refreshment before your meeting with Monsieur Salmon?"

"Monsieur Salmon? I thought our audience was with his majesty, not his secretary?" The duke looked down his nose at the equerry.

"I am afraid that his Majesty is indisposed at this time, and matters of state are being dealt with by his trusted secretary and advisor, my Lord Salmon." The equerry replied diplomatically. The duke cast a knowing glance at his companion, who raised his eyebrows in response.

"Very well. We shall avail ourselves of your hospitality. Lead on."

Sometime later the two men were shown through to an antechamber and from there to the grand offices of the Royal Secretary. A guard passed them through as they were escorted by the same equerry into a warm and well-appointed room. The walls were lined with ornate wooden wainscoting and thick piled rugs covered much of the floor. A beautifully coloured stained glass window was set high into the far wall, flooding the room with light from the gloomy early spring day outside. A brazier threw out a steady heat while a huge fireplace set against the far wall blazed against the damp Parisian air.

Two figures were engaged in a discussion over a table covered with documents as they entered the chamber. One was of slim build, in his early thirties with a scholarly air and piercing blue eyes that missed nothing and gave naught away. He was dressed in the height of fashion in embroidered silk of turquoise and gold, and his long blond hair curled to the nape of his neck in the current custom. Beside him was a youth, a boy of perhaps thirteen years of age at first appearance. His long nose bespoke his paternal lineage, but he had his mother's beautiful eyes and dark hair. He inclined his head, gazing across at the two newcomers. The duke was immediately reminded of the boy's father, Charles VI. But it was the older man who addressed them first.

"I bid you welcome, your Grace, and you too, Monsieur De Grisson. I am Pierre Salmon, at your service." He stood and moved across the room to greet them. "Allow me to introduce his Highness the Dauphin, Louis de Guyenne." The youth came forward and both men bowed. "I trust that you have been well looked after and are refreshed after your journey?" Salmon continued. He had a light, almost lisping voice, musical in quality yet strangely reassuring.

"We have, thank you, and we are much refreshed." The Duke of Burgundy was polite, suddenly aware of how powerful Salmon had become. Rumours had abounded of his rise in influence as the king had become ill, but he had not realised just what a tour de force the Secretary presented. "How does his Majesty?" The duke asked.

"His Majesty is ill," Salmon responded, ever aware of the royal connexion at his side, "While he enjoys moments of lucidity, he remains indisposed in matters of state. I bear the brunt of his duties, with the Dauphin as my aide in ensuring all is well within the realm."

The Dauphin was old beyond his years as was witnessed by his next comment. "My father believes that he is made of glass and will shatter if exposed to public life. Therefore we continue in his stead, counselling and governing for the day when he is ready to continue in his rightful place."

A loyal son and heir in these days of political turmoil. He will bear watching, the duke thought. Outwardly he commented. "We wish his Majesty a most speedy recovery, please God." The men crossed themselves and Salmon muttered a hearty 'Amen'.

"Now my Lords, may I offer you wine ere we commence our discussions?" Salmon took over, and the two men accepted the offer. With goblets of warm, spiced wine set before them, they settled down to hear the schemes that the king's secretary had planned.

"The message that was despatched to you in the king's name was agreed by the Ruling Council. It has long been acknowledged by all who love France that the stain upon her honour is the hold the English have on Calais. It is a blight, not only upon our good name, but upon the safety and security of our beloved country. I believe we are all agreed upon this view?" The two newcomers nodded assent, stifling their impatience as they waited to see what role they would be asked to assume in the coming events.

"Just so," Salmon continued. "In the king's more lucid moments, it greatly affects his Majesty's calm and equanimity to consider that one of his main towns and trading ports is under English rule. He has therefore urged me and the Council to undertake a campaign to re-take the town and return it to the rightful ownership of *la belle France.*"

"How is this to be achieved? Have plans been drawn up? Who is privy to them?" The duke demanded.

Pierre Salmon looked at the Duke of Burgundy with a benign expression on his face, a practiced expression that no doubt masked his true thoughts. "My Lord duke, we have already made extensive preparations in this regard – but alas they are not entirely complete."

He rose and beckoned the party to follow him to the large table beneath the stained glass window. He picked up a large parchment tied with a yellow ribbon and carefully unrolling the scroll, he placed paperweights at each corner to show a full scale map of Calais. The clear ink drawing showed the town with its walled emplacements and defences, the infamous sea-fed moat and the bridges and waterways that made it almost impregnable. The surrounding marshes were clearly defined, adding to the daunting prospect of capture.

"Let me begin with the established facts. Calais is a town of two parts: north and south. The sea feeds the main moat and is therefore tidal. The walls have been fortified since the English occupation, with new turrets and crossfire battlements. The main gates – of which there are three: the portside, the East across the marshes reached by a single road and a smaller entrance to the north – are all defended by water and drawbridges. Each proposed entry is naturally funnelled to one of these three access points, due to the lethal conditions of the marshland to either side. The moats are deep and wide, with no obvious crossing points. The islands in the centre look solid, but our engineers tell us that they are boggy and treacherous underfoot. They would not support a man at arms, let alone siege machines. They are also regularly denuded of all cover and well within bow shot of the walls."

Salmon paused to let all this sink in, and the duke snorted in disgust. "We know all this. Calais is apparently impossible to conquer, yet the English somehow managed it."

Salmon nodded. "They did it through siege and by starving

the population out. They also controlled the seaward side and therefore the port. It could not be re-provisioned and their guns of Satan cannoned the walls from high vantage points and embrasures above. It took them months of siege, during which the English Channel was as much a battleground as the landward side. Genoese pirates helped us, but still the blockade held true. Plague, pestilence and worse was visited upon the town." He shivered at the stories he had heard of people eating dogs, rodents and horses; high-born women prostituting themselves for food; disloyalty and treachery; the awful, forced evacuation of non-combatants who had been left to starve and die before the town walls, with neither side prepared to feed them.

He paused again, like a magician leading his audience to a point of expectation and tension. The duke frowned with impatience. He was tired of games and wanted action. Sensing a limit to his patience, Salmon continued.

"We do not have the luxury of time to mount a full siege. The town would be relieved before we could starve them out, although the sea will play a significant part in our plans. We have one main advantage; we can provision and supply our troops from the landward side and mount an assault on any or all of the main gates without fear of reprisal from the English after securing the area."

"But we still have to defeat the town's defences before the accursed English can relieve it," the duke commented.

"Yes my lord, you are as ever correct. Here", he stabbed a finger down to the north of the town. "It is here that we shall strike. Please note, my lords, that it is the widest entrance, and our engineers inform us that the bridge to the gateway is of arched stone. It would be impossible to destroy without substantial works taking many weeks – but here at the widest entrance, the moat is at its narrowest point. The surrounding ground is solid and capable of supporting great weight. We shall attack here with a mighty siege tower." He beamed at the duke and de Grisson.

"But my lord secretary, siege towers take months to construct. The garrison would be forewarned and re-stocked, fully provisioned to withstand a siege. How do you propose to retain the element of surprise?" De Grisson asked. It was here that the Dauphin showed his mettle.

"We already have begun the construction of our siege engine – in secret, at Saint-Omer."

Chapter Seventeen

Westminster Palace, London.

The dovecote was located high up in one of the Palace's many towers, and as part of the Royal Aviary it offered more than just a home for doves. The courtier wound his way down the spiral staircase, clasping a scrap of rolled up parchment in his hands. He reached the ground floor and made his way through the maze of corridors to Sir Richard's offices. Knocking, he went through the oaken door to the outer office that was guarded by his secretary.

"A message has just been delivered to the aviary. The bird carries French markings. My Lord Richard will wish to see it directly."

"Indeed he will," the secretary replied. "My gratitude. Remain in the main hall in case there is a return message." The courtier was aware of the court rankings; he nodded a bow and left the outer office. Alfred walked through to his master's inner chambers, moving across to pass on the scrap of parchment. A frown crossed Sir Richard's brow, as he had asked not to be disturbed.

"My Lord, a missive. We believe it comes direct from France."

"Thank you, Alfred." The frown disappeared as Richard stood and took the message, carefully unrolling the long, thin screed. He produced a magnifying glass and carefully deciphered the code, writing the reformed words onto parchment as he did so.

CALAIS THREATENED PLANS MADE AID NEEDED IN HASTE GODSPEED MONK

Sir Richard looked at the message again, sat down and rubbed his temples, hoping to ease the slow pulse of a headache that was rising there. *So,* he thought, *it has begun, the French are on the move. They make plans, and we need eyes and ears there to tell us what they plan to do. Jamie lad, it is time for you to start earning your keep.* He tore off the bottom of the page and threw the deciphered note together with the original message into the fire.

"Alfred, is Master James within the Palace?"

"I believe so, my Lord."

"Summon him, there are urgent matters to discuss. But do so discreetly, for we have enemies as well as friends within, of that I am certain sure."

"Of course, my Lord." Alfred left Sir Richard and went in search of the page who had delivered the coded message. He engaged the messenger in conversation, and the two men sauntered together towards the Great Hall, looking for all the world like colleagues engaged in a discussion of little import. Upon entering the hall, Alfred appraised the room, seeing courtiers in huddles, ladies flirting gently with knights and pages, conspiracies blossoming at every turn, some more malign than others. A colourful pageant of silks and gowns; pourpoints elegantly gilded and stuffed with bawdekin, their long sleeves hanging almost to the floor.

Their presence was noted by everyone, even those who seemed oblivious, but such was the nature of the court; everyone was capable of listening to two conversations at once, and no one's eyes missed anything. Alfred and the messenger appeared to wander aimlessly, making small talk with various groups as they passed, then lastly, as if by accident, they came to Jamie's assembly and smiled in gentle acknowledgement, as if engaging the participants in a harmless jape. Alfred walked off, while the page said quietly: "Sir Richard's chambers as the hour pleases, Master James," before catching up with Alfred.

A vague smile by way of acknowledgement and a subtle nod was Jamie's only outward response. The two passed on, their mission accomplished.

On their way to Sir Richard's chambers, they passed an open doorway, which heralded the sound of noisy exercise. The room was appointed as a gymnasium, and within it a group was cheering a wrestling bout. Alfred and the messenger noted a lean figure in striking garb, taller than his peers, surrounded by lords eagerly cheering the two contestants on to greater efforts between gulps of wine from their gilded goblets as the refreshment flowed copiously. The two exchanged glances: "The prince is clearly enjoying himself."

"Shall we?" Alfred offered. "For nought else but to add verisimilitude to our peregrinations."

"Let us indeed," The page responded, and the two of them sauntered into the gymnasium, appearing aimless as they moved towards the tall, elegant, figure. They bowed deeply as they approached:

"Your Royal Highness, I bid you good day," Alfred said.

"And to you, Alfred. How does my Lord Whittington? Thriving I trust. Does he ever cease from his toils? Encourage him to rest, or bring him to watch this fine spectacle."

The prince's voice was rich, and his words were delivered in with the light-hearted confidence of a man who was completely at ease with his surroundings and safe in the company of his favourites. Although tall, he was broad of shoulder, his pourpoint failing to hide the hard musculature of his shoulders. His long, thin, angular face was happy in repose, but marred by the thin puckered line of an ugly scar on his right cheek. He sipped from his goblet and laughed encouragingly, clapping Alfred on the shoulder.

"Now this new fellow, he wrestles right well. A Cornishman, by God. They breed them well down there, it seems." His meiny turned as one to view the spectacle before them.

A series of mats had been set down in the centre of the wooden floor and the two wrestlers were clad in the familiar white jackets of Cornish wrestlers. One was blond and broad of shoulder, showing incredible musculature and perfect balance. The other had curly hair, and whilst he matched the other in height, he was lighter of frame, but showed a wiry strength and greater fluidity of movement. Their strengths were different, yet they were a good match. As they gripped each other's stiff canvas jackets, the men fought to secure the crushing, dominant grip that would enable them to succeed with a winning throw.

Each gripping the other shoulder to arm, they circled clockwise, bending at the waist, drawing each other forward in an effort to pull the other off balance. The darker man stamped suddenly with his right foot forward. Using the momentum, he kicked with the flat of his left foot at his opponent's shin, pulling sharply with his arms.

It was a good move, and it caught the blond opponent off balance. But instead of trying to pull back and resist the move, the man went with it, bending the leg, dropping to his knee and extended his left leg sideways between his opponent's legs. As he did so he tugged hard with his right hand, pulling the darker man over his back in a surprise counter-move. Lifting his left shoulder and leg, he completed the move, and his opponent somersaulted to land flat on his back with a satisfying thud as he hit the floor.

To shouts and cheers, the blond giant stood smiling and helped his hapless opponent to stand.

"By God, that was a clever trick." The defeated opponent exclaimed. "I've not seen the like and I have never been beaten from that counter before."

"My father taught it to me, and his before 'un. It works well when movement allows. Difficult to pull off, if'n you aren't both standing still." They clapped each other on the back and parted in good grace as Prince Henry and his retinue approached.

"Cornishman, may I offer you my congratulations. That was as sprightly a move as ever I did see." The prince said.

"Thank you, your Highness." The wrestler stammered, dropping a deep bow.

"I must pass my respects to the Carmelite Guardian when next I see him. Come now, how are you known?"

"Mark of Cornwall, ere it please your Highness."

"It pleases me well, Mark of Cornwall." With that he turned to his secretary. "Have Mark added to the lists, for he shall represent me. Mark, what say you? We have a wrestling tourney of sorts with the French, which is better still than fighting them, I feel. Should you like that, to go to France and whip the cowardly *crapauds*? They'll cheat, mind, but you'll do, for certes."

"Your Royal Highness, I should be most honoured." Mark spluttered, not believing his ears.

"Excellent. We shall hear more of you, I am sure. Ralph, see to it."

"As you wish, my prince."

"Now, master Alfred, let me accompany you back to your master and see if we can pry him from his lair and dissuade him from his labours to enjoy some of life's pleasures for a change. What say you?"

"An eminent suggestion, your Royal Highness. Sir Richard shall be delighted to receive you." The prince waved away his retainers and strode off towards Sir Richard's quarters with Alfred almost running to keep up with his long stride.

Upon entering Sir Richard's offices, the prince's demeanour changed abruptly. Gone was the affable princeling, and in his stead was a shrewd and perspicacious statesman.

His almost foppish tones were replaced by a more direct approach; affable enough, but there was steel in the tone.

"My lord Richard, a good day to you. You toil as ever, I see. You send your man abroad on seemingly frivolous acts. Should I be concerned that something is afoot?"

"Ah your Royal Highness, you are as perceptive as ever. I have news from France, and an ill wind it is that blows across the channel."

The prince's brows furrowed: "Reveal to me the cause of your concerns."

"It is as we suspected, and as was revealed to us at the council in January. I am informed by one of our agents that the French have plans to take Calais." Sir Richard paused, awaiting the questions that would no doubt come from this news. In this he was not disappointed.

"Is your source reliable? We have heard rumours before, yet nought appeared."

"My agent in question is proven loyal, and I doubt any perfidy on his behalf. His nature and resource are beyond impeachment. However, the information is scant and I am wont to try and gain more news of French intentions as a matter of urgency."

"How would you propose such an undertaking? Any new insertion at this point would surely cause suspicion."

"As you say, my prince. Howsoever, my agent lodges in the town of Saint-Omer to the southeast of Calais. This will be our point of origin. I shall send someone to liaise with him and discover more on the nature of the plot. You need not be afeared, your Royal Highness. I shall engage the cleverest of subterfuge, and none shall be suspicious of our cause or the identity of our agent."

The prince smiled tightly, the strain upon the peril of the kingdom telling upon him. "I too shall be abroad, and may seek out information of mine own."

"My prince, I would strongly advise against this course of action. Perchance this treachery against your realm is real, and the result could be catastrophic should you be caught and should war ensue. Think, my prince, I urge you, think on. Your father is not recovered and you as the royal figurehead must be here to lead."

Anger flitted across the prince's face for a brief second at the rebuke, then reason returned. He clenched a fist and punched his palm in anger. "A pox on these French curs. They ruin my sport with their talk of war against us. Alas, Sir Richard, you have the right of it, though reason flies from my mind. I shall send my wrestlers without gracing them with my presence," he decided reluctantly. "Now, tell me, how does my father the king? He will not receive me and believes I am a viper in the nest. By God, though, I am true." He declared.

"My lord prince, he wavers. He suffers – some days worse than others. His mind is racked with pain and sores assail his body. His strength wanes, and to think he was once the most perfect knight in all of Europe, undefeated in the lists. It pains me to see him thus, but I strive to serve him as best I can."

"I know, Sir Richard, and your service does you credit. When we are king I shall ensure that you are rewarded." With this, he gently squeezed Sir Richard's shoulder in a rare show of courtly affection. "I will leave you now to your planning, but keep me abreast of all that passes."

As though reading the indecision in the prince's mind about travelling to France, Sir Richard gave a parting warning: "For sure. my prince. May it please you, do not sally abroad. I fear for your safety."

The prince snorted with a faint grin etching his lips. "You know me too well. But I shall heed your words." He was about to leave when Sir Richard motioned to another figure near one of the pillars by the fireplace.

"Ere you leave, my prince, may I introduce an esquire?"

Realising that there was more here than just a simple introduction, the prince studied the tall, muscular youth who stood before him.

"I have the honour to introduce James de Grispere, son of Thomas de Grispere of our guild."

Jamie came forward and bowed to the prince. "Your Royal Highness," he said.

The prince nodded and frowned. "That is Sir Robert de Umfraville's livery, is it not?"

"It is as you say, my lord prince. I have the honour of serving Sir Robert in his absence whilst he guards our Scottish borders."

"You served Sir Robert on the borders and trained with him in knighthood? You would doubtless have seen combat up there, keeping the heathen Scots rabble at bay," he said with a slight grin. "I rue the day I released Douglas and Murray to plot with that duplicitous cur Albany. My brother John is in straits for lack of funds at Berwick, he writes. Yet Sir Robert and Sir Thomas Beaufort brought a masterful raid to ram home to the Scots that we are still masters."

"I was privileged to be party to that raid, my lord, and we gave them a drubbing they shall not forget in a hurry. It was a fierce and instructive school, my prince, and I learned much under Sir Robert's tutelage."

"You were there, lad? Then Godspeed to you, and with it my blessing. It was a fine hour in English history." The prince said.

"James has agreed to help us with our venture abroad, my prince," Sir Richard interceded. "We feel that his endeavours will be of great service with the coming trials in France."

The prince looked again at Jamie, seeing the strength of purpose and determination in his face. "Then we are grateful to you, master James, and I wish you well in your task. But I caution you, have a care. The French are guileful and devilish cunning."

"I will heed your warning, my prince, but I shall do my best to serve England's cause."

"Then Godspeed, and I wish you well. Bring us back reliable information and you shall be well rewarded. I must away, before my presence here is noted and tongues wag like the tails of hounds at feed. I bid you all good day, and I will see you on the morrow at the council meeting, Sir Richard."

"As you say, my prince." Sir Richard replied.

With that Prince Henry stepped from the room to join a courtier awaiting his return at the door.

Chapter Eighteen

Saint Omer, France; April

The early spring weather had so far been kind, and an unseasonably warm sun shone down upon the Duke of Burgundy and Jean de Grisson as they rode along the main road into the town of Saint-Omer. The six day journey from Paris had been uneventful but tiring, with poor roads from the harsh winter slowing them down. Now the end was in sight, and the town of Saint-Omer, as part of the duke's lands, would guarantee a warm welcome for the party. The duke had sent part of his meiny on ahead to make preparations.

As they passed along the main highway that cut a swathe through the heavily forested region, they caught the occasional glimpse of the magnificent cathedral for which the town was famous through the cuttings in the trees. As they got closer, the frenetic activity outside the castle walls became more evident. A thriving wool and cloth industry prospered here, close to the Netherlands and Bruges, and a freely available and plentiful water route from the River Aa flowing on to Pas de Calais also gave it excellent transport links.

The looming castle and town walls rose above them, and John the Fearless nodded approvingly. It had been his father, Philip the Bold, who had strengthened and added extra fortifications to the town. The strong smell of sheep pervaded the air, mixed with tanning solutions and dyes and the odour of dung. The two men wrinkled their noses in disgust and wrapped their cowls around their faces until they had passed through the gates of the city walls.

"Ye Gods, those peasants stink!" De Grisson muttered beneath his cowl.

"They do indeed, but their labours produce the revenue for my estates. I needs must suffer excessive ordure for the sake of my purse," the duke responded with a grin. "The close distance 'tween my estates and Bruges means that the wool trade thrives here. Without it there would be little other than an abbey and a cathedral. Now let's to the Bourg, where my chatelaine had better have prepared our welcome if he wishes to keep his head. My arse is sore and my stomach thinks my throat has been cut!"

De Grisson laughed and added: "A hot bath, good meal, some of your excellent wine and a wench to warm your bed. You'll be a new man again."

With that, both men spurred their horses through the town, paying no heed to the peasantry they barged out of the way or the cries and curses their actions provoked. Some recognised the duke and doffed their caps, but he ignored them and pressed on through the cobbled streets.

The chatelaine welcomed them as they arrived with a clatter of hooves through the tower gateway guarding the Bourg. The man appeared well padded through years of good living. It was an easy life in Saint-Omer, a prosperous town with well-fed inhabitants and a thriving economy.

"Your Grace, you are bid most welcome." He said with a deep unctuous bow. The duke grunted in acknowledgement, dropped the reins of his horse and strode away to refresh himself, followed by de Grisson.

The following morning, as the light shafted through the slats of the shutters, the duke groaned as the little man in his head began hammering against the inside of his skull, testimony to the wine he had consumed the previous evening. He turned to his left and untangled himself from the dark long locks that were strewn across his neck and torso. The wench at his side sighed and locked her arms around him, snuggling into his chest, inhaling his scent of rose water and sweat from the previous night's lovemaking. The duke pried himself loose from her, and swinging his legs over the side of the bed he sat up and groaned again as the blood sang in his head. He grasped the flagon of water by his bed and drank deeply, the cold liquid splashing down over his bare chest.

His bed companion muttered gently and twisted deeper into the bolster, un-moved by his exit from the bed. Her hair splayed out in a dark fan against the white of the sheets. Her arse rose seductively as a hump under the white linen and seeing it, the duke smiled maliciously and slapped it hard. She jumped, squawked and swore, before resuming her slumbers.

"Bloody whore," he muttered and made to stand, a move he instantly regretted as the room span and the man in his head with a hammer pounded harder.

"Ye Gods, I am dying." He groaned, holding his head in his hands to steady his balance. It was a full hour before the duke's sanity was somewhat restored by a hearty breakfast and a gallon of water. He was still pale under his tan, but at least he now felt vaguely human.

"How was that comely wench you squired yester eve? By the Gods she was well hung ere she filled her gown." He muttered at Jean over breakfast.

"I misthought her for an alley cat, the way my back is

shredded and hurting to the point of ague. How was that minx you skulked off with?"

"Passing fair and skilled; more tricks than a conjurer." With more laughter and ribald jokes the two men continued until their breakfast was interrupted by a messenger. He bowed to the duke and presented a sealed missive. Puzzled, the duke broke the seal and tore it open. As he read, his brow creased then his whole face turned red with anger.

"What is it, John?" his friend asked.

"Those whoreson Armangacs have formed a new league. A treaty has been signed by Berry, Bourbon and Orleans. The bastards! I should have had them all assassinated along with the duke," he raged. "They're calling it the Treaty of Gien. The Treaty of Gien!" he shouted. "By God I'll have them banned and slaughtered. They say it is to save and protect the kingdom of France and all who endeavour to besmirch the *"welfare and honour of the king and kingdom"*. The duke waved the parchment under de Grisson's nose to emphasise the treason he read there. "They are targeting me as an enemy of the king. I will destroy them."

He crumpled the parchment and threw it to the floor, from where de Grisson picked it up to read for himself and understand more clearly the intent. "God's legs, this is full rebellion, civil war," he cried.

"I know too well their motives and what they hope to gain. Even now they will be plotting and with the hell-spawned English, I'll warrant."

All thoughts of breakfast were forgotten. Cursing loudly, they marched outside. They were met at the stables by grooms, who had readied their horses and were standing patiently awaiting their arrival. Mounted, they set off in the direction of the grand cathedral.

The morning was fair and they took their time walking

their horses through crowded streets that were familiar to the duke, for he had visited his fiefdom on many occasions. At length they turned a corner and both men feasted their eyes upon the glorious and majestic building that was Saint-Omer cathedral. It had begun as a small chapel, built by monks some 700 years earlier, but it had grown with each passing generation, and this morning it shone in the spring sun reflecting the light magnificently, its Ashlar stone appearing almost white in the brightness of the day. The drumming of hammers and chisels sounded in the air as they dismounted and entered through the primary nave. They strode into the main aisle of the church, with de Grisson marvelling at the internal glory that was set out before him. He gazed in awe up at the beautiful vaulted ceiling of the cathedral. They only managed to get halfway along the central aisle before they found their way barred by wooden scaffolding and canvas screens, from behind which came the sound of workmen hammering and sawing.

Two guards stood on duty, armed with halberds, each in mail and a shining cuirass. It seemed to the casual observer that it was an inappropriate amount of force for such a benign project. The duke and his companion marched forward. One guard went to block their way but the other, recognising the duke, bowed.

"My lord duke, you are welcome to our humble church. Do you wish to enter?"

"Of course," the duke snapped.

"One moment, my lord. I will seek the master mason, for it is often dangerous within, with falling debris."

With that he disappeared through a wooden door set into the structure. He returned a short time later accompanied by a solid man of medium height. His rolled up sleeves exposed forearms of knotted teak, with huge gnarled hands and swollen knuckles. He was covered in wood shavings rather than stone dust, and smelled of sweat and the sap of new timber. He was a proud man and although he showed deference to the duke, he was neither cowed nor subservient.

"Your Grace, we are honoured to have you here. Please follow me through into the chamber, but I would warn you of dust and rubble." The two noblemen followed the mason through the low-beamed door into the noise and dust beyond. As they passed through one door, there was a small ante-chamber before a second door opened into the body of the cathedral once again. Although they had some knowledge of what lay beyond, they were still taken by surprise at the sight that lay before them.

Instead of construction work on the new nave and extension to the main aisle as the populace of Saint-Omer supposed, the army of workers toiling away before them were working in wood, not stone. Large planks were piled high in stacks; thick oaken *bressumers* were stored vertically and were being pinned into place one at a time to form the central tower for what would eventually be a huge structure when completed. Most telling of all, the base plate, forming a stable structure for the whole assembly, was mounted on axles and huge wheels, with a harness yoke positioned in readiness to be attached.

"By the Gods, a siege tower!" De Grisson exclaimed.

"As you say Jean, and what a tower. Once we have re-taken Calais with it, it will be our route to defeating the Armagnacs too."

The seamed brown face of the master mason split into a wide grin, delighted with the reaction of the two noblemen.

"She will be a wonder when she is finished, and the accursed English will rue the day they captured Calais." He spat.

Chapter Nineteen

The Council Chamber, Westminster Palace.

The Council that was governing in the king's stead convened the day after Jamie's presentation to the prince. The men around the table were some of the most powerful and influential in the land and included Sir Richard Beauchamp, the Bishops of Durham and Bath, Richard, Earl of Warwick, Sir John Cornwaille, Thomas, Earl of Arundel, Sir John Tiptoft, Sir John Prophet, Sir Thomas Erpingham, his uncle Sir Henry Beaufort and Sir Thomas Percy, among others. They all stood as the prince entered the chamber, bowing.

"My Lords, thank you for attending, please sit, we have much to manage and debate. First, my Lord Henry, may we extend our sympathies to you on the loss of my Uncle and your dear brother, but we are right glad to have you back with us in this time of need."

Henry Beaufort nodded to accept the acknowledgement of his prince, who continued. "Let us begin apace, for I am aware of a pressing need abroad, and the tide waits for no man. Sir Richard, will you instruct us?"

"Thank you, my prince." Whittington answered. "My Lords, your Royal Highness, we have received intelligence from France that there is a plan to re-take Calais by the French and reignite their war with England. I know that we were appraised of this in January, but now the intelligence is more precise. One of my best and most reliable agents, embedded deep within France, has provided this information. He has asked for help and I am about to send someone to aid him in his cause." Sir Richard paused here and awaited any response from around the table.

It was William Stokes, a financial spy and advisor to the Council on all matters pertaining to taxes and commerce, who spoke first. He ran a network of investigators and spies throughout the kingdom in all ports and areas of trade. He was a sallow-faced man with a sharp-set features and deep set, searching eyes that missed nothing, seeming to see through everything they gazed upon. "Sir Richard, your methods are without doubt effective, but could this be a trap? Are we certain that the French cause is real? And if so, where do we suspect the assault to begin?"

"I have little doubt that the intelligence is true. The agent I have in place, if captured and tortured, would have given a different signature to his note, as we had agreed. This leaves me with a certainty of the French intention to attack Calais. Since the death of Louis of Orleans, our power and influence in the area has waned. My feelings are that the Duke of Burgundy will be behind the plot."

Sir Thomas Beaufort spoke next. "If they mean to attack, would this be the same means that they used to break the Treaty of 1396? How could they attack in surprise? It would mean a siege of many months, and we could re-stock and fortify the town with relief forces ere the siege was capable of taking the town. It took us many a month to drive the French out, and we have since fortified the town and made provision for a defence the like of which has not been seen before. How is it to be done?"

"Traitors within, perhaps?" Tiptoft replied.

"My lords." Sir Richard begged for calm. "We can merely speculate at this juncture. There are as we know many ways to bring down a town, and we can but plan and make provision for all conceivable eventualities. Our navy is now at greater strength than it has been for years, for which I give thanks to my lord..." Here he nodded towards the prince. "We can re-provision with greater ease than when we blockaded the port in the past. Moreover, we are better equipped to fight off Spanish or Venetian pirates who may seek, under French employ, to hinder our relief."

"As Governor of Calais," Sir Thomas Beaufort began, "I have heard little credible rumour of such a plot. There are of course the usual mutterings, from ale houses to the court, but little that bears credence or close scrutiny. Yet if you are certain sure, I must forthwith return in all haste and make preparations."

"My lord, I caution you not to alert unduly any forces that may be aware of what is afoot," Sir Richard cautioned.

Sir John Tiptoft asked: "Who shall you send, Sir Richard? It needs must be a well disguised party, for the French will be on their mettle."

For some reason Whittington hesitated, glancing to the prince, who gave an almost imperceptible shake of his head, his eyes sending a warning stare. "That has yet to be decided," he said. "I have agents in mind, but may send more than one to probe each possibility of offence."

Tiptoft's eyes focused keenly upon Sir Richard's face, but he realised that he would obtain no further information, and that to pursue the matter would cause suspicion.

Sir Thomas was the newly appointed Chancellor, and he re-entered the fray with a valid point on commerce.

"Needs must that we keep the port open at all odds. It is our doorway to the wool trade and for exports through France to the Netherlands, the import of which cannot be stressed too highly. We have, as you are all aware, transferred wealth amounting to a greater proportion of profits to the defence of the town, and this must not fail. To lose Calais would be a catastrophe." He warned.

The debate became more general, and the conversation turned to the king's health. All looked with interest at Prince Henry. "My father the king remains in fragile health. His body wanes, yet his mind remains active and seeks to help us reign over England. Please God that he may soon be among us again to govern in his rightful place." He finished.

The other lords nodded in assent, whatever their true feelings may have been, and a series of amens swept around the council table. At length, all articles of governance were completed and the Council sought to disband the meeting. Prince Henry looked across at his friend and confidant Sir Richard Courtney. With a nod of his head the prince rose, followed by Courtney and John Prophet, Keeper of the Privy Seal.

Sir Richard was one of the last to leave the chamber, speaking almost in whispers as he walked from the chamber in the company of William Stokes. In his incisive rasping voice Stokes said: "We have two priorities: continued trade and security of the realm. The two are interwoven and they begin and end with Calais."

Their discussion continued along the corridors, muting at times when a courtier or knight passed them.

Chapter Twenty

Southampton quayside.

The waters of the English Channel appeared calm and unthreatening on this mild spring day. A gentle breeze pushed a few clouds across the sky as a light south-easterly blew towards the shores of France. Two men stood apart from the bustle of activity at the edge of the stone wharf, one looking unhappily at the gentle swell of the sea as its green waters lapped against the quayside, causing the cog moored there to rise and fall minutely in time with the motion of the water.

The taller of the two looked across at his companion and placed a gentle hand on his shoulder. "Have cheer, Cristoforo, the wind is but a gentle breeze and will transport us to France in no time, God willing."

Cristoforo grimaced at the thought of crossing the Channel again. "I promised your father that I would guard your back to honour his saving my soul. But dear God I seem to have acted unwisely and not considered this journey. If only the Almighty would grant me wings for an hour and fly me there!"

In the weeks that followed their introduction, the two men

had grown to be good friends – at ease in each other's company, sharing a love of combat and training with weapons. They had shared techniques and trained with daggers and swords, Cristoforo's falchion a match for Jamie's broadsword despite the extra reach, and a bond had grown between them. At his father's urging, Jamie had accepted the offer of a companion he knew he could trust to watch his back, as John had done for his father over the years.

In quieter tones Cristoforo continued, as much to take his mind off the journey as anything else. "I am glad that Sir Richard deemed it more fitting that we should depart from Southampton, not London. More time on land and less at sea."

"Yes, there are too many eyes and ears in London. I still feel that I'm being followed from time to time around the court – a nest of vipers, as Sir Richard said. By God's troth, I'd rather battle the Scots on open ground with a sword in my hand."

"I prefer the shadows," Cristoforo answered. "Secrets and stealth are my world – so fear not, I will be at your back."

"Aye, and I shall be grateful of that ere this journey is over, of that I'm certain sure."

At which point their concentration was interrupted as the first of the huge wool sacks was hoisted from the quayside by the wooden crane, swinging in the breeze and with the motion of the gantry. The steeves scurried around, steadying the load with a trailing rope and guiding it into the hold of the deep-sided cog.

The noise and calls were all in English, a language that Cristoforo was beginning to master quite well, although he was still far from fluent. The regional accents of Southampton gave him a few extra problems, and his equilibrium was further disturbed by the arrival of a group of five or six young men, dressed in better clothes than those of a country bumpkin, despite the fact that their accents were not of the gentry. They moved towards the quayside in a garrulous group. Despite all being broad of shoulder and well-muscled, one blond giant stood a head taller than most. His easy gait belied his size as he rolled up to Jamie and Cristoforo.

"Good day masters," he said. "Begging pardon, but be this the boat for France?" His accent was so thick and to Cristoforo's ears unusual that he barely understood a word and looked at Jamie for help.

"Aye that she is, and sails with the tide once we're loaded," Jamie answered, smiling.

"Thank 'ee. I will inform master Swynford." With that he nodded respectfully and moved back along the quay, presumably to fetch his master.

Jamie's brow creased in a puzzled frown. "I'm sure I've seen that Hercules somewhere before." Cristoforo shrugged. Once he had assured himself that the man was not a potential threat, he became of little consequence.

"He and his friends will help to give the boat ballast, for as you say, he is a Heracles." He laughed, giving the Italian name for the fabled hero of ancient Greece.

They retired to the local inn, leaving Will, his headman, and two of his father's other servants to supervise the loading of the ship and await the rising of the tide.

As Jamie and Cristoforo were enjoying a flagon of ale, the door to the inn was thrust open and a well-dressed figure appeared. Silhouetted against the light, he stood for a moment letting his eyes adjust to the gloom within. A wary man by the look of him, Cristoforo noted. The newcomer was well dressed. He was obviously a nobleman, judging by his expensive and beautifully cut clothes and the rings that adorned his fingers. With a flourish, he removed his hat, which was of crushed velvet and sported two ostrich feathers.

For all his dandified appearance, both men noticed the

sword at his hip. In itself the sword was nothing unusual – many men carried swords – but he wore it with a carelessness of use that bespoke skill with the blade. Like Jamie, he wore riding boots which were splashed with mud as if he had travelled far. Jamie looked at his neck and shoulders, which were shrouded by a thick, woollen cloak. They were, he noticed, muscled in the same way as his own and uneven from long use of arms. The man was a knight, or an esquire at the very least. Arrogance seeped from him like an aura as he strode across the crowded tap room towards the bar, yet he moved well, remaining alert at all times. He ordered ale from the landlord, and turning he leaned on the bar to take in his surroundings.

His eyes alighted on Jamie and Cristoforo who had deliberately averted their gaze, not wishing to be noticed. Cristoforo had the trained ability to seemingly disappear at will and render himself almost invisible. To any onlooker, Jamie and Cristoforo were just two men engrossed in an intense discussion, oblivious to those around them.

They felt the stranger's eyes settle briefly upon them and then move on, subjecting the room to his study. He then chose a settle and sat with his back to the wall.

"He is a wary man indeed," Cristoforo commented quietly to Jamie.

Some time passed and the door was pushed open to admit a sailor of rough and weather-beaten appearance who cried out, "All those for the So'ton Maid, she sails soon."

With that he disappeared, closing the door to the inn. A number of men made to rise, including the well-dressed knight in the corner of the room: Jamie and Cristoforo exchanged glances.

"A fellow traveller," Jamie muttered.

They hefted up their baggage, including Jamie's leather warbag, and left the inn, proceeding to the cog, now risen in the water with the tide. They saw that Jamie's followers and servants were already aboard, leaning over the side and waiting for the final passengers to embark. Cristoforo crossed himself, muttered a prayer and stepped across the swaying gangplank, his knuckles white as he gripped the rope rails that prevented the unwary from dropping into the water between the quay and the ship, where they would be ground to a pulp by the movement of the vessel. Once aboard the craft he relaxed a little and went immediately to the forecastle, looking out to where the wide estuary of the River Alre joined Southampton Water as he strove to regain his equilibrium.

Jamie let him go and looked around, seeing the group of hearty youths he had met earlier. Among their number was the gentleman the blond giant had referred to as Master Swynford. He was of middle age and Jamie recognised him immediately from the Court. They had not been formally introduced, but each nodded to the other in mutual recognition. Swynford was elegantly dressed in the livery of Prince Henry and around his neck he wore an "SS" collar, identical to that which Sir Richard had bestowed upon Jamie before leaving for France, which was now concealed in his baggage.

Sir Richard Whittington's words came back to him now: *"Guard this well. Few are given by the king, and then only to his most faithful servants. It is the highest mark of loyalty and faith in the crown. Though heed me well, it marks you as the king's man – and with that you are in peril in foreign lands. Use it only as a means to identify yourself to my agent and keep it well hidden from prying eyes when you get to France. Remember to all purposes you are merely a merchant's son acting in his father's stead abroad on matters of trade. You will have your father's letter of authority, and that is all you must show if challenged."*

The stern words of warning had rammed home the serious

nature of his quest, and Jamie was now permanently on his mettle.

The sound of a whinnying horse shook him from his revere. He was startled. Rarely did a man transport his own horse, except when going to war. It was the usual practice to hire a mount on the other side of the Channel. This meant that the rider was serious and valued his ability to be well mounted. He looked across to see the knight from the tavern stroking the animal's muzzle and patting its neck. Feeling eyes upon him he turned around, meeting Jamie's glance with a pair of piercing grey eyes that offered no window to the soul: they were dead. Neither man backed down from the stare, each recognising in the other a vital life force and an equal at arms. Their staring match was interrupted by the cry of the captain.

"Cast off! Belay the lines."

With that the ropes and cables were thrown from the quay-side and a small rowing skip began to heave to, the toughened oarsmen pulling with all their might to right the cog for its exit from the harbour. Sails cracked as they caught the breeze and the huge rudder astern was pulled to full tilt by the helmsman. Almost imperceptibly the vessel moved away from the shore, gaining a life of its own as it followed the wind and the water. At a right angle to the quay, the mainsail caught the wind and billowed to its full extent, the ropes straining as the wind caught the huge sheet of canvas.

No longer needed, the towboat slipped away as the cog began to move on its own. The captain called out more orders as the sailors scampered about the ship with practised ease. Calls from the crow's nest carried down to the crew below and were acted upon accordingly. Gradually the cog glided free of the harbour and sailed out into the open sea. The spray from the swell rose up and drenched all on deck in gentle showers. Jamie found it exhilarating, whilst Cristoforo muttered on the upper deck with his eyes closed, praying continuously. Jamie noticed that two men in stiff leather jerkins were mounted both fore and aft, each with a crossbow at the ready. He asked Will if this was normal.

"Aye, master James. Pirates are rank about the Channel. The French and even the Spanish plunder these waters, ever ready to take a ship. The new Navy has helped, but there's no guarantee we'll be safe 'til we reach Calais."

"Have you been attacked before?"

"Yes, but we outran them and were saved by an English warship that frightened them off. Not that John wasn't keen to set about them. They lurk near French harbours and run upon English ships retuning with gelt, not wool. I pray that we do not meet them today, for we are poorly arrayed for battle."

Jamie nodded in agreement and thought back to John's warning. He looked about at the horizon and instinctively felt for the hilt of his sword at his side. He wore no mail or armour, for only a fool did that at sea, and many a man at arms and even knights had fallen to a watery death in sea battles for just such a reason. John had counselled him from an early age to forgo such protection, that he may swim rather than sink. He looked across at his warbag, reassured that it was within easy reach in a central hold away from the salt water. He and Will passed more time discussing their actions and their journey after they arrived in France, then moved on to check on the other servants and the cargo.

Jamie eyed the mysterious knight who was engaged in a similar occupation across on the starboard side. He too wore a sword but no armour, although he had brought a shield on board, Jamie noticed. It had been wrapped in a protective oiled cloth, and he had been unable to see any heraldic device or arms, so he was no wiser as to the man's identity.

As though at an unseen signal, the knight walked back

towards his horse to calm him, and his path took him past Jamie's position. Jamie, ever well-mannered, nodded and greeted him. "Good day, sir. A fair day for sailing."

The knight heard his cultured tones, and looking at his tailored dress decided that it would not be beneath him to respond in kind.

"Good day yourself. Indeed, with a fair wind we should be in France by mid-afternoon, God willing."

"You know this route well?"

"Well enough. I travel to France from time to time. And you?"

"As a youth I travelled with my father, and now in his stead. He grows frail and likes the journey less than he did in days past."

A slight frown crossed the knight's face. He had surely marked Jamie down as more than a merchant's son, and looking down pointedly at his sword he asked, "They are your wool sacks aboard?"

"They are. Trade is good and we flourish. Long may it continue in peace with the French."

The man snorted in reply. "I would not gamble even the throw of dice on such a hope. The peace between the two countries is as frail as a maiden's smile and twice as guileful."

Jamie smiled at the jest. "Then we needs must make hay – or even wool – while the sun shines."

"For certes. Tell me, have I seen you at court? I am sure you are familiar."

The alarm bells sounded in Jamie's head. "Possibly, I deal on my father's behalf and errands sometimes take me to the Palace. James de Grispere at your service." He bowed.

The knight responded in kind, bowing in turn. "Sir Jacques de Berry of Languedoc. Although I have chosen my side and support King Henry."

Chapter Twenty-One

The French Court, Paris.

The Duke of Burgundy, lately returned from Saint-Omer, strode into the private chambers of her majesty Queen Isabeau. The guards made to prevent him crossing through to the outer chamber, and despite his obvious rage they held their ground. A queen outranked a duke, even an angry duke.

"I demand to see her majesty." He shouted. One of the guards opened the door and slipped inside. He returned with a lady-in-waiting, who curtsied.

"Follow me, your Grace. Her Majesty will grant you an audience."

He said nothing and trailed in her wake, outwardly fuming. Shown through to the inner chamber he bowed low to the queen. "Your Majesty, a thousand pardons for my intrusion upon your presence." He greeted her, kissing her outstretched hand.

"My lord duke, how entrancing you look when you are angry." She teased, completely unabashed by his apoplectic demeanour.

"Your Majesty, I beg a private audience with you." He continued through clenched teeth. She dismissed her ladies in waiting, who scurried away gossiping, hiding their thoughts and smiles behind raised hands. Once they were alone, he closed the distance to hold both the queen's hands in his and look longingly into her eyes. The queen, now in her fortieth year, still retained much of the beauty of her youth. Blessed with high cheekbones and large wide-set eyes, she would have seduced most men half her age. Her lush hair was taken back and swept up under an intricate wimpled hat, adding further inches to her height. At the sight of her beauty, the duke's anger melted and he pulled her towards him in a crushing embrace, kissing her deeply.

After a brief moment she pulled away, placing a single finger on his lips and whispering: "The walls have eyes as well as ears, my beau. Later, come to me later. Now tell me, what ails you so? The heat of your anger goes before you like a burning brand."

The fire reignited in his eyes. "The treaty! You have heard of the whoreson Armagnac's new treaty? They do not spell my name, but they point a finger at me and by association with you, my queen. They declare that they are for France, when really they are for themselves. They are conniving to seize power. They ran rampant through Paris once before, my lady, trying to ruin your good name. They plot for the crown, I am sure of it."

Queen Isabeau adopted a calm expression, enunciating clearly with an accent that was still strongly inflected with her Bavarian roots. "You must calm yourself, John. We shall prevail, the Armagnacs have lost their hold on power. You saw to this. You have Paris with you, and nothing can harm either of us with the Parisians at our backs. The Armagnacs may cry and gnash their teeth, but it will avail them naught. A treaty such as this will only cause unrest in the provinces, and the capital will remain secure. I hear that all the main signatories of the treaty have retired to their estates and lands to re-group. The power – the real power – lies here in Paris, where we can control it. Now think on, where is their weakness and how can we best exploit it?"

The duke was finally mollified by the queen's words. "You are right as always, my love. We will rally in Paris. Divided, they will be weak, and will be forced to regroup their forces before they can march or move against us. Meanwhile we are here as one with all Paris at our backs. I will know in advance ere they move, for I have spies within their camp."

"Excellent. We shall control through government and absolute power. Remember I am still Regent in his majesty's name, and I shall wield my power absolutely. That includes the ruling council, who will do my bidding. Now tell me, how go the plans for the siege tower and the taking of Calais?"

"I was there but days ago and the tower prevails at a pace. Ten days, maybe a few more and she will be ready to be deployed against the English."

"Good. The timing will be perfect. For now we have an *entente cordiale* with our English foes. Indeed, they have sent an embassy of wrestlers for a tournament here at the palace."

"Does the prince accompany them? If he were here at the start of hostilities it would be the perfect opportunity to hold him hostage ere we sack the town."

"It would not be an honourable move, John. Think on it."

"I care not a fig for honour in war." The duke snapped, clicking his fingers to illustrate the point. "They lay false claim to our lands, seeking a greater foothold in France. I say we take the prince as hostage to fortune and be damned."

"Have a care. The Armagnacs have links to England still, and such an action could be a beacon to which they might rally.

It would divide, not unify our kingdom and potentially place the Armagnacs in control, rather than us. Think carefully before you act." The queen cautioned, thinking two moves ahead on the chessboard of the court.

"As you wish, your Majesty," he acquiesced – a little too readily, to the queen's ears. "But once I have taken Calais and I am pardoned for the death of the whoreson traitor Orleans, I will ensure we retake full control." He swore.

The queen for her part drew a veil over her features, as her role in Orleans' murder still wounded her and she would not let the Duke of Burgundy see her painful remorse over a dead lover. She was only too aware that she was a woman in a man's world and retained power through a perception of strength. To admit weakness or emotion would see her house of cards come tumbling down.

Chapter Twenty-Two

The English Channel

When the cog carrying Jamie and his party was midway across the Channel, the wind changed direction suddenly, sweeping in from the northwest. The cog lurched forward with the extra impetus provided by the wind and the mainsail strained harder against the ropes that linked it to the mast and body of the ship, which creaked under the strain. The change in pace caused Cristoforo further dismay, and he gripped the rails tighter, grabbing a rope and tying it about his waist for extra security against falling overboard. He clasped the crucifix about his neck and prayed to God that he be safely delivered to dry land.

Jamie smiled at his friend's histrionics and asked the captain as he passed how the journey was proceeding.

The seamed mahogany of the captain's face parted in a faint smile. "Now don't fret ere your friend on the fo'c'sle be screaming afore we're done, sir. The signs be good, an' I saw two swans ere we left, riding side by side. A good sign, sir, a good sign. This breeze will bring us about right 'andy, we'll see port afore expected if'n this keeps going." He gazed upwards at the billowed sail and trailing pennant at the top of the mast.

"Well done, Captain, I'll aid my friend if needs be." He assured him, and the Captain moved swiftly on. Jamie watched with interest as the party of young men accompanying Master Swynford found a clear patch of deck and began practising locks and moves to pass the time. The blond giant who had addressed him earlier stood slightly apart, leaning on his quarterstaff, watching the two pairs of wrestlers with interest. Jamie went to engage him in conversation.

"You come to France for a contest, I believe?"

The giant turned at the question. "Aye sir, that we do. On behalf of his Royal Highness Prince Henry. We are to be pitted against the French in a tournament to help celebrate our lasting peace, I'm told."

"Indeed, that should be entertaining. Does the prince attend?"

"He was to, but I'm told 'e is unwell and cannot travel. A shame as I'd 'ave liked to show him we do well on his behalf, to thank 'im for his patronage."

"I had not heard of the prince was of ill humour. May God grant him succour."

"Amen to that. And you, my lord, you travel to Paris as well?"

"Yes, Paris and other parts to trade with the French and Flemish in wool and yarn. Whilst the peace holds, trade goes well," Jamie commented.

"Aye, my father farms in Cornwall and we breed sheep. The price is good and we prosper, long may it continue."

"Indeed. Yet you left to wrestle in London?"

"That is so my lord. A long story it was, what took me away–"

"Sail ho!" came a cry from the crow's nest, cutting short

the giant's conversation. All eyes looked upwards first, then began to scan the horizon in the hope of spotting what the keen eyes of the lookout had seen. More information was shouted down.

"Ship from the North West a port, captain, heading direct towards us."

"Can you make them out?"

"Aye just one, I think. A skiff, two sails. On our course."

The Captain cursed, then barked out orders in rapid succession: "Bowmen, ready the brazier. Hoist shields men, quickly now!"

Jamie looked about at the activity, yet he was surprised and puzzled. One thing all sailors feared was fire at sea. It was a terrible danger and something to be avoided if at all possible. He saw the crossbowmen on the raised platform of the forecastle go to a small enclosed cauldron attached to the deck and with care strike a flint to the kindling within. He watched as with a little blowing they produced a muted flame which was carefully contained within the device and showed very little danger of engulfing the rest of the ship. All eyes were now straining to the distance as Jamie saw the crew bring forth thin wooden shields with various heraldic devices emblazoned upon them, but this puzzled him further as he did not recognise any of them. The shields themselves looked odd to his trained eyes. They appeared flimsy and incapable of taking a solid strike from a sword or mace.

A voice sounded behind him: "They are false, as you suppose, but serve well to fool the knaves into thinking we are a war cog with knights aboard, not wool and traders." Jamie turned and found himself facing Sir Jacques de Berry.

"And will it serve, sir?" he asked.

"Mayhap, depending on the pirates' numbers and how determined they may be."

As if to herald further dismay the lookout called down again. "Two ships, cap'n, running fast towards us."

"How long?"

"A league, maybe less and they'll be upon us."

The captain shouted "helm, five points a-starboard."

"It'll be a close-run thing," Sir Jacques muttered to Jamie, as everyone aboard sensed the slight change in direction and the increased speed as the cog was turned to run directly before the wind. Cristoforo, who had exceptionally keen sight, shouted down to the lower deck in French. "They are Spanish. I recognise their sails and craft."

"Are you sure?" Jamie called back

"Yes, I recognise the base born *bastardi!*" Cristoforo confirmed.

"What does he say?" The wrestler asked.

"He says that they are Spanish pirates."

"Is 'e Spanish hisself, your companion, or a Saracen?"

Despite the tense situation, Jamie could not help but smile. Cristoforo was forever being accused of being a Saracen, a heathen or a Spaniard. "Nay, he is Italian, and don't let him hear you say he is a Saracen, or he'll gut you like a common fish."

"I'd like to see 'm try," the wrestler muttered, looking up at Cristoforo's light frame and seeing the discomfort writ large upon his face.

"You mistake him," Jamie countered. "He dislikes the sea, but fears no pirate. My father saw him kill three robbers in as many seconds in Calais and hired his services on the spot."

The wrestler offered Jamie a grimace of disbelief, then went to join his companions at a call from master Swynford.

The two foreign craft bore down upon the cog steadily, gaining yard by yard, their sleek shape cutting through the choppy waves of the Channel with ease as they appeared to skim across the water, leaving a frothing white wake behind them. They were running almost parallel to each other on an intercepting course designed to offer the pirates the best vantage for attacking the cog. It was now possible to make out the features of the crew as they lined the sides of the caravels, whose twin triangular sails were filled to bursting, dragging the ships along at a good few knots faster than the more sedate cog. The pirates were jeering and chanting war cries, brandishing a mixture of weapons.

"Now!" shouted the captain when they were within two hundred yards, turning to the two crossbowmen in the forecastle. "Aim for the sails."

Despite the close proximity of the attackers, Cristoforo looked on with interest, watching as the crossbowmen selected longer than usual bolts, the ends of which were wrapped with pitch soaked tows that were wired just beneath the bolt head. Each man cocked his weapon then briefly placed the tip of the bolt into the burning brazier. Within seconds the tow caught alight and the men quickly slotted the bolts in place, took a hasty aim allowing for the rocking of the cog, and fired. Two bright arcs of fire sprang across the distance between the ships. The wind took the bolts slightly off target towards the end of their trajectory, one missing the mast and flying through the triangular sail of the first ship to fizzle harmlessly into the sea; the second, fired on the down drop of the cog, went low and thudded into the front of the caravel, where it immediately set fire to the wooden superstructure. Two pirates ran over, one raising rags to subdue the flames while the other poured water onto the blaze, causing it to flare further.

A few seconds later two more bolts were shot from the cog. Again, one flew through the sail, but lower this time, starting a small blaze which was set upon by the crew. The fourth bolt aimed at the ship already afire was lucky, striking the mast halfway up and immediately setting fire to the sail. The flames leapt across the canvas and the crew panicked as the sail started to flap, fanning the flames yet further. The crew tried to climb the ropes to reach the flames, but to no avail, and as the canvas disappeared, the ship slowed perceptibly, leaving only its fellow craft in pursuit of the cog. The crew cheered as the odds halved. They would only have one pirate ship to deal with now.

Watching the impending arrival of the caravel, which was now only fifty yards away, Jamie unclasped his thick cloak, went to his leather war bag, unbuckled the straps and reached inside. He produced a simple open-faced Bascinet helmet and padded leather coif, which he tied under his chin before thrusting the helmet on top. Next, he removed his battle axe: it had a double head, and a sharp and wicked looking point protruded from the end of the shaft. A leather loop extended from the bindings of the handle. He placed his palm upwards and slipped the loop over his thumb, rotated his hand so the strap went across the back of his wrist and grasped the handle firmly in his palm. In this way the strap enhanced his grip, secured the weapon in case he lost his hold while offering no possibility for an enemy to pull him off balance as if it had been attached to his wrist with no means of speedy release.

The blond giant watched with interest from his group a few paces away. "An axe?" he queried.

"My old teacher instructed me in ways of fighting with one aship. A sword won't answer. There's no room to swing and its close quarters we'll be at, I'll be bound."

With that, Jamie drew his long dagger with his left hand, span it in the air and caught it deftly so that the tip now pointed forwards. He gave the axe a few experimental twirls using his wrist strength, enjoying the feeling of confidence it gave him and ever thankful to John for his advice and training. John had fought many a battle at sea and prepared Jamie accordingly in its more specialised martial arts. He looked up at the sword the giant had drawn and nodded to his quarter staff.

"You'll be better off with that staff. I'm sure you need no instruction, but a longer reach will avail you more than a sword point or slashing."

"Thank 'ee, I'll fare better with it I'm sure." Then frowning, he asked. "But I thought 'ee were a merchant?"

Jamie offered the Cornishman a wicked grin, the lust of battle in his eyes as the second caravel closed the distance between the two ships. "I am," he lied, twirling the axe again. "Wrestler, tell me, how are you called? 'Tis good to know a man's name in battle."

"Mark of Cornwall." The man responded.

Jamie saluted him with his dagger. "James de Grispere at your service. Now let's to battle and show these Spanish scum the error of their ways."

Behind him, Sir Jacques de Berry had watched the arming and byplay with interest, and was as puzzled as Mark. *A merchant? By the rood I think not!* He thought, hefting a short arming sword and a small leather buckler reinforced with bands of iron.

Then the ship was a broadside, and the pirates were flinging hooks and ropes, intent on locking the two vessels together. The cog slowed under the sudden tow of the caravel, whose crew had drawn her sail now that she was attached to the English ship. Jamie stood braced against the side rail, the blood singing in his veins and a lust for battle beating in his chest. His war cry came unbidden in a harsh and joyous battle tones: *"An Umfraville! An Umfraville!"*

The old summons of his patron knight drove him on as he slashed down at the rope attaching the two ships, daring any to come and challenge him. Two pirates clad in surcoats, one brandishing a mace and the other a long stabbing dagger launched themselves at Jamie. He laughed as the battle madness took him and everything appeared to move more slowly as his mind and body reattuned themselves to battle through hours of practice and wars on the Scottish borders.

The mace bearer swung forward on a rope to Jamie's left, bringing his weapon crashing down with murderous intent. Jamie ducked under the stroke, his axe a blur as he cut the arm off at the elbow, sending a bright shower of blood from the severed limb. In the same movement he continued his turn, driving the dagger, now held underhand, into the stomach of the second assailant. The pirate screamed, clutched his stomach as the blood spurted and fell backwards into the sea. The movement of the two ships grinding together destroyed the man's body, sending blood across the flanks of both ships and staining the water below. Jamie turned his attention to the man with the mace, kicking his legs from under him and bringing the cutting blade of his axe down across his face in a killing blow.

Jamie looked briefly about him as the battle continued. Raising his eyes to the forecastle he saw Cristoforo cross dagger and Falchion to defend against a downward stroke from a scimitar, locking the weapon's blade. The Italian disengaged and sliced his attacker's throat open. Another attacked him, and Cristoforo bent his knees and threw himself backwards in an agile summersault, landing in perfect balance on the balls of his feet. The pirate tried to follow him, but he was off balance. Cristoforo brushed his blade aside almost delicately and brought his falchion down upon pirate's exposed neck, sending his body spinning into the sea. He looked for Jamie and found him. He saluted, smiled and continued his lethal work.

Looking about him, Jamie saw that Mark was in trouble, pressed by three men at once and barely managing to keep them at bay with his quarterstaff. He parried a blow from a dagger and carried the movement downwards, catching the man between the legs and heaving with all his immense strength. The pirate's face took on a look of surprise as he flew into the air as if gravity had for a moment forgotten about him, before crashing to the deck headfirst and lying still, his head at an unnatural angle but the look of surprise still writ upon his features. The move opened Mark up to an attack at his upper body, and seeing the exposed torso the second assailant lunged with a short sword. Mark barely had time to bring down his staff to block the stroke as he saw the third man about to slash across at his head.

"Drop, Mark!" Jamie shouted in English and Mark saw a sight he would never forget as long as he lived. Jamie appeared above, swinging his axe in a wide arc where his head had been, blocking the sword stroke and bringing his arm around in a blurred figure of eight, taking both men's heads in an arc of death. Jamie laughed, a manic and mirthless sound. The madness of battle was upon him and the red mist had descended over his vision. He jumped forward, shouting *"An Umfraville"* at the top of his lungs. Men cowered before him as he cut a swathe through the unarmoured ranks of the pirates. His axe was light as a butterfly's wing and lethal as a scythe, beating and falling, slaughtering as he went, a red rain of blood spraying from the wet blade.

For a few seconds Mark stood watching Jamie's fighting prowess in awe. Then as suddenly as it had begun, the pirates turned and fled, realising that they would find no easy pickings here. They fought for plunder, not glory or honour. They fled, leaping over the side to their ship, cutting ropes as they went. They had lost at least half their number and now their oarsmen pulled hard to disengage the ships putting distance between them. The men aboard the cog cheered and shouted at the departing Caravel, waving their weapons in victory. The sounds of the wounded at their feet calling in agony and moaning in their death throes brought them down from the height of battle. Jamie looked down at the slaughter at his feet, as the red mist of battle slowly dissipated. He shook himself and rolled his shoulders releasing the tension caused from the fighting, checking that none of the blood he was spattered with was his own.

"A good day's work." he declared stoically, then looked about to see to his servants. "Will, how goes it?"

"Master Jamie, Tye is down and close to death. All others are standing, but two are wounded."

"Where is Tye?"

"Aft. They swarmed across there and we was hard pressed 'til you cut through. By God, man, you fight like a demon! John taught you well, but I've never seen the like, even from John in his prime" the old retainer commented.

Jamie acknowledged the compliment with a tight grin, then passed on to seek out Tye. Finding him, he knelt at his head. The mortally wounded man was barely conscious and moaned at the pain from the wound in his stomach. Jamie saw the length and depth of the cut and knew the blow was fatal. The blue of the man's intestines showed through the cut in his tunic.

"Tye, it's Jamie. You fought well, lad. Be proud."

"Thank 'ee, master Jamie. Did...did we prevail?"

"We did indeed, and right royally. Now rest easy, we'll bandage you up and get you to a chirurgeon once we dock," Jamie promised.

"Aye, master but the pain...the pain is fearsome..." With that he sighed as a red froth came to his lips, and he slipped away in Jamie's arms. Jamie crossed himself, said a quick prayer over the man and covered him with a cloak. He rose to see Cristoforo skipping down the steps from the forecastle, all thoughts of sea sickness forgotten. His thoughts were temporarily interrupted by the Captain's gruff voice.

"Slit their throats and throw 'em over the side, the lot of them." The Captain ordered, looking around at the dead and dying pirates on the deck with no sanctity for human life.

Mark baulked at this. "Kill 'em in cold blood, cap'n?"

"Do it. I did'n ask 'em to attack my ship! They'd kill you as soon as look at you or take you as a slave to sell at a market for a slower death. Strong 'un like you'd fetch a fair price too. Far as I'm concerned the only good pirate is a dead 'un." He spat, moving on and heaving a slumped figure over the side.

The captain gave another order to his crossbowmen, who fetched more of the long bolts and dipped their pitched points once more into the brazier. Taking aim on the caravel, which was still within their reach, they fired their flaming bows at it, not stopping until the pirate ship was blazing and men were screaming or throwing themselves over the side as the ship began to list.

"If any of 'em swim this way, kill 'em an' leave 'em dead in the water." The captain said. He gave a nod of satisfaction, looking further astern to where the first caravel was now just a dot on the horizon, well out of range. Jamie watched him shake his head and mutter to himself before calling for the crew to take the wind and make for Calais.

A tough fighter like his fellow wrestlers, Mark was inured to the trials of combat, but he could not bring himself to kill the dying so cold-bloodedly. Sir Jacques had no such compunction, and seeing a wounded man about to lift his dagger for a sneak thrust at a crew member he ran him through, and heaving him by his long hair threw him over the low guard rail. He wiped the blade on another dead man's shirt before sheathing the sword and helping to eject other dead and dying pirates from the cog's decks. He spied Jamie and Cristoforo talking together and walked over to them.

"Master de Grispere, I've n'er seen the like," he said. "Your axe work was a wonder to watch – but if you're a merchant I'm a mule's arse. Where did you learn such skills?" He demanded. His tone was good humoured, as such qualities were to be admired.

Jamie responded in kind. "Thank you sir. I am indeed just a humble merchant's son, but my father has a man-at-arms who has fought many battles. He normally accompanies us, but this time he could not, so he taught me the rudiments, the better to protect myself."

Sir Jacques looked from Jamie to Cristoforo, believing not a word, but decided to leave well alone and make further enquiries when he was at court in France. Master de Grispere would bear watching. He contented himself with a final comment. "Then I should like to meet your father's man and mayhap he too could show me how to use an axe as you do."

Chapter Twenty-Three

Calais

The voyage across the channel met with no further incident, and the ship docked safely in the English port and was
soon in the process of being unloaded. Cristoforo watched
from the dockside, glad to be back once more on solid ground
as all his fears of sea travel had returned as soon as the battle was
ended. Jamie joined him and the two men watched the huge,
heavy sacks of wool being hoisted onto the wooden gantry
cranes, which loaded them directly on the waiting waggons that
would transport them inland to Paris and beyond. They were
soon met with a sadder sight – that of Tye's body, swathed in
cloth and being unloaded for burial. Both men bowed their
heads and crossed themselves as the body was carried past them.

"Now, for the love of God, I saw you almost killed as two
pirates attacked on the fo'c'sle. How did you tumble over backwards so?" Jamie inscribed in the air the backward somersault
that Cristoforo had managed with apparent ease.

"In our society our families train us from an early age, as
you are trained to knighthood," Cristoforo replied. "Our

training includes the ability to tumble and roll like acrobats. It is," here he struggled with the French word "...*fondamentale?*"

"Fundamental?"

"Si, fundamental to our training. Much knife work is about balance and movement, not strength." At that point, their conversation was interrupted as the giant presence of Mark of Cornwall loomed down upon them.

"Sirs, I beg your pardon, but we depart now for Paris." He waved a thumb over his shoulder at the party of wrestlers and master Swynford, waiting impatiently amid the stamping of horses' hooves. "I needs must thank 'ee for saving my life. If it weren't for you my head would be off my shoulders. You are passing quick with an axe, master Jamie, that I declare. And I'm right grateful to you. If ever I can be of service, you just have to ask." Mark stammered out his heartfelt thanks.

"You accounted yourself well with your staff and added to our number. Do not trouble yourself with thanks, just serve our gracious king well and whip the French in his name." Jamie responded modestly. He clapped the giant on his shoulder, feeling the solid bulk of muscle there. "Ere you depart may I introduce my companion, *Signor* Cristoforo Corio, who is in my father's employ and acts as my bodyguard on this seemingly perilous journey." Mark nodded in acknowledgement to Cristoforo and they shook hands, Cristoforo wincing at the strength of the other's grip.

"Well, *Signor* Corio, you took your toll of pirates too, I'm bound. Gentle sirs, I must now depart as my party awaits. I hope to see you again in Paris." With that he waved a salute and marched off towards master Swynford and the waiting party of wrestlers.

"He's built like an ox, that one." Cristoforo commented massaging his crushed hand.

"Yes he's a lusty infant I'll grant you, and I'll wager he'll give the French a hefty fall or two. Now we too must away as soon as the waggons are loaded. Father has engaged lodgings for us in Paris in a sennight, so we must move swiftly to arrive in time. First we must visit the constable in Calais, for I've letters of State from Sir Henry Beaufort informing him of our mission."

The two men moved off, pausing only to talk briefly with Will and explain that they would catch them on the road in two days' time as they could move much faster than the loaded waggons. They were surreptitiously watched throughout this by Jacques de Berry, who was curious as to the progress of Jamie de Grispere, a merchant with the ability of a master-at-arms. *You will bear watching, de Grispere, and I wonder what your business in Calais really is?* He muttered to himself.

As they entered Calais through the gates from the harbour, Cristoforo was aware of how much the months in England had changed him. No longer did he feel alien in this city of England in France; what was once strange now felt familiar. From the architecture to the sound of English voices and accents, everything was somehow comforting. It was the onward journey into France – more particularly Paris and the fear of discovery, however slight – which concerned him.

They moved through the streets, heading south to the second part of the city, divided from the first by an *enceinte*, an internal moat and drawbridge that gave them access to the heavily fortified inner bailey. Passing under the portcullis, Cristoforo remarked on the regimented streets, set out in regular lines in the Roman tradition. In the southwest corner they saw the towering turrets of the Keep. They made their way towards it, dismounting and stating their business to the guard at the Keep entrance. They were shown through to the Great Hall and thence to a private solar on the upper floor.

The room was well appointed, with wainscoted walls and

other luxuries to enable an easy life in all but the hardest of times. A fire burned in the open hearth and before it stood a man warming his hands against the blaze. Sir Geoffrey de Haven turned as they entered and they saw a man of middle years, prematurely grey, with a well-trimmed beard and crinkly hair. He was well dressed in hose and gambeson in the latest fashion. A jewelled belt bearing a delicate dagger cinched his waist.

Jamie and Cristoforo walked forward and bowed before him: "James de Grispere and *Signor* Cristoforo Corio at your service, Sir Geoffrey."

Sir Geoffrey cast an eye over both men, marking Cristoforo as an unknown factor, but passed no comment. "You are welcome sirs, and well met. I trust that you had a safe journey?"

"We arrived unharmed, Sir Geoffrey, but we had the misfortune to be waylaid by Spanish pirates in the Channel."

"Pirates! They become more troublesome and audacious as the weather improves. I trust that you escaped without loss?"

"One of our men was killed and two wounded, my lord, but we taught the pirates some manners, and they will know better than to attack good English ships again. They ran like whipped curs to lick their wounds and think twice about it."

"May God be praised, but it does my heart good to hear it. They are a plague upon our shipping and continue to harry trade when they can. Now, tell me, what news have you and how may I be of service?"

"We bring letters from Sir Henry Beaufort and the Great Council, my lord." Jamie reached into his gambeson and retrieved a scroll sealed with wax, which he passed into Sir Geoffrey's waiting hand. Sir Geoffrey broke the seal and read of the impending attack on Calais –his frown deepening as he did so.

"By the rood," he exclaimed "do we have any further intelligence? This bodes ill indeed. We are strong here. The fortress is strengthened beyond belief with new supplies and armed by coin from the new budget. But any threat is serious, and we cannot lose Calais, I need ill inform you of this fact. You are your father's son and well understand the commerce of the town and its bolster to England's wealth and trade abroad."

"I understand full well, my lord, and this is our part to take. We seek more information and plan to meet with Sir Richard's agent in the hope that he guides us to the core of the plot."

"Where do you meet him and who is this *insidiori*?" Sir Geoffrey asked, still deeply concerned.

"We have a meeting point arranged, but pardon, Sir Geoffrey, we were bid on pain of death not to reveal his identity to friend or foe on Sir Richard's express orders. I despair of being able to assist my Lord, but they are my orders."

"Do not concern yourself, de Grispere. I can see the value in such a tactic and will not press the matter. I am grateful for your time in bringing me the missive. Is there any other favour I may grant to assist you in your quest?"

"I think not. Although may we prevail upon you for two more horses? Those upon which we are mounted are at best adequate, and needs dictate that we shall be riding hard and fast to gain Paris as soon as we may."

"Of course, I will summon my steward who will see you well mounted and speed you on your mission."

They ate at the Constable's private table and had no sooner finished than they begged leave to depart. The Constable was as good as his word and two fresh mounts were bridled and ready for them, as they planned to ride and lead for the long journey to Paris. The horses were of excellent quality, and looked fit and full of running to Jamie's experienced eyes.

As a parting gift, Sir Geoffrey gave them letters of introduction to any who would aid assistance including inn owners along the way who were loyal to King Henry and would give them good lodgings. As they cantered out of the bailey, Sir Geoffrey rubbed his beard pensively and returned to his quarters to write a letter.

Chapter Twenty-Four

London

The Council members gathered in the Palace, including Prince Henry, who had been smuggled from private chambers to attend secretly as no one wished to alert any French spies that he was in fact fully well until such time as the wrestling competition was under way in Paris.

Every council member around the table was only too well aware of the severity of the situation should Calais fall. They all felt that this meeting was in effect a council of war. The prince stood to address them, acknowledging their presence and turning to Whittington.

"Sir Richard, you are our eyes and ears in this matter. Is there any further news from your agent in France?"

"None, my prince. But we do have news that our party has arrived safely. However, their vessel was attacked by two Spanish pirate ships in the Channel, which to my eyes is highly suspicious."

"What! Did they escape unharmed?"

Others around the table threw questions, including an

equally suspicious Sir Henry Beaufort, who in his position of Governor of Calais was always eager to seek news of his main responsibility. "How came you by this information?"

"The sources came from public gossip and were verified by express messenger. One death and a few injuries, but the company were by and large unharmed and the pirates were given no mercy. Apparently Sir Jacques de Berry was aboard. I thought I had missed his presence at court." Sir Richard commented obliquely.

"But he is just one knight."

"According to the captain's account, Sir Henry, it was James de Grispere and his Italian companion who fought their way through a great swath of them, killing some ten or twelve men single-handed, if indeed the tales are to be believed."

"Did he by God? So the young lion can roar," the prince commented.

"Indeed, I believe we have chosen well and he will give good account of himself. Sir Robert and John trained him well."

"John? Is that the same John who fought with my father and saved his life at the Siege of Vilnius? But he must be ancient now and bowed."

"If your Grace values his ears, I would not say that in his hearing for he seems to be emulating the great Marshall for longevity and fighting spirit."

The prince laughed good humouredly at the gentle rebuke. "You have the right of it; I've seen John in battle and even now would not wish to cross swords with him. Praise God that all is well and all are safe. Needs must we be patient until news is heard and pray they succeed.

"Now, tell me Sir Richard, is there any more news of the Lollard rising, or those who would usurp the blessed rights of the Holy sacrament?"

"None my prince of which I am aware."

"Then may the Lord guide and protect us."

Chapter Twenty-Five

Paris: The Royal Palace.

Jamie and Cristoforo's journey from Calais was uneventful, and by missing a night at an inn they managed to shave a day from the normal journey time of six days. They had overtaken the waggons at the end of the first day, but left them to their slower pace whilst they pressed on ahead. They had made plans for how they were to proceed throughout their journey.

They passed through the same western gate that Cristoforo had escaped from a few months previously with no more than a glance from the guards on duty. After the peace of the road, the noise and commotion of the thronged streets was an assault upon the senses. Pedestrians barred their way moving only slowly to allow them to pass. For Jamie, it reminded him of the busy commercial streets of London, but the language was strange and the smells subtly different. Indeed it was the smell of the city that assailed their senses the most: the press of human habitation produced unpleasant odours that would only get worse as the days became warmer. There was, Cristoforo noticed now that he had spent time in London, no sewerage or running water from pipes in the French capital, and the streets were strewn with all manner of animal and human excrement. Coming directly from the clean country roads it was all the more noticeable. He wrinkled his nose in disgust, pulling up part of his silk scarf to cover his face. He spoke in English, at which he was becoming more proficient, albeit with a markedly strong accent. "By God they stink, these French. Is there no sewer?"

"No, there are only sewers in London," Jamie replied with a smile. "I see you begin to appreciate your new home city. It is certainly rank here, and these are some of the better streets of Paris." They moved through the streets and as they did they both felt uneasy. Lives spent constantly in danger either on the battlefield or in clandestine circumstances had given them a well-developed sixth sense whenever they were being watched or followed. Jamie looked across at Cristoforo.

"I have that itch at the back of my neck, as I did in London when I was being followed. Do you feel it?" He asked.

Cristoforo snorted gently with a grimace. "I do, and have done since we entered through the gate. I would swear that eyes are upon us, and are not friendly to our cause, I'll be bound." He looked around surreptitiously, scanning the crowded streets for a familiar face, making mental notes of those about him, hoping such a catalogue would produce recognition at his next scan of the street.

"Let us bear left at the next street ahead, then slow down halfway and pretend that a horse has cast a shoe. I shall dismount whilst you seek our followers." Jamie muttered through half closed lips. Cristoforo nodded, and a hundred yards later they gently eased the horses to the next left hand turn, maintaining the same easy walking pace. The street was less crowded, with the shops of milliners and clothiers populating each side, clearly aimed at trade rather than retail to the general populace. Halfway along, Jamie mimed a cast shoe on his horse's near side fore and slipped carefully out of the saddle, glancing full backwards as he did so. He looked back in Cristoforo's direction but focused deeper into the distance. "Yellow and red cowl, short man. Disappeared before I could see more."

"Did he have a brown cloak and straw coloured hair?"

"Indeed, I am sure he did."

"I spotted him earlier. He will be wary now and fall back. Let us examine the wares here, for they are to your calling of silk and woven cloth."

Jamie agreed and the two men feigned interest in the various businesses along the street before sliding down another narrow side street and from there onto a parallel main thoroughfare. The feeling of being watched left both men and they proceeded to the lodgings reserved by Thomas de Grispere in advance. Upon arriving, Cristoforo let out a gasp of recognition.

"Why, these are the same lodgings at which I met your father months back," he declared.

"Aye, that would be right. He has been renting these since I was a boy and first accompanied him upon journeys in trade such as these," Jamie agreed. Once installed in their lodgings and having taken care of their horses, they washed the travel from their bodies in two wooden bathtubs provided by servants attached to the house and planned their next move.

"Where do we go on the morrow?" Cristoforo asked.

"We attend court and seek out those acquaintances that are allied to my father and attend to his trade. We play the part of merchants whilst we await connexion with the friar who is loyal to Sir Richard."

"How will this friar know us?"

"Sir Richard has made us known to him through our names and trade. My father is well known at court and has, despite the natural enmity between France and England, managed to forge strong links by trading on his Flemish ancestry."

"And tonight?" Cristoforo asked hopefully.

"Tonight? Why tonight, we address ourselves to pleasures and delights of Paris," Jamie said, at which both men laughed, intent upon enjoying what may well be their last carefree night before their lives were turned once more to the urgency at hand.

The following morning saw the two companions making their way with slightly thick heads towards the Place Royal, the Hotel des Tournelles and the home of the French court. With his father's head man Will at their side they approached the gates, seeing the famous turrets with flags fluttering in the breeze. The guards sought their business, and with letters of authority produced they were admitted to the French court. The inner courtyard was awash with human activity, from farriers to cooks, courtiers and messengers running in all directions.

The buildings were grander and more ornate than those of the English court, the grey stone of the buildings offering a strange sense of being inside a fairy tale castle. They proceeded through to the inner bailey and asked for direction to the offices of two merchants known to his father. It transpired that one of the two men was already in audience with the king's officials, but monsieur Henryck Danckant was in his office two stories above the courtyard. As they proceeded up the stone steps, Cristoforo asked how his father knew Danckant.

"He comes from an old Flemish family – indeed our families knew each other in Flanders, when my grandsire still lived there many years ago. He now has a permanent position with the royal secretary, securing cloth and wool for the royal court. He still trades, of course, and we shall more than pretend to conduct business with him. He is a valuable connexion, and one with whom my family continues to trade on a regular basis."

The door opened to an office that was warm but smelled musty and airless. Two clerks scribbled with quills at adjacent desks. Deeper into the room a larger desk stood, and behind this sat a hunched figure. If they were of a similar age, Cristoforo considered that this man had fared worse in aging than Master Thomas. He had a shaggy head of hair and large bushy eyebrows, from under which he now peered.

"Ah, master James, so you have come to see me. How delightful. By the rood you've grown. When last I saw you, you were but this high." He held his hand at waist height. "Come, come, sit down by the fire, for it is still chill at this time of year."

Introductions were made, although Monsieur Danckant was clearly already acquainted with Will. They discussed cloth and wool, and settled at length upon a fair price for a large proportion of the wool Jamie had brought from England. All the discussion had so far proceeded in French, yet here Jamie now switched to Flemish, much to the consternation of Cristoforo, who spoke not a word of it.

"Monsieur, tell me is there a friary within the walls?"

A puzzled expression flitted briefly across monsieur Danckant's face. "A friary? Why yes, there is a small group of friars that attend here. They are specialists in herbal lore, and act as healers and producers of medicines. Some would say that they do better than the quack mendicants who pose as doctors here." He chuckled at his own wit. "But why would you wish to visit them? Are you ill?"

"No, nothing of the kind. Be not alarmed. My sister

Jeanette takes certain herbs for a persistent migraine, and my father procures them for her when he visits the city. I wondered if there was a friary within that produces them. Due to our climate in England such herbs are very difficult to find and cultivate."

"Ah I see. Of course I would be honoured to facilitate an introduction. and I will show you the way in person," Monsieur Danckant offered.

"No Monsieur, please do not trouble yourself. You are a busy man and we have other business to attend to ere we visit the friary. There is no immediate urgency."

"As you wish. But do come and visit me again ere you leave. You are bound for Flanders after Paris?"

"Indeed. We leave by the weekend for Saint-Omer and the weavers there."

"They are producing fine cloth in excellent weaves. You will be amazed at the price they will fetch in England."

With that, Jamie offered their farewells and made to leave the older man. Once they were safely at the bottom of the stone steps, Cristoforo asked what he had been discussing.

"I needed to ensure that the clerks were not aware of my questions. As typical Parisians, it would be unlikely they would speak Flemish. The friar that we seek is based here, and now we need to seek him out but carefully. First, we shall visit the court to learn as much as we may of the latest developments between this country and our own."

Chapter Twenty-Six

Entering one of the great chambers of the French court, both men were dazzled by the gaiety and sophistication that lay before their eyes. Before them was a glorious panoply of fine lords and ladies, hangers-on, troubadours and musicians. Swathes of silks and tapestries graced the arches of columns with bright splashes of colour and light. The noise of conversations was far louder than the subdued murmuring of the English court. Everyone here seemed to be trying to outdo each other in terms of prominence and ostentation.

Having been raised in the cloth trade, Jamie's eyes were particularly drawn to the bright hues of the ladies dressed in flowing *côte-hardies* with long *tippets* edged in striking contrasting colours of white on black or cobalt and red, all edged and interwoven with gold thread. The elongated gowns seemed to defy gravity, giving their wearers an added grace, as though they rode on air as they paraded through the hall. The scene appeared magical to Jamie's eyes, as if he had been transported to a land of fairies and elves. Cristoforo was more sanguine, as many of the fabrics had been imported from his native Italy, where the colours were naturally more flamboyant.

"Ye gods, we have entered a magical kingdom," Jamie exclaimed in awe. Yet he was also aware of the undercurrent of intrigue that resembled that of the English court. Whispers were everywhere, in huddled groups or held within an interrogative glance. A courtly smile could mean anything too, but friendliness and discretion was a currency much in demand.

Looking around the hall, he spotted Sir Jacques de Berry in deep conversation with an important looking noble, a man with an aquiline nose and dark, hooded eyes. Behind them stood the two thrones, one of which was empty and the other graced by her majesty Queen Isabeau of France.

"So the French king is still indisposed, it would seem." Jamie whispered to Cristoforo, who merely nodded as his eyes were fixated on another lady, a woman with dark hair, olive skin and almond eyes

There was a sudden lull as the music stopped, to be replaced by a blare of trumpets announcing a new entertainment. Heralded from opposite corners, there entered two lines of players. They were no ordinary men, and Jamie and Cristoforo both spotted the blond giant from the ship: Mark of Cornwall.

"The wrestlers," he exclaimed. "It would seem our arrival is timely."

The parade of wrestlers came to a halt in front of her majesty and bowed to her. They were introduced by the master of ceremonies, each man standing forward as his name was called. As Mark was last in the line, Jamie had time to notice de Berry looking at him speculatively and commenting to the dark man at his side. He would have been even more concerned at the conversation that took place between them.

"That man, he was one of those from the ship that fought well against the pirates," de Berry whispered. "And from the quality of their intimacy he is friends with the merchant who I suspect carries another role beneath his woollen cap."

The dark haired man looked hard at Mark. "Dost think he spies for the English crown?"

"'Tis possible, I cannot be certain, my lord. But I will seek out the merchant, James de Grispere, and see if they find themselves in each other's company. The wrestler bears watching and 'twill soon become apparent if he can really fight or is but a fop."

"Have him watched. And the merchant. I know the name de Grispere. His family hail from my lands near Flanders and his father is a regular visitor at court. He does indeed trade in wool and cloth, so mayhap your suspicions are unfounded."

De Berry shrugged as if to say he knew what he had seen, and no merchant's son was capable of such prowess at arms.

"Howsoever, nothing is known at court of our plans at Saint-Omer apart from a chosen few, and that is how it must remain. Watch him closely."

"Should he appear at court, my lord duke, I have made plans to see that he is diverted."

"Good," the duke responded gravely.

Cristoforo had been eyeing a lady-in-waiting. He knew one of his countrywomen when he saw one and excused himself to beg an introduction with the lady, who was coyly pretending to both ignore and encourage him in the same action. It was artfully done, and successfully lured the moth to the candle. A beautiful oval face, framed with twists of black hair escaping from a rich velvet hennin beckoned him, and Cristoforo approached her as she giggled with another maiden, and then in a moment of seeming surprise he bowed deeply, before addressing her in Italian.

"*Mia signora, ho il piacere di presentarmi. Signor Cristoforo Corio al vostro servizio.*"

The lady's mouth opened in surprise as she heard her native tongue spoken so elegantly. She quickly regained her composure and curtseyed to Cristoforo. She hid her face briefly behind her fan, so only a huge pair of almond brown eyes were visible and murmured to her companion.

"You are impudent, *signor*, and I know you not. Yet you are a native of my land. From where dost thou hail, Sir Bold?" she quipped.

"From Firenze, my lady. But pray tell me what city could produce such beauty as stands before me. Even in *Italia* you must be revered."

"Fie upon on you! And speak in French so that my companion may understand your saucy tongue." Cirstoforo switched to French and repeated the compliment in that language.

The woman's companion arched an eyebrow. "Should I take pity upon this strutting cockerel and put him from his misery?" She quipped, smiling artfully at her companion, finally continuing as Cristoforo squirmed. "You have the honour of addressing la Contessa Alessandria di Felicini, milady-in-waiting to her Royal Highness, Queen Isabeau."

"My lady Contessa, I shall be forever in your service and your thrall," Cristoforo continued, bowing deeply again. The Contessa's eyes sparkled at the audacity of the man before her, yet she was not unaffected by his grace and manners.

"Well *signor* Corio, I hail from the fair city of Bologna to the north of your home. How does a Florentine land upon on these shores and find himself in the French court? Mayhap you are employed to entrance all women who fall prey to your charm?"

"No my lady, 'twas only to fall under your spell that I ventured forth. For I am not of the court, but serve the son of my master, Thomas de Grispere, a merchant of England. We trade here for a few days before moving on to Flanders."

"Ah, a Wight. I knew it, Matilda. For sure he will sequester our hearts and leave, never to be seen again," she teased. At that moment of mirth, she looked across the hall to see her majesty, who beckoned the two women with the merest imperious glance. Offering Cristoforo a brief curtsey they swept away, leaving him with a swish of skirts and a wonderful scent of jasmine and other exotic perfumes lingering in their wake. He shook his head, sighing, watching their passage towards the queen as he returned to Jamie's side.

"Victor or vanquished?" Jamie asked, smiling.

"Ah, Madonna. The Contessa, she bewitched me, *una vista bellissima!*"

Jamie laughed and made his way forward to the crowds that were forming around the area that had been set aside for the wrestling matches. Heralds sounded their trumpets again, and the first of the matched pairs came forward. Introductions were made by the umpire of the match. The traditional words of the Cornish wrestlers were not said here. The men just shook hands and the umpire called upon both to wrestle.

As the first match progressed it soon became obvious that the contest was never going to be run to the same sporting standards as those native to England would have expected. The two combatants appeared to those watching to be involved in something that was not far short of a brawl, their numerous fouls not called by the umpire. At length the Frenchman went for a deep hold at the waist and in doing so led with his elbow, which made contact first, winding his opponent who instinctively folded forwards in pain, enabling the Frenchman to take a strong top grip with his other hand. Off balance and doubled over, the Englishman was easily pulled forward into a flying hip throw which saw him land squarely onto the canvas and lose the match.

Having seen the line-up of contestants, Jamie realised that Mark would be last to compete, and motioned to Cristoforo to slip away with him, leaving the crowd to its excitement. They left the hall quietly amid the noise of the spectators and made their way through covered cloisters to the friary that faced onto the main outside courtyard. Passing under the archway, Jamie asked the way to the infirmary, claiming a rash on his neck which was irritating him. At the double doors of the infirmary they were met by a benevolent friar of kindly visage.

"Brother friar, I seek one Sebastian of your order," Jamie said. "I was advised to seek him by Monsieur Danckant, a family friend."

"Ah yes, Monsieur Danckant, a good man who serves us well with cloth. Please follow me and I shall introduce you to Friar Sebastian."

They followed the friar through a curtained opening to another chamber, where another monk was tending to the dressing of a sick patient.

"Brother Sebastian, I have a visitor for you and someone who ails. He was recommended to you by Monsieur Danckant."

The friar finished dressing his patient's arm and dismissed him, turning to face the newcomers. They were met by a pair of small, ferret-like eyes, that were wary and keen. He was thin and wiry with an inner strength that shone through his plain robes.

"Indeed, I trust Monsieur Danckant is well? How may I be of service?" He asked rather curtly, smiling at his brother friar, who bowed and moved silently off.

"Monsieur Danckant fares well and sends his compliments," Jamie continued a little warily. "I have a complaint of the skin. A fierce rash has assailed me and is rubbed raw with irritation. I pray thee, dost though have a salve that could ease my suffering?"

"Where does this rash occur?" Brother Sebastian demanded.

"Beneath my cowl here at my neck," Jamie replied.

"Then remove it and show me the cause."

After a slight hesitation, Jamie untied the lacing joining his cowl and pulled it aside to offer a view of his neck.

"No man, that will not answer. I prithee, remove it completely." The Friar ordered as he probed beneath the cowl. "I need good visage to..."

He halted, clearly alarmed, as first his fingers found, then his eyes saw, the SS collar around Jamie's neck. It was formed of beautifully tanned supple leather, embossed and decorated with a series of gold and silver esses at intervals around the collar. The crowning glory was the Lancastrian rose in gold, hanging as a medallion. The friar bit back a gasp as he fingered the collar. He looked around furtively.

"Mayhap....mayhap I shall be able be the better judge in the daylight. Follow me through to the gardens beyond."

With this he beckoned Jamie to the back wall, where a small door led to the gardens that supported the friary with its medicinal herbs. The doorway opened out on to a vast array of raised beds, offering every conceivable herb known to mankind that could be grown in the benevolent French climate. The garden was criss-crossed with paths and bordered by a high protective brick wall that offered shelter to the herbs. It was still, calm and peaceful, with wonderful fragrances and scents emanating from the plants. Once outside the friar ensured they were alone and closed the door to the infirmary.

"You take a great risk coming here thus," he rebuked Jamie and Cristoforo. The two young men merely shrugged in acceptance, as if such risks were part of their normal lives.

"We are just sely merchants, here on the business of my father. We seek to bring no harm or suspicion to anyone."

"I would adjure you take great care. There are spies everywhere. We cannot speak here for long ere someone becomes suspicious. Who sent you and how are you known?"

"We are here on the orders of Sir Richard Whittington. I am James de Grispere and this is *Signor* Cristoforo Corio, at your service."

The friar was circumspect and wasted no time with words or courtesy: "Where do you lodge?"

Jamie gave the friar the address of their lodgings, and he said that he would arrive that evening after compline. They returned to the infirmary and in a louder voice Friar Sebastian continued: "Apply this salve twice daily and it should assoil you of all that ails you." With that he offered Jamie a small jar of ointment.

Chapter Twenty-Seven

The two men returned to the Great Hall and sought the anonymity of the crowded area surrounding the tournament. They found that they were in time to see Mark's bout, and watched as he was called out to face his French opponent. The man was a hulk, with no perceivable neck, a rash of red hair and ears that had been ribbed and distorted by a history of heavy blows. Cristoforo saw this and laughed, commenting in English.

"Ha, look! He has the ears of a *cavolfiore!*"

"A what?"

"It is a vegetable from Genoa. White with rough textured florets and green leaves. Looks just like his ears."

Behind him he heard a tinkle of female laughter, and turned to see Contessa Alessandria. She had overheard his conversation and had clearly understood the allusion to the vegetable. "*Signor* Corio, you are incorrigible. Verily the poor man hast no help for his lumpen visage," she chided him in a mocking tone.

"Ah Contessa, you have returned and my heart is once again complete," Cristoforo replied artfully.

"And I see that your tongue has returned to its state of encomium."

Jamie watched the byplay, amused at this new side to Cristoforo – that of a suave suitor, steeped in courtly romance.

"Contessa, a thousand pardons, may I introduce my companion, James de Grispere, lately of England. Jamie, may I have the pleasure of introducing Contessa Alessandria de Felicini of Bologna." Jamie bowed and the Contessa curtseyed.

"My lady Contessa, I am at your service," Jamie took her hand and raised it to his lips.

"Mark's contest begins," Cristoforo commented. They turned to watch the last bout of the day.

Mark and his opponent, who Jamie could only think of as a *cavolfiore,* met with a crash of bodies as each sought to obtain the better grip. The score between the teams was currently lying three to each country and the day's sport would be decided on this final bout, a fact of which that Mark was only too keenly aware. The Frenchman sought and found grips on both Mark's arms, one below the triceps. Thus placed he drove his arm upwards with all his might, surging his power into the move and crying out to force more strength from his body. Instead of resisting, Mark went with the move and pulled backwards, surprising the Frenchman, who planted a slab-like foot down with a splat that anchored his weight and prevented further forward movement.

Amid the grunts of exertion, Mark sensed a change in his opponent, like an experienced rider feels through the reins of a highbred stallion, sending messages as to what might happen next. Sure enough, the Frenchman surged now with the other arm, forcing it up and back – but Mark was ready. He chose a different response, and locking his arm straight with all his massive strength, he prevented the move as soon as it had begun. But now Mark had an advantage, for he held the upper grip at his opponent's collar.

With the Frenchman's legs placed forward and back, Mark stepped forward, sweeping inside first the left leg then the right, which moved as the Frenchman corrected his balance. Twice more at a fast pace Mark repeated the moves, and each time the Frenchman retreated his stance became wider and more vulnerable to a frontal assault. Then in the graceful movement Mark pushed backwards and pulled forwards again, all within a split second. The Frenchman reacted as he hoped, resisting and unintentionally going with the pull. Mark pivoted on one leg presenting his back to his opponent, dropping his legs and throwing him over his hip in a flying mare.

The Frenchman was experienced and sought to ride out the throw, pushing off the hip, so Mark raised his outside leg, wheeling him in the air. His opponent tried to grab Mark's jacket, maintaining contact in an attempt to bring him down. Mark obliged him, continuing the movement and following the Frenchman's body closely to the floor. The two huge wrestlers crashed into the matting as one, to the audible crack of two ribs popping.

Mark was unhurt, redoubtable in his success. The Frenchman rolled and gasped in agony. It was his ribs that had been broken in the fall, and he was also badly winded. He curled into a ball to draw air into his lungs, all the time clutching his ribs.

"Hah! *Signor Cavolfiore* is not so great now eh?" Cristoforo mocked, laughing at the cries of dismay from the spectators that their man had failed. The Frenchman was game, but gaining his knees it was evident that he could not continue at the match, and the competition went to the English. The cheers of Mark's fellow combatants echoed loudly around the hall against the subdued response from the French.

Queen Isabeau – whom many courtiers felt still considered herself Bavarian –maintained a regal equanimity and offered a small tight smile which gave nothing away. Each team of wrestlers was brought forward and the queen dispensed a chain of victory to the English combatants with the help of an aide. At the end of the brief ceremony the teams were clapped and cheered as they made their way from the centre of the court.

At the side of the presentation area Jacques de Berry and the Duke of Burgundy stood apart. "Now, mark the blond giant, for I swear there is an intimacy between him and the merchant's son."

As they watched, Jamie and Cristoforo made their way through the throng of spectators to congratulate Mark.

"Mark. By the rood that was well done. Monsieur *Cavolfiore* was well turned. He'll rue the day he crossed paths with you." Jamie exclaimed, clapping him on the shoulder. Mark turned in delight and questioned the naming of his opponent, which Cristoforo gleefully explained.

From the other side of the hall, the three seemed good companions to de Berry and the duke.

"What say you? Good comrades in more than wrestling, I'll warrant. I worry that de Grispere was seen in the infirmary today. What did he do there? He looks hale and hearty to mine eyes."

"The infirmary? Many of the monks there have ties to my estates in the north, including Saint-Omer. You say de Grispere has connexions at court?"

"I have word from Sir John Tiptoft that he was followed after leaving Whittington's quarters. He is what he claims – a merchant's son – but no one of that ilk handles weapons like a trained knight. For he has a skill at arms of which I have not seen the like. His battle cry was *"an Umfraville"* when he fought. That name means much, as you and I know. Our Scots friends in arms rue the day when Sir Robert de Umfraville strikes into their heartland. He has ruined many a rebellion from the north, and de Grispere bears watching and questioning."

"Not openly," the duke adjured. "Force at court will not serve, we do not need hostilities with no cause to open us up or expose our intent. Let us use a weaker link in his chain. We will pressure the wrestler, and if they are friends as you suspect, this should prove the more propitious way forward to assoil him of suspicion. As to the merchant, use more subtle means."

"A clever ploy, but I have just the trap for master de Grispere," de Berry confirmed.

The two Frenchmen watched carefully as the three men continued a cordial discussion. Then Jamie and Cristoforo broke off their engagement with Mark, vowing to meet up with him later. Cristoforo made his way back to join the Contessa, amusing her with an outrageous story. He was repaid with laughter and her beautiful smile. At first Jamie grinned ruefully at Cristoforo's antics, then shaking his head he turned away as he sought to gain the attention of another merchant whom his father insisted that he meet. As he turned, his shoulder collided with someone who was passing from behind. There was a squeal of pain and a flash of turquoise as the figure sank to her knees.

"Oh my lady, a thousand pardons." Jamie cried, appalled that his actions should have hurt a lady so. "I pray thee tell me that you are not hurt," he urged. The lady's maid shooed him away as she bent to minister to her mistress.

"Away, you malapert beast! For verily you have injured my lady."

At that moment the lady in question blinked to reveal tears of pain. But Jamie saw only the eyes in her face. Never had he seen eyes like them. They were an extraordinary shade of amber with gold flecks within and a leonine quality. This was further enhanced by a trail of golden hair that had fallen from beneath her wimple, which had been knocked askew in the collision. She sighed then parted her lips in a delicate smile.

"Fear not, my lord, for I believe that I shall live. But it is a great wonder that I do, for are your shoulders made of steel?" She offered Jamie a demure smile from beneath eyelids that were hooded with promise.

"I am no lord, my lady but your humble servant James de Grispere, and I beg forgiveness for my clumsy manners."

"Aid me in helping my lady, you oaf, and I adjure you caution and not to compound your act," her maid scolded.

Jamie was cowed by the maid and gently helped the lady to her feet. She appeared as if she might swoon and begged a seat at a nearby table. Once safely there, Jamie offered to fetch some wine.

"Oh that is kind sir, I feel rather faint."

"As my lady pleases." And with that he rushed off to return with a goblet of fresh white wine, presenting it to the seated lady. She sipped it delicately and professed to be feeling much better. "My lady, is there anything further that I may do to aid you in recompense for my clumsiness?"

"No sir, all is now fair with me. I need but a little time to recover and shall be full well again. I prithee do not concern yourself."

"May I sit with you awhile to ensure complete recovery? I am at your service. Whom do I have the pleasure of addressing, my Lady, if I may be so bold?"

The lady beamed up at him with a stunning smile that was all white teeth and sparkling eyes. He felt the full force of it, and melted a little before her gaze. She offered her hand to be kissed.

"I am Lady Monique Nemours." She announced. "Pray sit, do."

She turned to her maid. "I will be fine, Claudine, but perhaps you would fetch my silk shawl for my neck and shoulders." The maid bobbed a curtsey.

"Yes my lady, I shall return in a trice." At which she threw another scolding glance in Jamie's direction before scurrying off. Monique brought the full charm to bear. "Now enlighten me as to your business here, for I perceive that you are not from France." She commanded.

"No my lady. I am English, from London. I am here as my father's emissary to trade in cloth, wool and silk."

Cristoforo and Alessandria watched the two of them from a distance with interest and differing thoughts. Cristoforo was amused.

"Ah, I strive and yet Master Jamie has them fall at his feet."

"Pah!" That was no accident. *La donna di seduzione* is victorious again," Alessandria commented.

"It was intentional, you suspect?" Cristoforo questioned.

"I have seen her a work afore. Men are wont to fall at her feet, the like of which defies all logic. She twists and turns as like to make an eel jealous."

"*E Vero*? Then I must look out for Jamie. For certes he's a brave man and a great warrior, but by the rood I suspect his defences are weak when a maiden weaves her web."

"Hah, master of love, yet you are not susceptible?" She teased.

"Oh my lady Contessa, I am susceptible only to your immutable charms."

"Rogue! I am awash with your compliments and fear I may drown ere I reach the shore. Now come, let us rescue your companion afore he is completely snared, for he shall be ere much more time is passed."

They strolled across to where Jamie was paying court to Lady Monique, who appeared fully recovered from her stumble and was hanging on his every word, seemingly entranced. Jamie responded in kind, falling deeper under the spell of her bewitching eyes.

As they approached, Cristoforo gently applauded in mock adulation: "Ah my lord prince of the dance, only you could nearly slay a poor damsel then seek to make love to her."

Jamie had been completely unaware of their approach, so utterly absorbed was he with Monique's attentions. He turned, startled as one leaving a trance.

"Cristoforo! Why you startled me, you Italian jackanapes. Forgive me, my lady, may I introduce my companion in trade, *Signor* Cristoforo Corio, who is in my father's employ, and with him the Contessa Alessandria di Felicini of this court."

Cristoforo bowed deeply and both Monique who had risen and the Contessa curtsied to each other. To any man skilled in womanly wiles there was seemingly no love lost between the two women.

"Forsooth, my lady and I are already acquainted, for the court is such a small place." Alessandria commented.

"Indeed it is, Contessa, and the common friendships one makes are passing quick," Monique responded.

The undertones were not lost on Jamie, who glanced from one woman to the other. His experience at the English court had prepared him for the ebb and flow of courtly undercurrents and to pick out any shadows of suspicion wherever they lay. He was a little perplexed as to what might be the cause of the vexation between the two women, but Cristoforo saved the awkward moment by stepping deftly in. "Jamie, we are needed. Monsieur Danckant has been asking after you on some matter of price," he said.

However besotted Jamie might be with Monique, he was not slow to comprehend Cristoforo's meaning and made his apologies to the lady, begging her pardon once more for the collision and asking if he might attend upon her during his time at court.

"I do so hope that we may meet again, for you are engaging company and I do so wish to learn more of England. 'Tis a place I have never visited."

"As it pleases you, my lady. We will meet on the morrow."

With that the two moved away, the Contessa accompanying them to the door where with Cristoforo's promise of a later assignation she departed, leaving the two men to talk.

Jamie was a little bemused by the proceedings. "Pray thee, what occurred to draw me away from milady? For she is bewitching and her company would be fair for hours to come. Why didst you draw me away?" He demanded.

"Jamie, I promised your father I would guard your back, and that is my duty. By the rood, that lady is not all she seems. The Contessa believes she has strong connexions to the house of Burgundy and that meeting was no accident of fate. It was engineered by her and you were her dupe, I swear."

"Nay. I agree that I'm a novice compared to you, but I've tumbled my share of wenches, and I am beyond my first calf love. Think ye that she planned our encounter?" He asked.

Cristoforo raised a cynical eyebrow, tilting his head at Jamie's naivety.

"Come, let's away and find a lively inn for supper and a flagon of wine and I will explain to you the world of women. Now when..." Cristoforo was on fine form from seducing the Contessa, and he proceeded to offer Jamie the benefit of his considerable experience in all matters of courtly love.

Chapter Twenty-Eight

Some hours later, when Jamie and Cristoforo were back in their lodgings, Cristoforo made his apologies to Jamie, swearing that the Contessa's heart would break if he did not meet with her this evening.

"It is my duty as the Contessa's countryman to ensure that she is protected from this wicked world. *Dio mio*, you would not have me abandon her, would you?"

"No," Jamie declared, laughing. "But think of me with the wizened Friar Sebastian when you are with the beautiful Contessa, and ask yourself who has the best of it."

"Ah, the sacrifices we make for our sins." Cristoforo laughed. With that, he bowed gracefully and retreated through the door with a skip in his step.

Jamie shouted an insult at his departing figure and then the humour left him. He estimated that Friar Sebastian would be arriving within the hour and realised that he must make plans for every contingency in case he was betrayed. He donned a thick padded gambeson that would withstand all but the sharpest blade; withdrew his sword from its scabbard and laid it on a trestle covered with just a light cloth, the hilt within easy reach. Then he summoned his headman.

"Will, a friar will arrive within the hour," Jamie said. "Admit him but no one else. Have a care when he knocks that he is alone. Trust no one and I will prove his identity from the window above ere he knocks. Once he is inside, bar the door and have two of the lads ready with daggers in case they're needed."

"As you please master James. Do you fear deceit?"

"I know not, Will, but forewarned is forearmed."

"We will be ready, have no fear." Will assured him.

A little before the hour of nine o'clock Jamie heard a rapping at the front door of the lodgings. He went to the window opening directly above the door to the street, and there in the dim light stood the hooded figure of a friar.

"Who goes there?" Jamie called softly.

The figure looked up, and he recognised the pinched features of Friar Sebastian. "Let me in forsooth, I must not be seen." He called upwards.

"Will? The door, our visitor has arrived."

Jamie left the landing and descended to the lower floor. There before him was Friar Sebastian, who was not at ease. He pulled his cowl back from his head to reveal a tense face that was fraught with worry.

"I bid you welcome, and have no fear. You are safe within these walls." Jamie did his best to calm his visitor.

"Good evening, my son. I dare not stay; my presence will be missed ere long. I needs must be brief and impart my news. The information you seek is this: they are building a siege engine at Saint-Omer."

"At Saint-Omer? But that is near where we must travel to meet up with my father's connexions. What type of machine is this, and where is it constructed? For an attack on Calais it must be huge, yet not easily concealed. How can such a thing be achieved?" Jamie rattled off questions as if he were thinking out loud.

"It is indeed huge, and I have seen it with mine own eyes. It is being constructed within the cathedral itself!"

"The cathedral?"

"Yes. It will be run on wheels but can be easily dismantled once fully completed – which be soon. When I was there two months ago, they were proceeding apace. They seek the spring for an attack. It is in the heart of my Duke of Burgundy's lands and he seeks the prize of the crown, with Calais as his lever. To deliver the news back to Sir Richard would take many days, and may be in vain. Action must be taken forthwith to prevent a disaster, and the tower must be destroyed ere it can be used. I would adjure you leave with all haste and find a means to thwart their planned assault."

Jamie's mind reeled. He had imagined passing information and reporting back to Sir Richard. "Why did you not impart the full information to Sir Richard?"

"I could not. The birds are watched closely and pigeons are netted or shot if seen. I believe I am under suspicion for my ties to the cathedral and I do not have the trust of all my fellow brethren."

"Your pardon, Friar Sebastian, I did not seek to cast aspersions upon your loyalty. But we must away with all haste to Saint-Omer and see what might be achieved.

"I would ask that you take me with you, sir, for I am afeared of rumour and suspicion within the court that might fall at my door."

"No one would dare to assail a man of the cloth upon holy ground, surely?" Jamie asked.

"You know not of what you speak. There are as you know two Popes of the apostolic church, and they in turn serve two masters: God and the power of the Holy See which is given by man. Do not underestimate the power of the crown in this matter," He said.

"Once again I crave your pardon, Friar Sebastian, I merely sought to dissemble the matter. Of course you may accompany us hence."

They were interrupted at that point by a disturbance at the rear of the lodgings, and Cristoforo appeared, looking vexed and fraught.

"Jamie!" he exclaimed, "Friar Sebastian," he nodded, "there is much afoot. Mark of Cornwall is taken, arrested on charges of espionage and spying."

"What?"

"Aye and more's the fool that would rush in after him. For I have it on good authority that he is but a snare to entice the real game, a tethered goat for the slaughter. We are the main course, I'll wager. And even now, I saw a watcher in shadows opposite, seeking news of anyone who enters here."

Knowing Cristoforo's ability to slip abroad like a wraith in the night Jamie did not doubt his friend's observation.

Friar Sebastian was aghast at the news. "Then I am undone!" He cried.

Cristoforo was unperturbed on his account and as nonchalant as ever.

"Fear not, friar, for I have a way out to the rear that will offer you a secret passage, but may I suggest that we secrete you abroad now ere you are missed?"

"Hold. For we may yet need your assistance further, Friar, and I would not ask if our need was not so great," said Jamie, then turning to Cristoforo he demanded, "Tell me, how you came by this intelligence?"

"La Contessa. We had a tryst for this evening in her private apartments, but ere I arrived she informed me of Mark's arrest.

The charges are spurious and by association she believes it is you and me who are the targets, for he is but a pawn to entice us into an attempted escape. She overheard this from the queen's quarters, and the Duke of Burgundy was the action's architect. He is apparently in league with Jacques de Berry. We must ensure Mark's release, no? For we cannot in all conscience allow him to rot at our expense."

Jamie thought quickly, summarising in his mind the events of the past few days. He cursed himself for his skill at arms on the cog, and for his open display of friendship with Mark.

"Of course we cannot, but we have an advantage."

"*Perche?*"

"They will expect us not to hear of Mark's arrest until the morrow, at which point they will anticipate either representation, protest or maybe an attempt at rescue. They will not expect us to act tonight. So we will do exactly that. We act now. Does the Contessa provide a clue as to where he may be held?"

"Indeed. Tis passing strange for he is kept in private apartments within the palace awaiting interrogation on the morrow, so rumour has it."

"Dost the Contessa know the exact location of the apartment within the palace?"

"I am sure that she can find the location. Why?" Cristoforo asked, although he suspected that he already knew the answer.

"We go in tonight. They will expect us tomorrow once we have heard the news. They would not for a moment suspect that we would hear tonight. No, it is now that we must move. Friar Sebastian, can we scale the wall and be safe in the garden ere you let us in to the friary? The palace will surely now be closed for the night." The friar nodded; a worrying look on his face.

"Good. Cristoforo, can you get us around the grounds once we are within?"

"With ease," the Italian replied, shrugging as though he had been asked to open a door with a handle.

"We must plan this carefully. We cannot go too soon, for if we do the discovery will be made early and we will have no chance of escape. I shall inform Will of our plans, so that he can be ready to travel at first light and be on the road from Paris ere the gate opens at dawn."

With Will informed and plans made, they ushered the nervous friar out to the rear entrance and into the safety of the dark night, having advised him of the hour at which they would arrive. Friar Sebastian scuttled off into the shadows and found with Cristoforo's guidance a street running parallel to his route home that provided good cover away from the prying eyes of the man watching their lodgings.

They made their final preparations and saddled horses ready for a speedy departure. Just before their leaving Cristoforo fetched his leather satchel that was never far from his side and withdrew a cloth bag secured by a drawstring, which he slung diagonally over his shoulders. Jamie was puzzled, but time was pressing and he asked no questions. For his part he wound a length of rope around his waist, ensuring that is was hidden from view beneath his cloak.

In the early hours of the morning the two figures made their way furtively across from their lodgings to the French court. No one was on a war footing, and no guards within the court had been made aware that anything untoward might occur. It was just another boring night on guard duty, approaching the hour of four o'clock when everyone was at their lowest ebb. Jamie and Cristoforo scaled an outer wall that led to parkland and the rambling grounds of the estate. It was only the inner areas that were well guarded, and they found their progress unimpeded until they reached the outer wall of the friary herb garden.

They moved carefully around the wall, seeking a small wicket gate that Friar Sebastian had advised them of earlier. Locating it on the south side they found it gave to a hard shove and moved inwards on greased hinges. The figure of Friar Sebastian emerged from the darkness, cowled and hunched. He said not a word, but motioned them to be quiet and follow him across the paved gardens. He took them to another dark corner and through a doorway into a secluded part of the friary, which in turn led out onto the cloisters. Once in the free area of the inner court, they could see that there were signs of activity from guards patrolling and the occasional courtier moving to and fro in the early hours, bearing messages.

The two men moved quietly, keeping to the shadows yet trying not to appear furtive, looking as though they belonged. Cristoforo was as ever a past master at moving unseen. He merged effortlessly with shadow and shade, making not a sound on his padded feet. They proceeded in this manner until they found their way barred by the doors into the royal area of the palace. The gatehouse was guarded by two soldiers, and from here internal walls curled away, interspersed at intervals with small turrets which gave the palace its name. The tops of the walls had small crenulations that were more ornamental than functional. The walls were only about twelve feet high. Looking upwards, Jamie loosened a rope he had tied around his waist, spreading the looped end, which he threw to engage with the top of the wall. On the third try it snagged one of the upright castellations. Jamie gave it a proving tug, and the rope held. He began a quick ascent up the stone wall and upon reaching the top saw that Cristoforo had followed suit, climbing carefully with his cloth bag slung about his shoulders. They curled over the wall and hung by their hands for a second before dropping lightly to other side.

Cristoforo knew exactly where he was going and Jamie followed, padding lightly after him. They entered through a side door as the guard ambled by, staggering a little as if he was having trouble staying awake. Inside the palace everyone felt safe, and the internal doors were unlocked. They moved quietly along a corridor and a door opened from an apartment, the light from a candle spilled out onto the corridor. There was no time to hide, Jamie merely bluffed it out.

"So I urged the little strumpet to give more, and what a tumble she was! By the rood I'll never be the same again!" He commented in a slurred voice, lurching along the corridor in a manner of apparent inebriation.

Cristoforo laughed at the ribald commentary as they passed the courtier, who gave them barely a glance, suspecting nothing, seeing only two gentlemen the worse for drink making their way back to their apartments after an evening's ribaldry. Once he was out of sight, Cristoforo looked behind him and nodded. They dropped the merry act and proceeded along at a pace.

"So many people here, if you look as if you belong and proceed as normal, you are naturally accepted. You have to just play the part."

The corridor led to another turret and a staircase that spiralled upwards. Cristoforo motioned for Jamie to follow and they ascended to the second floor. He counted three doors along then knocked in a certain way, using a preordained signal. The door was opened carefully and The Contessa's beautiful veiled face appeared from within.

"*Caro, vieni, vieni, subito!*" she whispered.

The two men slipped in inside and she shut the door quickly.

"You are safe, praise God. There are guards everywhere, but they are all relaxed and no one yet suspects what is about to happen. I only heard because my maid had a tryst with one of the men guarding your countryman, *Signor* Jamie. They took him quietly when he was by himself. Your master Swynford is both puzzled and afraid, for he knows not where Mark is being held, nor aught of his fate. Tomorrow, my maid tells me they intended to torture him to reveal what he knows about you and any plots there may be to undermine France."

"Forsooth, what gave them the idea that he might be privy to any such information?"

"It is but a ruse. They know that he will attract you and Cristoforo. It is you they want, and he is the bait. The Duke of Burgundy and Jacques de Berry are behind it. The duke is the most powerful man in France."

"Hell's teeth – the duke and de Berry? I thought that de Berry was an Armagnac name, and the Armagnacs hate the Burgundians. Burgundy had the Duke of Orleans assassinated, did he not?" Jamie exclaimed.

"*Signor* Jamie, you are correct, but de Berry is the poor relation. His father was wrongly accused of seceding the surrender of his castle, and the duke's family have never forgiven those responsible. He pretends to side with the English, but secures favour with the duke to regain the lands and status his family forfeited. Now he follows whomsoever will pay him to further his cause," she cautioned.

Jamie cursed again: "Of all the people to have as a travelling companion, it would have to be de Berry."

"'Tis passing strange. is it not? I would suspect that this is no coincidence, Jamie," Cristoforo cautioned.

"You may have the right of it, and is something to appraise Sir Richard of upon our return to London."

"First we must rescue Mark from the clutches of these

duplicitous scum," he muttered.

The Contessa pulled a light cloak about her shoulders and moved towards the door.

"Where dost thou go?" Cristoforo asked, tenderness and concern in his voice.

"It is difficult and you will become lost. Come, all will be well," she urged.

They followed the Contessa out of her chamber and along a series of winding corridors until they reached a lower level on the other side of the palace. At either end there were the inevitable turrets, both of which offered spiral stairs that led downwards. She paused and urged them both closer the better to hear her words: "Directly below is a corridor identical to this one," she whispered. "Halfway along you will see a room with a guard at the door. That is where he is being held."

They nodded their understanding. Then, with her leading the way, they proceeded down the first flight of stairs of the turret. They crept softly down the last of the stone steps and halted. Jamie, who was leading, peered cautiously around the newel, and what met his eyes filled with him disappointment. There was not one guard, but two. He motioned the other two to back up.

A few steps up Jamie whispered: "There are two guards, one here at the foot of the steps and another outside the door. We cannot close the distance ere one is alerted to raise others. It is all of forty or fifty yards to the middle of the corridor. It is useless," he finished in dismay.

However, Cristoforo was not perturbed as he motioned that they rise further back up the staircase to prevent their voices carrying below. Once above, he explained his plan.

"Jamie, stay here and allow me a count of one hundred in your mind. This will give me time to ascertain my position. Be careful and look around the stair, you will see me and we will act together. You take the guard below and I shall deal with the other at the door." He finished simply, as though his plan was self-explanatory and perfectly obvious.

"How in God's name do you intend to cover fifty yards? Sprout wings and fly?" Jamie asked in exasperation. Cristoforo gave a hint of a smile and lifted the cloth bag from around his shoulders, adding to Jamie's puzzlement. Pulling open the drawstring he pulled out two pieces of equipment no longer than eleven or twelve inches and only half discernible in the dim light. He passed the bag to the Countess, who was equally puzzled, and proceed to locate the two pieces together with discernible metallic click. He then produced a slim length of what appeared to be cord, attaching each looped end to the cross bar he had just located in place. The Contessa gasped, putting her hand to her mouth. "*Assassino!*" she hissed.

Jamie uttered a gasp: "A crossbow! But the like of none I have seen before."

Cristoforo brought it up to the light of a flaming torch, where the wicked weapon looked almost like a toy. Jamie could now see that while the stock was made in the traditional manner of wood, the crossbar seemed to be a laminate of steel and horn, hinting at great power despite its small size. It was, he knew, no toy but an assassin's weapon that would be deadly at short range. On closer inspection he noticed three razor sharp bolts attached to the bottom of the stock.

"She is deadly at up to sixty yards and fabulously accurate. Who needs wings?" he grinned, white teeth showing in the gloom.

"You're going to kill the guard?"

"What else? He needs to be silenced and quickly," Cristoforo answered with no hesitation. "You will need to deal a similar fate to the other man. My lady Contessa, you must go now, or this will become dangerous for you," he urged.

She was in a state of shock, never having realised that the peacock who had charmed her at court was the same lethal assassin who stood before her now. She tore her eyes away from the evil looking crossbow.

"No, I will stay. You will need a guide to get you out. Now go. Hurry!" she said.

"Jamie, as soon as I go start counting." Cristoforo quickly kissed the Countess before she could object, span around and almost sprinted away on silent feet, at home with the night. Jamie bowed and departed back down the spiral staircase again to await Cristoforo's emergence at the other end of the corridor. He slid his dagger from its sheath and waited, calming his breathing, counting to the moment at which he would strike. It was a strange feeling, he reflected. He would kill in battle, a duel or a known enemy with no compunction whatsoever, yet he felt a tinge of regret here. The guards were only guilty of being on the wrong side, and to kill in cold blood seemed wrong. Then he shook himself mentally. If it was the guards' lives or Mark's, there would be no choice to make.

Cristoforo ran easily to the end of the corridor and down the steps, then stopped. He placed the end of the crossbow against the wall, wedged the stock in his stomach, bracing his muscles and pulled the cord back using both hands until he heard the soft click as the catch caught the cord. He released one of the bolts from beneath the weapon and placed it in the flight groove. He peered carefully around the corner of the stairwell. The guard was facing the opposite wall, with his back to Mark's cell some forty yards away. Cristoforo spotted Jamie's head at the opposite end of the corridor. He was ready. He raised his crossbow, but at that very moment both guards moved as if to an unseen signal and began to walk towards each other to change places. Just in time he withheld his shot – a question burning inside him: shoot now or wait? The longer the wait, the more chance there was that both of them would be discovered. He saw that Jamie was hidden from view by the other guard. Now, he thought, it had to be now. He re-sighted, aiming for the back of the guard's neck to silence any cry, inhaled, held his breath, exhaled and pulled the release trigger. There was a slight twang as the cord flew forward and a soft whistle as the quarrel flew through the air, both of which sounds were masked by the guards' footsteps. The barbs bit home and the guard gave a brief croaked gasp as the quarrel severed his spine.

At the other end of the corridor, Jamie sprinted a few feet to close the gap as the other guard froze in shock, seeing his companion struck down, seemingly unable to move. Jamie's left hand clasped the guard's mouth, while the right pushed the dagger upwards between the lower ribs, killing him almost instantly. The man's blood poured from the wound and he slumped and fell twitching at Jamie's feet. Once the deed was done, Jamie felt no remorse. It was just another French enemy gone.

"*Bravo*, Jamie, *buon lavoro!*" he applauded.

Jamie shrugged and hefted the dead man upright, propping him against the wall so that he looked to be sleeping. Cristoforo did the same with his dead body. He listened carefully as he had been trained for any untoward sound or disturbance, closing his eyes to aid his sharp hearing. Nothing could he heard, and he nodded to Jamie, who moved to the door and slid back the bolts at the top and bottom. Luckily, they were greased and did not squeak. Both men were aware that relief guards could arrive at any time. Easing open the door they peered into the gloomy interior, illuminated only by the light thrown from the flaming brand without. At first they saw nothing then Jamie whispered: "Mark?"

He heard a moan from the far side of the room. Cristoforo

brought the brand down from the wall and held it high to shed more light on the interior of the room. It was not furnished as a cell, but as an office or a guard room. There was a sturdy table and a number of chairs strewn about the floor. A window was set high up in the wall but offered no light at this hour. A candle stood on the table and it spluttered into flame as Cristoforo lit it with the brand.

There at the base of the table, shackled to one of the legs, was the huge form of Mark, curled up in a ball. They saw in the dim light that one of his eyes was swollen shut and a gash had been opened above the other. There were mottled bruises on his bare chest. He pushed down with one arm to help raise his torso and groaned. Cristoforo and Jamie rushed to his aid.

"They did this to you?" Jamie asked.

"Aye," he answered through mushed lips. "That bastard I beat yesterday, they let him at me while I was tied. I'll 'ave him back one day, just you see if I don't." Jamie no longer felt at all upset at killing the guards. "Bloody *crapauds!*" Mark finished.

They raised him gently into a sitting position, but the shackle prevented further movement. It was locked with a seemingly crude mechanism.

"Who has the key?" Cristoforo asked.

"Cap'n of the guard, I thinks."

Cristoforo reached to his boot, pulled out one of the slim throwing stiletto knives and worked it into the large keyhole of the shackle. A few seconds later there was a click and the mechanism released.

"You never cease to surprise me, Cristoforo," Jamie muttered. The Italian smiled and replaced the knife in his boot-top.

"Can you stand, Mark? We must make haste."

"Don't 'ee worry. Takes more than a Frog to better me. Old Bertha, our carthorse at the farm, trampled me this one time an'

195

that were worse'n this. Gave 'er a slap and rode the ol' bitch 'ome. I'll be grand soon enough, just get me out of 'ere," Mark urged.

They paused at the doorway then left the room, walking down the corridor as fast as Mark's progress would allow. At the end they climbed the staircase and found the Contessa waiting for them.

"We must hurry," she warned them, "They will be sure to change the guard with the dawn."

With her as their guide they soon reached the inner wall they had scaled earlier that night. Jamie threw the rope whilst Cristoforo bade goodnight to the Contessa, who this time returned his kiss, hugging him tightly.

"*Torna presto, caro mio,*" She told him. She was rewarded with a flashing white smile and a courtly bow. She scuttled off with a rustle of skirts into the darkness of the night.

The rope was looped over one of the crenulations and all three men hauled themselves up and dropped to the orchards within the grounds. Mark stood for a moment, hands on his knees. The exertion had caused blood to drip from his battered face. They retraced their route back to the friary without discovery. Jamie was dismayed to find that Friar Sebastian was nowhere to be found.

"We dare not tarry to search for him," he whispered to the others, "It could be our undoing." With regret, yet forced by necessity, they slipped quickly and silently across the herb garden, through the wicket gate and from there back into the city streets the town.

Mark was wheezing a little, but he pushed on, not wishing to be caught again.

"Can you ride, Mark?" Jamie asked.

"Aye, I can and I will. Nothing will persuade me to return to that place."

They finally reached the lodgings, where they found three horses waiting for them in the rear courtyard. Will was there with two other servants armed with swords, and they were relieved to find it was Jamie who returned rather than the Watch.

"Master Jamie, praise the Lord. You fetched him out, then?"

"That we did Will, that we did. Are you all ready to move? For we needs must be at the Westward gate by daybreak, and that will not be long in coming." Jamie looked up at the dawn that was creeping into the night sky. Cristoforo disassembled his crossbow, which he had kept ready in case the need arose to use it against pursuers.

"*Sì*, the dawn she will arrive soon," he muttered.

They bustled to, and within minutes the party was ready and on the route to the gate and the road to Calais beyond. They were first in the queue for the opening of the gates, each holding his breath for the hue and cry they were half expecting, as it had been at least half an hour since they fled the palace. The guard checked their papers and passed them through, with Mark hiding in the bed of the waggon covered in cloth and silks. Once through and out of sight of the sentries, they extricated him and he remounted his horse.

"Will, press on for Calais; there may be riders sent for all those following this road. Delay them as you may with misinformation, but not at your own peril. Is that understood? If needs be, tell them we left for Flanders."

"Aye, master Jamie, will do. They'll not catch us 'til much later today for we'll set a fair pace, be assured."

"Thank you Will, and Godspeed to you."

With that, Jamie and his two companions rode off northwards to intercept the road to Saint-Omer.

Chapter Twenty-Nine

The Duke of Burgundy was alerted when the guard changed in the early morning, and his temper erupted in a way his staff were well used to.

"Find him!" he raged. "How did he escape? Find out who helped him. For he could not have achieved it by himself. I want their heads, do you hear? Their heads! How did this happen? He surely had help from within. Did the other English party of wrestlers help him, I wonder?"

"No, your Grace, we had a guard on the door to their chambers all night and none left the room."

"How were the guards dealt with at the Englishman's door?"

The hapless captain explained about the fate of the two guards and the manner of their demise.

"A crossbow bolt?"

"Yes my lord, but smaller than a normal size, and strangely contrived."

"So we seek a demon dwarf with a crossbow. He should not be hard to find. Or the others. Find them, imbecile. Go!"

The captain of bowed and retreated from the chamber, happy to be gone.

Alone with Jean de Grisson in his private chamber, the duke cursed aloud. "Who helped? For surely the man must have had help?"

"My lord are we certain that the merchant de Grispere was at his lodgings all night and saw no one?"

The duke stopped to wonder for a moment, his rage calmed, his thoughts beginning to clear. "Find the man we sent to watch his lodgings last night, Jean. Question him again about all that happened yester night. And send the captain of the guard with four men to investigate their lodgings, to see if they are still within. If not, have them ride straight to gates without recourse, and look to the north west. Follow anyone on the Calais road who may be with the English party."

"As you wish, John." De Grisson left in search of the captain of the guard and the errant watcher. The duke then sent a courtier in search of another whom he thought may be able to help, and before long a visitor entered his chambers.

Sometime later de Grisson returned with a report for the duke.

"I have news. Our little spy reports that all he saw the whole evening was one visitor, an old man in a hooded cowl which may have been that of a monk or friar."

A frown etched itself across the duke's forehead. "Did this mysterious visitor stay the whole night?"

"Apparently he did, and no more visitors were seen either entering or leaving the house for whole period."

"Hmm. And he is certain sure?"

"Aye, I grilled him hard on pain of death. He remained diligent all night, so he swears, and left his post to return here at around the hour of four in the morning, after the watch retires."

"Four, you say? This crosses with the time of attack on the cell. I wonder... could it have been achieved – to the friary, now," he snapped. "Let us see if we can rattle a cage or two. It would have taken two men to release the wrestler; two skilled men – de Grispere and that mysterious Italian companion of his mayhap."

The two men strode out of the chambers at a pace, and pressing the guards to follow them they rushed down the steps and directly to the friary. They demanded an audience with the head of the order in Paris, Guardian Martin. Upon questioning him they found that nothing untoward had occurred the previous evening and all the friars were accounted for, either at prayer or working in the precincts.

"Why do you disturb our peace here, my lord duke? Nothing will serve bar the disruption of our sanctity. Have you a purpose that you could impart that I may aid you more specifically in your quest?" The guardian offered with an ill-concealed tone of impatience.

The duke considered him from under dark brows and decided upon a whim to change tack. "For certes you may, Guardian, for my search concerns matters pertaining to Saint-Omer. The base of your order is there, is it not?"

"Indeed, in the abbey of Saint Bertin where Abbot Augustine presides. Yet I fail to see how this affects us here."

"Well you may. Yet could you inform me who here hails from that area and more specifically has strong connexions with your brethren there?"

The guardian sensed a trap and wisely obfuscated, pleading that many of his friars here were at one time or another privy to attending the Abbey at Saint-Omer and all had connexions to the area.

"Bah, we will interview the inmates here ourselves," the

duke ordered. With that, both he and Jean proceeded to the inner friary.

On the road north west from Paris, Jamie, Cristoforo and Mark bade Will and the waggons goodbye and made a faster pace on the road leading to Calais and Saint-Omer. They were hard pressed and had little time to talk among themselves, galloping wherever they could. The roads upon which Jean and the duke had passed some weeks earlier were now drier, leaving rutted tracks that would lame a horse if care were not taken. After a day's hard riding in which they changed horses twice along the way, they finally reached an inn some fifty miles north of Paris. Here they stopped for the night and arranged for new horses to commence the following day's ride.

As he slid awkwardly from his horse, Mark groaned at the pain from his bruised muscles and staggered for a few steps despite his great strength.

"By the rood, I'm spent. The beating they gave me pains me still," he moaned, stretching as best he could. Jamie placed a steadying hand upon his shoulder.

"Easy now. We shall rest here, and I will order a hot tub to ease your damaged limbs. Then we will talk, for I'll be bound that you have questions and we too should like know what occurred."

Later, as Mark languished in a wooden tub that was barely large enough to contain his huge frame, the other two men joined him in his room to discuss the events of the last twenty-four hours as well as other matters away from prying eyes and eavesdroppers.

"When did they take you?" Jamie asked.

"I was summoned to attend what they said was a private celebration and an audience with her majesty Queen Isabeau. A courtier led me to a chamber and once I was in it I was struck from behind and fell unconscious. I came to all trussed up like a chicken, and before me was the wrestler I beat in my match. By the good Lord, he hit me fearsome hard, and I'll neither forget 'im or forgive 'im in a long time. I was pleased when the captain of the guard came and stopped it."

"So when they were beating you, did they demand of you any intelligence about my whereabouts or the conversations in which we had engaged?"

Mark looked puzzled: "Nay. The bastard just snarled how he was going to break me so I'd never wrestle again. Then the captain of the guard came an' called him off, like I says. Tol' me I'd see my friends in the morning then be freed. I asked my crime, and he laughed in my face. Said my crime was bein' English, which I thought right odd." He paused, easing his muscles in the hot water. "By God's breath I'm right grateful, never was I gladder to see two English faces afore – even if one of 'em were Eye-talian," he said with a grin and they all laughed, easing the tension.

Cristoforo smiled at the reference. "So, as we thought, it was a ruse to deliver us into their hands, with you as the bait."

"Aye, Cristo... Cristopher... How're you called again?"

"Cristoforo Corio, at your service."

"That's hard for me, Cristofo...but I'm right grateful to you," Mark finished lamely.

"Now more than ever we must away to Saint-Omer as swiftly as we can travel to ruin their plans," Jamie interrupted. "There will be a pursuit as soon as they realise we are not within our lodgings or with the waggon train. We leave at dawn tomorrow, and with two fresh horses apiece we'll make Saint-Omer ahead of them."

"I'm still puzzled. What part did I play in this?" Mark asked. "Other than beating that Frog bastard. And why do we travel to this Saint-Omer place and not straight to Calais and English soil?"

At which Jamie explained in full the reason for their being in France, leaving some details out but apologising for inadvertently involving him in their mission. "As to Calais, this is the same road but we veer off to head for Saint-Omer. This way we buy a good day's ride if not more. We then have a choice: slip into Calais and return to England or make for Bruges or another port within Flanders that will avail us safe passage to England. But first we must destroy this siege machine ere the French re-take Calais and all is lost."

"Well then, master Jamie, it seems that I owe you my life twice over, and I'd repay the debt by helpin' you foil the French. It seems an honourable role to play, and they ain't no friends of mine if'n this is how they behave, so I'll gladly aid you in any way I can," Mark assured them.

"Well said, Mark of Cornwall. And as to aiding me, think nought of it. Rest and return to full strength ere we have need of you yet," Jamie urged.

With this they retired to their rooms and met an hour later for a supper of roasted lamb and a strong red wine that revived their spirits and tired limbs.

"I have warned the landlord that we shall leave at dawn and he will have our new horses ready. He appears a little curious, if not overtly suspicious, but there is little we can do to prevent that. I suspect pursuit will be hot on our heels, so speed is our best weapon, not secrecy."

The other two nodded in agreement and retired to their beds early, avoiding other guests in the inn.

It was midday when Jean de Grisson returned to the palace with the captain of the guard to seek out the duke. He found him pacing his private quarters in an evil temper.

"Well? What news?" The duke demanded as the two men were shown into the chamber.

The captain of the guard bowed, then explained that they had found the lodgings empty. Following his orders they had given hot pursuit to the English waggon train and overtaken them some hours along the road.

"Yet there was no evidence of the English whoreson de Grispere or that Italian whelp he travels with?"

"Nay my lord, yet the captain at the gate remembers them well, as they were first to past this morning. The master of the train declares that they departed pressing on for Calais to catch an early ship."

"Just the two of them? The Englishman and the Italian? Not the English giant, the wrestler?"

"No, your Grace."

"He was dissembling for sure. They would have smuggled the man out. Yet where do they go? Where indeed would they go? Could they know of our plans, Jean? A monk, a spy – and we saw two this morning, both hailing from Saint-Omer. I had a report from my Lady Monique Nemours. It seems that de Grispere was indeed a merchant, or so he claimed, and was to visit connexions in Saint-Omer for purposes of trade. The Italian, it seems, had become besotted with the Contessa Alessandria di Felicini. I wonder, think you that she would have aided their cause?"

"A lady in waiting to the queen?" De Grisson said doubtfully.

The duke made a decision. "Take five men at arms, and proceed in all haste to Saint-Omer. Send a galloper ahead, he may yet arrive first. For I warrant they are going to seek the tower. Hell's teeth, they must be thwarted at all costs." He punched the palm of his hand in exasperation. "Go now Jean, and I will interview these two monks here and send a message by pigeon to the constable of the town ere I know more."

"By all the saints, you believe they seek to destroy the tower?"

"Destroy? Nay, for it is well guarded, but seek intelligence and impart it to Calais and have our allies there prepare to help. Our man in the town may still debase their cause. I will arrange for a squadron of men to guard the road at Tilques in case they escape. The road narrows there and it is almost impossible to avoid."

Chapter Thirty

Saint-Omer

Jamie, Cristoforo and Mark had pressed hard for three days, halving the time that De Grisson and the duke had taken to reach Saint-Omer there weeks earlier. On the second day they rode so hard that they found themselves between inns as night fell and camped one night on the road, sleeping rough in a small copse by the wayside, wrapped in their cloaks for warmth and with the comfort of a fire. Mark was young and his aching body healed quickly, enabling him to suffer such privation and speed their journey.

On the fourth day they were presented with the vision of the glorious cathedral bathed in a glow of crimson, as the early morning sun cast a pink wash across its walls, making it appear as though it was constructed from a glazed confection.

"The smell of that tanning water's bad enough to make a grown man weep," Mark declared at the rancid fumes that assaulted their olfactory senses as they passed the outskirts of the town.

"Aye, it's an acquired taste, and not one I'd care to get used to," Jamie agreed, pulling up his cowl to muffle the smell as they passed the riverside tanning sheds.

"Once we are inside, do we make directly for the cathedral?" Cristoforo asked.

"Aye. We'll find an inn nearby, stable the horses and visit the Cathedral at vespers like any humble pilgrims. We'll see the lay of the land and make our plans from there. We can do nought 'til we comprehend the layout of the building. The area holding the tower will be guarded, as Friar Sebastian advised. If I recall right, the location of the siege engine is at the end of the eastern nave..." he mused. "Time is against us. I fear pursuit and we will not have another day in which to act."

Once beyond the gatehouse, they pushed their tired horses on through the streets of the town, guided by the dominant edifice of the cathedral up ahead. They found an inn close by. The landlord was curious, as most men of his calling are, seeking news of Jamie's business within the town.

"I am here to trade. My family was originally from this area. Their name is de Grispere," he offered. "Now I travel in my father's stead as he is frail with age. Perhaps you could direct me to the weaver's guild and *messieurs* Van de Veld and Vermulen's places of work, for I must meet with them."

At this the landlord became more gracious, and not for the first time Jamie was pleased that he had the authenticity of his trade to use as a cloak for his mission: *Sir Richard has advised me well,* he thought. The landlord gave them directions on how best to arrive at the area where both men lived, for which Jamie thanked him and requested a meal for later in the day when they returned.

Stabling the horses at the rear of the inn they walked the short distance to the cathedral, which appeared even more magnificent close up. The edifice rose above them, a buttressed leviathan of bright ashlar stone reflecting the sun's rays in splendid majesty, dominating the town.

At this early hour, morning prayers were just ending and the three of them split up upon entry, and took the chance to briefly scout around the building. Despite their mission, the internal beauty of the building with its ornate frescos and vaulted ceilings was breathtaking. Even Cristoforo, who was used to the elaborate decoration of the Florentine churches, was impressed. They mingled with the early morning worshippers and left without being noticed. They returned to the inn and sought their meal. In a private corner of the tap room they discussed what they had found.

"Two guards at the door main door, mailed and armed. They will be too far away to aid those within when our action begins." Jamie concluded. "This leaves us the problem of how to foil the two men at the far end, which will offer us access to the main vault where the machine is being constructed."

"What raises concern in my mind," Cristoforo commented, "is not dealing with the guards without, but if there should more within the main nave. We cannot permit any knowledge of our combat outside to permeate the area in which the engine is being constructed ere our presence is known there."

"Aye, that is true enough," Jamie agreed. "And even you cannot shoot two men at the same time with your crossbow."

Cristoforo tilted his head to one side, acknowledging the fact. He shrugged and offered Jamie a thin smile. "No, but I think I can find a way. Two men are suspicious, one is not. I will be upon them before they know it."

So great was Jamie's confidence in his newfound companion that he merely accepted the fact and moved to the next obstacle.

"So we needs must gain entry through the door to the nave. My worry is that it may be locked within, should guards be stationed there. Howsoever, I may have a ruse to bring them out if that is so."

Here Mark interceded. "That door didn't look too strong to me. Just put up to keep prying eyes out. Main thing is the guards. One good shove and she'll be in and off 'er hinges, then we can face what we find with surprise on our side."

"Well said, Mark. If you're right you'll earn your keep yet."

So with a plan made, they left the inn to wander the town and see how their escape could be made without access to the various gates which would be locked and barred against the night. Jamie also had two connexions of his father to meet with and discuss business, purchasing cloth and agreeing new contracts for delivery of English wool. Like many towns, certain businesses were collected in a given area of Saint-Omer. The cloth merchants were all located on the Eastern side of the city near the River Aa, and Jamie used the meetings to scout the area. Many small gates gave access to waterways powering the mills that were located beyond the walls. They were small enough for limited ingress and egress for personal use but not for public use or traffic. One such access point led off the yard to the rear of Vermulen's house and premises.

As they left the man Jamie commented: "We'll not be able to take the horses, through the gate, but we'll go on foot once we're through and make for Watten. 'Tis only a few miles away, and there we can arrange new mounts, for my father has another man of trade based there," he assured the others. They wandered around the town a little more to familiarise themselves further, finally returning to the inn during the late afternoon.

When evening came, the three men left the inn and made their way to the cathedral. They entered through the main doors at the western end and proceeded down the main aisle towards the crowd of people praying and partaking of vespers.

The sound of the monks' voices blended beautifully, and the chanting added to the majesty and awe-inspiring grandeur of the building. It was a wonderful, other-worldly experience as the choir's voices soared, filling the vaulted building with praise to the Lord. The three stood transfixed, so affected were they by the perfect cadence. Then the music ended and prayers began. Mark and Jamie seated themselves halfway down the aisle while Cristoforo found a pew near the front, away from them.

The Abbot's incantations continued for another half hour, then with the final prayers and blessing said, the congregation began to disperse. At length there were just a few monks left tidying the church and the two guards in front of what appeared to be final section of the main nave. Eventually all fell silent, and while Mark and Jamie continued to bow their heads, apparently deep in prayer, Cristoforo approached the two guards, noting their haubergeon mail coats and open-faced helmets. Closing the distance and in a whisper of hushed reverence he asked in Italian if he could see the main area behind. They could of course understand little of what he said so he switched to French. They denied him access, claiming that the works were unsafe and that no one was allowed in at any hour, least of all this time in the evening.

"Ah *scusi*, perhaps another time. I am visiting from *Firenze* and appreciate the beauty of your magnificent church." With this he half turned, extending his arm to encompass the whole church. In doing so he gave it one final check to make sure no one else was present. As he turned again to face them he seemed to lose his balance as he placed a foot on one of the two steps leading up to the nave directly in front of the guards. He brought both hands down to steady himself, brushing the tops of his boots as he did so. Upon righting himself his hands flew upwards in a blur of speed, driving forwards, aiming for their exposed throats.

Cristoforo's religious conscience would not allow him to commit murder in church if it was avoidable, so it was not the blades but the hilts of the daggers that drove into the guards' larynxes. The blows achieved the desired effect nonetheless: their mouths opened like beached fish, unable to form a word or sound, gasping as they struggled with the lack of air, eyes wide in terror and pain. Cristoforo stepped forward and smashed their helmeted heads together twice, and both men fell limply to the floor.

Jamie and Mark wasted no time, rushing forward as soon as Cristoforo began his action.

"Bravo, Cristoforo, bravo" Jamie whispered. The guards' faces were flushed bright red, yet their breath still rasped, testament to Cristoforo's judgement and skill.

The three of them paused and listened for any untoward sound, and once they were confident that they had not been discovered, Mark stepped up to the door that was barring their way. He tried it and concluded that there was some form of wooden latch that could only be operated from within. From the way it moved under the slight pressure of his hand, it was a token gesture only. He inspected the door more closely in the candlelight. It was obviously a temporary structure, something that was there only for the duration of the construction, to be removed upon completion of the works when the stud wall was taken down.

He sought the iron hinges and crude raised stud heads of the bolts. Next his fingers found the edge of the ill-fitting door and gained a good purchase on it.

"Cristo," he whispered. "As I lift this door, be ready to slide your knife in to raise the latch." Cristoforo produced one of the knives from his boot, which glinted wickedly in the candlelight. He nodded in readiness. Mark braced himself and exerted his huge strength. At first nothing happened, then inexorably the door moved up and slightly outwards, offering a slim gap between the frame and the door. Cristoforo inserted his knife and pushed up the latch while Mark pulled, keeping the door raised up off its hinge pins and taking the whole weight on his arms. Once past the jamb with the latch kept up from its keeper, he soundlessly let the door drop to the base of the pins: they were in. Mark rolled his huge shoulders as he relaxed from the strain and turned in time to see the exchange of expression between Jamie and Cristoforo.

"By the rood I would not have believed such a thing possible," Jamie hissed, amazed at what he had just witnessed.

"Now we go through," Mark said softly. "There's another chamber and a door on the other side. Here, pass me that candle, Cristo," he beckoned.

They entered the intermediary chamber and found themselves in a small room no more than about ten feet square, which appeared to be acting as little more than a dust and sound barrier to the temporary wall, preventing any curious visitor to the cathedral from looking within at the construction. There was no secure latch here, just a simple wooden bar with a finger hole that allowed it to be opened from either side. Cristoforo blew out the candle, slid his finger into the hole and carefully lifted the wooden latch. There was no sound, so he gently eased the door towards them. He caught a muted sound of boots – to his trained ears at least two guards were patrolling within. The vast inner chamber was alight with candles and brands throwing ghostly shadows against the walls, spectral and unnaturally elongated. He heard one of the guards pass by and waited until his footsteps faded. He sensed that the guards were not alert, performing what they saw as a perfunctory duty in a safe and loyal town. Night after night they would take the same patrol, with no noise or rumour of danger. It had been this false sense of security that had enabled Cristoforo to perform his deadly trade on many occasions without fear or redress. Both Mark and Jamie were close behind him and he held up two fingers and then rotated his hand in an Italian fashion. *"Più o meno,"* he whispered.

Two guards, more or less. They understood his meaning as he slid forward like a wraith in the night, following the guard, taking two steps for the guard's one. The halberd was balanced on the guard's shoulder as he strode along on his usual route through the nave. He was relaxed and obviously bored. The trick, Cristoforo knew, was to disable him without the halberd falling to the ground. Jamie and Mark stood just inside the door, watching with their breath held as Cristoforo slid his arm around both the guard's neck and his halberd, pushing the bone of his forearm straight and hard against the larynx. He then placed his right arm straight against the back of the guard's neck, clasped both elbows and squeezed, rotating the left arm to dig deeply into his victim's throat. There was a brief struggle and slight thrashing of arms, but the guard was unconscious in a matter of seconds.

Cristoforo allowed him to slump gently backwards to the floor, carefully placing the halberd up against a buttress. His two companions came forward to his side. Then he glanced around, taking in for the first time the huge wooden edifice before him.

"Dio mio!" Cristoforo exclaimed in a whisper, crossing himself. Before them stood the finished siege tower, looking like some dark monster from Hell in the flickering candlelight. It oozed menace and seemed to take on life of its own to the three men who were dwarfed before it. The wheels and axles which Jean and the duke had seen weeks earlier were now complete and the entire thing was ready to be moved. The three men shivered involuntarily, thinking what it would do to the citizens of Calais.

"Hell's teeth," Jamie whispered, "that must be destroyed."

At that moment the reverent silence of the cathedral was shattered. The wooden door which they had passed through moments ago was flung open and Jean de Grisson stood there, his eyes bloodshot, his clothes travel-stained and a sword in his hand. At his back were a party of ten men at arms, weapons raised and ready to attack the three interlopers.

"It seems we have come just in time, malapert churls," de Grisson said. "Do you surrender? If you lay down your arms we will spare your lives and we shall not spill blood in God's holy house."

"To be tried a by a French court?" Jamie responded. "I think not, sir. I'd as lief die in battle than with a French rope around my neck." With that he drew his sword and dagger, the heft and balance of the weapons giving him confidence. As always, a period of calm followed, for as the blood sang in his veins, everything seemed to slow down in the few seconds before the battle madness took him. Behind him, Jamie's companions fanned out to form a small triangle with Jamie at its head. Mark had armed himself with the halberd of the fallen guard, which was much like his quarterstaff except more lethal. Cristoforo withdrew the falchion from the scabbard on his back and one of his boot daggers. Each man readied himself in his own way, relishing the fight. They spread further apart giving each other more room.

"So be it," de Grisson snarled. He advanced, the men at arms behind him spreading out into a semi-circle. When they were within a few feet they ran at the trio, but they were hampered by their halberds, which could not swing in the restricted space or in the close proximity of their fellow men at arms. It was a battle of reach, with the halberds' extra length giving the advantage to the men at arms.

De Grisson and Jamie met head on, each armed with a

sword and dagger. De Grisson had heard Jacques de Berry's account about the battle on the cog that had led to initial suspicions being raised about Jamie, but gave little thought to it now. He was exalted to find his prey after a hard ride from Paris, and was keen to kill him. He thought the account of Jamie's prowess exaggerated, and strode forward meaning to finish him quickly. It was not to be.

One of the men at arms closed the distance with his halberd, lunging to disembowel Jamie, who took an upper half guard and seemed to swipe the wicked spike aside almost casually. By sidestepping, he placed the man at arms between him and de Grisson. The blade of the halberd passed him by, committed to the lunge. Jamie rotated his wrist and struck down at the straight arm, breaking the elbow through the mail, then drove his dagger into the aventail of the neck, the sharp, slim point piercing the wide links, killing the man instantly. He kicked him contemptuously off his dagger and lunged straight at the furious de Grisson, who bounded back and in doing so lost his guard, turning to his right as he did so.

Jamie seized the opportunity, leaping in and aiming for the throat, and found de Grisson's shoulder protected only by a thick gambeson. The point slid home, driving into the bone, and de Grisson dropped his dagger, howling in pain as his left arm bled. Jamie sensed a second attack as another man-at-arms launched an overhead strike. He crossed sword and dagger, blocking the blow up high, then stamped forward, kicking the man in the stomach. The man immediately dropped forward, retching, and Jamie thrust his dagger into his unprotected face before leaving him to drop.

Jamie spun around, slashing backhanded into the face of the next man, taking him across the eyes. The man dropped to the floor blinded and screaming, his hands raised to his bleeding face. Jamie looked to see how his friends were faring. He was in time to see Mark deliver a whirling strike with the stock of his halberd between a man's legs then drive the blunt end straight to his windpipe. He fell to join two more at his feet, and Mark too looked up. Dismayed, he saw that the second guard from the cathedral had come from the rear unannounced and was rushing to attack Cristoforo whilst he tackled his man.

"Cristo!" He shouted. Hearing the warning, Cristoforo sliced upwards, ducking under the strike of the man at arms' sword and pivoted in the same movement to see the halberdier charging him. His arm flew backwards and a second later the guard stopped dead as though he had run into a wall. Cristoforo's dagger protruded from his neck, and Cristoforo briefly saluted Mark with his falchion before spinning around to face the next man.

The fraction of time it had taken Cristoforo to complete his action gave Jamie pause for thought. He knew that more men would arrive soon, so he pulled a burning brand from a sconce mounted on the wall and threw it at siege tower. It caught in a cross member and flames immediately licked at the dry wood. All action stopped as the men-at-arms saw the flames begin to take hold. They were torn. Carry on fighting or save the tower and probably their church? Jamie seized the moment and found de Grisson, who was bleeding badly from his wound and eying the door to main church. Jamie knew that there must be no escape or warning or they were all doomed. With this in mind he ran towards de Grisson, cutting off his escape.

"Yield and I'll not kill you," Jamie said.

The Frenchman snarled, then seemed to relax. He shrugged, looking at the flames that were now starting to devour the wooden tower. He dropped his sword arm, appearing to agree, then swept forward aiming for Jamie's legs in a wicked cross sweep. Without armour Jamie was light and many had been the times John or Sir Robert had trained him for all manner of treachery in combat. He merely jumped up with both his legs, avoiding the blow. As he landed he pushed the point of his blade into de Grisson' face, catching him the cheek below the left eye. The point of Jamie's sword exited from the back of De Grisson's neck by a good foot, and he fell at Jamie's feet, dead before he hit the ground.

Pulling back his sword, Jamie looked about. The tower was now well ablaze as sparks and shards of wood began collapsing like the structure of a freshly-lit bonfire, landing on the floor. As he watched, two elegant tapestries caught fire and ancient rugs strewn about the floor started to smoulder. The whole place would, he realised, be an inferno in minutes. A terrible heat was already being produced by the roaring tower and they would have to pass close by in order to escape by another route. He looked upwards, following the lines of the orange tongues of flame licking towards the ceiling, only to see roof timbers start to catch alight.

"Come," he shouted, "or we'll all be roasted alive."

The three remaining guards gave up the combat now that they were evenly matched, and ran towards the doorway to seek help from the town.

"We are lost Jamie, we cannot escape," Mark warned.

"No, we can go this way. The doors are bolted from the inside and there are at least two more doorways. Follow me." With that they raced past the blazing tower, shielding their faces from the intense heat as they did so. The tower had become a spitting, snarling, fire breathing beast, showering sparks and flaming spars with equal abandon down upon the nave.

The two men followed Jamie, Cristoforo kneeling to retrieve his dagger from the throat of the dead guard. They found a small door off a private chapel that opened out onto the street. A commotion was already starting, and chaos ensued as the men-at-arms began to alert the town.

"Come with me," Jamie urged. "Soon there will be disorder and we shall be glad of it."

They circled the cathedral through the back streets and came to their inn. Their horses, which they had previously saddled, stood waiting. Quickly mounting, they took a circuitous route through the streets of the town, loudly proclaiming that the cathedral was on fire to all who would listen. The citizens began to emerge from their houses, panicking as they saw the roof of the cathedral, which was already starting to smoke ominously as flames caught on the timbers.

They cantered to Vermulen's house and crept silently to the door. They took their baggage from the cantles and left the horses. Moving softly on foot, Jamie unbolted the door, which he had learned gave way to a walled yard and thence into the mill. They passed through, half expecting to be stopped at any time. But no one was there. A pair of double doors led out onto a lane taking them away from the town.

Jamie looked back briefly. Where the cathedral had proudly stood, there was a vermillion glow against the night sky. The roof was on fire, and showers of sparks flew high into the night sky along with a billowing and glowing cloud of smoke.

"I hope that the good Lord forgives me for this night's work," he said aloud.

"Amen to that," Mark added.

Cristoforo had broken his earlier vow not to kill on God's sacred ground. He bowed his head in the direction of the fire, muttered a short prayer asking for forgiveness and crossed himself three times – once for each of them, it seemed.

Chapter Thirty-One

The three men made their way to the lane that led from the mill and headed north towards the Watten road. From past experience, Jamie knew that this northern area was a series of wide marshes that had not been drained, and to stray from the marked paths meant a horrible death by drowning. He made his way forward carefully, prodding the ground with a long stick if he was at all uncertain of the pathway in the darkness. The other two followed in his footsteps.

It took much longer than he anticipated, and each time they looked back, the southern skies were illuminated by an eerie orange glow as Saint-Omer and its cathedral burned behind them. They hurried as fast as they dared, aware that as soon as the fire was under control, the town's citizens would be looking for the culprits with no mercy in their hearts.

An hour later they finally cleared the marshland and began to make faster progress, heading northwest in the direction of Watten. It took them four hours in darkness to travel the eight miles or so to the village. When they finally arrived it was near midnight, and rather than cause suspicion and alarm they made a camp a few hundred yards from the village near the banks of the river Aa. Thankfully it was a dry night and the heat from a small campfire was welcome at the end of their journey. As they seated themselves around the fire to warm their hands, Cristoforo opened his leather satchel and produced a small metal bowl. He stood and went to the river, filling it with water.

"You thirsty, Cristo? Here, drink your fill from my water bottle," Mark offered.

"Nay Mark, I have a small scratch from the fight."

Jamie looked round. "You're injured? Here let me see," he said.

"In a moment, let me set this first."

With that, Cristoforo set up a crude tripod using green sticks that would not easily catch fire and contrived to cantilever the top spar to support the bowl by the thin chain that was attached to it, so that it might hang over the flames. This done, he unbuckled the thick gambeson he wore. In the firelight they saw that it was darkly stained on his chest.

"My God man, that is more than a scratch," Jamie observed. "Here, let me aid you ere you re-open the wound."

As they tried to remove the gambeson they found that the dried blood had stuck it to the Italian's torso, and prying it off caused the wound to bleed again. At this, Cristoforo took a sharp intake of breath against the pain. His linen shirt beneath was stained dark red, and dried blood covered most of his chest.

"God's legs, but that is not good," Jamie exclaimed.

"It is nothing. The *bastardo* with the halberd, he caught me with a cut before I could stop him. But he can tell the tale to his ancestors tonight ere he sleeps with the dead," he finished. "Please pass me my satchel."

Rummaging inside, Cristoforo produced a suede pouch, and untying the drawstring he removed some strips of clean cloth and tiny phials with cork stoppers. One of these he emptied into the water heating over the fire. The other two men looked on with interest. When the water started to boil he removed the bowl from the fire and carefully dipped a piece of the clean cloth into it, then removed it, allowing the cloth to cool slightly. He washed his wound carefully, revealing a cut which crossed his pectoral muscle. He flinched with the heat and the pain as he removed all the dirt and dried blood from it, and Jamie and Mark saw in the firelight that a film of sweat had appeared on Cristoforo's brow.

"Now this is the part I like the least," he declared. With that he took a small leather flask from the satchel and handed it to Jamie. "I will lie back and you can pour some on my wound, *va bene*?"

Jamie nodded and removed the stopper in readiness. Cristoforo lay back, exhaled and said: "*Vai, vai.*"

Jamie poured a little of the liquid onto the open wound as Cristoforo flinched and cried out: "*Aiii, Dio mio*", then relaxed. To Jamie's nose the liquid smelled of strong brandy as the fumes hit him. Looking down, he saw that Cristoforo's torso was crisscrossed with the scars of old wounds, including one that was curiously shaped as a long, thin puckered line which crossed at intervals with smaller scars.

"Please Mark, in that pouch there is a poultice wrapped up. Wet it from the water and place it on the wound, then rip my shirt and bind it to my chest," he instructed, sitting upright. Once it was securely he place he relaxed visibly, but was obviously still in pain.

"How do 'ee know the art of healing?" Mark asked, curious from his time with the friars in the herb garden.

"My great, great grandfather travelled to the Holy Land many years ago, and saved the life of a healer when he was ambushed on the road by bandits. He could not save the man's family. who were already dead or enslaved, but he himself had been left for dead. The man proclaimed that his religion bade him repay the debt with his life as his God decreed. He returned with my grandfather to Firenze and taught him and our creed all he knew of healing lore and medicine. To this day we practice this, and we prepare ourselves for the occasions when we are injured in such a manner." He concluded, pointing to his chest.

"There is a mighty strange scar on your ribs. What manner of weapon caused that?" Jamie asked. Cristoforo looked down at his side.

"Ha, no. It was a common sword. But if a cut is too deep to heal, the healer showed us how to close a wound using a fine needle and silk thread. Then when all is healed you remove the thread and *eccoti!*"

"By the rood it is marvellously done. Does it seal the wound with no pus or rotting?" Jamie asked.

"The healer said that all the implements must be inserted into boiling water or the spirit that you just poured upon me ere they are put to use. I know not why, but I follow his words and all has so far been well," he explained.

"Well, whatever he taught seems to work, and you're still alive, so all is indeed well." Mark commented sagely. They looked at Cristoforo's scars for a little longer, discussed closing the wound with a red hot iron and then Mark took Cristoforo's stained gambeson down to the river to wash it clean as best he could. He only partially wetted it, as he knew that the thick wool padding would take an age to dry. Returning, he set it up by the fireside and rigged a frame to face the garment to the flames. It would take two nights to make it dry enough to be worn again.

"Here is the willow you asked for. There was a good supply down by the bank. It reminds me of home by the pond on the farm. What do 'ee want it for?" Mark asked.

Cristoforo snapped and split the thin supple twigs of the

willow and with a knife removed the mushy pith from the centre of each twig. "*Il midollo?* How do you say?"

"The pith," Jamie answered.

"Yes the pith, it has qualities to reduce fever and take away the pain. It tastes awful but it works *molto bene*," Cristoforo answered.

"By all that's holy I've learned a good deal here tonight," Jamie declared. With which he peeled back the sleeve of his own gambeson which had been sliced by a halberd that had caught the muscle of his forearm. It had bled profusely but was nowhere near as dangerous or deep as Cristoforo's wound. He took the flask of spirit and poured a little onto his cut. It stung like a hundred wasps and he gasped at the sharpness of the pain and bound the wound tightly with a clean cloth.

They retired for the night. Cristoforo, wrapped in a clean shirt and his thick cloak, settled down closest to the fire and fell into a fitful sleep, disturbed periodically by the pain from his wound but eased by the willow pith. When he woke, he fed the fire then drifted back to sleep again. As dawn broke, he was relieved to be on the move again and ease his aching chest.

They broke their meagre camp and walked into the large village that sprawled on either side of the river. There was a fortress tower and small bailey where the constable would be stationed and they studiously avoided this, heading for the house and mill of monsieur de Lange, whom Jamie's father asked him to visit if time permitted. Knocking upon the door of a large house and mill, they were admitted by a servant and met by de Lange himself, who lived up to his family name, being as broad as he was tall with a huge belly and a double chin.

"You are most welcome, master James, and by the Lord you have grown. It was many a year past when last I made your acquaintance, and you were merely a child. But tell me, how come you to be afoot and in a sorry state of repair, if I may be so bold?"

Jamie gave a story they had rehearsed of being set upon by rogues on the forest path who stole their horses and after a brief skirmish had retreated with their booty. De Lange immediately accepted the tale. "Indeed there are *routiers* about, lost from the wars and ever keen to relieve a traveller of his goods. But come and break your fast with me and let us do what we can for you. How does your father? Well I trust?"

And so the conversation progressed and Jamie indicated a wish to proceed as he did not want the previous night's incident to follow him before they left De Lange's hospitality. They discussed terms for a consignment of cloth to be exported to England and then agreed a price for the hire of three horses to take them to Dunkerque.

It rained during the day's travel, and the back roads to the coast had become slippery and uncertain under the horses' hooves. It was a cold rain, and the previous warmth of the sun was entirely absent. Cristoforo had started to slump in the saddle. Jamie had led them away from Watten heading for Dunkerque, which he knew was much closer.

"Do you expect trouble from *routiers* and such like, master Jamie?" Mark asked.

"Aye mayhap, yet the roads to Calais will be guarded by men-at-arms awaiting us, I suspect. Word will have spread faster than wildfire of our deeds at Saint-Omer and for certes the Duke of Burgundy will have placed men on the roads to waylay us. Dunkerque is shorter by a few miles and we can get a ship from the port there." He looked up at the rain which had increased steadily in the last hour since they had passed Spycker. "Barely a few miles to go now," he assured them. "Cristoforo, how goes it? Do you suffer, man?"

"Yes. The wound I fear is infected by the cursed French

steel! I will be better when I can rest and take some more broth and change the poultice. She will help me most to draw the poison, for by the saints it throbs."

"'Tis but five miles now to Dunkerque, and we will find respite there whilst I seek a ship to transport us back to England."

"Ahh, a ship. *Madonna,* I would rather curl up and die here than face the sea again. By all the Gods, please let me die ere I sail again."

Mark and Jamie could not help but laugh a little, as these false histrionics showed that their friend was better disposed than they had thought. "Aye, some good French cognac and you'll be mending better for it," Jamie said. "No *crapaud* was yet born that will get the better of you, Cristoforo. I just hope that Will and the others in our party returned to England safely."

"Aye and the rest of my mates with master Swynford. Please God that none befell my fate or worse," Mark intoned.

Chapter Thirty-Two

The Royal Court, Paris

The Duke of Burgundy had been left in a state of deep anxiety by the abrupt departure of the English party and the freeing of the wrestler. He had received no word from Saint-Omer for two days and had demanded a private audience with the queen concerning her lady-in-waiting.

When he was finally admitted to the queen's private solar, he swept in and bowed deeply in front of her.

"Your majesty, you are looking as radiant as ever," he began.

"And you my lord, with your bounteous praises, come hither with news or boons to be granted. Which is it, I pray?" she replied, not all deceived by his flattery.

"Your majesty, I have your interests and those of the kingdom at heart as always, and this is what has brought me to your presence."

"Fie upon you, John. A pretty coil you do set before me, I'll be bound."

"Your majesty, could I ask a boon for a private audience?

For in part my news concerns your meiny," He said, looking pointedly around the chamber at the two ladies-in-waiting and guard at the doors.

"I am out of humour, and wish only to hear what you have to discuss in company."

The duke cast his eyes to the floor and gave a small sigh of disapproval. His posture stiffened and for a moment he forgot that he was addressing the queen.

"As your majesty wishes. I do verily seek your council on two matters that I believe are connected," he proceeded cautiously. The queen raised an eyebrow but made no comment, and the duke continued. "A few days since we received intelligence that there may be a plot against France from within. Suspicions were raised and we took steps to secure the court. The suspected spy was one of the English wrestlers who performed for your majesty. However, we believe that he has accomplices and that he attempted to use the wrestler as a lure to entrap them." He paused, letting the significance of the information register with the queen.

"I should like to know the outcome of this interrogation. Stop prevaricating and inform me of your findings," she ordered.

"Would that I could your majesty, other than to say that we were thwarted in our quest."

"How so?"

"The arrest was made late three days past, and we were to interrogate the man more closely the following morning. Ere we could commence our questioning to obtain the names of his accomplices and the nature of his mission, he was sprung loose."

"From within the palace? How so?" she demanded.

"Your majesty, if it pleases there were two other men aboard the cog that transported the wrestlers from England. An Englishmen and an Italian. The Italian paid court to your lady-in-waiting La Contessa Alessandria di Felicini – who of course is also Italian."

"Upon such a tenuous coincidence you would associate the Contessa with this coil of intrigue? Surely theirs was but a short-lived acquaintance and there can be nought to her actions that you would condemn her so. And why do you suspect the Englishman and his companion of spying in the name of England?" She asked, sensing that the duke was presenting her with only half the truth. The duke continued, explaining the incident aboard the cog that had been witnessed by de Berry and the link between Jamie's connexions and where he may be planning to go from Paris. This he explained to the queen, together with his suspicions of the friary. He swore that the connexion with Saint-Omer and the sudden departure from Paris of the English party gave him no significant cause for concern.

"I give you great leave in your duties, Duke John, but to indict my lady Contessa of aiding and abetting a spy is to treat her harshly. Genevieve, fetch Alessandria hence forthwith, I should like to speak with her." Turning once more to the duke she declared. "I feel sure she will be assoiled of all accusations of wrongdoing."

Moments later the Contessa Di Felicini appeared in the solar and curtseyed deeply to the queen.

"Your majesty, how may I be of service?" she asked prettily.

"The Duke of Burgundy has concerns concerning your connexion with the Italian and the Englishmen whom you met in this court a few days since. Pray thee give us an account of all that occurred," she asked.

"For certes, your majesty. You will recall that I mentioned *signor* Corio to you after the wrestling match and begged permission to treat with him over supper." At this the duke began to colour in anger, realising he had been baited and trapped as she continued. "He was very charming and an impossible flirt. Yet of course as a countryman of mine I was pleased to be able to converse with him in my native language. I am sure that you understand, your majesty?" She begged, playing on the fact that Queen Isabeau had never lost her Bavarian accent and still preferred her Germanic tongue to French. The point was not lost, and the queen nodded in understanding indicating that she should continue.

"We engaged in conversation and indeed I met with his employer Monsieur James de Grispere and my lady Monique Nemours, who were also engaged in a quality of intimacy, I declare." With this she glanced across at the duke meaningfully, feigning diffidence behind her fan. At which mention of Lady Monique, the queen began to understand how the accusation had come about. "Then we retired to witness the wrestling competition: I, *signor* Corio, Monsieur De Grispere and of course mademoiselle Nemours together. Was there fault in this?" she queried, offering the duke a direct look of wide-eyed innocence over her fan.

With a nod and impatient shrug Duke John indicated that she should continue with her narrative.

"We continued our intimacy, and *signor* Corio begged to be able to return that evening for supper. I acquiesced and he escorted me thus. I was at your majesty's right on the lower table you will recall, my queen," she pleaded.

"And afterwards?" snarled the duke.

Unperturbed, the Contessa sprang her fan once more and looked over it coquettishly, fluttering her eyelids. "My lord duke, why of course he returned hence to his own apartments ere the evening was full gone. Forsooth I would not condone his suit on first acquaintance and unaccompanied. For certes the guards at the gate will support my story."

"I will ensure that they do," he muttered.

The queen, who had watched this by-play with interest, was beginning to run out of patience. "Duke John, prithee what ails you? The Contessa is clearly assoiled of whatever you may suspect her in terms of wrongdoing. Now, have the courtesy to render account and apologise to the Contessa."

"A thousand pardons, Contessa. It is my duty to verify all cases that are put before me. I merely wished to ascertain the whereabouts of certain suspects and thought that you might be able to aid me in that quest."

"Most certainly, my lord duke, and yet I appear unable to so do. What has occurred, may I ask, to vex you so?" She continued, heartened by the queen's response yet still wary of a trap.

"A suspect whom we detained was sprung free two nights since from within the depths of the palace. We believe that he was aided in this mission from within. And, as close companions, the Englishman de Grispere and the Italian, your suitor, are suspect. Therefore any association is by its nature perforce to be investigated." He barely held his temper and only by a supreme effort of will did he manage to look away from the Contessa and bow graciously to the queen. "If your majesty permits, I wish to attend to matters of State concerning the fugitives."

The queen nodded her consent and he bowed again, backing out of the chamber.

"My dear Contessa," the queen said when he was gone, "you play a dangerous game, and whilst I am wont to believe and sympathise with your position, have a care. The duke is a very dangerous man and made all the more so in that he is beloved by Paris. Within that regard lies his power. Even queens are sometimes wont to feel the draft of uncertainty and the breeze of power about their necks. Beware, for if ever proof certain came to light – fabricated or real – that you were involved in this conspiracy, I would not be able to save you. Perhaps a spell in warmer climes may be propitious? Now go, and consider well my words."

"As her majesty pleases," the Contessa replied with a deep curtsey.

Chapter Thirty-Three

23rd April. Westminster Palace, London.

At the reconvened parliament it was hard for those present to reconcile that the man before them was King Henry, who in his youth had been one of the greatest knights in Christendom. The man before the gathered members looked twice his forty three years. The king's stooped posture was little more than a loose-limbed frame for his clothes and his slack features were those of a man resigned to his fate. His nose and cheeks bore boils and sores that were repellent to those who met his gaze and his left arm seemed withered and disjointed, as though he could not move it properly.

Some looked at him in pity, others with avarice, thinking how they might benefit from his death and which side they should now be choosing. The petition from the Commons included eighteen articles that were being put before the king and the reformed Council. The king previously read through all the articles but stumbled again at the fifteenth, which attested to the bribing of royal officials and had been agreed by the young Prince Henry. The king signed and agreed to all within the document.

"Father, your Majesty, I have here another article which was not included in the original charters," Prince Henry adjured. He produced a separate scroll with his own personal seal and handed it to his father, and as he did so he steeled himself to look into his father's rheumy eyes with no pity. For Prince Henry the kingdom was everything, and he knew that it could not continue as it had been.

The king grasped the rolled parchment firmly as if in anger, dreading yet not perceiving what may be contained within. "What is this? Another means to trap and contain me? Have I spawned a gaoler and an advocate that would pass judgement upon me thus?" he scowled and tore open the seal. Those around the throne held their breath for some were aware of the contents and expected an explosion. As the king read the article his brows furrowed and anger creased his features. Some signs returned of the terrible force that he had once been. Then perceptibly he slumped his shoulders and rubbed the bridge of his nose between finger and thumb as if accepting the inevitable. He had neither the energy nor the where-withal to fight this final emasculation of his power. In a last act of defiance he threw the parchment to the floor in front of the prince.

"As you wish, usurper, pebble hearted whelp of mine. But take heed, for everything comes to take account and by the Lord Almighty your day will arrive," he shouted in a strained voice.

The prince's face was stone, and none could read any expression there. "As your Majesty pleases," he said, picking up the article from the floor.

"Aye, I do please. Get you gone from my throne, for I am still king in name even though your work here is a curse upon my reign and undermines me at every turn."

The prince and his meiny, including all the council members, bowed deeply three times and left the chamber. Once they had departed the king looked at his private secretary, his face pained at what he perceived as his son's distrust. "Prepare us for a journey to Lambeth, for we will not sit here and watch our kingdom crumble into dust."

In the Commons, the Chancellor read out the new names of the Council, a list that included the king's own cousin, Henry Beaufort.

"What say you to the exclusion of the Arundel and Tiptoft, my prince?" asked Sir Richard Whittington.

"They had reasonable causes to be excused and had incurred my ire. Now let us commence with the new government of this land," adjured the prince. "I wish to include both Bishop Henry Chichele and the Earl of Warwick to the Council," he looked around at the Commons and other Council members, daring them to object. The assembly either met his gaze by agreement or looked away, too worried about the changing times and their own futures to show any dissent to the warrior prince.

Chapter Thirty-Four

Dunkerque

The fever had grown in Cristoforo as the day's journey to Dunkerque progressed, and Jamie made the decision that they could not embark upon a sea crossing until such time as his friend's condition improved. They had bespoken rooms in a house within the town close to the harbour that benefitted from a good sea breeze. Three days later Cristoforo's fever had broken but instead of radiating heat, he shook with cold.

"Mark, help me pull the cot closer to the fire, for he is now shivering despite blankets and we need a new balm. I fear his body has transduced from melancholy to phlegm. Ere he burned afore now he freezes, yet it is ungodly warm in here."

"For certes, Jamie." Mark and Jamie lifted the wooden cot as easily as carrying a child, moving it closer to the hearth. Disturbed by the movement, Cristoforo rose from a deep yet troubled sleep. He was clearly very ill, yet was desperate to speak.

"I need you to get some...ingredients for a... mundificative..." he mumbled. He shivered some more, his face pale under his natural tan.

"Tell me, Cristoforo, I am here," Jamie urged.

"You must obtain white bread. It must be white...then barley flour, honey and turpentine oil." He fell back a little and gave a list of herbs. They tucked him back under the covers and stoked up the fire, making it almost unbearably hot for them.

"I will go into the town and find the apothecary, for we must have the herbs that Cristoforo described ere we mend him properly. Answer the door for no one even if you hear a knock, for I fear the longer we are here the more likely we are to be discovered. They will know we have not ventured to Calais for there are spies within the town I doubt not. Vengeance will be the spur that drives them and they will want our heads."

"Will you be safe here? The town is rife with suspicion," Mark asked.

"Aye, fear not. I am known here through my father, and those that know me not will think me local to the area for my accent is of these parts when I wish. It is home to my family – or was two generations past. Though held under Burgundian rule, many here are sympathetic to the English and trade continues unabated – often without custom or excise tax being paid," at which he winked. "They'll not jeopardise the flow of trade and my father's name still holds sway here, for the Duke of Burgundy is not liked."

Mark was familiar with the trade in smuggling. It was part of the upbringing of even the most God-fearing Cornishman. He ginned as Jamie buckled on his sword and secured his cloak and cowl against the rain which had not stopped since they entered the town. Having sought out another of his father's connexions, a monsieur Alyten, with whom he passed an hour or so in a convivial goblet of strong spiced red wine, he obtained directions to the apothecary. The town he knew was essentially a huge oval island with walled fortifications and a wide natural moat. It was set out on regular cross-sectioned streets and was therefore easy to navigate. The architecture was at once familiar from his travels, yet different from his native London. Jamie found his way easily enough and bought essential supplies from various shops throughout the town. With a borel sack slung over his shoulder he made his way to his final stop at the apothecary. Jamie already had a good ear for the slight change in regional accent and employed it here with the old man in the shop.

With a suspicious look over his half mooned spectacles, the man quizzed Jamie. He was nosy and invasive in his questioning, and Jamie was uncomfortable.

"How say you that your companion gained this cut to his hand?"

"His knife slipped whilst carving new leather," Jamie replied. "Now I need to leave and see how he fares ere his fever returns." Jamie continued, the impatience showing in his voice. Having made his purchases he quickly exited the shop and began to make his way through the crowded streets in the direction of the harbour and his lodgings. There were to his mind more soldiers and men-at-arms on the streets than would seem normal and they seemed to be stopping citizens at random at checkpoints on street corners. *Our deeds at Saint-Omer seem to have caught up with us,* he mused. He pulled his cloak tighter to disguise his sword and took a side street hoping to avoid the checkpoints. Then a call came.

"Hoi, wait there monsieur!" The accent was French, not Flemish, and Parisian if his ears did not deceive him.

"*Oui* monsieur," he replied, accentuating his Flemish accent. Turning, he found a guard of three men led by a sergeant-at-arms. They came in a state of readiness and he saw a fourth figure approach from a side street, blocking his escape.

Jamie continued his pretence of innocence, putting a pleasant smile upon his face. He knew that he could in all probability take all the guards and had indeed plotted the moves as to how he would achieve this, yet he held his hand. His thoughts were for Cristoforo, who could not be moved easily.

"Where do you go?" The sergeant asked aggressively.

"Why to my lodgings, and thence to the stench of London to trade and please God I return to Ghent and home in a sennight."

"London? What do you do there?"

"I am a merchant, and my father is a master weaver from Ghent. We need wool and I seek to place orders for our cloth. The English fools cannot produce a weave as we do, despite trying to steal our secrets."

The sergeant started to relax, accepting Jamie's story, which matched his stylish mode of dress and his Flemish accent. They had been told to look for three men: two Englishmen and an Italian. Then a thought seemed to occur to him. "Yet you travel alone? No servants to aid you?" He asked suspiciously.

"My meiny has already sailed, but my brother is sick with a fever and ails still. Pray God that we catch the tide on the morrow," he lied. "England will not help his cause for it always rains and London is a damp and foggy place. They hate us, but trade is good and we shall not stay longer than we need to drink one of their alehouses dry and futter a wench or two." He continued affably, seeking to bring the sergeant onside, knowing that he too would hate the English.

The men around him relaxed at this ribald comment and sympathised with his cause.

"Godspeed to you then," the sergeant said. "I hope that you cheat them, but 'ware the unclean sluts of London. *Au revoir*." He slapped Jamie on the shoulder.

"Thank you, we always do. *Au revoir*, sergeant." Jamie

saluted and made to turn away and proceed on his journey. His heart was beating faster and the feeling of being watched stayed with him until he turned the corner. Yet a niggle of doubt crept up on him and instead of returning to his lodgings he carried on back to the workshop and house of monsieur Alyten and went straight within as though he belonged there. As he did so, he saw out of the corner of his eye one of the men-at-arms peering from behind a pillar.

"James, you return, is all well?" Monsieur Alyten asked, surprised to see him back again so soon.

"I am sorry to disturb you," Jamie said, "yet I am vexed. I had the strangest feeling that I was being followed and sought refuge here so I can spy who may be after me. It troubles me that I have coin in my purse and may be targeted." His tongue was as glib as ever. With this, Alyten summoned two servants to look about and insisted that one escort Jamie back to his lodgings, for which he offered thanks. He decided that the guise of a humble merchant was as trying as fighting against great odds; yet could not resist an inward smile thinking of what Sir Robert would say to see him ducking a fight.

They set off together, and Jamie lost his feeling of being watched. At length they returned to his lodgings and he thanked monsieur Alyten's servant for watching over him and paid him with a silver shilling. Checking once more, he rapped on the door and called to Mark who let him in.

Mark had been concerned by his long absence, and Jamie explained about the soldiers.

"We need to be gone, and soon. Every moment we stay increases our danger of discovery."

"I think Cristo is easier. His breathing is steadier and he no longer shivers, yet the wound still appears hot."

"Then let us prepare the mundificative."

Jamie produced a metal bowl and hung it across the flames,

then added the turpentine oil and a little water. As the liquid heated they gradually added white breadcrumbs, flour and honey, stirring the contents until it gently simmered over the fire.

"It has had a while now, and we must allow it to cool, so Cristo says," Mark commented, "then we apply it as before with a clean bandage and strap it in place."

"Hopefully a good night's rest will ease him enough that we may travel, for we may not tarry here, I fear. I shall book passage on a ship for the morrow and hope that he is better."

With that Jamie left again and walked the short distance to the harbour there to arrange passage for them back to England. He found an English cog bound on the morning tide for Dover with space enough for them.

"We sail on the ten o'clock tide mind, so do not be late," the captain said. Then as an aside he added, "Yet watch your back, lad, for the watch is about and Englishmen is what they seek and an Italian too, I'm told. If them's you, I'd get 'ee aboard soon as you like, for I've no love for the *crapauds*." He spat overboard to emphasise the point.

"Thank you captain, I am doubly grateful. Yet we have a friend who may be on a stretcher ill from the bad humours abroad. If we brought him early to get him settled, would that be in order?"

"Aye, it would, and he can berth below. Bring him by the south quay, less traffic there and we'll have him aboard in a flash."

"Thank you. I will ensure that you are amply rewarded for our safe passage," Jamie assured him.

The following morning they disturbed Cristoforo early from his slumbers. Sensing the urgency, he staggered to his feet and stumbled down the stairs to the main hallway.

"He will never make it on foot, and if we stretcher him it will draw more attention," Jamie mused.

Mark was not perturbed: "Fear not, Jamie, aid him onto my back and I'll carry him for a piggyback as we did when we was children." With that the giant crouched and Jamie helped Cristoforo onto his back. Mark stood as though Cristoforo was but a child.

"Wait. I'll cloak him, and he will barely be discernible as anything more than a woolsack." With that he raised the cowl and pulled it to fit snugly. He tugged at Cristoforo's cloak, which Mark pulled tightly against himself, and with Jamie leading the way carrying their bags they arrived at the harbour unchallenged. Once there, the captain stood waiting and urged them aboard. Mark took the gangplank easily despite his load, and deposited Cristoforo safely below. Jamie shook his head in amazement. Mark was barely breathing heavily and seemed as strong as ever.

"Ye gods man, but you are an ox. You carry him with ease," he marvelled.

Mark gave him a good natured smile: "Cristo? Why he's just a slip of a thing, now if I'd've been carryin' you..." he smiled, clasping Jamie on the shoulder with a huge hand.

Chapter Thirty-Five

The French Court, Paris.

Five days after the fire, a soiled messenger arrived at the palace, exhausted and travel-stained from his journey. The queen was in conference with her ministers, including the Duke of Burgundy. From the council chamber, a commotion was heard in the main chamber without. The council members were all seated around a large table and turned almost as one towards the chamber doors. The queen, who was seated at the head of the table and facing the doors questioned: "What is that garboil without?"

The doors opened as if in answer and a guard appeared, bowing deeply and begging her pardon for the interruption.

"Your majesty, a thousand pardons. A messenger begs an urgent audience with his Grace the Duke of Burgundy. He has come from Saint-Omer and will not be dissuaded from his course. He states that it is of the utmost importance."

The queen arched an eyebrow. "It seems, Duke John, that you are now sought above royalty itself. Very well, bring him forward and we will hear what is so grave that it bears the cost of the court's time."

The messenger staggered forward and the duke recognised him as the man he'd sent to Saint-Omer a week ago. He began to fear the worst.

"Well man, what news do you bring? Are the fugitives caught?"

"No your Grace, yet there is... worse news that I bear... evil tidings."

"Well? The duke demanded icily.

"The cathedral at Saint-Omer was set alight and half the town was destroyed. It was terrible to behold. The captain of the guard sent this," he offered, proffering forward a sealed scroll.

The duke snatched the scroll from the messenger's hand, breaking the seal to read the short message, then crumpled the parchment as his face suffused with blood as his temper flared. "No!" he cried.

The queen, who was braver than the rest of the assembly, asked, "What is the full account?"

"The siege tower is completely destroyed. Ten men are killed. Jean de Grisson is dead and the three of them escaped. Christ on the cross, I'll have him hung and quartered as God is my witness." He shook, raising his fist upward shaking it skyward in rage.

"Whom do you mean? The Englishman?"

"Both Englishmen and the Italian. By God he is no merchant, but a killer in disguise. De Berry warned Jean, and he must have the right of it, for he called him deadly and so he must have been to better Jean, for he was excellent with a blade. That Italian jackanapes too I'm bound is an *assassino!* I want their heads. Your majesty, with your permission I would excuse myself as I needs must send more men to capture them, ere they escape to the God-cursed isle of England."

"Pray thee, but do you not feel that they may have already absconded aboard a ship and sailed?" The queen asked gently.

"No. I would have been informed of such a thing, for we have strong connexions with Calais and watchers within. I made plans that they should be stopped at all costs. I know that De Grispere's retinue and that of the wrestlers sailed days past, yet they were not amongst those leaving. I have pirates ready to board them ere notice is given. No, I am convinced they still linger on our shores," he finished emphatically.

"Then pray go and find them, and seek them out with no mercy," she ordered.

"Majesty," the duke bowed deeply and left the chamber.

Once he had left, the queen turned to her councillors. "Lords, *messieurs*, we would adjure that we leave matters of state for now and continue when we can concentrate more freely in the knowledge that our realm is once more secure."

They all agreed readily and left the chamber. Queen Isabeau retired with one of her ladies-in-waiting. "Adele, ask the Contessa to attend us immediately in our private solar," she ordered.

The servant left, and some minutes later, seated by the window gazing across Paris, Queen Isabeau heard a knock at her door. Adele and Contessa Alessandria entered curtseying.

"Your majesty," Alessandria offered.

"Adele, leave us." When the other woman had left the chamber the queen continued. "Are you aware of the latest news from Saint-Omer?" She asked, her eyes seeming to pierce the Contessa's soul.

"If your majesty pleases, Adele informed of this terrible crime there against the cathedral."

"Ah just so. Yet there remains a problem for you closer to home. Here in the court, in fact."

"Majesty?"

"Duke John is certain that the culprits are the two Englishmen and your countryman. It is a heinous crime, and he rages quite rightly against the perpetrators. By God's grace he will catch all three and make examples of them. Yet think on, should the duke fail to apprehend these villains, his wrath will be doubly fired. His mind will then turn to all those who did – or may have – aided them. He will have need of a scapegoat as his power and popularity rely upon a successful campaign against the English. The Armagnac faction will seek to reduce his power and seize an alliance with England. Paris, and therefore the realm, will be at their mercy all because the plan to take Calais was thwarted."

"*Madonna!* Majesty, are you asking me to leave the court?" Alessandria asked in dismay.

"Child, we speak candidly. Think on it. The duke is vindictive and his vengeance will be unremitting. Everyone he suspects will be punished, or worse. We have already said that even with all our power we cannot protect you fully. Think on how you may accidentally slip on steps one night; or fall prey to poison or simply disappear with a false story of travel? Worse, you could be found guilty of treason and executed. Do you wish to live your life looking constantly over your shoulder for the assassin's blade?"

The full import of her words hit the Contessa as hard as a mailed fist.

"What would you advise, your majesty?" she asked timidly.

"We would adjure you to plan for travel directly, before any action against you can be taken. Decide where you wish to go ere the duke finds his quest unsuccessful and his birds already flown. Think on it carefully and make a decision, and we will of course assist you in any way that we are able. Then, should all be well and should the perpetrators be caught, you will be safe. If they are not..." she left the words hanging in the air.

The Contessa chewed her bottom lip involuntarily, frowning at the royal ultimatum. She spoke the thoughts rushing through her head out loud: "To return to Bologna would be a different sort of imprisonment. My father would seek a cloistered existence for me, far different to that of the court. He would see me wed on a pre-arrangement and at twenty years old, and I am not ready for such a life. It is also a great distance to travel; fraught with dangers it provides ample time to catch me ere my destination is reached – which forsooth, I believe it will."

"Yet you will have no desire to be *enceinte*. Perforce what other choice do you have?"

The Contessa blushed at the queen's remark yet a thought came suddenly to her. "*Ecco*. I have it," she exclaimed. "My uncle is a banker who resides in London and aides the court, I understand, in matters of finance. He will I am sure be able to find a position for me as a lady-in-waiting, perchance with the king's wife –"

"What! The Spanish whore? My child that will put a spur under the duke's saddle ere it comes to pass. The duke covets her lands and children and there was a perfervid agreement between them concerning these terms. So in caution we ask, do you know your uncle well?"

"We are on distant terms, yet we have corresponded and he has indeed in the past invited me to England, assuring me that I should be made most welcome."

"Then set that as your course. But be aware, should you leave the court, you will be perceived by the duke to be guilty of aiding your countryman."

"I understand, your majesty, yet with your forbearance it seems the wisest course for me."

"Indeed. Then make clandestine preparations and should it be necessary for you to depart, we will have it known that you left for Italy."

Chapter Thirty-Six

London.

The five hour crossing passed without incident, and was mercifully smooth despite the wind being against them. Cristoforo passed in and out of consciousness, apparently unaware that he was at sea once more. Jamie decided that was probably for the best. Once docked, Mark left to seek out master Swynford and his fellow wrestlers, who were no doubt as anxious to see him as he was them. Cristoforo was transported by waggon to Thomas's house in Lawrence Lane. It was after midday the following day when he eventually woke, and Jamie found him propped up by pillows and being nursed by Jeanette.

"How does he, sister?"

"He appears much calmer. His fever seems to have abated and there is colour back in his cheeks. I do believe that the bile of evil humours has left his body and he will make a swift recovery from this point."

"Praise God that it be so, for he has proved a good friend and a faithful comrade in arms that I would be sore to lose. I have had the cook prepare a new mundificative, as he dictated that we should replace it daily."

"I will replace it as necessary, but now think I will rest and let him sleep more. I shall ask one of the servants to look in upon him." She rose and the two left Cristoforo's side.

Once below, Jamie sought out his father in his private solar. He found him in a seat padded with cushions before the fire, looking comfortable as he read through papers. Thomas de Grispere looked up, rubbing his eyes with his knuckles. Jamie noticed lines etched his face which he believed had not been there before. He looked drawn and tired, more with nerves than work.

"Are you well father. for you look weary?"

"I am weary indeed, lad. I've been concerned about you these past weeks and have had merchants to boot staying here as they trade. As you know, the government has decreed that no foreigners can stay at inns or lodgings and must be housed by those with whom they trade. 'Tis good for England, yet onerous upon me, for they are tiresome company and I yearned for my own peace again. Yet trade was good and needs must it be done.

"Now tell me of your time abroad. I wish to hear all particulars, as Sir Richard was at times concerned for you – and we more so when master Swynford returned with news of Mark's capture and your flight from Paris. Sit now, have some wine and tell me all." Jamie's father poured some spiced red wine into a goblet, still warm from the insertion of a hot poker.

Jamie smiled, realising how tired he himself was from the exigencies of his mission. He sat, reached up and raked his fingers through his thick, dark red hair, pushing it back from his forehead in two waves. He stretched back his elbows, releasing the tension in his strong shoulders, listening to the sinews crackle. He followed this by extending his legs towards the fire, pushing outward with all his muscles. It was good to be home. Jamie inhaled then sighed, finally relaxing his body as he felt the warmth from the fire radiate towards him. He grasped the proffered goblet, took a sip of wine and was silent for a while, mulling over his thoughts. His father respected this pause, waiting patiently, seeing his son in a new light, for he perceived that Jamie seemed to have grown up before his eyes, and displayed a new maturity in the wake of his mission.

At length Jamie took a deep breath and described the events from boarding the cog at the docks, the pirate attack, Jacques de Berry, Mark's match, and meeting with ladies at the French court. He paused for breath, seeking another goblet of wine, and continued with the later events from Mark's rescue to the fight in the Cathedral. Here his face clouded over in an expression of regret.

"Father, I killed men in God's house and know for certain how Thomas a Becket's killers felt. To commit sin within such a place and then to desecrate it by burning the cathedral to the ground, may God assoil me," he pleaded, crossing himself. His father saw his pain and sought to offer him solace.

"My son, do not trouble yourself. Thomas a Becket's killers slew an unarmed man of God in God's own house. You killed a treacherous Frenchman who would have killed you without a second thought. You acted in good faith to save our realm by defeating those who would besmirch God's house by using it to conceal the construction of a weapon of war. They are the guilty ones. Seek absolution if you must, but you did what you had to do. You acted with a pure heart in defence of the kingdom by fiat of God's anointed ruler on earth. Do not whip your own conscience with thorns of recrimination," Thomas urged.

Jamie looked across at his father, lightened by the approbation of his actions. "It gives me succour to hear you speak so, for when the battle madness comes upon me I see no reason and know not what I do. I took four men's lives in that church in less time than it took me to tell of it."

"You have a gift from God, lad. Be glad of it; use it always in his name on the side of righteousness and all will be well. Even John says he has never seen the like of your prowess and I adhere to his views."

"John? Why I have to thank him for his advice. A battle-axe aboard ship is a bonny weapon and we cut a swathe through the pirates. Of that I'm pleased and have no regrets," he chuckled.

His father was pleased to see Jamie's mood lighten and he asked for more details of his trade agreements and connexions. These Jamie supplied and advised that he had papers for his approval signed by the various parties with whom he had treated.

"What news here in England?" Jamie asked when business had been concluded. "How does the government and the Council? I hear that all is not well with the king?"

The older man sighed and began recounting the events over the past weeks.

"They called a new parliament and Council on the twenty-third of April. The prince introduced new rules and indeed new Council members, all of whom are his favourites. Parliament still convenes and will finish sitting on the fourteenth of May, so we are told. There is much ado as the king is a monarch in name only, for the prince and the Council rule in his stead and he is stripped of all real power. He has retired to Lambeth Palace and resides there a broken man by all accounts. Yet the king remains a thorn in the Council's side, for he continues to bear interest in all affairs of state and will not relinquish control of his position.

"His wife Queen Joan remains loyal still, God bless her,

though she resides elsewhere. The prince has remained civil in that regard as yet." He shrugged as though fearing the worst in the future. "But the realm is not a secure place and rumours spread quicker than wildfire. All seek to glean from the other, and power is dispensed as much through the quill as by the sword," he lamented.

"Yet for our cause the setting should seem strong, I feel," Jamie said. "For we continue to trade, and with the embargo on profits and income prevented from going abroad we continue to benefit do we not, father?"

"Aye son, we do, and the trade that you have garnered through these agreements," he indicated the parchments on the low table before them, "will aid our family coffers immeasurably. The agreements put in place with the Council of Pisa this year past stand good, and we can bank and trade with the Florentines and the Venetians. In that account we are most fortunate. Yet I still fear for the stability of the court and kingdom for we are caught twixt a king and a prince, where the vagaries of power may turn at any time and in any direction."

"I needs must visit Sir Richard and present myself to the court as I'm sure that he will want a full report of all that occurred. Though by the rood, I must eat first for I am famished," Jamie moaned.

"Yes, thank God that Lent has ended and we can have meat again. I have arranged for a bowl of chicken tredure to be sent up to Cristoforo. How does he fare?"

"He appears to be mending and is of a better hue than he was. Whatever evil humours invaded his body they are now being bested, praise God."

With that Jamie rose and accompanied his father into the main hall, where a table was set and wonderful aromas emanated from the kitchen below. John and his sister joined them soon after and the conversation strayed to France and their mission. John forgot the sensibilities of the table and soon asked searching questions concerning the action that had taken place.

"Ho, you dealt with four men and not a scratch, you without armour and they bearing halberds?" he asked, amazed.

"Three. One had a sword and was right lively with it too, although far too confident. Yet I did sustain a small wound. The blade sliced my forearm, yet 'twas but a scratch and some of Cristoforo's fiery spirit healed it nicely."

He went on to discuss the herbs and poultices that Cristoforo had used and the story of the Saracen healer who had instructed his great, great grandfather. "Yet John it was your lesson in axe work that saved me, for the weapon is most efficacious aboard a ship."

"Good. Forsooth we must practice halberd against sword as time permits. How did the wrestler account himself?"

"Passing well. He is a master of the quarterstaff, preferring it to the sword. As such a halberd is a natural extension of his skill. With the extra reach and immense strength the like of which I have rarely seen, he made short work of the French."

"Bravo for him. The only good Frenchman is a dead Frenchman." John opined emphatically.

"John!" Jeanette chided, pretending a sensitivity she did not possess. She had grown up around men and had even learned to fight with a wooden sword as a girl when her father was not around. John had taught her and loved her for it like his own daughter. As a response he snorted, not taken in by her maidenly modesty.

"Now I must away," Jamie declared "and report to Sir Richard, who will be keen to hear my news."

"You can take that evil red-headed beast of yours with you." John urged, "for he has nearly killed me and two grooms: well is he named Richard, for he has a temper to match the Coeur de Lion."

At which Jamie just laughed, thinking how much he had missed his destrier. Yet he knew that the request was part in jest, as riding a fresh war horse through crowded streets was to court trouble.

Chapter Thirty-Seven

Westminster Palace

It was good to be back in the English court once more, Jamie decided. He passed numerous courtiers and ladies, pausing to speak to some of them, catching up on gossip, rumour and scandal, flirting with the ladies and re-establishing his place at court. He had realised in the short space of time between his return from the Borders and his adventures in France that he had come to enjoy and feel very much at home in the swirl and sway of the palace with all its social mores.

He was not sure if he was imagining it or not, but there seemed more foreigners of Flemish, French, Spanish and particularly Italian origin in the court than before. They all seemed busy and preoccupied with favours and audiences with various officials. The prince's name was on everyone's lips and questions were thrown at Jamie: Where had he been for weeks? Had he been abroad? How was the French court? Had he heard about the fearful fire in the cathedral at Saint-Omer? And so it went on.

Jamie smiled inwardly at this last question, concealing his

knowledge by saying that he had heard rumours, nothing more. Wending his way through the corridors he came at last to Sir Richard's offices, where he was admitted by the faithful Alfred. He was escorted through to the inner chamber immediately and given a royal welcome, as Sir Richard was at that moment in private conference with the prince himself. The tall figure of the heir to the throne raised himself from his stooped position over a table piled high with papers and smiled at Jamie as he entered. Elegantly clad as usual, his was a bright array of contrasting hose, one leg red, the other blue in the latest fashion. The gold-brooched velvet doublet trailed to long pierpoints, fastened by buttons that rose to a high collar around his neck. He looked sleek and healthy to Jamie's eyes.

Whittington was not as dandified, but even so he was expensively dressed in a dark doublet of contrasting arms and torso with puffed sleeves. His bright gold chain of office hung around his neck, a mantle of authority. His face was impassive, giving nothing away, yet he seemed to peer into the very soul of those upon whom he glanced. His expression broke into a smile as he offered Jamie a hearty welcome.

"James, lad, come hither. By the Lord Harry 'tis good to see you. My prince, you remember James de Grispere?"

"Indeed I do, and you are most welcome sir, for your deeds precede you and they do you credit."

"Your royal highness," Jamie offered the prince a bow.

"Come, James, sit and tell us the whole of your story whilst we enjoy some privacy." The prince encouraged. Jamie was still tired from the exertions of the last few days, but he was in awe of the prince and picked up his energy to retell his story. At times the prince pressed him for details, asking for confirmation especially of the piracy, the duplicity of Jacques de Berry, the siege tower, its construction and the fire. Finally they offered concern for Cristoforo.

"How does your Italian friend fare?" Sir Richard asked.

"He does well, sir, and appears to be recovering, praise God. The wound became infected yet he was his own healer, a legacy of family bonds and medicine." Jamie was reluctant to give full airing to his friend's profession to the prince and Sir Richard.

"Yet both he and the wrestler, Mark of Cornwall, gave good account of themselves – and you would have been hard pressed to succeed without their aid," the prince said.

"Indeed my prince, for although we were thrown together by circumstance, all was well. Yet I wonder at the coincidences involved."

"How so?" Sir Richard demanded.

"Too many coincidences make me suspicious, Sir Richard. Consider, prithee: they take Mark and make him prisoner to entrap me. Why? What should have alerted them to my true calling? Of course the battle aboard the cog was enlightening for de Berry in that he saw my true abilities. It was unfortunate for me that I was unaware that de Berry was scheming with the duke. Also 'twas passing strange that he should arrive at a late hour straight from court for the voyage.

"Would the action at sea alone give him pause to suspect that we were in league, and to what end? I cannot help but believe that another informed upon us to cause such suspicion. I know that there are those at court – be they merchant or courtier, spy or informer – yet apart from Friar Sebastian, only the Constable of Calais knew something of our real intent and that we were serving England."

Sir Richard and the prince exchanged a silent knowing glance. "You have a good mind and press it well into the service of your trade. We have suspected for a while that Sir Geoffrey de Haven the governor of Calais, is playing us false. As yet we have no proof...."

"By the rood, I believe that proof is coming to pass, for who else could have informed the French of my true purpose?"

"He will bear watching. Rumour has it you have stirred a hornet's nest in France. The Duke of Burgundy I hear is mad with rage and vents his spleen against any who may be suspect."

"What of Friar Sebastian?" Jamie asked at once fearful for the man's fate as a shiver overcame him.

Sir Richard looked abashed: "We know not, for he has been arrested and no one knows of his fate – yet I fear the worst. May God protect him.

"I wish that I could aid him, for he served us well," Jamie said. "Yet what of de Berry? Will he return to England, think ye?"

The prince answered here. "Almost certainly. His family is old in its allegiance to England, although his father suffered mightily in our cause, giving his life after being falsely accused by the duke's grandfather. Yet it is not de Berry, but who he serves that is of import."

"You would let him go unaffected? Set a viper back in our midst?" Jamie was aghast and forgot himself to speak so before the prince. "Your royal highness I beg your forgiveness..."

The prince raised a hand and offered a smile of forbearance at the younger man's enthusiasm.

"You have a lot to learn, James." Sir Richard said. "Here we may feed Sir Jacques whatever information we will, and use his wiles against him. For it is as the prince says: it is who he serves that interests us more."

"Whom does he serve?" Jamie asked, "the Duke of Burgundy?" Before an answer was proffered, the prince stated that he had an important engagement with Council members. As he made to leave he addressed Jamie directly, looking down at him from his great height.

"It is a great service that you have done for your country, James, and it shall not go unrewarded."

"Your royal highness is very gracious, yet it was no more than my honour and duty and I was pleased to be of service to your cause," he answered, bowing and accepting the compliment proudly.

"Just so, yet the deed shall be heeded and made known to Sir Robert, who will surely be proud of his protégé."

With that he nodded to Sir Richard and swept out, energy and purpose surging from him. A tight smile etched Whittington's lips as he gazed at an awestruck Jamie, who recovered sufficiently to ask his question again. There was a pregnant pause before the answer came.

"Nay, lad. Not Burgundy. He serves Sir John Tiptoft," Sir Richard answered softly.

"The former keeper of the king's wardrobe?" Jamie was aghast. "But why?"

"That is a long story, and as yet we need proof certain of how deep and indeed what connexions he may have with those outside the court and beyond the realm." At this point Whittington sighed as though deciding where to start and how much he should divulge. "Sit with me, have a goblet of wine, for there is much to tell and it may have a bearing on what happens next in your life."

Jamie accepted, and sat in the chair that was proffered to him.

"I suppose that it began whilst you were still away in the north with Sir Robert. It is therefore important that you become acquainted with all that has taken place," Whittington paused, marshalling his thoughts. "The truth is that Tiptoft was – and is – the king's man. As the prince grew in power, his agenda was to change the course of how the country was to be run. You will agree that the security of the realm is of paramount importance to all who are loyal to the crown." Jamie nodded. "And this intertwines with the finances that enable such security to flourish. The chief concern is that Calais remains stable as a bastion of light and a symbol of our power in France. If it should fall our power base and security across the Channel will be lost. For this reason fifty percent of tax revenue is directed to the defence of Calais. This has in the past amounted to some £45,000."

Jamie raised an eyebrow in surprise at the size of the figure.

Whittington continued: "Now as you and more particularly your father will know, wool exports from France and Flanders depend on trade routes. If our links from Calais are shut, the livelihoods of farmers, merchants and traders such as your father will be destroyed forever. Yet kings are not wont to render account and nor do they heed privation or budget. With this potential for revenue shortfall his majesty continued to live in excess of his perceived means, and cuts needed to be made. The king made these cuts at Calais' expense, reducing its finances by half!"

"And Prince Henry, as Constable of Calais, was put out," Jamie interceded.

"That would be an understatement. He raged at the account, and the king did not back up the unfortunate Sir John Tiptoft, but instead rescinded his instructions. Tiptoft and Bishop Arundel were both caught in the maelstrom and were dismissed from their positions in December last year. Sir John especially feels hard done by and his bitter resentment at the way in which he was treated endures. Outwardly he bears it with stoicism, and no one would know aught was amiss. Yet inwardly and in private I suspect otherwise."

"Forsooth, the mission to save Calais from siege had more implications than first I thought." Jamie mused.

"Aye James, perhaps now even more than ever, for with the

thwarting of the Duke of Burgundy's plans he needs must seek another avenue to turn the focus away from him and to diminish the power of the Armagnac faction."

Here Jamie interrupted, puzzled at the mention of the Armagnacs. "Yet if I have understood aright, it is *John* de Berry who leads the Armagnacs, who surely must be related to the Jacques I met who supports another faction."

"You have the right of it. Yet Jacques plays a dangerous game and you will rarely see him and Burgundy together. Jacques de Berry is a distant relative of Duke John de Berry and I suspect that he will play both sides with equal skill until he decides who will be the victor. A dangerous game, but he seems to excel at it – at least so far.

"Yet there is more that I must impart to you. With the failure of his plans to re-take Calais, I believe that the Duke of Burgundy will once again strengthen his position with both Scotland and Wales, seeking to divide our realm and thus weaken it. Think on this: Tiptoft has estates in Worcester and is close to the Herefordshire holdings of Sir John Oldcastle."

"The Lollard knight?" Jamie exclaimed.

"I would adjure you not to describe him thus outside these walls, lad, for he is close to Prince Henry, who will hear naught against him. For sure he has Lollard sympathies, and some say he treats with Glyndower, yet nothing can be proved and proof be needed if we are to turn the prince against him. I know Herefordshire well as my father has estates in neighbouring Gloucestershire and the Marches. The lines of loyalty are vague at best, and can change overnight. I know that if Oldcastle could gain power and supplant his beliefs he would trade with the Devil himself whom he professes to denounce."

"You have given me much to think on, Sir Richard. I have but one question: what coat of arms does Sir John bear?"

"A white shield, I believe, with a red Argent and a saltire engrailed gules. Why do you ask?"

"Then it seems I have already incurred the displeasure of Sir John, for he had me followed on the first day that I attended you here." Jamie explained the events that had occurred when he had been followed home by the courtier what seemed a lifetime ago. When he finished, Sir Richard looked at him searchingly.

"You have changed, James, since the events in France and your mission. It is different to the battlefield, and you have grown in another way. You have matured, and now use your head as much as your fighting skills. For the life you have accepted, your wits will more often serve you better."

"Mayhap, yet you may be assured of my full assistance at all times, for I am devoted to the safety of the realm."

"Of that I have no doubt. But now you need rest. Come and see me in two days' time, for I want you about the court mixing with the squires at arms. Bring Signor Corio, for I would meet him. Another Italian at court would not seem out of place."

"Thank you, yet that depends upon my father rather than me, for he is in his employ and bonded to him."

"Is he indeed? That is passing strange, how came it about?"

Jamie gave Sir Richard an expurgated version of events in Paris, deliberately omitting the actions that led to the original introduction to his father. He explained that Cristoforo had been on a mission for his own father who was based in Florence, describing how he helped Master Thomas and played down his skill at arms, not wishing his friend to be considered as an assassin.

"And you say he received a wound within the cathedral when the guards sought to kill you?"

"Indeed, he was standing guard by the door on watch and

was surprised by a man-at-arms. A falchion is poor defence against a halberd. Though I believe that in the melee that followed the guard slipped and Cristoforo was able to silence him."

"Ah a falchion, then. How very fortunate," Whittington mused, studying Jamie's face intently. "Well he seems to have been a blessing in disguise and a useful fellow."

"That he was, for he was able to gain acceptance in the French court as an Italian where I as an Englishman was not. As such we complimented each other. He also acquainted himself with a certain Contessa Alessandria di Felicini, a lady-in-waiting to Queen Isabeau."

Whittington's interest was piqued and he demanded more information relating to their rescue of Mark and how it came about. Again Jamie was economical with the truth, glossing over certain aspects of the raid on the court, particularly Cristoforo's lethal skill with his crossbow.

"Just so," Whittington concluded. "Well when he is able I should like to be introduced and thank him on behalf of the king for the sterling service that he undoubtedly did for the crown. As you saw, your efforts have been personally noticed by Prince Henry. I know not what he has in mind for you, but I am keen to keep you in my employ."

Part Two
Wales

Chapter Thirty-Eight

London

As the spring days grew warmer Jamie rode Richard as often as he could, taking him out to Smythefeld by the West Gate to the grassed area used by knights and squires to exercise and train their mounts, who became restless if they were stabled permanently within the city.

It was a fine May day and they had left Lawrence Lane early, yet the streets were already a-bustle with pedestrian traffic and carts carrying tuns or cloth. The butchers along the Shambles opened early, with boys shouting out to passers-by that the quality of their meat was the best in London. The soil of the night littered certain streets, running down the central gutters where the new soil pipes had not yet been laid.

John accompanied Jamie on his own horse, as much to aid Jamie and for the joy of practicing with his old pupil. Most citizens looked up and moved quickly to see two mailed men riding warhorses through the street – and well they should, for Richard was in a fine temper.

"Ye gods, the brute is fresh." Jamie declared, as Richard

sidled sharply once again, startled by a fluttering banner proclaiming a tailor's premises. "I swear to God he is able to tell colours, for it is always blue he shies at." Jamie cursed as he bridled him, keeping his right leg in place, dropping his weight instinctively and correcting the wayward movement almost before it had begun. The huge chestnut snorted, blowing butterflies from his nose, and began another test, prancing left then right.

"He thinks it funny, and is always thus when fresh. Yet I've missed the old bastard." Jamie continued, a huge smile on his lips.

"I see now why the grooms hated him so. I have sympathy for their plight, for he's a bastard sure enough." Yet John was pleased. He had schooled Jamie since his first time on a horse as a one-year-old boy sitting in front of him at the pommel. Now Jamie was a master horseman in his own right, strong yet with soft hands that felt and did not strain.

"Aye for sure when he's like this, but wait 'til you see him work in earnest."

"He'd better improve or he'll not be worth the purse." John opined.

They skirted Smythefeld, avoiding West Smithfield Bar and slipping through the break in the wall into the vast area of Spitelecroft. The acres of rolling grass spread out before them, a fine mist rising like a dragon's breath as the sun burnt off the early morning dew.

Satisfied that Richard was sufficiently warmed up, Jamie prepared to give him his head. He looked across at John, who was well mounted, and nodded. Jamie grinned, feeling the build-up of mighty torque from the horse beneath him. A mere whisper of his leg and with a kiss of his lips the power came in: there was no jolt of a start, one minute they were walking and within two strides they had moved to a fast canter. The sheer ease of acceleration was effortless, and after a few hundred yards he looked across at John who grinned back at him expecting the old challenge, knowing what Jamie planned.

"First to the tree at the end yonder buys the ale!" Jamie shouted. He gave Richard his head and urged with his legs. The chestnut surged forward to full gallop, hitting his top speed of over forty miles per hour in a few strides as the ground thundered beneath him. Tears streamed from Jamie's eyes, and his mouth was drawn in a rictus as the wind pulled at him. He looked over his shoulder and saw John left behind as the large oak loomed upon them. Jamie sat down deeply in his saddle, drew his hands back gently, curbing the stallion, which responded with grace, finally bumping to a halt in a rump-locking slide with his hocks directly beneath him. Jamie turned Richard deftly to face John as he caught up.

"What, did you get lost? Or fall off mayhap and needed to remount?" he mocked.

John cursed him: "The Devil, but that horse has wings, he should be named Pegasus, not Richard!" At which Jamie just laughed, pleased with the beautiful monster that he rode and feeling better than he had in weeks.

They gathered the horses and returned to Smythefeld at a steady canter completing a full circuit of the huge Spitelecroft fields. Re-entering the training area they saw a few more squires and knights out practicing mock combat, entrenching the moves of battle into their mount's memories.

Drawing their wooden practice swords, Jamie and John proceeded to attack each other, miming the deadly dance of battle, prancing this way and that, cutting and thrusting, using their mounts as a weapon as much as their swords. At last both men withdrew at an unseen signal giving their mounts and sword arms time to recover. At which point a figure familiar to Jamie rode up.

"Kit, 'tis good to see you," Jamie hailed. "John, this is Christopher Urquhart, another esquire at arms attached to the court under Sir Miles Blessing. Kit, this is John of Northampton, my father's stalwart and master-at-arms.

"Your servant, sir."

"And yours. Urquhart? Are you related to Sir Geoffrey Urquhart, for you have his likeness?"

"He is my father, sir."

"Hah, that makes me feel old, for I served with him and the king in the wars abroad and in the Holy Land."

"I shall pass on your greetings when next I see him," Kit offered, then turned to Jamie. "Now, you malapert rogue, I heard you'd scurried off to France and rumours must be true that you are returned. What news? How was the French court? Were the ladies as beautiful as the tales tell?"

Jamie parried the ribald remarks and sought to downplay his mission as a mere trading visit on behalf of his father. The ribbing over, Kit looked more closely at Richard, who was fretting with impatience to run once more.

"So tell me, is this Richard of whom we have heard so much? For certes he looks and acts like the Coeur de Lion himself,"

"He is none other," Jamie replied.

"He looks large and lumpen. Can he move in battle?"

"Better than the misbegotten nag that's holding you up," Jamie commented, at which they agreed to take a turn against each other. Kit drew his wooden practice sword and saluted. "Kit, a warning, Richard is fully trained and will not hold back. I adjure you to be careful."

"What? He'll not turn faster than Griffin, I'll wager."

They attacked with wooden swords, the horses nimble in positioning their riders for the best strikes. They crossed each other, landing blows on mailed arms and torsos. The strikes were fast yet light; neither wanted a broken arm or hand. The beat of swords echoed across the field and a few stood to gather and watch, spurring the two men on. Jamie found his pace and revelled as always in battle – even mock battle. Yet he had to hold himself in check to prevent the madness rising and using the full force of his aggression against his opponent. With this in mind they rushed forward to make contact. The clash came in high-guard with the horses' impetus bringing them on, crossing swords and quickly disengaging, and Kit was carried through while Jamie executed a perfect *prise-de-fer*, dropping for a slash to the upper leg and making clean contact. Richard stopped and turned on a shilling, antici-pating the command to spin on the forehand and attack. Kit halted his stallion, thinking himself safe for a backslash on the turn of point on the quarter. He did not know his danger. Unbidden, Richard sensed the change and pirouetted on his forelegs, performing a perfect capriole and lashing out with his hind legs. Jamie realised the change and cried out, deliber-ately unbalancing Richard to limit the energy of the coming strike.

Caught mid turn Kit was surprised, thinking that no horse could react that fast, as the two hooves lashed out: one catching his own stallion on the neck and the other smashing into his sword arm as the weapon spun backwards into the air with the force of the blow. Kit cried out in pain. Richard snorted in anger, ready to turn and lash with his forelegs as soon as his quarters hit the ground.

"No you devil, no! Yield!" Jamie cried, curbing Richard harshly to save his friend from death. "Kit, is your arm broken?" he demanded.

Kit flexed the limb and cursed in agony: "Hell's teeth. But I believe not. By God's holy balls that horse turned like a moun-tain goat. I never would have believed it for a stallion that size.

Christ on the Cross, Jamie, I know you warned me, but by God I should have heeded you more sagely."

"Thank God he caught you on the arm and not your chest, or you'd be dead. I tried all I could to stem him. Now how does the arm?"

Both men dismounted and Jamie held the horses, keeping the two stallions apart while John came forward to check Kit's arm.

"Easy lad. Straighten it...slowly now..." John eased the limb towards full extension, stopping when Kit cried out in pain. For such a rough man he massaged the arm gently, seeking a break and feeling the tendons, using his vast experience with injuries in the past.

"You'll do, lad. The tendons are sprained and bruised but there's no break I can feel. You'll be sore for a while – rest it carefully."

"Thank 'ee John, I'll do that for sure. I declare it is not my first injury in training nor I doubt will it be my last."

"I have some ointment prescribed by my Italian friend Cristoforo. I'll bring it to court tomorrow. It'll ease your bruising. Can you mount, man?"

"Aye, hold Griffin and I'll be up in a trice." With that he slipped his left foot into the stirrup, bounced off his right leg throwing himself up, balancing himself with one hand. It was neatly done from long hours of practice and without full armour it seemed easy to him. The horse, sensing his unease, shifted slightly to let him obtain a good seat.

"Come, we will escort you back into the town." Jamie offered.

"Aye, but you can keep that monster away from me," Kit said. There was a grin on his face and a sparkle to his eye that robbed the comment of any malice.

"A thousand pardons. Richard knows not his own strength,

just like the Lion Heart after whom he is named." Jamie apologised. As the two men parted, he repeated his promise to bring the salve.

"On the morrow, Kit, I shall bring it to court with me." With that he and John turned away, leaving Kit and his party to return to the court.

"By the wonder, that is a magnificent beast. Brute though he is I'd rather have him for me than against," John commented.

"Aye, he is that, and I'd not trade him for a pot of gold." Jamie said, reaching for Richard's ears as the mighty horse pushed his head back playfully, rubbing his poll against Jamie's hand calm as a lamb.

"Aye, and to look at him now you'd think he was but a playful palfrey, not a fire-breathing dragon." John shook his head in wonderment.

Chapter Thirty-Nine

Cristoforo didn't feel well enough to attend the court and be introduced to Sir Richard Whittington until a further week had passed. Parliament was recessed on the fourteenth of May and the court was filled with gaiety and life. Upon entering the Great Hall, Cristoforo paused to take it all in, ever wary and more so as he still had not full use of his left arm, which he bore in a sling for fear of reopening the wound.

Jamie had become used to his friend's cautious nature and had learned the same trick, taking in his surroundings before relaxing, and not thinking it at all unusual. A minstrel was playing and courtiers stood in groups, gossiping, flirting and making overtures to the influential for audiences with the powerful. Undoubtedly plots were being hatched, as Jamie knew only too well. Jamie spotted Christopher Urquhart laughing with other esquires and walked over, introducing Cristoforo to the group.

"How did you injure your arm, Cristoforo?" Kit asked.

Having been briefed by Jamie he replied, "I fell from my horse, twisting my shoulder. It is yet sore."

"Ha, tell me it was not that beast Richard, for I still bear the pain of his hooves on my own account," Kit said.

Everyone laughed at this and made jokes at Kit's expense, for they had all heard the story of his encounter with Jamie's chestnut stallion. Jamie then looked down, feeling a presence at his side. One of the prince's deerhounds had sidled up to him and was awaiting an affectionate response. It was a striking dog, with a beautiful tawny coat splashed with white across the muzzle and chest. Its magnificent head was waist high and Jamie felt for its velvet ear, which he rubbed affectionately. Of all the hounds that lurked in the hall, this had become his favourite and she always sought him out. He left Cristoforo to banter with the esquires and went to one of the large tables bearing wine and sweetmeats. Surreptitiously he picked up one of the pastries and slipped it quietly to the hound, which swallowed it with two chews.

"Now away with you or I shall be in trouble," he urged the hound, who ignored his command and followed faithfully at his heels as he returned to the group. Jamie prised Cristoforo away from the small huddle and they made their way to the western side of the hall. Here a group of ladies were entering, and Cristoforo stopped dead.

"Contessa! *Madonna*, do my eyes deceive me? *Porca miseria,* tell me I am not dreaming." He beseeched her in Italian. The Contessa did not lose her composure. She had the advantage of knowing Cristoforo was in London and that he would in all probability be at court. He offered her a bow and rose quickly to address her.

"Ah, my peacock, you do not dream for I am of flesh and blood," she teased.

"That I never doubted, Contessa, yet how come you to be here? I must hear all."

It is a matter of delicacy and not for all," she advised quietly.

"I see that you are injured. Do you make a good recovery?"

Jamie interceded, bowing to her. "Contessa Alessandria, it is an honour to see you again and in my own fair country."

"Ah, *signor* Jamie, it is my pleasure to reacquaint myself with you. I trust you are well?"

"I am well indeed, Contessa. Yet you must excuse us for we are on a matter that is pressing for time. May I extend the hospitality of our home and mayhap invite you to sup with us at my father's house?"

The Contessa accepted with alacrity and gave Jamie her address. With an exchange of bows and curtseys the two groups parted company.

Cristoforo's mind was in a whirl. "*Dio mio*, I cannot believe it. Alessandria is here, and the sun she does indeed shine in England."

Jamie sighed and laughed at his friend's melodramatic response. Then he became serious. "Pay heed now, we must be wary to preserve your true purpose in Paris. You were merely an emissary for your father and became entwined with my father's business."

"Yes you have prepared me, fear not. Though Sir Richard is with us, is he not?" he asked a little puzzled.

"That he is, and yet he is cunning and discerns all affairs right quickly. For that reason alone I would not have him in a position where he may exert influence upon us, but especially you. Just be wary, yet there's the irony, for you are the wariest man I know. He smiles and welcomes in a most cordial manner, yet I perceive that behind the smile he always has an agenda of his own. That agenda is the preservation of the Crown and the realm at all costs. He will, I'm bound, sacrifice anything and anyone who may serve him in that need," he warned.

"I shall be on my mettle." He assured Jamie as they approached the last corridor that led to Sir Richard's chambers.

Contessa Alessandria had agreed to dine at the de Grispere home later that week, and when she came she brought with her a maid companion and an armed servant who were now in the kitchens below.

The table was full, with Jeanette, John and Cristoforo present. They had found many acquaintances in common.

"Had I but known that you were related to *Signor* Alberti I should have invited him to dine with us also." Thomas advised

"Indeed, when I informed my uncle Filippo, he was surprised that I should have made a mutual acquaintance," she commented in French, using it as a common language between them.

"Yet you bear a different surname Contessa?" Jeanette enquired.

"Please, call me Alessandria. Yes, my mother – may God rest her soul – was my uncle's sister. Like *Signor* Corio here, we hail originally from Firenze, but were exiled in 1401 because of jealousy and the political ambitions of other bankers' families. My father moved to Bologna and my uncle here to London, where he remains. I believe he is fortunate, and does not need to abide by the rules for foreigners of occupation."

"As banker to the king and indeed Sir Richard, I believe he has special dispensation in most matters," Thomas joked. "I believe he was at the Council of Pisa with Sir Richard, and was responsible for collecting the payment due to Peter Pence and the Pope."

"That is so," she confirmed. "He too, is your banker?"

"Like most merchants, we need funds abroad to pay for wares," Thomas answered, "and he facilitates the transfer of money in that regard. It is a good system and serves us well. I believe he still serves the clerics on missions for the Pope." The others were interested, particularly Cristoforo, who appeared slightly uneasy. Jamie guessed the cause of his concern and decided to reassure him.

"'Tis passing strange that your families knew each other not in Florence, so near yet so far." Silently Cristoforo blessed Jamie, knowing what he was trying to do.

"Not really, for you must understand that *Firenze* has nearly one hundred thousand souls and my poor family were *arti medi,* not of the upper class. We were and remain just traders and farmers, with our own small holdings, but not of the *arti maggiori.*" Cristoforo ventured, not mentioning his family's other profession.

With this he looked across at Alessandria to see if there was any trace of contempt written across her face at the idea of associating with base born *contadini*. She smiled delicately, sensing his purpose and replied to the unspoken question.

"I have always found it better to judge a tree by its fruit rather than its roots," she responded. Cristoforo's heart leapt at the reply and he gave a little nod of appreciation at her courtesy and manners.

"*Grazie, signorina* Contessa," he whispered inclining his head in gratitude.

Jamie was curious about another matter and sought to break into the pregnant pause as Cristoforo and Alessandria sizzled with emotion so hot that he thought he would be burned. "Perforce there is one story that we have not heard: how do you come to be in London? When last we met you were engaged with her Majesty Queen Isabeau."

"'Tis a great wonder and passing strange indeed, that I should be thus delivered at your door, for I believe it is your actions that caused it." She replied mysteriously.

"How so Contessa? For by the rood if we have wronged

you, please accept my deepest apologies and allow me to offer recompense," Jamie offered, mortified that he may have somehow caused her difficulties.

"Pray do not concern yourself unduly, Jamie, for it was by the merest bad luck and connexions. I was not discovered to have aided you, so you have no cause to worry. Mark though, that the payment for kindness is forever a penalty where the Duke of Burgundy is concerned, it would seem," she commented.

"How so?" Jamie asked.

In response, the Contessa explained in full the persecution of all those who may have had any association with foreigners to the French court, and how by implication, he considered that Jamie – and by association Cristoforo – may have aided Mark in his escape.

"So we did cause you grief through our connexions? Yet as you suspected, the link between myself and Mark was tenuous at best, and verily I believe that it was caused by more than common nationality."

"How so?" his father asked, perplexed.

"There was the incident on the cog, de Berry's late arrival at port and the constable at Calais, who was rather too inquisitive, Cristoforo and I thought. I felt that we were betrayed ere we ventured forth from court." Jamie continued to air his theories, yet restrained from echoing Sir Richard's thoughts on Sir John Oldcastle and Tiptoft. Cristoforo chimed in at times, supporting Jamie's suspicions.

"Are you now persona non grata at court?" Cristoforo asked out of concern.

"Her majesty advised me that I may be subjected to persecution if I continued to reside at court, and informed me that even her protection may not protect me sufficiently. I took this to heart, for the duke is a vindictive man and the court can be a perilous place to those who fall from grace. There is also my lady Monique Nemours to consider, for she was ever at his beck and call." Jamie blanched, thinking of his brief acquaintance with her. The Contessa continued: "he was in a furious rage when he learned of the fire at the cathedral in Saint-Omer. Dare I ask, were you involved in this?"

"May God forgive me but we were. It was our duty and we had little choice, for a siege machine had been constructed there. An object of war in the house of God, no less, set to unleash destruction and death upon Calais." At which point Jamie's eyes clouded over as he thought back to the lives he had taken in the church, which would forever lie upon his conscience. "As God is my witness it was a terrible choice, but sometimes in war we are given little chance to exercise free will."

"I think that if God had not wished it so, he would have frowned upon your mission and you would be in a Parisian gaol now, ready for public execution in Calais at the hands of the duke – *pour encourager les autres*," she gently consoled him.

"You are kind and gracious, Alessandria, and I thank you for your forbearance," Jamie responded.

Looking downwards in shame, Cristoforo finally turned to the Contessa, hoping for exculpation in his own right. "We are much in your debt, Alessandria, for without your aid we should not have freed Mark and he would still be languishing in a French gaol, and us with him."

The Contessa flashed him a beautiful smile, accepting his praise and acknowledging his appeal. Yet there remained in both of their minds questions as yet unanswered, for Cristoforo remembered her awe in the passageway when he produced the crossbow. He relaxed for now and proceeded to engage Alessandria in some outrageous story of how they escaped France and how he, whilst wounded, had half carried both Jamie and Mark to the boat. The whole party laughed at the implausible story, and the atmosphere became more relaxed.

The evening came to an end, and in a moment of private intimacy Cristoforo managed to escort the Contessa to the door before her lady and the armed servant arrived. He felt his heart shiver with tremors of emotion the like of which he had never felt before. Looking into her deep brown eyes he was suddenly scared that she would snub him as one from a different class.

As though sensing his fear, she offered a hand to be kissed, which he eagerly took.

"Contessa – Alessandria – may I have the honour to pay you court and call upon you?" he asked.

"You ask such a thing after the adventures that we had lately in Paris? *Mamma mia,* I thought you were made of sterner stuff. Are your bright plumes ruffled, my peacock?" She teased him, offering as solace only a dazzling smile. Looking up from her hand he caught it and realised that all would be well.

"It was as much for your uncle's sake as for your deference to my position."

"My uncle is not my keeper, and what he does not know will not cause him ill humours. So I believe that we will meet at court – or perhaps you can persuade Jeanette to accompany us, for I have found a friend in her and there are few I would count as such in this new land," she responded, reinforcing her streak of independence. At that point her maid and servant arrived and the conversation was cut short. Cristoforo switched to Italian: "Tomorrow, I will call upon you at court, tell me where and when?"

She gave him a time and place, pulled up her hood and was gone on a waft of perfume into the night. Cristoforo's heart soared.

Chapter Forty

The French Court

The fire at Saint-Omer had turned the Duke of Burgundy into a bitter and vengeful man who vented his spleen against anyone who even acted suspiciously. He was only too aware that his popularity was now hanging by a thread, and the king had sought his presence in one of his more lucid moments.

The King of France, Charles VI, was seated at the head of the throne room. Brocaded silk wallpaper adorned the walls portraying hunting scenes and fabulously coloured birds of paradise in full flight. Silk printed with a Fleur-de-lys pattern swathed the royal throne chamber with a huge canopy, casting shadows about the monarch. The opulent feel of the decor drew the small chamber in still more, creating an intimate area amid a festering sea of rumour and scandal.

Two lines of men parted as suddenly as the Red Sea. The doors to the chamber had opened, admitting a single visitor. The lush green patterned carpet silenced his footsteps as he strode forward with an arrogance that bespoke his place in the hierarchical order as only second in line of importance to any in the room. The mumble of courtiers' voices droned about his head as the duke looked out in sublime equanimity over his surroundings. He met no one's gaze and wore upon his face a haughty expression of resolute indifference.

Halting at the prescribed distance he bowed three times, maintaining eye contact with the king. He was shocked at what he saw, for it had been some time since King Charles had last been seen in public, fearing once again that he might shatter as if made of glass. Despite the strong nose his face had an effeminate cast, and to counter this the king had grown a small beard and wispy moustache, perhaps to prove to himself that he was not made of glass, but flesh and blood like all other men. Yet the features were haunted, the eyes wary with tension and a highly strung personality lurked just beneath the surface, ready to boil over.

With this is mind, the duke was as unctuous as ever where his cousin the king was concerned. "Your majesty is looking well and in good health, may God continue to smile upon you."

"Thank you, cousin. We are grateful to you for your kind regard and for attending us. To wit, we have intelligence that disturbs us greatly." He continued as one arising out of a sleep and perceiving events as though they had just occurred. "We hear that the cathedral at Saint-Omer is burned, and with it your ambitions for the recapture of Calais. Pray tell us this is not so?"

"I must beg your majesty's pardon and inform him that as ever he is well informed pertaining to matters within his kingdom. We were subject to an infiltration of foreign spies who pervaded the court, seeking to undermine our cause and gain advantage, trading upon your majesty's hospitality and honour. I know not where their information can have been gained, yet I am even now seeking redress against those I suspect may have aided them in their endeavours." He let the words hang with a strong air of menace in them, causing those amongst the council and inner circle to take breath, knowing how vindictive the duke could be.

"We would hope that you might have had more success in preventing them from succeeding in the first place, cousin John. Mark us well, we would see these traitors sought and dealt with. Perforce, where dost thou suspect that the plot originated? Mm, mmm? Speak man, speak." The king commanded a little querulously.

"Your majesty will be pleased to hear that I already have a suspect in custody and he has confirmed that the plot was first hatched in England, sire. For it was ever to their advantage to undermine us." Here he looked pointedly at the Duke of Orleans and the other Armagnac faction that were present in the chamber.

The king followed his gaze, drawing his own conclusions. "All very well, but how do we continue with our endeavours to rid our realm of the English, mm?" he interrupted.

The duke was well aware of the danger here and trod a careful line, not wishing to reveal his plans in detail to the Armagnac faction. "As your majesty pleases, I have resolved to cause dissent and division within England's realm and mayhap more, if my plans succeed." He resolved to say nothing more that might help anyone who would stand against his cause. "To this end I would request a private audience with your majesty to explain how this may be brought about."

"As you wish, yet we warn you, we shall not be easily swayed."

Hours later, the duke was in his private chambers in a deep discussion with Jacques de Berry. In public they sought to distance themselves, acknowledging no close acquaintance, with de Berry maintaining a secure relationship with his uncle and the Armagnacs.

"My uncle was furious at the private audience you obtained with the king, and would have given half his fortune to gain some knowledge of what occurred between you and his majesty."

The duke grinned mirthlessly. "Such news causes me great solace, for my plans would be thwarted ere they were known by your uncle. The Armagnacs continue to sue for lasting peace with the English, and seem happy to sacrifice Calais and all that we hold dear. So I have an errand for you of great import. You must return to England and thence to Scotland. I will have messages for you to deliver to the Duke of Albany at the Scottish court. Thence to London and see to other matters that I would like to see resolved."

A week later Jacques de Berry found himself at the quayside in Dunkerque. Early June had brought with it fair weather and the calm sea promised an easy crossing. He watched as his faithful horse was once more loaded across on to the waiting cog, its legs at first kicking out before the creature resigned itself to its fate, hanging heavily in the two slings strapped across its belly, using the head collar for balance. The whites of its eyes rolled, hating the experience despite having been subjected to it on many occasions. As the solid deck approached beneath him, the stallion flailed its legs in expectation of wooden boards. De Berry exhaled deeply, having unconsciously held his breath throughout. Satisfied, he walked forward himself to board the vessel.

Five hours later, the cog docked at Dover. It had been an uneventful crossing, and with the port reached the cargo was unloaded – all except Jacques de Berry, who remained in the upper hold of the ship with his horse, which was steadily munching on some oats which de Berry held in his hand. Not too many, he knew, for horses could not vomit as humans, and sickness at sea could result in deadly colic. The captain came down wooden steps to him so as not to be overheard.

"Three hours, sir, to reload. Then we shall be away again up the coast towards Edinburgh."

"How long will it take, Captain? I worry for my horse."

The man rubbed his chin, raising and replacing his greasy leather hat. "Three, maybe four days, depends upon the winds and such."

"'Tis too long. Mayhap you could dock for an hour at Lynn? Unload me there away from prying eyes, and I could continue my journey thence."

"Aye, that I could sir, for you pay me well and I'll have 'ee there by mornin'," he promised. "Though if'n 'ee be wantin' to slip in quiet like, I'd soon as see you landed at Skeggy. It's also on the other side of the estuary and it'll make your journey shorter by half a day."

The deal was struck, and an hour later the cog slipped its moorings and headed north around the English coast. The ship hugged the shore, keeping within sight of land the whole time, only moving further out to sea as night drew on for fear of unseen rocks. The following morning, to the relief of Jacques de Berry, they landed at Skegness harbour. The tiny fishing village and settlement was alive with small boats leaving and others returning from a night's fishing. It was all hustle and bustle, and one more cog pulling in raised no comment and went unnoticed in the throng of seagoing traffic. A small pier offered access for those with deeper drafts and it was this that the captain made for. There was no sling this time; instead, a wide plank with rails was slid out by two steves. With much coaxing and a blindfold, the horse was led ashore and onto the pier. Once on solid ground again it stamped, snorted and shook itself.

Jacques de Berry saddled the animal quickly, keen to be away with as little comment as possible. Once mounted, he urged the horse into a walk and clipped across the cobbled streets in search of the main road north.

Chapter Forty-One

London

The palace halls were cool against the pervading heat of the streets outside. Summer had begun early, with flaming June heralding the seasonal change. A series of informal wrestling matches had been organised for the entertainment of the courtiers, and as a keen exponent of the art of wrestling the prince himself had determined that he should take part in the sport.

He stood amongst his favourites, watching various matches taking place in the centre of the hall. He was to be paired with Mark of Cornwall, and had been wanting to try his strength and skill against the young man since he had heard news of his winning bout in France. The prince was as tall as Mark, though not as well built, although he had a sinewy strength from long training sessions with weapons since boyhood. His long arms were honed and tight and his body carried not a pound of spare fat.

Mark had spoken to Jamie and Cristoforo the day before,

and both had come to attend the fun with great expectations of being entertained. It was also a perfect opportunity for Cristoforo to spend time with Contessa Alessandria as they mingled in the crowd of courtiers. She was today dressed in a gown of turquoise silk, and wore upon her head a chequered wimple of black and white with a trailing veil to the rear. A touch of kohl emphasised her beautiful brown eyes, and Cristoforo was alive with admiration for her, and dared to insert his arm through hers in a declaration of courtly love.

Jamie smiled tolerantly, as an older brother might. Since returning from France he had been feted by the ladies himself as his prominence grew, despite protestations that he had nothing to do with the cathedral fire at Saint-Omer or had acted in any other way than as an observer at the French court. He had flirted with and paid court to various ladies, and one in particular had ignited a spark in him. She was Alice, daughter of Sir Andrew of Macclesfield. Despite this flirtation, he still did not share the love-smitten state of his comrade in arms.

"Come, witness you both, for the bout is to commence," he urged.

The prince and Mark had squared off against each other, and despite protestations that he must not let him win, both Jamie and Cristoforo noticed that the fierce concentration and determination they had seen etched on his face in Paris was not there today. In conversation with him on their journey back from France, Jamie had likened it to the battle lust that every warrior succumbs to before and during combat. Here Mark was concentrating, but he was not as fiercely competitive as he would have been if his life or the honour of his country depended upon it.

Jamie looked at them, trying to foresee which way the contest would go, when he felt the grip of a hand on his elbow.

Startled by the contact, which drew him out of his immersion in the contest, he looked down to see a courtier by his side beckoning him away from the press of people watching the bout. Once clear, the courtier whispered: "Master de Grispere, Sir Richard requires your presence urgently."

Cursing silently to himself, Jamie cast a final glance at the backs of the crowd of courtiers watching the match. There was a concerted 'ooh' as either Mark or the prince was thrown.

"As he wishes," he retorted irritably.

Minutes later he was in Sir Richard's chamber.

"Ah James, I am truly sorry to remove you from the contest, but I knew it to be an opportune moment to do so as all eyes would be on the prince's match, providing a perfect moment for you to slip away unobserved."

"Of course, Sir Richard. I understand."

"Now we must not tarry, for I do not wish your absence to be commented upon. Let me perforce further you with an explanation. Your excellent and successful mission in France has spawned another tentacle that threatens to clutch at the stability of the realm. I have an agent abroad in Wales who has failed to report to me now for some days. He is – or perhaps was – reporting from Adam Usk, who has long been attached to Glyndower's court. His last report suggested that there are rumours from the Scottish court that lead me to believe more dissension is planned from Wales and from across our northern border. My greatest fear is that these two actions could be coordinated. Not as Hotspur and Glyndower were at Shrewsbury, but by a pincer attack in two directions that would leave us open to a rear-guard action from the French. If this were achieved we should be in mighty peril, and our borders would be rendered suddenly porous."

"That would indeed be perilous, Sir Richard," Jamie opined, "Yet forgive me if I proffer my own thoughts on this, as

I do not have access to your intelligence. The king in each case holds sway as Glyndower's family – not just his wife but his children, including his firstborn – are held in the Tower against such actions. Meanwhile the Scots have an even bigger counterbalance against their behaviour, for their very heir is held here – Prince James, who will one day inherit the throne when he is released and crowned King of Scotland. Yet you say they will move against these bonds and risk all?"

"You think well, James, like a chess player watching the pieces on the board, seeing the moves before your enemy. I praise you for your perspicacity – yet think on. Prince James is indeed held here on pain of ransom, yet who holds the strings and stands to gain by his absence, but faces the butcher's bill if he be released?"

"The treacherous Duke of Albany," Jamie confirmed. Through Sir Robert's tutelage he had become well versed in Scottish politics and loyalties north of the border.

"Indeed you have the right of it. With Murdoch and Douglas in league with each other the triumvirate holds sway, and Albany would not wish his nephew James to usurp his power. And then we must consider Glyndower. Yes, his wife Margaret and his family languish in the Tower. Yet what chance do you think he perceives of seeing them again? Hmm? None. It is revenge he wants, and to be in power with strength enough to have them freed. That is his driving force. The catalyst here is the French, for they are bleeding and sore from the wounds that you inflicted – and inflicted well, praise God. Now I have heard that Burgundy is in talks with Albany, who if persuaded will link with Glyndower to coordinate our demise. Think how close they came at Worcester when the French invaded and we stood in balance on a pivot point. That must never again come to pass."

"Burgundy's hand is in this! By the rood I would like to

meet him in combat. Yet, I do not see how I may aid you in your cause. Do you wish me to return to Scotland?"

"No lad, I wish you to venture to Wales, seek out Glyndower, join his band and spy for me."

If Sir Richard had hit Jamie with a mace it would have had no more impact. "Wales?" he said. "I have no connexions there, nor reasons to go. How can I best serve you in this?"

"Aye, I can see how this may appear surprising, and with little wonder. I shall explain and you will see my route to the devil Glyndower. In this year alone I have lost three men, never to be heard of again, all executed and their bodies buried in the godforsaken land of the Welsh, I suspect. Yet I perceive the reason is this: each time a man sought to insert himself, he was alone and had little cause to be accepted. Glyndower is canny, which is evidenced by his continuing freedom despite the bounty that rests upon his head. Yet if men entered with good reason – as say, a party escaping persecution in England and with a legitimate hatred of the government here – they would I believe hold greater chance of success."

"I am intrigued, Sir Richard. Pray continue, for I wish to see what conjuror's trick you intend to perform here." Jamie replied.

"When you returned from France we discussed the Lollard knight Sir John Oldcastle, who has sympathies with Glyndower and whose estates in Hereford border the Welsh Marches, yet who remains a friend to the prince. Here I believe is your connexion, for you will pose as a Lollard sympathiser, exiled and in fear of your life for your beliefs. Glyndower's brother-in-law, Sir John Scudamore, has estates on the borders nearby in Ewyas and Monnington. You could perhaps visit him by accident on the road to add credence to your cause. Seek shelter and ask how you might meet and join Glyndower."

"You mentioned that a group stood greater chance of success. How should I achieve this? Whom should I take to feign my cause?"

"I believe it would be to your advantage to take allies. You achieved great success in France with two other men. Perchance you could enlist their help again. You would be a disparate group of no known association, and therefore more likely to be accepted."

"You would have me encumber Cristoforo and Mark?"

"Why not?" Whittington countered, and in his manner Jamie saw the ruthlessness that never lurked far beneath the surface. "They are anonymous, with no links to the crown or the court. Think on't, a disillusioned esquire, an Italian adrift on a sea of exile and a Cornishman friendless and far from home. A more perfect concoction one could not wish to mix and so unlikely to be contrived."

Jamie pondered the moment and Whittington's words. He knew instantly that Cristoforo would join him. As to Mark, he could but ask and see if he would agree. He also knew he could not ask for two better men to go with him into the lion's den. At length he answered, with Sir Richard ever patient, allowing Jamie time to seal his fate.

"I am as ever loyal to the crown, and continue to pledge my troth to aid you and thus the king in any way I can. As to the others, I can but ask and see if they agree."

"I am well pleased, James. Now go and return to the wrestling, for it is unlikely that you will have been missed. I shall send for you again when I have more news."

Jamie left the chambers with his thoughts in turmoil. Not looking where he was going, he almost bumped into the squire that had followed him on the first day that he had met Sir Richard.

"Watch where you're going, churl!" The equerry snarled in a fit of anger.

"I beg your p... you!" Jamie responded, recognising the man and seeing the coat of arms emblazoned on his jupon. It was the red argent and saltire engrailed gules of Sir John Tiptoft. Jamie's anger flew to the fore. He did not stop to think, but reacted as if in battle, for he saw the hand of the man drop to his dagger. Jamie took a step to the left, and as he did so he brought up his right arm, swinging from the shoulder. He kept the hand at ninety degrees and at the last minute rotated it to strike with the outer edge of the thumb, driving it into the courtier's windpipe. It was an evil blow and had it landed with full force in battle the man would have died with a crushed larynx. As it was he retched, his eyes popping open as he collapsed to the floor, wheezing. Two more figures approached, followed by a group of ladies. Jamie thought quickly, pretending concern.

"Quick, bring wine! This fellow seems to be having a seizure, I can barely hear him breathe," he urged in false concern. Then as if to aid him, he bent his head close to his ear and whispered: "Next time, whelp, I'll kill you. Tell that to master Tiptoft." Then louder. "That's it, fellow, breathe quietly. Steady now and I'll leave you to the ministrations of this good lady," he urged as one of the ladies in waiting approached again, this time bearing a goblet of watered wine. As Jamie looked up properly to take the goblet, he met the eyes of lady Alice of Macclesfield. The eyes were cornflower blue, framed by gold. A shimmering sheath of silk outlined her form against the backlight. Jamie was suddenly tongue-tied.

"My lady ... I am grateful ... or rather this fellow is."

"What? The elegant master de Grispere is lost for words?" Lady Alice replied. "Is this real, or do I dream? No, for here is trouble, and where trouble is to be found so is the redoubtable

Jamie," she commented, to peals of laughter from the ladies fanning around her.

Jamie recovered adroitly, "Ah my lady, I am on my knees – as is befitting in your presence, in readiness to serve. Yet I find it is you who serves me. How can this be, beauty serving the beast?"

"Ho! Fie upon you! You see, ladies, how he makes so quick a recovery?" At which another equerry bearing the arms of Tiptoft arrived to aid his companion and Jamie stood to rid himself of his burden.

"My lady, on what errand may I serve you wither you go?"

"We are lately returned from the gallery to better watch the matches below, and now we seek to praise the winners in their victory. I was surprised not to see you there. Were you drawn by a new assignation? Did some fair damsel need rescuing, mayhap?" She fluttered her lashes at him, then gently drew him away from the stricken man, sweeping him along towards the main chamber and the noise from the court.

Jamie and the group of ladies entered unnoticed into the cacophony from the courtiers, who were all commenting loudly on the matches they had seen, particularly that of the prince. As the other ladies talked and flirted, Alice quietly said as an aside: "You should know that the prince won by three falls to two against your friend, the giant Mark. It would not do for you to have been ignorant of the score." Here she looked directly up into his eyes, a challenge in her manner and all the artifice of a shallow damsel dropped.

Jamie arched an eyebrow in surprise. "My lady, you do me an injustice."

"Do I? You of all people disappear in a moment of excite-ment, probably to some clandestine meeting, to find yourself in a brawl dressed as an accident. By the rood, I am no coy flower to swoon and be deceived. Rumours swirl about you like mist in the dawn, yet no one can fathom your depth. I had the advantage of arriving slightly ahead of my party and observed the blow you dealt Crispin – ah no, do not deny it, I adjure you. He is an arrogant knave and will ever find his just deserts."

"My lady, your timing was propitious and I must thank you for your intervention and your discretion, for as you rightly say it was not an accident."

"May you tell me your tale? For certes you make friends and enemies right quickly," she remarked.

"I shall perchance, but not here, for there are ears and eyes abroad. Perhaps this evening at supper, if you dine at court?"

"I do, for my father returns this evening and I shall wait upon my mother."

"Then perhaps I may dance with you when the minstrels play."

At this point a voice floated across in mocking tones. "Ah the only squire I know who disappears on business only to return hence with a beautiful *signorina*. If only she had seen me first, for now my heart is truly broken," Cristoforo opined.

"We may still seek a clandestine tryst, for I hear that Italians are better lovers," Lady Alice responded.

"Yet they might not if a certain Contessa should hear of such a thing," Jamie interrupted. "I fear that your ... ears, shall we say ... would be forfeit at the very least."

"Ah you wound me, Jamie, you wound me." Cristoforo continued unabashed. Then quietly he whispered. "The prince won by a fall, in case you are asked."

Alice laughed at the aside: "I see my efforts were not needed, yet of course no air of conspiracy abides about you..." She mocked.

"My lady is as ever perspicacious," Jamie bowed. "Until this evening, my lady." He allowed her to move away amongst her friends. He watched her go with a sigh, as he realised he may be following Cristoforo on his road to amorous entanglement.

"What? The deadly swordsman has his heart pierced?" Cristoforo mocked. "This will be a fine tale to tell John. He will laugh 'til drunk, I'm bound."

"Away you rogue, ere I skewer you with my sword." Jamie hissed.

Chapter Forty-Two

Stirling Castle, Scotland.

Jacques de Berry had followed the river Forth upstream from Edinburgh, and at last found himself approaching his destination, Stirling Castle. The temperature had become progressively colder the further north he had ridden, and now a slanting grey drizzle drove in from the east, chilling his bones. His horse was tired and hung its head against the rain, dropping its ears in disgust. De Berry pulled his thick woollen cloak about him and hunched lower in the saddle. Surely, he thought, I will be there soon. Back at the last hamlet they had assured him in near incomprehensible French that it was but a few miles to the castle stronghold.

Then suddenly the road began to rise in front of him and a break in the weather revealed the ominous bulk of Castle Hill and the great crag of granite supporting Stirling castle. "Christ on the cross I'd not want to take that bastard hold," he swore to himself. The sheer face of the granite cliff rose vertically before him and above it, outlined against a grey sky, reared the outline of the castle itself, a huge behemoth dominating everything in sight. He shivered involuntarily. It looked forbidding and he was not yet sure what sort of reception he would receive.

Man and horse plodded on into the gloom and finally, when he had all but given up hope of ever reaching the top, the road levelled out and he was faced with an imposing gatehouse of two turrets bordering an arched gateway. The ground fell away to either side of the drawbridge, rendering the castle nigh-on impregnable to de Berry's eyes. Wearily he approached the guard at the gate, offering his name and business. A sergeant-at-arms was called and asked him in gruff tones to follow through the vast walls to the Nether Bailey. To de Berry it felt dark and imposing, a lifetime away from the French court which he had left only two weeks ago. Everywhere was grey, dour granite where neither light shone nor shadow fell.

A groom came to take his horse and he dismounted stiffly, to be escorted by a squire into the West Tower and the main living quarters. All around he saw heavy fortifications and large numbers of men-at-arms. He was ushered into the Great Hall and with the opening of the doors a trickle of warmth finally exuded from a great blaze in the brazier within. Despite its large size, the room seemed to be filled with people. Large hunting dogs lay strewn around waiting for morsels to be dropped by sympathetic owners. De Berry had heard reports that the Scottish court had begun to emulate that of the French court in Paris, with the accent on chivalric homage and courtly love. The fashions of the few women present he saw were similar to those in France, although the men were differently dressed, with many a kilt on display. Here he noticed that reds and greens were predominant colours, mixing with rarer yellows. Most men wore bonnets rather than the taller hats of the southern court.

Looking towards the end of the hall he gained his first view of Robert Stewart, Duke of Albany. The duke was remarkable, in that he had achieved such an old age when many of his kin perished before their twenty-first birthday. His back was still straight, but his features were now sagging. He wore a bonnet of Stewart tartan from beneath which untidy wisps of grey hair extruded. He stood at the head of his liege lords, and as the protector of Scotland he commanded their presence. The newcomer was announced, and all turned to stare as de Berry walked through the groups of courtiers. He found himself before the duke, who had a sword thane to either side of him, hands on the hilts of their swords in readiness against any treachery. The Scottish court was even worse than the English for treachery and assassination.

De Berry stopped and bowed to the old man before him. "My lord duke, I offer you greetings and felicitations from my master the Duke of Burgundy of France. He trusts that you are in good health and that nothing ails you."

"Lord de Berry, I thank you for your message and courtesy, and bid you welcome to my court. When did you leave France, man, for you look fatigued?"

"Two weeks ago – and aye sir, I am forsooth. My joints ache and will not bend to my will," he declared with a grim smile. "I am unused to your climate, sir."

"Then it's a wee dram of *uisge beatha* you'll be needing, laddie, tae ease your pain." The duke nodded to a servant, who brought forth a glass holding an amber liquid. Jacques accepted the offering and drained the whisky in one gulp, then coughed as the fiery spirit scorched his throat, making his eyes water. His voice when he spoke sounded strained.

"Well that will cure me for sure, I've no doubt." The others smiled at the reaction of those not used to their partisan tastes.

"Come now, we sup soon. It will serve ye well to get food inside you ere long."

"You are most gracious, my lord, yet ere I rest I have missives for you that must be served, if I may?"

"Of course."

De Berry reached into his leather satchel bag, noticing again the tightening of hands on sword hilts. He produced three scrolls of letters, ribboned and sealed with the Burgundy crest in red wax. He passed them over to the duke, who took them graciously.

"Now man, awa' and see to yourself, for we dine in half of the hour," he ordered. At which a servant appeared and led de Berry from the hall to a side door and his lodgings within the castle quarters.

As he left he heard the hubbub of noise recommence from all those present in the court, He was, he realised, the beast with two tails.

In London, Jamie chose his moment to approach Mark. He found the wrestler in a quiet corner, re-living his defeat at the hands of the prince with his comrades. He detached himself from the group at a nod from Jamie.

"I have a boon to ask you," Jamie began. "Yet you must not feel obligated to attend me, for it will surely put you in great peril. So I adjure you think ere you speak and hear me to the end."

The blond giant nodded and walked with Jamie through an archway into an open cloister and gardens where it would be much more difficult for them to be overheard. Still Jamie dropped his voice so only Mark could hear.

"We have come to know each other well since France, I own, and are firm friends, I believe," Jamie said.

"Aye, indeed we are, master Jamie, so you need do away with any airs, for I am straight of speech and would have it like a staff – true and straight. Ask me your boon," Mark replied. Jamie laughed. He had become so accustomed to the courtly language and managing everything with care, and found Mark's direct manner refreshing.

"Well spoken, Mark. Very well, I have been tasked by the Council – more particularly Sir Richard, for I know I can trust you – to journey into Wales on a matter of great import. I must seek out Owen ap Glyndower and spy upon him, seeking knowledge of a plot between the Welsh, Scots and French..." Jamie paused to see his friend's reaction. He was not disappointed.

"By the Holy Lord, your tasks are not for the faint-hearted. Yet to go against the Welsh would do my heart good, for they raid and pillage sometimes to Cornwall. They killed my uncle and his family on their farm. I am not alone, for no Englishman abides the Welsh. They are banned from our soil, and for good reason, so to raid theirs would seem fitting," he gave Jamie a wicked grin.

Jamie clapped him on the shoulder, feeling the solid mass of muscle there. "That pleases me well, for now I have two fellows to accompany me – and two better men I could not wish for to aid me in my travails."

"Cristo goes too, does 'ee? Well then, we'll make a fine mess of the Welsh, just you see if we don't."

Jamie sat down with Mark in the warm summer air of the cloistered garden, and explained all the points made by Sir Richard. Mark agreed that he would be ready to move whenever required, as the prince would surely release him from his sporting responsibilities for such a task. They stood and walked in the gardens once more, before Mark disappeared off to his lodgings from the south end, while Jamie moved back to the entrance whence they had entered. The cloistered garden was now empty of those who had previously walked around to enjoy the sunshine within the grounds and Jamie was in a thoughtful mood, much preoccupied with his own musings as he turned to leave. He was jolted from his thoughts as a figure appeared before him – a figure with a bandage at his throat.

"Ho now, sir knight of the cloth," the man said. "Where do you go in such a hurry? We must needs have words, for my throat is still sore from your ministrations three days back," he rasped.

"Out of my way. I give no ground to an empty knave such as you," Jamie snarled, his temper rising. But he saw movement from behind him and to the side as figures previously hidden came from behind the pillared arches of the cloister. There were in all five squires and servants, each in the Tiptoft livery and each bearing sticks or light clubs. This was the way, he knew, that gangs of servants would band together to repay those who had earned their master's displeasure. Men had been killed in this way, but if their master wielded enough power the servants were often pardoned and naught more was said of the matter.

"So now we have a reckoning," the man said, "and I pay you back for the damage you wreaked upon my throat. Let us see how you fight with broken legs and shoulders ere we're finished with you, sir knight of the weaver," he sneered. Jamie knew that he would be brought down and dared not draw his dagger. He knew that he would kill some, maybe all of them, and his coin of influence was not robust enough to withstand the consequences of such actions. He plotted his moves with one thought in mind – he would take the leader down and mayhap kill him with his bare hands before he was clubbed senseless. He had one advantage, he knew: they were many seeking one target, he was one seeking many targets. With this in mind he jumped to put a pillar at his back and then prepared for the onslaught. The cowardly leader – he remembered now that Lady Alice had named him Crispin – cried for the others to attack him, and they surged towards Jamie with their sticks and clubs raised.

The first stick fell, aimed at his head, yet the pillar prevented it from landing with full force as it struck the stone first. Jamie blocked it with his forearm, wincing at the pain, and grabbed the arm, pulling and twisting to put the man between him and his foes as a human shield. A second blow fell upon the luckless man's shoulders and he dropped to his knees, crying out. Jamie wrenched the stick from his nerveless fingers.

He kicked out and forwards, as he would in a sword fight, striking a knee and breaking his own stick over the head of a squire, who sank to the floor unconscious. He felt a sharp blow at his ribs that drove the air from his lungs. Crispin had lashed around in a horizontal blow from behind the pillar and Jamie arched his body in defence as another club landed on his shoulder and he started to collapse at the knees, knowing that he would now be attacked by many clubs and sticks. Yet as he fell he grabbed at Crispin's leg and pulled, seeking the kneecap. He drove the palm of his hand hard across it, feeling it shift and dislocate as his opponent cried in pain and stumbled backwards. The other three moved in for the kill, ready to rain blows upon the helpless figure before them, and Jamie made to cover his head with his arms as he waited for the clubbing blows.

They never came. There was suddenly a space around him as he saw two pairs of feet leave the ground and heard a sudden dull crunch. Both men had been lifted bodily off the ground and their heads smashed together. They dropped in an unconscious heap. A giant shadow loomed above him as Mark peered down.

"Are ye all right, master Jamie? I heard the commotion and thought I'd best return – and I'm right glad I did."

"I've been worse, but I'll mend thanks to you. Never were you more welcome." Jamie rubbed his head and felt his ribs delicately, wincing at the tenderness there. Of the attackers only the leader, Crispin, remained conscious, barely able to stand with his dislocated knee cap. Jamie looked across at him and rose to his feet.

"You whoreson dung-head. I should kill you for this craven attack, for you would like to have killed me ere your pride could not stomach that I bested you. Your bile will harm you yet."

Crispin cursed in pain and spat an oath. Jamie began to turn away, but on hearing the oath he spun around, driving his fist right to the point of the hinge of the other man's jaw. There was a snapping sound and Crispin's jaw dropped, assuming a strange angle. He sank to the floor, semi-conscious. Jamie knelt beside him, grasped the neck of his doublet and pulled him up until their faces were but inches apart. "Cross me again and I will seek you out and kill you, Tiptoft's protection or no," he said, and let Crispin fall to the flagstones of the cloister. He stood and turned to his friend and rescuer.

"Mark, let us away afore more such vermin arrive." Mark nodded and exhaled, the aggression leaving him. The two men moved on, with Jamie wincing at every stride.

Chapter Forty-Three

Stirling Castle/London

The following morning, Jacques de Berry attended the Duke of Albany in his private solar. The duke's council and sword thanes were in conference, discussing the contents of the letters sent by the Duke of Burgundy. Albany set the papers down before him and spoke to de Berry.

"So, Burgundy seeks my aid, in return for which he promises to grant me the north of the kingdom?" he muttered bluntly, cutting through the courtly language and chivalric overtures to summarise the Duke of Burgundy's terms.

"In essence he does, my lord. This to include a collusion with Glyndower of Wales. We would have a tri-indenture binding us all to rise against King Henry in one concerted effort, rendering it necessary for him to fight on three or possibly even four fronts, drawing his forces out and weakening them.

"There are those within the court who are not pleased with the way the English realm is being managed, and many more who remain loyal to the old King Richard. Many would rise from within to a different banner of leadership, creating confusion and poor morale." He left the words to hang and settle within the old man's head.

Albany pondered what de Berry had said and looked across at him, marshalling his thoughts in his head. "It's a fine picture ye paint of a divided England we might share to rule. Yet it poses as many questions as answers, as I'm sure ye'll ken."

They spoke in French at the court, yet the occasional Scottish word prevailed momentarily, throwing Jacques. "I am sure my lord will have concerns, yet what is chief amongst them, prithee?" He answered suavely.

"You'll know of my nephew James, the uncrowned King of Scotland? Well should he be freed and return across the border, my position would change considerably and I would be less able to help you, as despite my protestations he does not view me favourably."

The old fox wants his nephew killed or dropped into a dark hole somewhere so he can continue the clan Stewart with himself or his sons as king, de Berry thought, but he kept his face impassive.

"My lord, Duke John of Burgundy has given me *carte blanche* to arrange terms that are beneficial to us both. In this accord I feel he would agree to any request you may have concerning the...care and safety...of your nephew."

"Good. We understand one another. How would we liaise with Glyndower, for he has fought against us in the past and only our Celtic blood will draw us together for a common cause?"

"That is true enough. Dost thou recall that in the past, his majesty King Charles of France aided and fitted Glyndower with arms and men in his own cause? Any entreaty bearing French support would give you and Glyndower strong reason for putting old scores aside. In this I believe we can all accede.

The Duke of Burgundy would have you send two men, perhaps posing as merchants, to the Welsh court and there seek entreaties on Glyndower's behalf to fight with us. This would draw him forward, for he has an ineluctable desire to seek revenge against the injustices done to his family by the English. Duke John has already made addresses to Glyndower from one of his own agents and it would be a great wonder if he should not hear your cause favourably."

"Let me think on't, for it is a grave undertaking you suggest, and one that needs careful consideration."

"Of course, my lord. I am in service to your wishes. Yet I would add more intelligence to this consideration. We have other plans to divert the prince away to Calais by causing disruption there, leaving King Henry alone with only members of his council and none to follow into battle as a figurehead the like of which the prince would provide. For the king is well past his prime and very ill."

"So we hear, and it fits well for your proposal I'll grant ye. Even so, I must consider your proposals most fully and speak with my kinsman ere I make a decision. Now, dine with us and stay longer whilst we talk more."

In London, Lady Alice looked at Jamie with grave concern. "Jamie, I have heard the most terrible rumours, which if true give me much worry." Alice confided, as they walked among the other members of the court in the Great Hall.

"Pray tell me of such rumours" Jamie responded light-heartedly, although he had a very good idea of the news that Alice had heard.

"There are those who say that you fought with Sir John

Tiptoft's men in an argument over the Lollard rights. Can this be so?" She kept her expression light. yet there was deep concern in her voice.

"Pray now, don't be pebble-hearted, for there is a barrage of rumours flying hither and thither. People will hear what they wish to hear. I would adjure you to stay true to me – yet do not seek to defend me too strongly as I have no desire for you to be judged in my stead, nor become embroiled in what is to follow. I would just say this, my lady Alice: I am loyal to the crown, but oft we must use deceit to play the part and bring our enemies down.

"I pray thee do not worry on my account, for I shall be full assoiled in due course, but for now must play the villain and the fool. I am to leave soon for Wales. That much will become the knowledge of the court, yet if thou dost hear such stories I adjure you to affect surprise and dismay, as all others will."

Her hand flew to his arm and he felt pressure that caused him to wince as she touched the bruises from the attack a week earlier. "Oh I am sorry, forgive me. Does your arm still pain you?"

"Not to your gentle touch, my lady," Jamie smiled, "and not as much as my heart, should you think me a villain."

"My lord, you are indeed a knave," Lady Alice returned his smile. "Yet I worry still. Wales? A Godforsaken country where they say dragons still lurk."

"Aye, and well they might – yet I suspect they take human form. Fear not, for I travel with two good friends, Cristoforo and Mark. With them I could face an army of dragons and still win through, especially if I could return to you, my lady."

"Fie on you, for your chivalry will be the death of you."

"Mayhap, yet heed me well and distance yourself from my company. For you must not too stand accused by association. I adjure you, follow my lead, break from me now," he urged in no more than a whisper, "and admonish me loudly, then run off as though greatly upset."

"'Pon my soul..."

"Do this, my lady, I insist, for the sake of your good name."

At this she inhaled deeply and stepped back a clear pace, raising her voice as though in anger.

"Why then, sir, you give me no choice. You are a knave and I can give no credence to your suit. Now leave me be and do not offer yourself to my attentions again." She turned away from him in apparent disgust and stormed off, her face red with anger.

Jamie had no trouble appearing upset, blushing at the sudden attention of the court. He bowed briefly and swept out of the Great Hall, but once free of those confines he allowed a small smile to play across his lips. *It was well done, Alice, well done indeed. Now you are safe from my connexions.*

Two days later he attended Sir Richard Whittington in his chambers late at night.

"I'm sorry that you have been disadvantaged by the rumours we set abroad," Whittington said. "Perforce your set-to with Tiptoft's men was a godsend, and we can use it to our cause. It will mayhap work to your advantage in Wales, for if any rumour strays of a disenfranchised squire with Lollard sympathies, it will stand you in good stead. I have papers permitting your early departure through the gates even if they are barred." Whittington shuffled some documents and passed them to Jamie. "Friends and enemies alike can see it as a temporary banishment if they so wish. Let them believe we are giving time for tempers to cool, and let them believe that your friends have chosen to side with you against the court. I am right pleased that your friends will accompany you, for it will be a telling time. A disparate group you shall be – a wrestler, a Lollard squire and a roving Italian intent on fleeing his past. It will create as good a foil as any."

Jamie looked out of Sir Richard's window watching the dusk enfold the city that was his home, his rest and his sanctuary. "Where should we make for first, Sir Richard?" he asked.

"You will make haste to Worcester, where men will aid you howsoever they can under Lord Grey's banner. When in trouble or in need of aid, call him first. And mark this well – the Earl of Arundel is closer at Shrewsbury, but he is not to be trusted. He and that whoreson Glyndower were ever in the thick of each other and I'll not trust either for a pot to piss in over the difference between them. Arundel serves himself and takes whatever gains he can, all the while claiming loyalty to the crown. Loyalty and favour soar like a gull on the wind, tipping this way one minute and that the next, so beware." Whittington looked down and fiddled with a quill, aligning it with the edge of his desk before raising his eyes to meet Jamie's and continuing "Beware of Arundel's followers, too. John Wele, captain of Oswestry, Richard Lacon, captain of Clun and the two Corbet brothers, for they are knaves of the first order and you must trust them not. The Marcher Lords are a lawless lot and traitors, yet whilst they remain under Arundel's protection there is little we can do. The prince owes Arundel his loyalty until such pressure can be brought to bear that may split their growing power asunder. The local men there fear these traitorous lords as much as the Welsh. But Richard, Lord Grey of Codnor, is to be trusted, and you must liaise closely with him. He is effectively now unofficially the Earl of Worcester, and will reside there whilst you are secreted in Wales."

"He is the Chamberlain of the Household, is he not?"

"He bears that office and many more besides. He is a favourite of both the king and Prince Henry, which alone is a rare accolade. 'Tis fortunate that Arundel and Codnor do not treat well with each other, so Sir Richard can be trusted all the more. He has dealt with Glyndower before and would dearly wish to see him captured or finished."

Jamie nodded, taking in all the details that were necessary for his survival and asking as much of Sir Richard as he thought he could ever need. At length their interview was at an end, and Whittington wished him luck and Godspeed.

Chapter Forty-Four

Worcester

"What town is next, Jamie?" Cristoforo asked. "All is new to me and I seek a good bed for the night. By God's grace the sun shines and it seems that July has finally brought summer to England."

"We aim for Worcester, and should be there in good time ere night falls," Jamie replied. "I have been there many a time with my father, and it is a goodly city, loyal to the king and in a perfect situs across the River Severn. In many ways it forms a gateway to lands further west and Wales. It was on these western banks that last the French landed and made to attack the city from Abberley aided by the traitor Glyndower, so Whittington told me."

"'Tis good land, and rich for farming," Mark commented. "Rolling hills and filled with birdsong. Makes my heart right glad to be out of the city."

"Aye that it is, although there is also cloth production here within the city and nearby. The river powers the mills through a flute and 'tis grand country for wool. Father comes here oft to buy cloth and it's fast approaching the quality of the Flemish weavers. Gloves and gauntlets too, of doe skin – my sister has a pair that came from here and they are a marvel to behold. I may buy some for Alice, for she risked her position and reputation by her connexion with me and I'd as lief make amends."

"Aye," Cristoforo added, "for we are an odd triumvirate: a Lollard squire, a foreigner on the run for crimes following him from Italy and a wrestler fleeing for his life from vengeance out of Cornwall. And the Lionheart come back amongst us as a horse," he quipped, pulling out of reach of the chestnut stallion's teeth as it sought to nip his own mount.

The three men laughed at the jest and then fell silent as they reigned in their horses at the vista before them. They had left the Evesham road and started to ride down the main London road of Red Hill, cresting before the main descent into the City of Worcester, which lay nestled in a green valley. The city's magnificent cathedral was bathed in sunlight and the sandstone and yellow Cotswold limestone of its walls had begun to mellow with age over the last three hundred years as it rose to a pinnacle, the huge tower dominating the city below.

"By all the saints 'tis a wonderful sight, and God works miracles for sure," Mark enthused.

"Amen to that," Jamie agreed. "Let us not tarry, but hasten to see if the welcome is as warm as it looks, for a hot tub is what I need to ease my aching bones."

The three pressed on down the hill, with the trees on either side of the road standing guard like sentinels as they rode into the City. They passed rows of empty cottages in various stages of disrepair and collapse as they rode closer to habitation.

"Why so many empty houses?" Cristoforo asked.

"The Black Death," Jamie replied. "We lost half the population of England, so they say. 'Tis rare to see a full village and it will be many a generation afore we see England rising again as she was."

"Aye we had it bad in Cornwall too. My father told of whole villages being wiped out. 'Twas a bad time for all, so I'm told."

The smell of a thriving city began to assail them as they neared the Sidbury Gate, where midden pits had been dug and filled with the products of human existence.

"By the rood, the gongfermours have been busy with shit," Jamie exclaimed, raising his cowl to his face. As they passed the pits and drew closer to the gate the smell left them, as no waste was permitted within fifty yards of the red sandstone walls.

"Ye gods that's better. That was a rancid fetid ordure," Cristoforo commented

"Aye we're clear now and food beckons, if we still have the stomachs for it," Mark said with a grin.

They approached the southernmost entrance through the city walls, passing over the thirty-foot-wide moat surrounding the city and through the Sidbury Gate, which was dominated by two huge towers upon which sat a full watch of guards armed with crossbows. Cristoforo crossed himself seeing the heads of traitors and other nefarious villains raised on spikes above the gate. Two crows were gnawing at what was left of the eye sockets, cawing to each other aggressively.

The three looked up to the cathedral that loomed above them, which was even more awe-inspiring at close quarters. To the south of the cathedral, Edgar Street led to the castle entrance, and it was in this direction that they aimed their horses. Once within the city, ragged children started to run up to them, offering a place to stable their horses, a place for the night, the best inn at which to drink or obtain a meal.

"Penny sir, an oi'll show 'ee the best beer in the city."

"No 'e won't sir, I will!" another cried. It had been a ritual they'd experienced in every town they had ridden into on their journey so far.

"Scrawny little rascals, look at 'em. Barely enough to feed a rat." Mark commented, fishing into his purse and flicking three or four coins up into the air. The urchins swooped like locusts onto the halfpennies.

"Keep that up all the way to Wales and you'll fetch up one of them." Jamie chided him.

"Aye, mayhap, but I've been poor and hungry and t'ain't a good feeling," Mark replied. "One year our crops failed on the farm and we nearly took to eating the 'orses like the French. Praise God we survived, but it were a close-run thing."

"You've a good heart, Mark." Cristoforo praised now – using English as much as French, having become more proficient in the language.

Mark shrugged: "I hate to see young 'uns suffer."

The exchange brought them to the gates of Edgar tower, where they presented their intent and were shown through to the bailey. The castle itself was of Norman construction and lay adjacent to the cathedral. The newer buildings of the gaols were off to their right, while ahead lay the huge man-made motte atop which sat the stone keep. Stabling their horses, they passed into the inner bailey and up through the guardhouse to the keep itself, where they were given an audience by the sheriff, who acted as a constable for the castle. He was a man in his early twenties, squarely built and dressed in a bright doublet and hose. A chain of office sat upon his shoulders and he carried himself with an air of authority. As he moved forward, Jamie recalled that Whittington had said he reported to both the Beauchamps and Sir Richard of Grey and was loyal to the crown.

"Good sirs, I bid you welcome to Worcester. I am the sheriff, Clifford of Ombersely, at your service."

Jamie made the introductions and invited more comment as to their mission.

"Messages arrived from both Sir Richard Whittington and my Lord Grey some weeks ago advising of your coming, and telling me that I was not to heed any rumours I should hear told abroad. I therefore offer you any assistance that I may."

"Dost thou know of any rumours that have flown before us concerning our business in these parts?"

"No reports have reached my ears of anything regarding your company, though 'tis normal for rumours of Lollardy to float on the wind and dissent is often heard here on the borders with Wales. Often a man or two passes and goes over to Glyndower to seek sanctuary or redress against some imagined slight. As such, it will do your errand no harm – and may even aid you, I feel. Now explain as much as you are able of your intent and tell me how I may be of service."

Jamie carefully outlined their mission and told the sheriff of such plans as they had so far formulated.

"It would be a great wonder if we succeed and unearth all that may be suspected without being unmasked. Therefore, should the need arise, can we count on your garrison to aid us?"

"By all means, for I am at your service and in constant contact with Sir Richard Grey, who will be moving here from Codnor in due course and will then be better able to aid you ere the need occurs. He will fortify either Worcester or Stokesay castle nearer the Marches according to your directions."

"That will ease my soul, for we needs must have a force to call upon and cannot in all conscience depend upon my Lord Arundel or his cohorts."

"By the rood no, for it was ever rumoured that he deals as much with as against Glyndower."

"So Sir Richard Whittington warned us. We need a secure method of proving our message is verified. If it be one of us who returns, perforce they shall have this link of an SS collar on whomever we shall send." Jamie produced a link from Whittington's collar that was pinned to a small velvet patch as a brooch. "Mark it well, for without this trinket any entreaty to arms will be a trap and our lives forfeit."

The sheriff nodded at the significance of the SS link and suggested further ideas, to which Mark and Cristoforo nodded in agreement, so that before long they all fully understood the way in which they were to proceed.

"I know Stokesay well, for 'tis owned by a friend of my father's, Laurence de Ludlow, who trades on wool and treats with us often."

"Laurence is a good and trustworthy man, and will aid us with provisions and a base from which to call to arms. His estates are often raided by the Welsh, and yet he receives little aid from Arundel at Shrewsbury or Richard Lacon, captain of Clun. It is probably best that a message be sent there alerting us of any new intelligence. Yet enough for now, for I am sure you would like a hot tub ere we sup. I will arrange for you to eat here tonight and my servant will show you to a private solar." With this plan heartily agreed upon, the three left to be escorted to their room, and all plans were later finalised over supper.

Chapter Forty-Five

Jamie, Cristoforo and Mark left the castle the following morning. They followed the Deansway down to the River Severn and crossed the river bridge, passing through the gateway in the middle. They were seen through by hard eyed guards, wary of strangers so close to the contested border country.

"So it begins," Jamie commented. "Now we enter enemy territory – or so it seems, for the Severn is as much a boundary as a castle wall."

"We do not go now to Monnington and Sir John Scudamore?" Mark asked.

"No. They say he is acting against Glyndower, but his true loyalties are not known. If he were in fact Glyndower's ally he would hand us to him, but if not he would grow suspicious and turn us in to loyalist forces. We shall have to do what we can without his help."

"It seems there ain't nothing straightforward on the borders. It's all quicksand here, looking sound yet soft and treacherous underneath." Mark offered.

"Aye Mark, I believe that you have the right of it," Jamie agreed. "'Tis no great wonder that Glyndower has not been brought to heel, for who can you trust in this miasma? Many who claim to be English side with the Welsh to feather their own nests, and a man's loyalty can turn as quickly as a sword blade, according to whose purse he covets. Adam Usk is the only man who is the king's agent in the camp, and even he was turned like a coin."

"Amen to that," Cristoforo quipped. "This is my world. I am wise to the ways of assassins and spies – yet it might all be for naught if we cannot gain Glyndower's confidence and trust."

"Just so. Yet we bring what he desires. We are fighting men, and on that count alone we can satisfy him."

The other two nodded in agreement with Jamie's retort, both confident in their fighting abilities. They moved on at a steady pace, trotting and cantering at even intervals, letting the horses breathe and giving them time for recovery, aiming to by-pass Ludlow and camp in the open forest near Bishop's Castle by nightfall.

"We're making good time," Jamie remarked. "We should avoid any towns between here and Machynlleth so as not to attract attention, for we'll be across the border and in Wales by nightfall."

They pressed on through the heat of the summer's day, halting at a limpid stream to refill water bottles and then moving swiftly on. They arrived at Bishop's Castle in time to buy bread and meat, with Mark entering the tiny hamlet alone, the other two hiding in the trees outside the village. They pressed on into the woods and found a clearing off the road where they made camp. The horses were fed and hobbled for the night and they lit a fire upon which to cook the meat.

With a flagon of wine to drink, they settled down for the

evening as pink tendrils etched their final fingers across a fading skyline, casting long ethereal shadows amongst the trees. Soon there was only dim moonlight and the light from the fire radiating out into the darkness. Mark gazed into flames, mesmerised by the soporific glow and the warmth emanating from the hearth of stones surrounding the fire. Looking up briefly, he noticed that neither Jamie nor Cristoforo were looking into the flames.

"Don't 'ee like the fire? I see you never look at it directly. I find it soothing and comforting, reminds me of the hearth at 'ome."

Jamie smiled a slow lazy smile, glancing across at Cristoforo, their thoughts as one.

"Aye Mark we like it well enough," Jamie replied. "But in enemy territory I never blind myself to the light. Should we be ambushed now I would be blind if I looked away into the night, and in that moment might my life be forfeit." Cristoforo said nothing, but nodded sagely.

"Well I never. That wouldn't occur to me in a month o' Sundays," Mark said.

"'Tis something you learn. It was John or Sir Robert taught me the trick, I remember not which, but it's stood me in good stead."

"My father took me out when I was a boy and taught me all the tricks of the night," Cristoforo added. "What to heed, when to be afraid, and that the darkness is your friend if you learn how to harness its power."

"Aye well, there I'm with 'ee. I like the dark and all its creatures, 'tis man that upsets me most," Mark chuckled quietly. Then Jamie's keen ears caught a sound and he silenced his companions with a gesture. He tilted his head, straining his ears once more for the sound. There it was again; a rustle of branch against branch, almost imperceptible, followed by a slight keening sound. All three men were on their feet immediately, shrugging off their cloaks. Cristoforo drew his two daggers, and Jamie reached down and pulled his sword silently from its wooden scabbard where it had lain at his side. Mark too had drawn his old sword ready for combat. In a barely audible whisper Jamie said: "Stay here, Mark, by the horses. It may be a trap to lure us away. Cristoforo, here in the shadow," he beckoned.

With that Jamie melted away into the night, a wraith bent on destruction. Then he heard it again – a high pitched keening sound, drawing him forward twenty yards or so from their camp. Every sense was now fully alert, straining to breaking point. He lifted each foot carefully, placing it so as not to snap a twig or rustle a bramble, convinced that he was being drawn into an ambush.

He stood perfectly still keeping his breathing low and shallow, flaring his nostrils to pick up any scent on the air, but all he could smell was crushed grass and sap. Then he heard it again, a mewling sound, high pitched and alien. He took two more paces with his senses fully alert, then he heard the rustle of undergrowth to his left. He span and crouched into a fighting stance, awaiting the charge. It never came, and his line of sight was too high. He looked down as a bramble bush moved a few feet in front of him. A pair of silver eyes looked up at him, belonging to a creature that emitted a low, coughing wine. A dog!

"By all that's holy you scared me witless, cur," he said. "Mark, Cristoforo, come! It's a dog, by the Lord Harry, a dog."

With a rustling of undergrowth the other two appeared, their weapons still at the ready. Cristoforo, like most Italians, was wary of dogs and held back. Mark laughed at the sight, for it was not so much a dog, more a large puppy, or so it seemed.

Jamie handed his sword to Mark before kneeling to the

ground. The dog did not move, but as Jamie reached forward, its top lip curled in a snarl and he made to snap. "Ho!" Jamie cried. "The animal still has spirit. Can you fetch me my cloak or gauntlets? I've no wish to lose a finger to this beast."

Mark returned with Jamie's thick gauntlets. Jamie slipped them on and moved once more towards the dog. "What ails the animal, Jamie?" Mark said. "I cannot see what is holding him."

"Nor I, yet he is stuck fast." With that the animal growled as bravely as it could and snapped at his hand once more. This time Jamie was ready and caught the jaws, clamping them shut. He attempted to pull the dog towards him, but its rear leg seemed stuck and the animal yelped through its closed jaws. Feeling further back, Jamie found a rope snare fastened hard around its rear leg that had rubbed the flesh raw, almost to the bone. The stick post had been gnawed through, but the trailing end had caught in the undergrowth and the animal was stuck fast.

"By the rood, a snare! Easy boy," Jamie soothed the dog. "I'll have you free in a trice." Jamie pulled his dagger from the sheath at his belt. Feeling back, he pulled at the cord and sliced it with the razor sharp blade of the dagger. The dog whimpered as the undergrowth pulled at the trap with the dog's leg still in it, and the cut rope slid free, stressing the wound further as it did so.

"Easy boy, I've got you." And with one sweeping movement he enveloped the animal in his cloak, scooping it up into a swaddling embrace to avoid the teeth. The dog tried to writhe free, but Jamie crushed him tighter to his chest and the dog gave in. Jamie felt the air go out of him. Marching back to the fire, he bade Mark help him as Cristoforo was none too keen to get close to the animal. Jamie held the dog while Mark examined the torn flesh of the wound.

"Cristo, have you any herbs or medicines to help the dog?" Mark asked. "He has a bad wound on his leg." Mark asked.

"Heal a dog? Madonna, life is strange in these isles. *Porca miseria,*" he swore and went off muttering to fetch his leather satchel. He returned with a bowl of water, and a clean cloth. Jamie held the dog tightly and spoke softly to it, trying to calm it while Mark bathed the wound and bound it with a clean cloth. In the light from the fire, they got a better look at the dog.

"Look," Jamie pointed. "He has whip marks across his back, and the poor beast has been beaten and starved by the look of his ribs."

"'E probably ran away to save hisself yet another beating. Some bastards are right cruel to animals, and no mistake," Mark said. "What is 'e? You said he were just a pup, but he's a big 'un."

"He's...no hang on...he's is a she. A bitch. A Wolfhound bitch, no less, and underneath the cuts and scars she's well-bred, I'm bound. Ye gods, but she'll be huge when she's fully grown."

"What, bigger still?" Cristoforo asked. "She is a lion, not a dog."

"Aye, they're a tough breed, and strong," Jamie said.

"What will you do with her now you've saved her? She can't walk like that."

"I'll not abandon her to her fate here. I shall keep her and take her with us. She'll be a good luck charm, you'll see." Jamie assured Cristoforo, for he'd had a soft spot for animals since the days of his youth.

Mark smiled and nodded, while Cristoforo shook his head, claiming that all Englishmen were mad as the dogs they coveted. Mark produced one of the borel sacks that had held food, and they carefully eased the struggling, petrified animal into it, preventing her from escaping. Thus swaddled, Jamie held her close and she relaxed, easing down by his side to sleep, where she whimpered and shivered from time to time.

The following morning, the true condition of the poor dog's plight was much more apparent, which angered Jamie and made him vow more strongly to keep her and make amends for his fellow man's ill-treatment of her.

"What will you do with a forest dog like that?" Cristoforo asked. "Do you really mean to take her with us?".

"Aye I do. She'll ride up with me 'til her leg heals, and then she can run like she was made to do. She's a hunting dog, made for long journeys, and when full grown she'll be good company."

So it was decided, and they made off towards Machynlleth with the bitch sat before Jamie on the cantle of his saddle. Mark looked across and swore that he saw a certain glimmer of pride begin to take shape in the dog's demeanour.

They pressed on into the Welsh heartland, passing through the outskirts of small towns and villages. The going became harder, with sharper inclines, higher hills and deeper valleys. The roadway was carved into rugged grey rock, rising above the trees into scrubby upland.

"I have not seen a country more given to offering perfect cover for an ambush since last I was in Scotland," Jamie observed, remembering a time that seemed long ago, but was only the previous winter. He recalled the snow on the pines outside Peebles, the cold of the night and the screams of the dying Scotsmen. "Ye gods, you can see why we face such a tough time conquering Glyndower and bringing him to heel. A small band of warriors could hold off, harass and kill many times their number and slip away to fight again, with no loss and little danger to their own numbers. I feel as though we are being watched. What say you, Cristoforo?"

"*Si*. I cannot shake it and it makes me uneasy. I want to be up there," he pointed to the crest of the valley several hundred feet above them. "I want to be up there looking down, not trapped down here in the valley looking up."

They were more alert now, tense to any danger that may suddenly make itself apparent. The going had slowed them down and they had no wish to approach Glyndower's stronghold at Machynlleth in the dark. They reached a fork in the road at the village of Llanbrynmair, once again camping outside the confines of the settlement. Here they chose a high position in a small copse under a rocky outcrop. It was secure and sheltered. They made a small fire at the base of the escarpment, ate a hot meal, then moved away to conceal their position for the night in the manner of hardened campaigners.

Mark was bemused, having never campaigned or been hunted. "Be it really necessary to move?"

"Aye," Jamie replied. "The heat from the embers, the smell of food and the disturbance will attract all manner of animals – including the Welsh. Our presence will carry on the wind. Up here we are safe and we'll make a second camp with no fire, in a position of vantage. No one will sneak up on us unawares here."

"I'd never of thought of it but it makes sense. You too, Cristo?"

"*Si*, changing camps has saved my life many a time," the Italian agreed. "Now where is that godforsaken *cane della foresta*?" he muttered, looking around for the dog, never feeling safe when he could not see her.

"She'll have gone snuffling for food, I'm bound. She limps less today and I think she is feeling a tad better." With that Jamie walked down the rough track, and sure enough the dog was sniffing around their previous camp. Stretching his lower lip to his teeth and pushing out his upper lip he whistled a high pitched sound, at which the dog raised her head and limped towards him, her ears pricked. "Come here girl, come here, forest dog," he whispered. She came up and brushed her head against his leg, glad of human contact that did not attempt to beat her. They walked back up the track to the hollow that concealed their camp.

"Ha, you found the faithful hound then?" Mark joked. "Come, forest dog." He held out a piece of stale bread that he had smeared with meat grease from their supper. The dog was suspicious at first, then the hunger overrode fear and she lunged up, grabbing it and slinking back. The bread disappeared in two gulps.

"Still hungry? That dog eats more than you, Mark." Cristoforo joked, as everyone acknowledged that Mark could eat his own weight in food at any mealtime. The three of them laughed at this, ribbing each other on their individual idiosyncrasies as the bond between them strengthened.

"Now, ere we travel further into this Godforsaken wilderness, we must have a plan and know what we're about. Perforce they will take our weapons, for I would be most surprised if they were not suspicious of us arriving at their camp unheralded. Yet I suspect that you will be free from suspicion, Cristo," Jamie commented, adopting Mark's shortening of Cristoforo's name. "So this is what we shall do if all goes as I foresee..." he continued with his thoughts on how they should proceed.

Their strategy settled, they made to retire for the night. The hound was once more secured within the borel sack, which she accepted with a better grace, curling up at Jamie's side for comfort and warmth. Twice in the night she pricked up her ears, waking Jamie from his light sleep and causing him to reach for the hilt of his sword. Yet nothing came to assault them, and in the end he fell back into a dreamless sleep.

Chapter Forty-Six

They broke camp early the following morning, heading out along the main road for Machynlleth. This time the dog allowed herself to be bundled up into the saddle by Mark without showing her teeth.

"Ho, Forest Dog, up you come." Jamie encouraged, and once back in her customary place she settled back against his torso.

"I swear she thinks she's a queen up there." Mark joked.

"Aye more's the like," Jamie agreed.

Cristoforo shook his head at the bond between man and animal. Horses he could understand – they had their uses – but dogs, if not fulfilling some kind of function such as hunting or scaring up game, were little more than an irritant and a waste of time.

They made their way onwards with Cristoforo and Jamie feeling that prickle behind their necks as they came closer to Machynlleth. The deep valley roads followed the valley and estuary of the River Dyfi as it wended its way towards the coastal village of Aberdyfi some miles further on.

They rounded a bend, and with two rock escarpments on either side they were forced by nature into a funnel. It was here that their way was barred. The road was patrolled by a guard of three men on the ground and two above with war bows which they could fire from concealment.

"Halt," the leader called out, first in a tongue that none could understand, then in English. Realising that they were not Welsh, he continued in the English tongue. "Where do you go and what is your business here?"

"We seek one Owen Glyndower, and were told that we may find him here."

"Why do you seek him? What is your business with the Prince of Wales?"

Jamie held his temper in check, for Prince Henry himself had been invested as the Prince of Wales, and to him it was a blasphemy to call another by that title. Yet France had been a good school and he moved on without showing emotion.

"We seek both sanctuary from the English and to offer our services to fight in your prince's cause against the false crown of England."

The leader of the guards looked to his colleagues in disgust, as though he had heard these words before. "Who are you and from where do you hail?" he snarled in an unfriendly manner.

"I am James de Grispere, a merchant's son and lately an esquire. My companions are Cristoforo Corio, formerly of Florence and Paris, and Mark of Cornwall, whom we met on the road and persuaded to join us."

"Huh, we'll see as to that. Dismount if you wish to go further."

The three looked at each other and shrugged. They dismounted but kept a firm hold of the reins of their horses and mules. Richard began to paw the ground and snort, picking up the atmosphere that all was not well. His nostrils flared and his ears became erect – signs that Jamie knew only too well. A guard went to grab the reins and Richard's teeth found his arm, snapping the bone before Jamie could stop it. The man howled in pain and reached for his dagger with his undamaged left arm.

"Harm my horse and I shall kill you, even if I die in the act. Forsooth, you should know better than to take a stallion so from its master." Jamie shouted, halting the man in mid-action as his own dagger appeared from nowhere, its point an inch from the guard's eye. The guards could not comprehend that the action had occurred so fast, and the guard who had tried to seize Richard stopped as though he had hit a wall. For a brief moment nobody moved, and the tension built as they all realised that one false move would end in bloodshed. Cristoforo had dropped into a crouching position, ready to pick and throw a dagger from his boot, and Mark brought his quarter-staff down, ready to break a head, for they knew what reaction the provocation would cause in Jamie. The leader, amazed at the speed of the travellers' reactions, raised a hand, cautioning all and breaking the tension, for they were so close that even the bowmen above would be hard put to miss their own men if they fired downwards into the group.

"Aye, Ap, you should. Proves he's a warhorse if naught else." The leader said. "Right, leave the mules and lead you own horses, but afore ye do I'll take your swords and daggers. If you be who you say you are, they will be returned." Jamie, Mark and Cristoforo unbuckled their belts reluctantly and handed their weapons over. Taking Jamie's sword, the leader admired it. "I hope that you lie, I envy you a fine weapon such as this." His mouth split in a humourless grin.

Jamie did not allow himself to be baited and shrugged nonchalantly, promising himself that he would drive his sword through the man's throat before their business was finished. Cristoforo had managed to disguise his movement of crouching as a reflex action to avoid the archers, and thus managed to keep his own arsenal of weapons minus his belt dagger. The other two were comforted by this small victory and knew Cristoforo would bide his time.

They were led directly into the township of Machynlleth, facing wary expressions from all they saw. This was no easy going, thriving township. The populace was on a full war footing, ready to fight at any time. It must, Jamie thought, be very wearying to be constantly on the alert for attack at any moment, every hour of the day. The main hall was situated in the centre of the town, and here they tied their horses to a rail and the wolfhound to a stand. No Norman build here, Jamie saw; instead the hall was a typical Saxon longhouse of single story construction with a high truss and a pitched roof running the whole length of the hall.

Two men at arms with spears and shields stood guard at the doorway and only parted as the gruff leader muttered something to them in incomprehensible Welsh. They were a surly pair of typical Celtic men, and their demeanours suggested that they would slit your throat as soon as look at you.

Jamie suddenly realised the immensity of their task: put a sword in his hand and he feared no man, for the battlefield was his forte. Yet here, flying under false colours, he was pitted against a different foe, realising his friends' lives could be forfeit. The responsibility weighed heavily upon him, and he knew he would have to consider their next strategy with the utmost care.

The inside of the hall was more spacious than it had appeared from the outside. Ancient, smoke blackened timbers supported the roof in a classic cruck construction, cantilevering out from the solid walls. The floor was of smooth stone flags lined with clean rushes. A pall of smoke hung in the air as there was insufficient ventilation to release all the warm air produced by a blazing brazier, despite the mid-summer conditions.

Despite its size, the huge hall was seemingly diminished by the large number of people within it. Welsh nobles and ladies were clustered in groups in a way that was very similar to the English court, yet the fashions were subtly different. There were fewer fine colours, and the darker hues reflected the more sombre nature of the company. Most of those present had darker hair that was typical of the Celtic race, and there were very few blond locks to be seen.

Conversation stalled to a few murmurings from the bustle of voices they had heard on first entering the hall. They were suddenly the centre of attention, yet all three held their heads proudly high, confident in who they were and refusing to be intimidated by a court of enemies. Members of the court stepped back, clearing a path for them to be brought before a figure who sat in a large carved oak chair. It was not a throne, but it was still as an imposing piece of furniture, with runes and figures carved into its sides and back.

Jamie had not known quite what to expect – a brigand maybe or a haughty peasant with ideas above his station – but he saw that there was a quality to the man before him, sure signs of breeding and grace to his face. His hair was not of the popular fashion; it was long and curled outwards at the ends over his shoulders, which were broad in the manner of a knight. The planes of his face were drawn and tight as one who had campaigned for much of his life and was literally worn to the bone with not a spare ounce of flesh left upon his body. There was a perceptive tightness about the mouth that bespoke of tragedy and loss replacing what once might have been a ready smile and a generous soul.

He would, Jamie estimated, be around fifty years old every year showed in his grey streaked hair and beard. When he spoke it was with a deep, rich voice more of a bard rather than a soldier. The accent was one Jamie had not heard before; one possibly more suited to song and poetry than plain speech.

"So, who do we have here?" he asked.

"My prince, these men are from England and seek to enlist in our cause, hating the English, so they say," answered the leader of the guard bowing ere he spoke.

"You are a man missing," Glyndower looked accusingly at the guard, "Where is Ieuan?"

"This man's horse bit him, sire," the guard pointed at Jamie, "and his arm is broken. The women tend to him as we speak,". Glyndower looked at Jamie, who could have sworn that a ghost of a smile threatened to surface in the older man's face.

"That will teach the impetuous fool how to deal with strange horses and even stranger men," he said. "Tell me of yourselves," he demanded.

Jamie repeated his story and the explanations that he had furnished to the men at the gateway to the town. Glyndower listened impassively, asking questions here and there to clarify a point or two of their stories.

"You say that you sought me out for my supposed connexions with Sir John Oldcastle, and were persuaded that this would aid your cause?" He asked sceptically.

"As you say, Prince Owen, for Lollardy is a perilous station to own to in the English court, and only Sir John seems to be immune," Jamie replied.

"I would doubt that, for it is a coil that is difficult to embrace in any circumstance. You, giant, how come you here? Didst slay a man in a wrestling match?" He spoke in English to Mark, who winced involuntarily at the charge, adding credence to his case yet meeting the prince's eyes unabashed. "And you are now a man who shrinks from life to flee such consequences as may be attached to his past actions. What of you, Italian? From whom do you hide?"

Cristoforo hid his anger with effort and shrugged. "I hide from no man – especially those who would do me harm and would unfairly judge me," he responded.

Glyndower laughed openly at this. "A good answer, Italian. So I ask you all this: why should I trust you? You come to me unbidden, and the opportunity is there ere my back is turned to murder me and secure the gratitude and forgiveness of the English as benefit for my death. How do I know that you speak the truth? How do I know that my life will not be forfeit?" He demanded.

At this point Cristoforo looked across to Jamie, aware that the next action would seal their fate one way or the other. It was time for a high risk strategy. Cristoforo turned back and waited.

"Well?" Glendower continued, "The proof awaits your actions."

Almost unheard Jamie hissed: "Vie!"

Cristoforo shrugged in that nonchalant way he had perfected, and in an apparent extension of the move he crouched, scooped and with blinding speed, flung a dagger at the beam above the Glyndower's head. It buried itself in the beam above the Welshman, vibrating with a twang as it exhausted the energy of the throw.

Glyndower, to his credit, realised that any movement of avoidance would have been futile and would also have appeared as a sign of weakness in his own court. He held himself rigid, his eyes meeting Cristoforo's. His bodyguards were taken by surprise, and drew their swords in grumbling confusion, shocked at the speed of the attack.

Jamie shrugged, his arms open. "He could have chosen which of your eyes to put that dagger through. If we'd wanted you dead, my lord prince, we would have achieved our aim. My companion is an assassin, but not of you."

The members of Glyndower's court seemed to release their

breath as one, muttering oaths at the travellers, yet Glyndower stilled the voices in his court by raising his hand to demand quiet. The dissenting voices were silenced as soon as they began.

"You are both brave and foolhardy," Glyndower said. "You walk into my court unannounced to show an old man his vulnerability. You are passing quick, Italian, and your skill is a sight to behold, for never have I seen the like. You make fools of my men to have allowed you to come bearing arms under my roof. I would punish them if your horse had not done so already." A few laughs rang out at this, and the captain of the guard cast his eyes to the floor. "Get out of my sight, man, and take your foolish companions with you," Glyndower shouted at his captain. "If such a thing happens again you will find yourself captain of shovelling shit from my court and nothing more. Go!" The captain bowed and scurried from the large room with his men.

"It was merely to prove a point, my lord prince," Cristoforo assured him. "I mean you no harm and am perhaps more skilled in the art of concealment than your men gave me credence for."

"If you make fools of my men you make a fool of me," Glyndower responded. Anger flared briefly in his eyes, and tension increased around the hall as everyone waited for his reaction. Then he laughed. "Yet you are audacious and have courage. I like that in a man. Come then, join us for food and wine and let me better understand your circumstance."

"My prince?" Cristoforo questioned, "a small favour?"

"Well?"

"May I retrieve my dagger?"

"Ha! Set to, boyo, set to. Would you like me to aid you?"

Cristoforo smiled and looked at Mark, who linked his hands. Mark knew exactly what was required, and moved closer to the prince, saying: "With your permission, my lord prince."

Owen Glyndower was puzzled, and moved to one side with

no inkling of what was to come. Mark stood just in front of the cross member where the dagger was buried in the wood, his hand forming a sling. Cristoforo skipped forward and sprang into the cradle of his hands, at which Mark boosted him upwards as though he were a child. Cristoforo was launched high into the air. He plucked the dagger free and somersaulted backwards in an extravagant display of acrobatics, landing lightly on his feet as he touched the ground. He bowed deeply to add to the drama, sweeping his arm wide. The hand, with the dagger at its point, described an arc before Glyndower, proving again that he could have killed him where he sat. Glyndower remained motionless, his eyes once more never leaving Cristoforo's. After a few seconds he smiled and applauded Cristoforo's antics.

"If you fight as well as you perform, we shall beat the English with ease," he declared. There were smiles at this around the room and any remaining tension ebbed away. Jamie kept his face impassive. He knew underneath that nothing had changed and they would still be watched warily for a while, until their loyalty had been proved in the heat of battle against his kinsmen.

Glyndower sent men to stable their horses, and the dog was brought in to meet the dogs of the court, who skulked hither and yon, seeking scraps or attention as their owners settled down to eat at long trestle tables, which servants proceeded to fill with thick cuts of meat. The food was plentiful yet plain, bearing none of the rich sauces favoured by the English court.

Seated near the prince was a gaunt man who looked as though he had lived through hard times. A grey pallor coloured his features, and there was a wary look to his eyes. Glyndower introduced him, saying: "This is another of your countrymen who has come to my aid. Adam Usk, esquire James de Grispere and his companions Cristoforo Corio and Mark of Cornwall."

"At your service, sir." Jamie offered. "Are you lately of England or do you stay here for a longer period?" *So this was the infamous English spy who trod a fine line for both sides,* Jamie thought. *He looks like a scared ferret. Whatever Whittington says, he will bear watching and I'll trust no one with my life here.*

"I have abided here for some years. Are you from court, for I have not heard your name ere now?"

The conversation went back and forth, with nothing missed by the keen eyes of Glyndower, who it seemed noted, every glance and nuance of meaning. Once the meal was over the three were shown to their quarters by a soldier of Glyndower's meiny. The dog jumped to its feet and followed Jamie. Glyndower himself stayed in the hall to discuss other plans with his captains. He called Usk back: "Have enquiries made in court, for I trust no one who arrives here unannounced. Mayhap I am too suspicions, yet I fear treachery at every turn. The Scots envoys arrive soon, and we needs must we be wary."

"Indeed, my lord prince. I think you are wise. De Grispere is glib and canny, yet I know nothing of him nor of his past. Do you wish me to spy here as well?"

"No, for I have put in place a course of action that will secure knowledge for myself. De Grispere is too aware. There is a more subtle way to storm that fortification, and it plays forth as we speak."

Chapter Forty-Seven

"Cross now, Mark. Yes, that's it, now twist and release," Jamie instructed. "It is as much about timing as strength. You tell me wrestling is the same, not just a matter of brute strength but skill and how it is applied. Well, apply now the skills I am trying to teach you. Despite your strength I will beat you every time because the angle for me is provident. Again," he demanded, wielding the practice sword before Mark's eyes.

"You be worse'n my own father," Mark moaned at Jamie, taking a stance again, holding his blade at cross guard. He had for once forsaken his quarterstaff and forced himself to put in more sword practice to appease Jamie.

The wolfhound puppy had become Jamie's dog, and followed him everywhere. She now sat watching the practice, having had to be restrained at first, perceiving that her master was in peril. She lay down, still wary, with her head between her huge paws, eyes missing nothing, a thin cord securing her loosely to a post, tied at the other end to a new collar.

They had settled down to a meal with the Welsh court on that first day, and all had appeared to be going to plan. Lodgings had been provided, and more importantly their weapons had been returned to them.

Mark had struck up a friendship with a young local widow woman named Amwen, whose husband had died of the flux a year before. All appeared to be going well until the second week, when a raiding party led by one of Glyndower's knights, Huw of Gwyneth, returned victorious to Machynlleth.

He rode into the town from the south as Jamie and others were practising their sword play. They broke from their labours in the harsh sunshine to seek shade and relieve their thirst as the first sounds of the war band were heard to joyous greetings. The welcoming committee included Prince Owen himself, who had been visiting the latest fortifications on the east road.

The practice area was behind the main hall on a small square of flatted ground that had been set aside for the purpose. They were for the most part hidden from view when they heard the noise of the returning war band. Two of the Welshmen moved off to greet the warriors and Jamie, always curious, followed a little behind to take in the sight, yet remaining at a distance from the proceedings. The hound had slipped her leash and stood by his side rubbing against him, whining.

"All right, Forest Dog, all right." He whispered as he petted her, watching the war band's entrance into the town.

The band comprised about fifteen men, all mounted on shaggy Welsh ponies. They were well armed and tough looking, their skin drawn tight across their faces and tanned to the colour of old leather. All wore their hair long down their necks, and their helmets were toggled to their saddles. Their war bows were held in long sheaths attached to the cantles. Two of the men were wrapped in bloody bandages, and as he watched Jamie saw one fall from the saddle in exhaustion, to be deftly caught by two women who rushed forward before he hit the floor.

Despite this, their attitude appeared triumphant and the pack mules trailing behind were laden with plunder. Arms, cloth and chattels hung from the backs of the beasts. The greetings and comments were all in Welsh and therefore incomprehensible to Jamie, or to Mark and Cristoforo who had appeared at his side to watch the parade.

"They look to have been successful," Cristoforo commented wryly.

"I wonder how many poor English souls they've killed?" Jamie asked rhetorically, thinking back to the Scottish borders and the carnage he had witnessed there against his countrymen. He knew he would have to hide these thoughts and curb his temper if they were to survive.

Mark looked across at him and spoke quietly: "Aye, I've seen a border raid such as this, and lost a cousin and his family to it. Whoreson Welsh," he muttered.

"Careful Mark. Amwen, good day to you. How do you today?"

Mark was startled and looked down to see dark brown wavy tresses framing a tanned face, with deep blue eyes and a mouth filled with tiny teeth as she smiled up at him. She inserted herself beneath his huge arm, then sprang back quickly, wrinkling her nose. She spoke only a little halting English, yet the meaning of her flurry of Welsh was clearly comprehensible. The other two men laughed: "I don't think she likes honest sweat, Mark lad, mayhap you need a wash," Jamie said

"Yes," she added, her accent thick and lilting. "a wash. Ugh!"

Their banter was disturbed as Owen ap Glyndower came to embrace the newcomer, clapping him on the shoulders. Then after talking for a few minutes he spotted Jamie and the others. Changing to French, he continued. "Huw, let me introduce you to our new men at arms."

A Knight and a Spy 1410

The leader of the war band looked first at Prince Owen then at the three newcomers. Jamie saw the slant to his cruel eyes deepen, and there was no friendliness evident. The scar on his upper lip from a past encounter gave his mouth a slight sneer in repose, heightening his sinister appearance. Jamie decided that he did not like the man, and the feeling appeared to be mutual.

With the introductions made, Jamie and the other two bowed as Glyndower began to explain how they came to be in camp. Yet he was cut short by a growl from Jamie's side. The Forest Dog's lip curled upwards in a snarling growl as she bared her teeth.

"What?" cried Huw. "My dog, you've got my dog. Where did you find the whelp skulking? I lost her ere we went raiding, as you may recall, Lord Owain. Come here, damn you, cur." he cursed, reaching to grab the hound.

Jamie had not understood the words, but the intent was evident. He grabbed Huw's wrist before he could lay a hand on the wolfhound.

"No! Forest is mine," he answered coldly. "We found her on the road in the Forest, and so is she named."

"Unhand me, or by the cross I'll skewer you!" Huw cried, pulling free his dagger. Prince Owen pushed the arm upwards. "No, Huw. They came to aid us, not to be killed by you." He ordered, fixing his eyes upon Jamie. "Where did you find this dog?"

"Outside Worcester, near Abberley," he lied, pushing his own dagger back into its sheath, using the first place he could think of. The battle there stuck in his mind.

"Well that is a goodly distance, and you have a likely cause to claim ownership. I see this easily settled. Amwen, bring the hound hither."

Amwen, who had developed a soft spot for the young dog,

341

gently bade it follow her to the spot indicated by the prince. Forest followed her, hiding behind her legs and growling quietly.

"Huw there, Jamie there." Glyndower indicated two places some yards away on opposite sides of the dog.

"The answer is simple. Amwen, move away. You two, call to the dog in whatever name you have. Jamie has only known her a week by his reckoning. You Huw, since birth, but let the dog itself decide. Amwen, fall back now." The Welshwoman did so, and the wolfhound shivered at her possible fate.

"Call her as you will, messires." Glyndower ordered.

Both men called her by the name they had given her. The frightened puppy looked one way and the other, then kindness won. At the words: "Come Forest Dog", she sprang forward to Jamie and away from Huw's curses. Jamie could not resist looking up with a smile of triumph upon his face which he was unable to conceal. Huw spat at the dog. The spittle hit her coat and he swore in Welsh. "This is not over, Englishman," he said. "We shall have our reckoning, you and me."

Despite encouragement from the prince, he strode off to his band.

"Beware, James," Glyndower said. "I love him as I would a brother, yet he has a fierce temper and will not account this well. I cannot afford you any protection on his account. I have known him years and you only a few minutes. I owe him much and he is a loyal captain of my guard."

"I understand, my prince, and I will sleep lightly."

"Do that. I wish no discord on this matter, but be sure where my opinion lies," He looked Jamie squarely in the eye to drive home his point. He then turned abruptly and left to reconcile his estate with Huw. In the background, Cristoforo surreptitiously slid his dagger back into his boot top and Mark relaxed hold on his staff.

Huw Shot Jamie a final look over his shoulder, and it spoke volumes. There was pure malice in that look, he had been belittled in his eyes by a dog that was once his, and worse by a strange Englishman. Jamie knew he would not rest until both had been made to pay.

Chapter Forty-Eight

Hereford.

"So, three men, you say?"

"Aye, an English esquire named James de Grispere, and a huge man of Cornwall – a wrestler. Now I don't for certain sure if'n 'e be of the court or no. Master Usk 'as sent a man to Cornwall to trace 'im there. The third be a strange one, an Italian of someplace called Florence or such. Seems to be in close friendship with the esquire."

Like most men of reasonable intelligence who could not read and write, Harold could remember facts and details well, and he stored them away in his memory to recall when he returned to London. The men spoke in English, yet Arthwes – the man providing the information – was half Welsh, being of an English father and Welsh mother. He was wary of betraying his Welsh lineage, which could result in persecution and suspicion at best, for the Welsh were banned from England and could hold no land or rights, such was their low station in the eyes of the English, who hated them to a man.

"You say they came through Worcester and travelled the

road from London?" Harold asked. "Well someone will have seen them without doubt. This Cornishman, when did they meet him on the road?"

"I know not," Arthwes replied. "Mayhap they met in London an' chose to travel together. Oi'll find what I can assemble of their station an' background, an' I will report it back to master Usk for him to dissemble."

"Right, but now I must away back to my lord Oldcastle's manor and thence to London on the morrow. I will return hence in a sennight and meet you here on the noon," Harold offered.

In Machynlleth, Cristoforo was complaining about the weather. "Ye gods, does it stifle all the time in Wales?" he moaned, slapping his face and exposed skin against the swarm of gnats and midges that bit him at every opportunity. They floated in pillars surrounding the camps and the town, becoming worse once anyone was foolish enough to enter the sea of bracken and coarse undergrowth surrounding the valleys.

"You should try visiting Scotland," Jamie responded, raising laughter from the surrounding Welshmen.

"I thought it hot in Italy, Cristo, be it not?" Mark asked.

"It is, with a dry heat that leaves you mellow and content. Italy does not buzz with base-born insects that hate me with a vengeance that makes a Saracen seem forgiving. I swear by the almighty I'll learn to swim and dive into the river."

"You cannot swim?" asked Collen, one of the knights of Glyndower's court with whom Cristoforo had struck up a friendship in the weeks that had passed since they had entered his service. Both favoured the dagger as a weapon and enjoyed tracking off across country scouting together. They had sparred with each other using wooden daggers, each learning a trick or two from the other.

Mark found the whole idea of Cristoforo's terror of water hilarious, considering that he feared nothing else. "Aye, 'tis passing strange for he be afraid of nought else but God's life-giving water."

"*Madonna*, had God wished me to swim, he would have given me fins."

"I'd have thought with hand speed like yours you'd have swotted all these flies ere they could land," Collen continued. The backhanded compliment reflected the fact that he had never seen the like of the Italian's reaction time. However, Cristoforo had deliberately held back from showing him the falchion, neglecting to wear it for fear of detection as he only wore a shirt in the heat and losing the potential advantage should a propitious moment come to use it. Collen continued, "fear not, the lower the little bastards come, especially close to like this, means rain is coming. We'll 'ave a storm soon, mark me. 'Twill be good 'un and all, for I've never seen an August like it, so close and humid."

"That will be a relief, for I never thought I'd see the day when I prayed for rain."

At this statement there were more ribald comments and ribbing from the Welsh. Jamie was pleased they were fitting in well and the suspicion that initially surrounded them was beginning to dissipate. Yet there remained the spectre of Huw of Gwynedd. When sober, he shot fierce scowls in Jamie's direction, but twice now when in his cups, he had made scathing remarks and veiled threats that caused Jamie to bite his tongue. Everyone knew that a moment would come when the matter would be settled with swords rather than words, and that it was a matter of when, not if.

That evening it arrived.

The evening meal had started well, with ale and mead flowing with convivial company added to by the arrival of two of Owen ap Glyndower's captains including the famous Black Rhys.

"Who is that?" Jamie asked of Collen as a flamboyant figure entered the hall. He was broad of shoulder and had flowing black hair, which he wore long, and a generous black beard that was just starting to fleck with streaks of grey. The man wore a long red cloak and his gambeson bore the heraldic crest of a black raven on a red background. He greeted many with laughter and shook many hands ere he made his way to Glyndower's great chair.

"That? He is my lord Rhys Ddu, or in English, Black Rhys. He is Prince Owain's main captain and commander of arms. He is from Cardigan and was once sheriff there. The English have put a substantial price upon his head, for he has sent many of their knights to meet their maker. He is fearless in battle and always at the van."

"He seems a goodly knight, and well made for certes. I have not seen his like – other than in my friend Mark." Jamie commented at the larger than life figure dominating the hall.

"Aye, and he likes to wrestle too when he is of a mind."

Mark heard those words and was curious. He had gone a few rounds with the men of Glyndower's camp and much to their chagrin had beaten them all with little effort. It wasn't just his strength, it was the ability he had to read a man and see what moves he would make before he knew himself what he would do.

"Why does he come now, is there a special event to celebrate?"

Collen looked slightly askance at the question, but shrugged, deciding that it was normal curiosity. "With the price on his head he moves around a good deal, like the prince himself. Yet important matters must be discussed I fear. Tomorrow we break camp and move on, for we've tarried here too long." He hesitated and Jamie felt there was more to be said, yet asked nothing further for he knew when to press and when to leave well alone.

They watched as the black haired figure moved forward to embrace Glyndower as an equal, and a long conversation in Welsh ensued. Then turning to greet others, the prince offered an introduction to the three newcomers, who greeted the captain in turn. When Jamie was mentioned, two words floated across the hall at his name that he was meant to hear: "*lleidr cŵn!*"

Jamie knew not what the words meant but he surmised that they were an insult, for they had been spoken by Huw of Gwynedd. He reddened at the words. "What did he say?" he demanded of Collen. The warrior looked away and then down before finally raising his eyes and answering Jamie's question: "Dog thief."

Jamie's face froze into a hard mask as the battle madness rose within him. Like an alcoholic smelling his first whisky after a period of sobriety, he recognised the signs in himself. He wanted it, he welcomed it, he needed combat. Jamie's mouth set into a tight-lipped grin that had no humour in it whatsoever. Looking directly at Huw he said, "better to be a thief that than a beater of dogs, women and children, for that is all you could manage."

Collen looked up at him aghast: "Do you know what you are doing, man, for Huw is fierce and a champion?"

"Translate for me. Tell him!"

Collen repeated the words in Welsh so that the meaning could be clear. Everyone heard them, and looked from one man to the other. Huw jumped to his feet, spilling his wine. "No man calls me that! I claim the right, my prince, I claim the right. His life will be forfeit, by Gods Holy body it will." he screamed. By Jamie's side Forest looked up pitifully and whined sensing that all was not well.

"Do you know what you have done, lad?" Owen ap Glyndower explained. "You can only retreat by apologising and mayhap returning the dog. For I warn you, he will kill you. It will be single combat on foot, the old way. No armour, just a sword. Do you stand?"

"I stand. Let us do it now, for he needs a lesson in manners." Jamie retorted, deliberately baiting the Welsh warrior, whom he knew would understand his words. Rhys Ddu actually laughed, a big bellied sound, for he loved nothing more than to watch a good fight – except perhaps to be in the thick of the fight himself.

"Well go to boys, go to. Clear the tables, make space now, for we'll have our sport," Rhys shouted with glee.

The tables were cleared to form a rectangular arena. Cristoforo came behind Jamie bearing his sword, which he had fetched from their hut.

"Kill the whoreson Welsh bastard," he urged in Latin. "Yet watch, for he will charge through I feel, using his strength and low centre to best you."

Jamie nodded, all his concentration on the fight and watching his enemy, fighting the rise of adrenalin, he did not want his muscles to seize. He was wearing nothing save a linen shirt and breeches, and these he kept in place. He pulled the sword from its scabbard and twirled it from his wrist, feeling the perfect balance.

"Thank you, Cristoforo. Mark, keep a hold on Forest. I don't want her harmed and she'll like as not attack this bastard as soon as we start."

"Aye, Jamie, fear not," Mark leashed her, gripping the cord tightly.

As Huw readied himself, Black Rhys regarded Jamie carefully. Then he said as an aside to Huw, "Watch him, Huw, there is something here I do not like."

"Him?" Huw snorted in disbelief. "That snot nosed whelp? I was killing Englishmen afore he was pupped."

Black Rhys was not sure. He marked Jamie's stance and attitude, noting that there was not an ounce of fear in him, despite the fact that he was in the midst of an enemy camp with Welshmen all around him. He was pitched against an older, more experienced and battle hardened knight, yet he demurred not even a little. He was, Rhys knew, either exceptionally skilled or full of boastful self-belief. They would soon find out. Both men came forward with no protective arms or gambeson, just the shirts on their backs and the hatred in their hearts.

Glyndower stood between them. "You know that this be to the death. Honour has been impugned by both of you, now let this be resolved! When I signal, you start."

Jamie felt it rise then, and he could not have stopped it if he'd tried. The battle lust rose in him; he wanted to kill with no mercy; he wanted the carnage to commence.

"Fight!" Glyndower cried.

Fighting without armour was different, as Jamie knew. This was how his training had started, with John in the yard behind his house for as long as he could remember. Wooden swords then, and many was the time he had come in with welts on his arms and back, for John spared him nothing. Later, as he put more power into the strikes he found that even a wooden sword could cause cuts and lacerations. Now it had become second nature. There was no thought, he just *was*; he became a machine brought to life to deal death with a sword.

They crossed twice, each testing the other, and Jamie found

Huw's weakness: he disliked the right cross guard attack from low down. Jamie saw something flicker in Huw's eyes: *was it fear?* He hoped so.

They disengaged, circling, Huw had a high guard, holding the pommel of his sword by his face two handed. It was an invitation to attack and a trap Jamie knew only too well. He lurched up with the point from a low guard crossing the centre line, and Huw's blade flashed down to meet the cross guard of Jamie's sword. Jamie twisted left and stamped hard with his foot, putting power into the block. Grabbing a handful of Huw's hair he pulled hard, driving the boss of the pommel into his face as he flew past. The move had been exceptionally fast and unexpected, and to those watching it seemed that an unseen ghost had grabbed Huw and pulled him by strings.

Blood gushed from a gash on his right cheek, colouring his chest red. He raised a hand to check the wound, astounded that someone could have caught him so. Jamie stood waiting, his sword in high guard, point backwards. Huw's point flicked out at his eyes, and Jamie retreated one step and rotated his wrists, meeting his opponent's sword halfway down the blade. He stepped forward and rotated his wrists again through one hundred and eighty degrees, slashing inwards towards Huw's face. Huw barely recovered, driving his right arm upwards with his blade above him.

Again Jamie's wrist rotated as he performed a perfect disengage. His sword was a bright arc of steel as he brought it round in a semicircle, moving under Huw's raised guard and slicing hard into his ribs, slicing back to meet the last attempt by Huw to cut through his defence as he crumpled to the floor with his side in tatters. Jamie did not think. There was no mercy in him the red mist descended as he drove the point down and straight through Huw's exposed chest. With final heave of breath, Huw was dead. Jamie withdrew the blade, panting a little from exertion.

The court had expected a match of sorts, not the slaughter of one of their champions in less than a minute. Their minds reeled; they had seen Huw in battle, a crazed madman who was afraid of nothing, slaughtering twice his number. Yet in this simple, brutal combat he had been bettered with apparent ease and with a speed of movement that far outclassed his own.

"By the Gods," Rhys Ddu exclaimed, "I saw it, yet I do not believe it. He dispatched Huw without pausing to draw breath. Look at him! He hasn't even broken a sweat. Who are you, boyo, who are you?" He exchanged glances with Prince Owen, whose incredulous expression mirrored his own.

Gradually the court returned to life, still unsure that their eyes had not deceived them. Wailing, Huw's wife ran forward and dropped to her knees beside her dead husband. Jamie looked on, his eyes still hard. He then turned back to Cristoforo and Mark, who had Amwen by his side. Jamie could not read the expression upon her face. Her hands clasped Mark's arm so tightly that her fingers had turned white.

She muttered in Welsh: "And I looked, and beheld a pale horse! And his name that sat on him was Death, and Hades followed him. And they were given authority of the earth, to kill with a sword."

Cristoforo nodded. To his eyes it was a deed well done, yet he still marvelled at his friend's skill. He performed to his eyes with the precision of a chirurgeon.

Mark said, "Like me in a wrestling match, you knew what you were going to do within two moves, did you not?"

"I believe so – yet I don't think, I just am. The opening comes. I take it and react. I cannot tell you how," he answered.

Chapter Forty-Nine

Two days after the duel, Glyndower's court was still awhirl with rumours and everyone was giving Jamie a wide berth.

"Why do I have the feeling that this matter is not settled?" he asked of Cristoforo, absentmindedly stroking Forest's ears as she sat beside him in blissful contentment.

"It is not and never will be. The prince will keep you close now, for despite your prowess he will be wary of having someone as lethal as you in his camp..." Cristoforo let the comment hang in the air.

Jamie shrugged and changed the subject. "This gathering of captains and forces bodes ill for us, yet I cannot see what may have altered. Mark has no intelligence that may help, for Amwen is a clam who hears all yet dispenses no wisdom. I fear for him that he may fall too deeply for her."

"I too, for I would not wish to lose him here. I share your belief in her sorcery, for she has cast a spell on our giant and sways him this way and that. Yet I trust her not."

"Nor I. Perforce I have turned my mind to the barrier to our plan that may benefit both Mark and our cause. When we have news to send back to Sir Richard Grey, how should we do it? Whichever one of us leaves the camp will be suspected and overridden before he can make Stokesay castle, and will alert the Welsh that we are spies. To that end I have a plan that may serve both problems: to untwine Mark and leave us free from suspicion."

"How so?" Cristoforo asked, puzzled.

Jamie explained how and when he should start to play a part which he had in mind.

The following morning, Owen was greeted by a newcomer who was shown quietly into the hall.

"What news have you for me, Arthwes, for our time grows perilous and I pray that it be good?"

"I have news, my lord prince, yet I know not whether good or ill. Harold has lately returned from London where he sought answers to questions." At which Arthwes looked sideways at Adam Usk, his spymaster.

"Proceed, man, and fear not. You must pass on all, exactly as you told me. For the truer the tale the fewer that tell of it."

"As you command, my lord. Harold sought the council of Sir John Oldcastle, who was latterly at court. It seems there was falling out between James de Grispere and the tradition of the church. He was ostracised, banished on pain of death for views of Lollardy, and Sir John was advised by the prince himself that he could not tolerate such views at court. To wit, I have a missive written by Sir John for your eyes, but fear not for it is neither addressed nor signed for fear of interception. Harold said he believed that you would comprehend the meaning, my prince."

Glyndower tore open the seal and read the cryptic script. He reread it to be sure of its intent.

"It confirms that de Grispere was at court and well regarded, yet seems to have become bound by Oldcastle's religious views by default. T'would appear he was given little choice: to leave or be burned ere his custom was made public. He has been scorned by the prince and lost his love. The Italian was de Grispere's father's servant, and arrived under circumstances most strange, that are shrouded in mystery." He paused, looking into the mid distance, as if to grasp the full import of the words, seeking to read between the lines. "So far the intelligence given bears out well with the story we have been told. Despite all, we have no news or intelligence of Mark of Cornwall, for Sir John knows aught of his existence. We shall see what we may learn from Bodmin, whence he claims to hail.

Perforce we have nothing to dissuade us from the facts put forward by de Grispere and his companions, yet still I wonder. Needs must that we accept the facts such as they are and sleep with one eye open, for I never thought I'd see the day that Huw would be so easily dismissed."

"Huw is dead?" Arthwes cried in surprise.

"He is indeed. He forced a dual upon de Grispere over a hound of all things, which became a matter of honour. Forsooth it was not the manner of the circumstance that chills me so, but the manner of his passing, for 'twas less a match than an execution. Poor Huw, despite being the challenger, stood not a chance in hell."

"De Grispere must be passing fair with a sword, then, for Huw was as fierce a warrior as ever I did see, and was never bested on the field of battle."

"Amen to that, yet he met his match here and no mistake. Now needs must we make haste to meet our lords from Scotland, for they arrive by the morning tide at Aberdyfi. I would that we could meet with them and form an alliance to drive the English back and raise Wales as a mighty princedom once more.

"We move at first light, for I have tarried here too long and fear a surprise attack. Come, let us rally and move forward on the morrow." Glyndower straightened from his ornate chair and stretched, easing old bones and muscles, suddenly aware of the toll that constant roaming and worry placed upon him.

Arthwes left the hall and returned to his cot, still aghast at the news of Huw's demise.

A short while later, Jamie was called to an audience with Glyndower and advised that he would join the party travelling to Aberdyfi the next morning. Returning to his cot Jamie sought the company of Mark and Cristoforo.

"Glyndower's army travels on the morrow for Aberdyfi. I know not what the cause, yet I am summoned to attend," he advised his friends.

"We shall be ready, Jamie. What time do we depart?" Mark asked.

"Ah no, you mistake me, it is just I who shall accompany Glyndower and his party." he stated to the concern of his companions.

"What, is it a trap?" Cristoforo demanded.

"No I think not. I believe it is a council of war to decide the next step in the campaign against the English. A coming of captains and knights has been ordained, together with an envoy from Scotland, I am told. Only battle leaders and knights are to be present."

"Should you wish I can follow and aid your escape if it proves to be a trap." Cristoforo offered.

"Nay, though good your offer may be, I fear not a trap. That will come later I perceive, when they put me in the van to try my mettle and loyalty to their cause."

Cristoforo was not to be easily dissuaded. "Yet I fear for you, for to divide us is to defeat us."

"Fear not, Cristoforo, all be well. This is but a test. Later the challenge will come. Stick fast here and learn all you can whilst I'm away."

The following morning Glydower's army fell quickly into place, captains rallying troops ready for the march along the line of the river Dyfi that would take them to the fishing village of Aberdyfi. Sweethearts and wives lined the roadside in farewell, and Jamie bade goodbye to Mark and Cristoforo, with Forest whining as her master left without her.

The gentle summer rain had persisted, keeping a low mist about the area. Brief squalls swept in from the sea, soaking the party as it made its way westwards. The road they followed was an old one, originally forged by the Romans to gain access to the western port at the estuary of the river Dyfi. It wound its way along the shore below grey cliffs that were shot with shards of yellow, bronze and ochre as metal ores showed through the rock in streaks of colour.

The party followed the north side of the estuary, and not for the first time Jamie realised how easy it would be to hold off an army many times the size of the defenders simply by blockading the road. He could see why it had been so difficult to hunt Glyndower in his homeland and gain a decisive victory. It was only a short ten mile journey, and as they rounded the last of the twists and turns of the Dyfi, they crested a slight rise and saw the village below them. It was set out in a sweeping crescent, away from the flat beaches and sculpted sand dunes swathed with long grasses that swayed in the gentle breeze.

"It is beautiful, even in the rain," Jamie enthused to no one in particular. It was Collen at his side who answered.

"Aye it is. Many's the time I've sat and fished here, in a boat offshore. 'Tis even fairer when the sunshine's out, mind."

They passed down into the village, taking a single sweeping road that followed the curve of the seashore. One or two tracks cut up into the hills, giving access in-land, where a few cottages had been built on the slopes, offering stunning views across the bay and out to sea.

The tide was retreating, and for the fun of it some of the men, including Jamie, proceeded down to the wide sandy beach to give their horses a run. Richard had never seen the sea, nor been on sand like this, and with the salt smell, wind and rain Jamie was expecting some dissent on his behalf. He was not disappointed. Richard shivered, his whole body trembling. He snorted at the sea, planted all four legs and locked stock still as if braced against an unseen enemy. Jamie urged him with leg pressure and he sidled, half passed, dropped his shoulder and as the other horses leapt forward to a canter he threw his head up in a twist that in the early days would have head-butted Jamie and doubtless broken his nose. Now he was ready for it, and he slipped to the side, knowing what was coming next: the quarter muscles bunched, torqueing up power that was released with a sudden surge as Richard shot forward. The stallion hated to be beaten, and the sight of a group of horses ahead of him over-rode the fear of the unknown and reminded him that he loved to run. Within a few strides the magnificent chestnut had caught the tail end of the group, and with tears streaming from his eyes, Jamie laughed at the sheer exhilaration of flying on the wind as they passed the leaders. The harbour jetty was two hundred yards off and Jamie shouted out a variation of the old challenge: "Last to the jetty buys the ale!"

Yet he nearly lost, for as he approached the jetty he saw that boats had been pulled up on the shore, one of which had a blue pennant fluttering from the mast head. Richard swerved violently and bethought it funny to unseat his master, who kicked free his stirrups and rolled out whilst Richard slid in the sand and waited for him. Jamie cursed, then saw the fast approaching horsemen, grabbed the cantle and bounded back up into the saddle. Without any urging Richard was off, the blue flag forgotten. Even before Jamie had regained his stirrups they were at full gallop again within a few strides. The others caught him by the jetty and made ribald comments at his expense: "What ails you, Englishman, can't you sit a horse?" one of them mocked.

"Aye, by the rood it appears not. The old goat will have his fun. In aught but combat he fears blue, I know not why. Once in battle he cares of nothing except to fight, and does that right well. Yet here abroad and in play, he is a nightmare," Jamie explained. "But even as I was unseated, I recovered and remounted and still managed to beat you all, did I not?"

They laughed, offering similar stories of errant horses they had known, and made for the inn on the shorefront, where they awaited Glyndower and his captains, who had resisted the urge to race their horses. There was much mirth at Jamie's expense, and it served to break the tension that had pervaded since the fight with Huw. For a short while Jamie relaxed and almost forgot he was amongst the enemy. Then it all changed.

Two figures came out of the inn bearing tankards of ale. They were wearing plaid tartan and kilts, with bonnets on their heads with a feather cast at a jaunty angle. They spoke in French, yet the accent was unmistakable, straight from across the border Jamie knew so well. The Scots had arrived. They had no armour, Jamie noted, but long dirks sat at their waists and they had a wary look to their eyes. Both had a hard-eyed look about them, despite the humour of their comments.

"Yon man, master of the horse, I see." They joked, having witnessed Jamie's fall.

"Aye, but he sprang back up right lively. Credit to him," the taller man said. "Yon's a bonny stallion. I've not seen the like, and fast too, we saw."

Jamie replied in kind, and bore the ribbing with equanimity.

They were introduced as Patrick of Laidlaw and Corin of Dumfries: merchants, Jamie was told, on business from Scotland to trade for wool. Jamie smiled and accepted the obvious lie. He looked closely at the men and saw scars on their knuckles and arms that were similar to his own sword marks. They had a heft about the shoulders that was not of a woolsack's making.

He knew that he would unfortunately not be party to the talks that were to ensue between Glyndower and the two Scotsmen, yet he wished with all his heart that he could be. *Merchants? By the rood, I think not.* Jamie thought: *So Sir Richard had the right of it, the Scots are in league with the Welsh, and the French are behind it for sure.*

The main body of the party moved away to a private room bespoke by Glyndower and his captains. They alone were to be privy to the conversation between the Scotsmen and the Welsh. There was no opportunity to overhear the discussions. For hours men wandered the shore or visited the only other inn in the village at the furthest end, away from the direction from which they had come. Then Jamie had an idea. Calling at the main taproom of the inn, he procured a flagon of ale and secured it to Richard's saddle. The Scottish delegation would have travelled by boat; he would find which one and engage in amiable conversation with the owner. Looking towards the main pier he spotted one craft that stood out by its difference in design and seagoing ability. It was larger than the other boats in evidence, and Jamie wandered down to seek out its crew. The captain was absent when he called aboard for any sign of life, but he was met by a youth who was annoyed at being left aboard by the captain and the two other crew members, who had both been to the inn to partake of ale.

"Ahoy the ship." he called in French as the common language. He had a rudimentary knowledge of Gaelic, but he did not want the man to know.

A deck hand appeared from below coiling a rope as he walked up to Jamie. "Aye, what're ye wantin'?" he replied.

"The captain said if I was exercising my horse to bring this for ye."

"Did 'e by God? Well bless 'im for a heathen. I find the French difficult, so do you ken English?"

Jamie smiled, a godsend indeed. "Aye, for 'tis spoken a good deal now and they use me for such trips to that heathen land on account of my ability with the tongue."

Untying the flagon, Jamie proceeded to glean what information he could from the suddenly garrulous shipmate, whose name he found was Ailig. The words came tumbling out as he grumbled about the Scottish Lords who had travelled with them. *So they are not merchants*, Jamie thought, and pieces of the puzzle began to come together. With more discourse he was nearly undone and had to cough over his ale to hide his reaction as Ailig continued: "'Twas all because a man came from France – an Englishman mind, and we dropped him at Liverpool, horse an all, for he was a knight. I hate horses aboard, they're bad luck, but he would have none of it and was stubborn."

"I've known a few knights from my days at court. Can you recall his name?" Jamie asked, not daring to breathe, expecting the answer that came. Just then footsteps sounded on the jetty.

"Hoy, what goes on here then?" a voice called in Gaelic.

Jamie turned calmly: "Captain, I was passing and brought your man some ale to share with me. I am with Glyndower's party and he asked me to keep watch o'er the sea ere they converse within."

"Ah I see. Well Ailig, get back to your work you'll be falling down drunk afore long, and we've a sharp return due tonight, ye ken?"

The downtrodden Ailig scowled tugged his forelock at Jamie and turned back to his work.

"Best keep the lad away from the ale," the captain said, "for his head's not strong."

"Well, here I must patrol and keep a watch, so I'll bid you a good day, captain." Jamie swung up on to Richard's back and cantered off down the beach. The seaman looked after him with his eyes narrowed in suspicion, before shaking his head and heading off to berate Ailig some more.

Chapter Fifty

Calls rang out in Gaelic as the two Scotsmen returned to the ship and departed with the high tide from the Dyfi harbour. Jamie made sure that he was somewhere else when the ship cast off its lines; he did not want his presence commented upon by the captain to either the Scots or Glyndower. Once they were a few hundred yards out, he cantered back to the centre of the village to see what new plans had been made.

"We are moving, men," Glyndower ordered, "despite the late hour. It is Glandyfi and the castle for us tonight."

Jamie was swept up with the others in the general exodus from Aberdyfi as Glyndower led the company back along the estuary, crossing downstream of Machynlleth as Glyndower was ever wary of staying too long in one place. Once on the south side of the river they made good speed and arrived at the castle at Glandyfi by late evening. It was a simple wooden palisade castle set upon a motte and bailey with a stone keep. Despite the fact that it lay just outside the village of Glandyfi, it was named Aberdyfi castle.

Once they were within the walls of the castle, the war party

– for that was what it was – dismounted and settled into the keep for the night, secure in the knowledge that they could relax, easily forewarned should an English search party approach. Around a huge table, the captains that had joined Glyndower by prior arrangement gathered.

There was a discernible sense of reserve about the tables, as if nobody was sure whom they could trust. Jamie was wary, not knowing how to read the mood of the company. He was curious as to their stay at the castle and quietly asked Arthwg, one of Glyndower's men-at arms how long they would be camped here.

"As long as it takes," he answered. "We wait 'til all the captains and knights assemble, and a tidy number t'will be. For we be assemblin' for war."

"'Tis good, for I shall look forward to wetting my sword once more," Jamie responded, but inside he fretted. Over the next three days, as Arthwg had predicted, more men arrived with small retinues of sword thanes as bodyguards.

On the third day the assembled company gathered around a huge table for the evening meal. As the evening progressed more of Glyndower's captains and knights arrived. Some asked after Huw and were pointed in Jamie's direction as the slayer of their friend and champion. There were more than a few glances askance at Jamie who began to feel uneasy for the first time since joining Glyndower's ranks. He tightened his hand on his dagger, vowing that if he were to go down he would take a few of them with him.

In the end his fears proved unfounded, for he was called to the table of captains to take his place and be appraised of intelligence concerning the proposed raid. *Finally* he thought *it has come, the time for action.*

All fell silent as the leaders were seated and Glyndower showed the qualities of his leadership in an impassioned speech, embracing all and advancing their cause with heartfelt thanks to those whose aim was to set Wales free.

"My friends and captains all. We have striven to free our land, the land of our fathers into which we have ploughed our blood and souls. We know the cost of our venture, yet now it bears fruit, and our vision will compensate for the sacrifices we have all made. Now though, we have a great opportunity and the time is ripe for our cause. This time we strike not alone, but aided by allies from the north, for the Scots seek freedom as we do. The King of France too is on our side and aids us in our fight. Alone we can no longer succeed, but united we will prevail." He finished his speech to a crescendo of voices and crashing of ale tankards onto tables. There was a hubbub of voices and Glyndower raised a hand, calling for silence once more.

"In four days' time we shall meet again at Bishops Castle and make our final plans for the attack. We will begin our foray into the heart of England to bring the English to heel and take back what is rightfully ours: a free Wales governed not by English whoresons but free of all predisposition and over-lord-ship. We will govern our land and take what is rightfully ours, secure in a future of freedom."

Jamie listened askance, aware of the furore that Glyndow-er's impassioned speech was causing. He looked sideways at the bright, sweaty, sheened faces of men who found themselves in the grip of ale and battle fervour. *Ye Gods,* Jamie thought, *this is a full blown revolution, anarchy against the king and realm.*

The rhetoric continued, and Jamie cheered with the rest of them as he tried to find some clue as to where the first point of attack would be. If the rallying point were Newtown itself, with its chequered history, it would prove a valuable striking point for raids into England.

Where would they strike from there? Jamie wondered, his

mind a whirl. Clun was close, but went against Whittington's reckoning. He'd said that they were secret allies of Glyndower. Ludlow was too strong a fortress for an initial foray and would take weeks to storm and secure, by which time help would arrive to relieve the castle. It would have to be somewhere in between. Then he had it: *Stokesay! A strong and prominent holding place, and a great point from which to sally forth. I must warn Sir Richard de Grey*, he realised, and for that he needed to be back at Machynlleth to send forth a message.

The company awoke to a hazy mist that drifted upward in the light of early morning as the nascent sun drew moisture from the wet earth, forming wreaths of swirling silver grey that shrouded the fields. Rays broke through, offering paths of light that looked for all the world like celestial passages to the other side. The smell of warm wet soil pervaded the air; birdsong broke out, heralding a new day, a day that was filled with hope – but not for Jamie. The daunting prospect of his task stretched before him like a boulder-strewn road. He was drawn from his reverie by a clap on the shoulder as Rhys Ddu appeared at his side.

"Well lad, tell me, is it James or Jamie?"

"My father and family called me both before we split, and either is equal to me. I care not. All that is past now, and a new life beckons here with Prince Owain," Jamie replied.

"Well that may be, man, but worry not for we'll secure you a place within our ranks and you'll live a good life. You could do worse than follow me back to Cardigan. 'Tis far away from the borders, and no one'll find you there." Rhys said.

"That is a fair offer, and after this raid mayhap I shall be able to take you up on your generous terms. I've always had a hankering to live near the sea, and t'would suit me well.

"Let's win this fight first, and see how all goes, eh?"

"Amen to that." Jamie agreed, feeling a little rueful despite everything, for the offer had been made in good grace and for a moment he felt guilty and a little torn, finding it hard to hate the man, despite being him being a sworn enemy of England.

"Think on't, and we'll talk again," Rhys clapped Jamie on the shoulder once more.

Others began to move around too, fanning fires and setting tables for hot meat ere the day's march began. Rhys Ddu moved off, leaving Jamie, who happened to glance around, the feeling on his neck worrying him again. As he passed back to fetch and saddle Richard, he saw that Rhys was now in deep and whispered conversation with Owain. Neither saw him pass by as Glyndower listened carefully to what Rhys Ddu had to say.

"Well, what was his response?" Glyndower asked.

"I offered as you said. He seemed well pleased with the thought, considered his family and told me that he relished the idea of living by the sea. Yet there is something...I know not what. Do as I say and put him in the van when we attack. That will prove his mettle and loyalty, for if he kills bastard Englishmen as well as he killed Huw, then he is our man."

Glyndower nodded and looked up to see Jamie's back as he passed towards where Richard was tethered.

"I will mark him well, and his slippery Italian friend. Come, let us to war."

Chapter Fifty-One

Westminster Palace, London

A feast had been planned for that evening to celebrate a good harvest, as the perfect weather had heralded an early gathering of wheat and hay. The court was full of colourful figures cast in gold, silks, brocades and jewels. The newest fashion of lower cut bodices was 'very daring and all the women wished to embrace the exposure and allure of décolletage.

The men wore different coloured hose of bright, bold colours, and sported elongated pointed toes to their shoes. Minstrels played and a full court encouraged gaiety, led by Prince Henry himself, who appeared not to have a care in the world. Outwardly the prince was in an ebullient mood. Calais had been saved, and no news had yet been heard of any further invasion plans. The kingdom appeared secure, although the spectre of his father still lingered above him like the sword of Damocles. Inwardly, he kept close secrets with the council and with Sir Richard Whittington.

"What news, Sir Richard?" he asked as they paraded around

the great hall, smiling at everyone, yet at the same time aware that the fate of the kingdom was held in balance.

"None, my lord prince, save that Sir Richard Grey is in position and waits to hear what news is brought out of Wales. I fear for James, yet there is nought we can do but trust in the good Lord to aid us."

"Amen to that cause..." The prince's discourse was cut short as the Contessa Alessandria swept by, with two other ladies accompanying her. She curtsied before him and he etched a bow in response.

"My lady Contessa, how do you do? Is all well and are you settling into your new home?"

"Your royal highness is most kind to ask after me. I find the court so filled with diversions that I could not but be entertained and made welcome. Everyone seems most generous of spirit that I would hardly fail to find my new home most welcoming," she replied prettily.

"That is as it should be, yet if there is any further courtesy of service that I may be able to extend to you and your uncle, you have only to ask and it shall be granted."

"My prince, you are most kind," she fluttered her eyes behind her fan, "yet I hesitate still to request any favour or trade for my own advantage upon my uncle's acquaintance."

"Pray thee, ask away, I adjure you," the prince encouraged.

The Contessa dropped her voice so that only Whittington and the prince might hear. "I do have a quaere concerning a countryman of mine, and one who I presume to hold dear." The prince said nothing, yet cast a sidelong glance at Whittington.

When the prince finally responded, there was a little flint in his voice: "Pray tell me more."

"Ah, I perceive a misalliance of circumstance and would not wish to trespass upon your good nature, sire, it was merely to enquire if there may be any news of one Cristoforo Corio, late of Florence and of this court who travelled abroad, to aid a... friend...who may be friend to you, my Lord?" at which she nodded towards Sir Richard Whittington, who coughed discreetly then responded.

"My dear Contessa, I am assured that all is well with all our subjects abroad from these lands, and if anything untoward should occur we are as ever mindful of their safety and would be apprised of any such unfortunate events. Suffice it to say that we have heard nought of anything that would give us cause for concern here at court," Whittington finished, his strong and discerning eyes piercing hers. She was however not disconcerted, and was about to continue her gentle interrogation when the prince interceded, looking over her shoulder.

"Ah, my Lady Alice, you look very fair tonight my dear, I trust you do well?"

The blonde vision coming towards him blushed at his address and curtseyed low. Her hair was netted this evening with emeralds that sparkled in the candlelight and her gown of gold brocade shimmered as she moved.

"My lord prince," she murmured, "Sir Richard."

"Now Contessa, where are my manners, for I perceive a mutual acquaintance here that you should explore. May I introduce my Lady Alice, daughter of Baron Andrew of Macclesfield? This my dear, is La Contessa Alessandria di Felicini, late of France, now happily ensconced within our court. Ladies, if you will excuse us we needs must move on, for there are festivities to be enjoyed." The prince finished in a manner that was polite yet brooked no argument, and together with Sir Richard they moved off, leaving the ladies to talk.

The Contessa and Lady Alice eyed one another, unsure of how to begin after being left adrift with little cognizance of each other's position. "How vexing of the prince to leave us so lately introduced," the Contessa offered, as if to break the ice.

"Even so, yet there is no accounting for princes and their whims, I'm bound," Lady Alice responded. "Pray tell me, his highness said you were of France, yet I perceive you are of Italian descent. Forgive me if I appear curious, for I have travelled to that land with my father and it seems that you have the same accent."

"I do indeed, and no offence is taken. I was enquiring of the prince after one of my countrymen who was lately of the court and now travels to the farthest shores of this land. I sought news of him, yet all seems mysterious and I brood and fret for his good health and his safety."

"Where has he travelled?" Alice asked, although she had a good idea of the answer.

The Contessa searched her face before she answered a little warily, realising why they might have been introduced by the prince. "Why to Wales, a far flung land of dragons, or so I am told."

Alice raised a hand to her mouth in shock: "Your countryman, is he by name Cristoforo Corio? For if so, I now perceive the prince's game."

Chapter Fifty-Two

Wales

"So what didst pass between them?" Jamie asked of Ffili, one of Glyndower's teulu as they walked across from the stables behind the great hall in Machynlleth.

"As I declare, Mark came upon the Italian talking to mistress Amwen, looking deeply into her eyes in that foreigner way of his. I've seen him courting many a lady at camp, and they seem to melt afore his gaze. He has a way with the women, that's for sure."

"Aye, that he does, I'll not deny it," Jamie acceded.

"Well, as I declare, Mark took it ill and bemoaned his suit, claiming Cristoforo was poaching where he should not."

"Pray tell," Jamie urged "what was Amwen's response to the Italian's advances?"

"Why 'tis passing strange, for rather than deny it she flirted and stood aback, seeing which way the wind blew, if you know what I mean? For a woman's way is strange to men, I declare."

"And in this discourse did they speak English or French?"

"Well, there you have me, for t'was odd, yet they spoke the cursed Sais tongue, begging your pardon, Jamie."

"Odd?"

"Aye, as Amwen seemed to comprehend all, and found it right pleasing that two men should fight over her."

"Thank you, Ffili. Your words will aid me, and I shall settle this 'tween my friends," Jamie replied showing none of his thoughts.

"Good luck with that, for ere a woman is part, the whole is never thus," Ffili commented.

"Amen to that," Jamie responded with a chuckle and walked off to find his friends.

Cristoforo was behind the hall, practicing as ever with Collen. Daggers sang in the air, to be caught as the start of an attack or for defence.

"Cristoforo, how goes it?" Jamie called as his friend's face broke into a wide smile.

"Jamie! By the good Lord I thought you had gone for good. How was the sea? Cold and wet I'll wager."

"Aye that it was. Come walk with me and we'll talk of the sea and boats." Cristoforo bowed to Collen and took his leave, seeking time alone with Jamie. Once out of earshot Jamie confided: "It seems you've done right well as we planned?"

"Aye, too well. That Amwen is a canny wench and not to be trusted. What started as a brief conversation became upon her encouragement a courtly attachment, far beyond anything we had planned. I am sure that she comprehends far more of the English tongue than she admits to."

"I suspected as much from that which I gleaned from Ffili. 'Tis all around the camp that you and Mark have had a falling out, I'll be bound."

"'Tis true, yet it breaks my heart, for Mark is a goodly man and not one I should wish to hurt on purpose, for he has become as a brother to me..."

"Fear not, all will be resolved ere we can declare our true colours again. Now there is much to tell and the quality of your intimacy with Amwen gives fuel to what must occur tonight. For by the rood, much mischief has been fomented; you must leave forthwith and warn against the war party that will be unleashed against our borders."

"So soon?"

"Yes, tonight, upon excuse of garboil with Mark. Leave this evening in a grand rage and seek nought from us save a farewell. Yet have care, for my belief is that we are as much at risk as ever, and trust is a currency not easily minted in Welshmen's hearts. I suspect I shall be tested ere long, and perforce will be found wanting. I suspect they will set me in the heart of battle and watch for me to take English lives. I will be wearing my hauberk and cuirass of Sir Robert's colours in the foray, and pray to God that I am well marked, for I do not wish to serve as a pin cushion to my lord's archers. Now, take this." Jamie pressed the SS brooch into Cristoforo's hand and explained all that had occurred and the plans that were made at Aberdyfi Castle.

"Hell's teeth, it bodes not well. I must make haste and be there to Stokesay well afore the war band arrives. Shall I leave silently or make my displeasure known?"

"I think it would be best served to leave openly and advise that you make for Shrewsbury, there to sell your abilities. For my Lord Arundel is not badly disposed to Glyndower if all is to be believed, and 'twill serve well. I for my part will stir the pot a little more and provoke one final confrontation twixt you and Mark ere you depart. It grieves me to vex him so, for he is of true heart, yet he would not easily dupe Amwen or any others if our true intent were known, for 'tis not in his nature."

"Aye his manner is as straight as the staff he wields so well.

Needs must I shall make obeisance to him once this cursed errand is done." Cristoforo promised.

The two men discussed all that Jamie had found out, including the Scottish lords arriving and Jacques de Berry's involvement in Scotland. They made final arrangements and then split up. Cristoforo returned to his practice with Collen and Jamie set off to visit Mark. Jamie moved around the cots to the one he shared with the other two men, passing between the lines of dwellings. As he neared his own quarters, a shadow of grey appeared and his hand flew to his sword unbidden. The shadow became a flash and launched itself at him, striking for his chest and knocking the wind out of him, nearly lifting him off his feet.

"Forest! By the gods I swear you've grown much in four short days." He cried as the wolfhound proceeded to lick his face in greeting, her tail wagging below her upraised body supported solely on her back legs, as two huge paws rested upon Jamie's chest. A deep bark emanated from within her body that ended in a sort of mournful howl. He ruffled her ears playfully, at which a large figure emerged from within their quarters.

"Mark, by God's grace it is good to see a friendly face again. How goes it?"

"I be well, Jamie, and you too for time seems to have passed slowly ere you were away and someone has missed you," he nodded meaningfully, looking at Forest.

"Hah so I see. Come with me while I walk off stiffness from my ride back, for Richard was full of himself and up to his usual tricks."

The two men fell in side by side and walked around the camp. Jamie threw a stick for the dog.

"Truth to tell I have had an ill time of late, and it offends me to tell of it. For all is not good 'tween Cristo and myself. We seem to have fallen out, and it grieves me, for once were such close friends."

"That is ill news. How so? For I would lief as make it well again with you both."

"It started as nothing, for I saw Cristo talking with Amwen on more than one occasion and they seemed to have an air of intimacy about them. Truth to tell I was jealous, and I never thought I would see the day I fell out with a friend over a girl. For myself I supposed myself to be mistook, yet there was no gainsaying what I saw and it filled me with anger and pain."

"So, prithee, how did Amwen show herself when you aired it with her?"

"'Tis passing strange, for she seems distant and aloof of emotion, she just smiles and tells me naught is wrong and passes it all off as fun. It eats away at me something cruel. Tell me, Jamie, are these the ways of Italians?"

"Perhaps 'tis so, Mark. But I am right curious, how do you talk so deeply with Amwen? For I bethought she spoke no English, you no Welsh and had but a little French between you."

"Well, 'tis passing strange, for her grasp of English seems to have come on right quick, probably as I talk to her all the time, babbling on, and she seems to have a gift, for't."

"Does she, by the rood? Strange indeed, yet beneficial to ye," Jamie opined with a touch of irony that Mark missed. "Hear me now, for I will speak with Cristoforo and engage him in discourse on the matter, which can hopefully be resolved to the benefit of you both. There is more that I would impart to you, for I believe our time to be tested has come. A raid is planned into England, and will take place ere long."

Mark was surprised to hear that war would come so soon, and was torn between getting back to England and leaving Amwen, who had inveigled her way into his heart. Jamie saw within him the indecision and sought to sway him subtly, with all the detail of the events that had occurred. It was de Berry's name that caused Mark to defer to Jamie more than anything, yet still in his mind, Amwen held some sway.

"Mark, there is something else that I must impart, for I value you as a friend and would not bring your life to forfeit for that reason."

"Pray tell?"

"This raid will be a battle, and a big one. It will be a mêlée the like of which you will never have seen before. It will be nothing like we faced in the cathedral, for there will be chaos on all sides with no quarter given and arrow storms...how should I explain? War is different to combat and less the certain for it. It requires training and a mind for the kill."

"Why do you tell me this?" Mark asked, worried.

"When we go to war I will be playing two parts, and cannot be worried for your fate, so I would ask that you stay off the field and keep Forest safe, for she will try to save me in her loyal stupidity and would die in the attempt."

Mark interrupted, aghast: "I cannot leave you to fight alone."

"You can and must: consider that you have no armour or mail, not even a helmet. Your sword work is fair, but needs practice, and whilst your ability with a staff is unparalleled, a staff is not for the battlefield. Needs must I will tell Cristo the same. You have the skill in fair combat, his is the silent world of the assassin. The field of battle is my world, and I've trained for it all my life. So I beg you as a friend, promise me you'll stay clear, 'pon your word?"

Mark looked crestfallen, but on hearing that Cristoforo would be absent, he agreed and swore an oath to that effect.

"Good, then we are agreed, and thank 'ee for it. My heart settles lighter now that I can rely upon you to do this."

Chapter Fifty-Three

That evening new captains and men arrived to swell the ranks of Glyndower's army, including Phillip Scudamore and Owen ap Tudor, and there was feasting in the hall. Jamie sat next to Rhys Ddu, who continued to gently probe about his background, with offers of spoils and a livelihood once the raid had been completed and they had entrenched themselves into English lands.

Jamie played the part and showed enthusiasm for the roles that Ddu outlined for him. "I have given great thought to your offer, and would like to live at Cardigan, it seems a goodly spot away from the pressure to practice what I believe in and what I feel is right by God," he commented.

"I care not what god a man prays to as long as it not be a heathen god. All I ask is that he has a strong right arm and a sword in his hand when the time is right," Rhys answered. Jamie was about to respond when a commotion broke out at a lower table – in English.

"I will not sit and bear witness to you making sheep's eyes at my woman," Mark shouted at Cristoforo, who had seated himself opposite the couple on a long table. Cristoforo stopped, a goblet of wine half raised to his lips. His eyes took on a hue of slate, his face became an inscrutable mask.

"It is not I who makes with the eyes of a *pecora!* From my vantage here I see nought but a comely woman who would not dissuade my suit," Cristoforo responded calmly, intent upon striking home a point and riling Mark the more for it.

"By the rood I'll not take this ill-mannered jibe," Mark snarled, rising, his face suffusing with anger. As matters started to head towards an irreconcilable point, Jamie arrived at the table in an attempt to calm the troubled waters. Amwen, he noticed, had said nought – and worse, was looking upon Mark and Cristoforo with a whimsical smile playing upon her lips.

"Hold fellows, hold, for this is no way for friends to commend themselves to each other. Come, we must not fight amongst ourselves. It is the English who are the enemy, not our own good company."

"Tell him, not me, for my manners are not at fault," Mark ranted.

"*Porca miseria,*" Cristoforo began and continued in incomprehensible Italian, of which the gist if not the exact meaning was gained by all present. He rose, slammed his goblet to the table and strode from the hall, a look of disgust upon his face. Jamie called after him to no avail; he merely flicked his hand over his shoulder in a wave of dismissal. Jamie looked at Mark, and shrugged apologetically for his friend before following Cristoforo outside. Glyndower had been an interested witness to this exchange and looked first to Rhys, then to Collen, whom he beckoned forth to his side. Amwen caught a look from her prince and an imperceptible nod passed between them.

Once outside, Jamie ran to Cristoforo. "You did well, my friend, mayhap too well, yet none could doubt your intent."

"Aye and there's the rub, for I have treated Mark ill, and I feel the wound as keen as a cut to my own skin. If I do not live to return, please God make my peace with him in my stead." He pleaded.

"Fie now, none of that, for you'll be there to embrace him ere long. I'll impart that you are for Shrewsbury, for 'tis the same road as Stokesay, and they'll not suspect anything more than a wronged friend and the horns of a cuckold."

Cristoforo smiled with a flash of white teeth in the evening light and made to saddle his horse, gathering his leather satchel and a small sack of food and stowing it behind the cantle. He strapped the scabbard onto his back and slid the falchion into it. "I feel better now and complete again."

"Travel in God's care, Cristo, and heed all signs, for danger lurks in every shadow," Jamie urged, at which a voice floated out into the evening.

"Cristoforo, wait, where do you go?" It was Collen, who saw that he was saddling his horse ready for departure from the camp.

Jamie shot Cristoforo a look that was full of meaning. "Collen, why I have had enough forsooth, and depart to find friendlier climes."

"Where do you make for?"

"I am for Shrewsbury. I have not yet seen the town, and I hear that the Earl of Arundel is seeking men."

"Let me bear you company on your journey – at least in part. For I know the trails well and can show you a quicker, safer route than you may otherwise find. The prince has given me leave and it would be my pleasure to give you a fair journey under the circumstances of your leaving. We will make to Welshpool, and thence your journey will be more straightforward."

Cristoforo thought quickly, knowing that to refuse would

cause much suspicion, and that from the map Jamie had drawn Welshpool was less than a day's ride from Stokesay. Not as direct as Newtown, but it would have to do.

"Await my return ere I fetch my horse." Collen offered.

"Aye that would be right gracious of you, for I could do with company on the road and for sure I should become lost in the hills and forests away from the main route."

As Collen left to fetch his horse, Jamie gave Cristoforo one final word of warning: "I know that you are aware, yet I would adjure you, trust him not, for Glyndower's motives are always suspect to me."

"Fear not," Cristoforo said. "I have taught him little of what I know and gained more from him than he has from me. What's this, a leaving party?" He added, as Forest slid silently from Jamie's side as if to say goodbye, sensing with an innate instinct that all was not well. In their time at camp, even Cristoforo had been won over by the hound, and had favoured her when he thought no one was watching. He rubbed her ears and stroked the fine head that was developing well.

"She will be a horse when I see her next," he quipped.

"Aye, that she may," Jamie agreed, and as Collen returned, he finished with an adieu. "Fare thee well, Cristoforo, and please God we meet again soon, for Mark will be sad in the morning and wish to mend the bond again."

"Mayhap he will. Stay strong, Jamie and may fortune smile upon you."

With that the two men trotted off out of the town on the eastern road following the line of the river Dyfi.

"We'll head up towards the village of Mallwyd," Collen said. "'Tis only some twelve miles distant. Tho' we shall be tardy for a night within the village, and we'd be best to camp outside. I know a good place with water and soft moss for a bed, so all will be well." Collen assured Cristoforo, who acknowledged the timing and was happy to let him talk, playing the part of the hurt Latin temperament well. The two figures rode from the town, and with a turn of the bend they were soon lost to sight.

As Jamie returned to the great hall, he was aware that all eyes were upon him. He walked straight to Mark's side and voiced his displeasure.

"Cristoforo has gone." He spoke to Mark yet gave Amwen a look that should chill her bones. Yet for all the response he received he might have thrown a snowball into hell. She sat impassively, allowing no emotion to show upon her face.

Mark's face fell, and sadness was written there despite his earlier angry outburst. "Tis passing sad, for once we were good comrades in arms and it gnaws at my soul that he should depart thus. Where does he make for? Mayhap I should go after him and make my peace?"

"I would counsel you not. He heads for Shrewsbury to seek engagement there with the Earl of Arundel. Collen is with him at the prince's adjuring, so all will be well. Mayhap he will calm in the days ahead and return to us, for I am as a sad as you. Yet tonight it would seem wise to leave him to his own counsel."

Mark nodded, looking no happier. Amwen in response gently squeezed his arm in comfort, responding not to Jamie's words. Jamie left them and returned to the captain's table where he made his explanations and fielded the expected responses about hot blooded Italians not playing to the rules.

Cristoforo and Collen made camp by the side of the river Dyfi close to the village of Mallwyd. The evening had become a little chilly, and Collen set a fire whilst Cristoforo gathered more wood.

"You see?" he remarked as Cristoforo returned. "A comfortable bed of moss and a snug dell away from the road. What more could two travellers wish for?"

They settled down with a pot above the fire and a stew of rabbit set to boil and simmer. They talked companionably over supper, exchanging stories of travels past and experiences of combat. Then Collen rose from his cross legged position: "I'll check to the horses afore we sleep to ensure that the hobbles have not come loose that they not stray too far."

"Aye, go to, I'll settle here." Cristoforo agreed.

Collen quietly departed the glade and went to look at the horses that were hobbled nearby. Cristoforo looked out into the night as was his custom, and made to get his cloak ready for sleep. Collen's steps as he returned were soft against the moss-covered floor, yet Cristoforo's sharp ears detected the stealthy sound of steel against wood and the whirr of a blade, even if only a whisper, as he strained to detect the other man's approach. He rolled sharply sideways as the sword swept down to where he had been sitting, chopping into a log laid by the fire. Cristoforo's roll continued as one movement which ended with him on his feet, a dagger drawn. Yet Collen was full of tricks and followed him, as he had been trained to do. The distance was too close to throw the dagger as the movement would open him up to Collen's strike and result in Cristoforo's death, yet the closeness allowed him to deflect the sword's tip with a flick of his wrist. He fell back to avoid the full force of the strike.

Despite all this movement, Collen could not resist a taunt as he flicked out with the tip of his sword: "Too close to throw those daggers now, aren't you?" he said.

Cristoforo seemed to stumble and fall backwards, losing his

footing. He described a perfect backward roll with Collen following closely, not wanting to afford his opponent the opportunity to throw a dagger. Yet the downward position made it more difficult for him to catch and thrust at Cristoforo. As Cristoforo completed the move he arrived on his feet, one foot planted in front of the other in a wide stance, stretched forward in perfect balance. His falchion was now in his right hand, a dagger in the left and a savage grin upon his face.

"What? By Hades, whence did that come?" Collen shouted and struck downwards, cleaving towards Cristoforo's head. The dagger and falchion crossed just below the sword tip in a move he had been taught by Fiori dei Liberi, the Italian master who had instructed him years ago.

The falchion pointed to the left and the dagger to the right, trapping the sword blade. Using the strength of his wrists, Cristoforo twisted the sword blade to his right, off the centre line, the falchion directing it past him. Then reversing his grip on the dagger he drove it backhanded directly into Collen's chest, rotating his torso to increase the speed and power of the strike. He let go of the hilt and Collen fell to his knees, fighting for breath as bubbles of blood began to emerge from his mouth. He sank to the floor, gasping.

Cristoforo had left the dagger blade in place, knowing it would prolong Collen's life a little. He needed to learn as much as he could before the man died.

"Why Collen? I bethought us friends?"

"Aye, sorry I am...but the prince...the prince thought you a spy and ordered your death. Had to...obey. You're quick, too quick, like...Jamie. The sword fooled me...you cheated me..."

"I'm right glad I did or t'would be me there and you here. Now aid me and ease your conscience. Does the prince suspect Jamie or Mark?"

"Jamie...no one trusts him...too good. Of Mark, no, he is

only a wrestler, though Amwen be bad...watch her...Cristo... watch..." And with that his last breath rattled from his body, the blood frothed up from his lungs and his head hung back, pillowed against Cristoforo's arm.

"Amen brother, for you died well," he reached forward and closed Collen's eyes. "May the Lord receive the soul of a good man." He crossed himself and bowed his head in a quick prayer.

Laying Collen's head down, Cristoforo realised he had no means of breaking earth, so he formed a cairn of stones to cover his body. Afterwards, he extinguished the fire, broke camp, saddled both horses and headed across country towards Llanfair Caereinion. From there, according to Jamie's map, he could head south for Montgomery and the English border. It would be a long, hard ride of some thirty-five miles through the night, he guessed, yet with two horses to ride relay he should make it ahead of Glyndower's forces.

Chapter Fifty-Four

"So Jamie, do you relish the fight to bring home plunder from the Sais that have wronged you so?"

"Aye, that I do, for 'twill be good to strike back at them."

The next words from Black Rhys confirmed what Jamie had been dreading, yet they came as no surprise. "'Tis good, for you will be at the van with me. We shall charge the gates of hell together at Stokesay Castle, for that is where we are bound after a night at Newtown."

So I was right. Jamie thought. *I hope to God Cristoforo made his journey successfully, for with this host and caught unawares, such a rebellion will bring a slaughter the like of which will ignite another war.* "I look forward to the hour. Then after, do we make for Ludlow and plunder there?" he asked, entering his role enthusiastically.

"Steady lad," Rhys grinned. "We'll see how we stir the English hornets' nest first. For many are those who still need proof of our intent, and to see the flames of Stokesay light the sky will be a clarion banner to our cause. The Welsh will rise up as before, for so Prince Owain has promised them." Rhys replied.

It was their second day of travel, with Jamie and Mark leading the mules that carried his armour. At length they arrived at Newtown under cover of dusk, an armoured host of knights, foot soldiers and archers in their hundreds, with mules carrying supplies, cooks and a scattering of women. There were banners fluttering in the light breeze and the company were in optimistic spirits, for surprise was on their side and they had the advantage of numbers. Their late arrival had been deliberately timed, for whilst Newtown still lay within Wales, no one could be trusted and news of a large host would have spread like wildfire.

They camped beyond the town, for the host was too large to be accommodated within the confines of the settlement. Guards were posted and all roads were patrolled by armed watchers, who stopped all leaving and seized any who tried to enter the area.

Jamie managed to separate Mark from Amwen, who pouted at the suggestion of a private talk. However, Jamie pressed his suit, calling upon Mark to walk around the camp. Forest, who had coped well with the journey, trotted by their sides.

"How goes it Mark? For I've had little enough time to speak with you since Cristoforo left."

"I still have a heavy heart on that score, yet I am well enough, though aggrieved that you want me away from the battle, for I would as lief guard your back."

"No." Jamie said. "For all the reasons that we discussed. Keep Forest and yourself safe and look after Amwen, but if all goes ill I adjure you to escape this company and return to London and account to Sir Richard Whittington – who will assoil you of all you have done here and make you an Earl of Cornwall, no doubt." he joked.

"Aye, would that not be grand? Mark, Earl of Cornwall." He laughed, then became more serious. "I wonder how Cristo does? For I miss him despite all, and Amwen gives me little succour in that regard."

"Fear not, for he has more tricks than a necromancer and the night is his friend, as we know."

"Aye that it is, and I would fain as not wish to face him in the dark. He is a wraith indeed."

"Well then, you have the right of it, so be not afeard. Yet I would ask one more boon early tomorrow ere battle commences. I wish to be in full harness, so I can turn away the arrows and alert the English, so would you honour me by being my squire at arms?" he asked.

"Aye, that I would, and right proud I shall be – first a squire then Mark, Earl of Cornwall," he laughed.

"For that I am mighty pleased for 'tis impossible to arm oneself without a squire. So come with me now and see the parts, that you may be familiar on the morrow."

They returned to the camp, where Mark helped Jamie unpack the armour from the greased sacks lined with wool that held the full harness. They laid the harness along with the chainmail out upon an old cloak on the floor. Mark looked at the plate in the light of a brazier, puzzled and disappointed. "I expected it to shine," he commented.

"No, I dressed it in lanolin oil to prevent rusting – yet look here, flecks of rust from that accursed Welsh weather. I shall return," he muttered, rising and moving away in search of a cook. He returned a while later with a small flask of vinegar. Mark watched with interest as he applied this to a bag of sand from his war bag, and with a cloth began to work the metal, removing the rust and the lanolin coating.

Seeing how it was done, Mark said, "Here, let me set to. I'll not have my knight clean his own harness."

"What? The future Earl of Cornwall cleans the harness of a lowly squire? By the rood!" Jamie quipped, as much to lighten the mood as the two men knew that tomorrow could bring death to them both. Amwen came over from the fire, interested in the cleaning process, and Forest too looked on as if to learn the art of arming her master. In this way they passed an hour in companionable silence until the plate shone and Forest approved with a long drawn-out howl into the night sky.

"That will do well, and I'm set for the morrow. Now back into the sacks and it will just need a final polish afore I arm in the morning and harvest the English like ripe wheat," He grinned humourlessly at Amwen, trusting her not and playing the role he had taken for himself.

So it was that the company left Newtown early before the sun's first rays had broken through the grey mists of dawn. Even in the last days of August, their breath could be seen in the chill of the early morning. Those who ventured forth left signs of their passing in the heavy dew, and when the first light broke forth it sparkled on the patterns of silvered spiders' webs caught amongst the wayside bracken and gorse.

"Tis a good day for a battle," Rhys Ddu shouted to the company arrayed before him. "Jamie, do you have no mail?" he said in a lower voice, remarking upon Jamie's vestment of only a gambeson to keep out the cold and a sword.

"Fear not, I will be so ere we near our sport, but I have no wish to be a target for the English bowmen should they be about. I do not want to be dead before the battle is reached."

Rhys nodded, although he maintained a puzzled expression as he was in mail but as yet no plate, with his helmet toggled to his saddle. Above him his banner flew and a plumed helm was toggled to his saddle. He was without doubt the best equipped knight there, and even Philip Scudamore and Rhys ap Tudor would not be so well attired when battle came. Already Rhys Ddu looked magnificent with his red cloak, the black ravens defined against the crimson background.

"How far to Stokesay Castle?" Jamie asked.

"Why 'tis but a few hours ride. We'll be there well before the mid morn."

With that the company moved off and, despite being on the wrong side, Jamie felt his heart soar for it meant combat and battle whatever the day may bring. Richard, sensing his master's excitement, sharpened and side-stepped in expectation.

"Steady my beauty, for we'll have our sport yet, be not afeard." Jamie calmed him.

They came at length to the wooded hilltop that overlooked Stokesay castle. The view was impressive, yet the castle defences were not all that they could be. The walls were perfunctory and there was no moat. The castle had two fortified towers and crenulated walls. It was as Jamie remembered it from a visit with his father: more a fortified manor house than a true castle. Easier to capture, settle and plunder. The surrounding land was rich and fertile, and produced a good income for its owner Sir Lawrence of Ludlow, who was a fond friend of both his father and Sir Richard Whittington.

He mused on this as he set about the task of arming with Mark's help, sheltered from view by the wood atop the hill. Mark had found a secluded dell masked by saplings, and there he set out the full harness on a cloak as Jamie had the night before. Others had followed suit and were beginning their own arming process away from the sight of the castle below, although very few possessed full harness and none of the quality that Jamie was about to display.

Mark gave the plate a final polish to remove any traces of lanolin and it shone for when Jamie returned from a final *paroli* with Glyndower and the captains on the order of battle. Jamie now wore a lightweight gambeson and thin suede hose. They fitted him like a glove and the gambeson had laces stoutly stitched and threaded at various points throughout the garment.

"This is your arming gambeson you talked of yester eve?" Mark asked, his eyebrows raised "Yet they be just laces. Will they hold the full weight of your armour?"

Jamie smiled back at him. "They are of bowstring and treated with beeswax, they'll stand two hundred pounds – far more than the fifty or so of my harness. Let us commence. First the greaves..." This Jamie could do himself as he bent to show Mark the hinged pieces with proud locating rivets that would lock the two halves together. "Now we secure them with the leather straps and buckles. This pin here," he pointed "locates the cuisse." He picked up the upper leg plates and poleyn knee pieces that were articulated. These he also closed and strapped. "Now, see you how I tie this to the laces at the top of each leg? Try for yourself with the other side," he indicated, securing the top of the cuisse to the arming jacket.

Mark looked on, puzzled. "Why be this ridge here?" he asked, pointing at a vee-shaped lip of metal a few inches below the top of the cuisse.

"That? That be a rib stop. See here," he said pointing to the left leg that had a tiny indented crease in the front of the metal. "Some rabid Scot nearly took my bollocks ere this stopped the point, praise God." Mark saw the meaning and laughed, while Amwen looked on, blushing with embarrassment.

"By God, Jamie, it fits you like a well-formed glove."

"So it should, for it was made especially for me from measurements. Francis Court, one of the king's own esquires, visited Sir Robert and took my measurements back to his homeland and passed them to Gian Galeazzo Visconti, Duke of Milan and a master armourer reputed to make the best plate armour in Christendom. He returned months later with this," he gestured downwards. "My father, for my birthday of eight and ten years, paid a king's ransom for it, wishing his son and heir to be well protected."

"Aye, and by the rood he did right well."

"Now comes your time, for here I shall really need your help. First the maille under shirt." Mark slipped it over Jamie's head. Then followed the breastplate, which was hinged at the side and strapped into place. The plate fell to just below the sternum and had golden inlay and decoration engraved upon its body. It was a beautiful piece of workmanship, Mark noticed, as he belted Jamie's maille coat, placing more weight upon on Jamie's shoulders and allowing the skirt to cover his groin.

"Here is the hard part for me. Pass me that rope with the loop. Thank you. Now the plackart." Mark helped Jamie apply it his lower body, where the articulated sections allowed full movement and flexibility. Jamie secured the rope around his waist and pulled it tightly inwards, cinching his middle and pulling the plackart in with it. "You should find it easier to belt up the piece, and once you have done so I shall release the rope and all will fall into place."

Mark immediately understood and watched as the armour settled as it should. "Why 'tis perfect," he commented.

"Aye, it works well. Now the vambrace for each side is different, this for my left, and that," he pointed to the remaining piece on the ground, "for my right."

The upper and lower cannons were secured as for the leg pieces and knotted to the top of the arming gambeson. Then came the pauldron shoulder pieces which covered the maille, the lacings and the upper cannons so Jamie's body was protected and secure. Next Mark slipped the bevor around his neck and checked that the hinged piece moved properly up and down.

Mark helped him strap sabatons to his feet. Here, Jamie broke with current thinking and had designed a pair of his own, eschewing the current fashion for long points that he believed would hinder a knight should he be dismounted. The articulated steel shoes ended in a blunt edge that would not catch when walking and fitted neatly over his leather boots. Finally he pulled on his coif, and over this Mark lifted the open faced salette helmet with an aventail back. Jamie kept the visor locked open as he expected no arrows from the English as yet. He buckled a belt about his waist to hold sword and dagger. This was made of riveted, hinged metal links that could not be cut as a normal leather belt might be, and was locked in place by a securing pin in place of the usual buckle.

Amwen looked on, amazed at the transformation before her eyes, from squire to knight – and a deadly one at that. Even Mark had not seen Jamie fully armoured, and his friend appeared even more indomitable than ever.

"By the rood, Jamie, you frighten me and I am with you," he exclaimed.

"Well 'tis a good thing." Then he stopped still, for the old feeling of being watched had fallen upon him once more.

"What ails you?" Mark asked, seeing his demeanour change.

Jamie was about to tell him, then he saw that Amwen's curiosity had been piqued. He shrugged. "'Tis nothing," he said. "Nought but the thought of the coming battle on such a fair day as this."

Mark moved his head towards Jamie and whispered: "Aye, I feel it too, I must be catching it from you and Cristo."

The final straps were tightened and Jamie emerged, a knight in full panoply. Richard too had been armoured with peytral plate, shaffron over his nose and a crupper over his quarters.

"Now hold Forest firmly, for I'll not want her in the thick of things," Jamie ordered.

"Aye we'll take good care of her, fear not." Mark assured him as he leashed the hound, who pulled and whined, holding the opposite stirrup leather to ease the strain as Jamie mounted.

Once mounted Jamie left the wood, drawing glances from all: a knight in full harness and battle dress of the best Milanese plate money could buy, for his father had fitted him out well. He wore a tabard over his cuirass bearing the arms of Sir Robert de Umfraville: *gule crusily* and a *cinque Foyle* set upon a *baston azure*. The bright blue of the diagonal stripe showed garish against the red as Sir Robert had intended.

Owen looked at Rhys, who looked back amazed, for Jamie was transformed and looked omnipotent and invincible. He saluted Glyndower, who looked plain in comparison in a gilded Bascinet helmet and a hauberk of fine chainmail, which although burnished to a shine paled in comparison to Jamie's harness.

"By God's holy legs, Jamie, you look fine and no gainsaying it." Rhys swore.

"Thank you my lord." Jamie acknowledged. "Now, shall we to war afore Richard charges by himself?" he joked, nodding down at his horse.

The company moved off down the hill towards the castle at Glyndower's command. Glyndower himself held back, for he was too old and valuable to be in the van, and stayed in the rear to command. Amwen, Mark and a number of his teulu remained with him.

"No combat, Mark?" he asked.

"No my lord prince. I fear no man in a straight fight with

staff or with my hands, yet Jamie – who has tutored me and knows well the art of war – ventured that I would be a chicken for the plucking out there. More so ere I have no armour that could fit my size and no arms save my old sword. I will join battle if it is to my advantage, for I am no coward, but this would be certain death"

"Aye well, he probably has the right of it. But we must mend that lack of ability ere long, so you may join the spoils and gain harness and ability with a sword." He quipped.

The attacking company emerged from the woods that shaded the hillside and spread out as they made ground across the lush pasture that surrounded the castle. Sheep that had moments before been grazing peacefully now scattered, bleating in fear and drawing the attention of a shepherd and his dog, which barked aggressively as the host came into view. The man stood stupefied, not believing what his eyes were telling him, finally managing to gain voice and shouting: "Attack! We're und –" There was a *thunk* as an arrow sprouted from his chest, fired by one of the Welsh bowmen who accompanied Glyndower's band. The shepherd fell silent to the grass. His dog whimpered beside him for a second, then looking up at the approaching company it put its tail between its legs and ran for the castle faster than any armoured horseman could follow.

Jamie knew that it would be impossible to reach the castle before the gates could be shut against them, yet he was puzzled that no lookout had raised the alarm and ordered them barred against the invaders.

"Mayhap luck is with us," Scudamore shouted across to the others at the head of the war party."

"Please God we shall reach the gates ere they close!" The horses were at a fast trot, and Jamie suddenly had an idea on how he might distance himself from the pack and change sides.

"Let us charge now and secure the gatehouse ere they bar it, for they surely will."

With that, and before any could question his resolve, he pushed Richard into a fast canter. The others followed suit and started to gallop across the open turf, with clods of earth flying from the horses' hooves as they accelerated. Jamie heard a cry of "Wait!" from Rhys, but it was ignored as the knights' impetus grew with each stride, the battle lust growing in each of them. The distance between the men at arms and the foot soldiers behind grew with every stride, until some hundred yards separated them.

Ordinarily that would not have been a problem. The cavalry would work as a battering ram and the foot soldiers would come in after them. But at this point, even over the thunder of hooves, Jamie heard the familiar whip and whistle of bow cords released and arrows flying. An arc of arrows moved swiftly across the sky, their deadly barbed heads reaching their zenith and then falling towards the mass of lightly armoured Welsh soldiers below.

The broad field through which the Welsh army was advancing was lined with a hedge some three hundred yards to one side and a drainage ditch to the other. These places of concealment were suddenly alive with a second rank of men armed with war bows. As the first hail of arrows thudded home the second rank of bowmen opened fire, and nearly half of the war party fell in what seemed like a matter of seconds. Most of them were closely packed, lightly armoured and unable to withstand the full force of an arrow at that range. It was carnage, and the few sergeants-at-arms who tried to rally the men were picked off quickly and accurately. The soldiers panicked, turning to flee to the safety of the woods from which they had lately emerged.

The knights galloping forward heard the chaos ensue

behind, and looking round they tried to curb their horses. But before they could do so, the gates that were still open spewed forth a charge of fully armoured horsemen led by a knight bearing the arms of a barre of six silver and azure bands. "For Codnor!" he shouted through his open visor. It a matter of yards before they would impact upon the Welsh knights, and Jamie called to Rhys Ddu, giving him a final opportunity based on chivalry and the sudden feeling of guilt he felt at the chaos and slaughter that were taking place behind him.

"Surrender, Rhys Ddu, and I'll take your cause," he offered.

Rhys turned his horse, temper flaring, the full force of his anger directed at Jamie. "Whoreson traitor, English pig, I'll kill you ere I surrender."

With that he spurred his horse at Jamie, raising his famed mace for attack, his shield held firm in his left hand. The mace was a lethal weapon in the mêlée of close quarters battle when the wielder had a shield. Yet as Jamie knew, it had one disadvantage: the attacker was exposed as he raised his arm above his head for the strike.

Richard saw the attack and knew his job, for he too charged, bringing his master at right arm to right arm, meeting the attack. Yet he felt Jamie's subtle instructions and at the last second swerved left with his quarters, taking Jamie away from the crushing force of the mace and enabling him to utilise the length of his sword to deflect the strike. Rhys was forced to cover quickly with his shield. Again Richard executed a capriole faster than any large horse with a fully armed knight on its back should have been able to, jumping onto his fore legs and flicking up his hind in a flying leap. Unlike with Kit, this was done in anger and both hooves found their target, unseating the Welsh knight, who flew sideways out of the saddle with one foot caught in the stirrup. Rhys's horse too was well trained, and stopped at his command. He released his foot and stood, heaving with rage, his shield misshapen from Richard's kick, calling for Jamie to stand and fight him on foot.

The battle that had briefly raged about them was almost won, as the Welsh forces began to surrender. Philip Scudamore was unhorsed and wounded. They turned to watch the single combat that was about to unfold before them as Jamie waved away all offers help, a point of honour that would be told in tales to come.

He dismounted, ordering Richard to stand. Jamie then turned and beckoned Rhys Ddu forward to combat. His sword was in his right hand and he drew his dagger with his left.

Rhys strode forward as well as he was able, having bruised his hip in the fall from his horse. "So, the traitor stands and fights in some false show of honour, then," he scorned.

Jamie said nothing as the familiar feeling came over him. He was calm and all movement seemed to slow as every sense focused before the battle madness settled upon him. He knew exactly what his move would be without a conscious thought; he had rehearsed it a thousand times in training. The huge, black bearded figure closed the distance, his shield held in perfect defence, his mace arm rising, ready to strike at Jamie's head. He lumbered forward, awesome in his anger, bitter for revenge.

Jamie allowed the mace to rise and fall, watching the movement by gauging the arm action. Rhys tucked his shield in at the last moment, perfectly timed as the mace arm came flying down, his arm twisting from the shoulder. Jamie timed it to parry the blow mid-flight, deflecting rather than blocking, twisting at the hip and allowing the main force of the strike to continue its arc. A lesser man would have exposed his right side, but Rhys was balanced and spun the shield in time to cover himself, presenting no gap to be exploited. But instead of raising the mace to its full height again, Rhys swung on the pivot of his body, slashing up and across Jamie's guard in a roundhouse strike aimed at his helmet encased head. Had it landed it would have concussed him at the very the least. With his visor up, Jamie saw the blow coming and ducked, but again found himself facing the covering shield.

Rhys let the strike come around under its own momentum, driving the shield forward as a buffer, ready to bring the mace down again in a powerful overhead blow. But this time Jamie was ready to use the advantage of his longsword. He knew that Rhys would have to swing his shield back and across to allow the planned strike, and at that point it would do what every axe and mace wielder feared – expose the upper arm and armpit. Rhys had mail and cuirass, but wore no revebrace or gardbrace. He was protected only by mail and an arming jacket beneath. Jamie seized the moment, timing it perfectly. As the shield swung to the left and just before the mace struck, he drove his sword point upwards, aiming for and finding the line between the bicep and tricep. Such was the force and keenness of the tip that the sword drove through the mail straight into the upper arm, destroying the muscle and nerve points there. The effect was spectacular and instantaneous.

Rhys yelled, dropping his arm and the mace in mid-flight as his nerves failed, causing paralysis of the arm and leaving him writhing and keening on the floor.

Jamie stood dispassionately, knowing exactly what he had done. The battle was won, and the combatants stood watching in awe: three moves and the champion of the Welsh knelt wailing and cursing in agony before Jamie.

"I claim victory. Yield to me," Jamie commanded. Rhys Ddu looked up with hatred in his eyes, cursing in Welsh. Jamie shrugged. It was just battle to him, and he had played his part saving the kingdom from another tripartite uprising that could have dethroned the king. Yet he was sad to see such a brave warrior go down, and glad that he had refrained from killing him – although he feared that Rhys would face a worse fate at the mercy of his captors.

From the circle of warriors a knight in full armour bearing the arms of Sir Richard Grey rode up to him. His visor was up, and Jamie saw a strong face with stern lines etched around the mouth, yet the eyes were fair and bore no harshness and when he spoke it was with a cultured voice of the court.

"We give our thanks to you, for I presume you are James de Grispere, of whom I have heard much?"

"Aye that I am, my lord, and I assume that I have the honour of addressing Sir Richard Grey." Jamie bowed to the knight.

"It is a fine day's work you have done here James, and well met, for we would have been taken by surprise if your man had not alerted us to the coming attack."

"Thank you my lord, I trust Cristoforo is well?"

Before Sir Richard could answer, a scream of anger was heard from up on the hill, where Owen ap Glyndower, prince of the Welsh, had seen his last chance at victory shattered.

Chapter Fifty-Five

Owen ap Glyndower looked with joy at the advancing forces and then frowned with puzzlement as the vanguard, led seemingly by Jamie, charged towards the castle gates that remained open. Something was amiss, he knew, then a storm of arrows began to rain down upon his army and he knew he was betrayed. He watched as three conrois of knights in full armour issued forth from the gates and began a charge. The slaughter that followed was sickening to his eyes, and when at length he saw the single combat of Jamie and Rhys Ddu, he knew he was lost and betrayed and cried out loudly in his anguish.

Mark looked on in awe, for he had not been told what was planned for fear that Amwen would betray them. Inside he cheered, then looked up to meet the eyes of Glyndower, seeing them dark with anger.

Glyndower pointed at Mark. "Kill him!" he called in Welsh to his Teulu. Amwen, hearing the command, pulled back a pace, unclasping his arm which she had been holding in excitement. One of Glydower's knights withdrew his sword and urged his horse forward two paces in order to strike Mark down.

True to his word, Mark proved he was perfectly schooled for one-on-one combat. The knight saw that Mark's sword was still scabbarded and thought he had an easy prey. Mark moved swiftly, belying his size, and drove his quarterstaff upwards single-handed into the neck of his assailant, who was lifted from his saddle and flung to the ground.

At this, Glyndower himself drew a sword and swung forward, followed by two more of his guard. Mark grasped the quarter staff with both hands and struck the nose of Glyndower's horse as he approached. The terrified animal cried in pain, rearing and turning away. The two knights came at him from opposite sides, shields up and swords raised to kill. *So be it,* Mark thought, *but I'll take one of you with me.* As they came within striking distance he chose the left hand man to take, hoping to pull him in as a shield.

Then there was a sudden twang from the copse just behind them and the whistle of air, followed by a thud as a quarrel protruded from the forehead of the guard to his right. The knight fell backwards out of the saddle, killed instantly. The other knight halted and Mark shot one end of the quarterstaff into his stomach then up under his jaw, knocking him out cold. He whirled to face an attack from the two remaining knights, but it didn't come.

A familiar voice called out in alarm. "Marco, look out!"

Mark turned to see Amwen pull a knife from her belt and lunge at him. The blow never arrived, for a grey flash of fur shot forward with no growl of warning, and teeth crunched against the knife-wielding forearm. Amwen screamed in agony as the bone snapped, crushed between Forest's jaws.

Mark looked on in amazement. "Amwen! Why?"

The features that he once thought pretty were now creased

in bitterness, torn with anger and malice. "My husband was killed by you Sais, and now you betray us here," she screeched. "A curse on you bastard whoresons."

"But I thought he died of a flux, not in battle?"

"All you know," she screamed and freed from Forest's jaws, she ran to where Glyndower and his remaining teulu waited, fretting to be away before they could be captured. She was pulled up roughly behind the surviving knight and his horse bounded away, arrows driving into the earth at full range, launched from war bows in the field below.

Mark stood as though in a trance, not believing his eyes as he was heralded by his saviour. "*Marco, amico mio.*"

A smiling Cristoforo emerged from the nearby copse, his crossbow resting insouciantly on his shoulder, a cocky swagger to his gait and a smile upon his handsome face.

"Cristo. You! It was you, by the Lord God. I'm right glad you were there. I thought my head to be forfeit when that second bugger set to with his sword." he then paused as Cristoforo drew near. "Cristo, I'm right sorry for losing my temper over Amwen. She has proved that I was wrong."

"*Di nulla. Mia culpa.* We had to do it, and it is I who must ask forgiveness for testing you. I'm very lucky not to be wearing a lump on my head from your staff for vexing you so. Jamie and I did not trust Amwen – rightly so by all accounts, for she seemed against our cause and indeed spoke English better than me."

Mark clapped Cristoforo on the shoulder then embraced him in a bear hug. They stood watching the departing prince and his meiny, with the slight figure of a woman clinging to the back of the knight.

"A lump on your head? I could've taken your head off at the shoulders," Mark muttered good-naturedly.

"You'd never have got near me," Cristoforo replied.

"We'll settle that when we get ourselves back to Lunnon," Mark grinned. "But I fear my naivety is to blame, for I thought her true and knew not that she spoke English so well." He turned and looked down. "And you, my girl, shall have an extra bone tonight, for you saved my life and no mistake," he laughed, ruffling Forest's ears.

"Well met, *cane di foresta*, maybe there is something in having a hound about after all." Cristoforo said. Just then the ground reverberated to a thunder of hooves as a party of knights drew closer, cantering up the hill. In the lead was a huge chestnut stallion that snorted as he approached. Forest crept behind Mark as Richard slid to a halt at the touch of his reins, cutting the turf with his rear hooves.

"Cristo! Mark! You're safe, praise God. By the Lord I thought the fiends of hell were after you when I heard that scream."

"Aye, you're not far wrong, but it were just one fiend and she's long gone and good riddans to 'er. Jamie I'm right sorry, I saw nought but what my heart told me, and I was a fool."

"Fie man, never. You were ever true and straight as always, and if a man's heart was never strained by a wench then he'd be no man to love. Come, we are all reunited again and it is I who must apologise for playing the part of a knave and using Cristo so, to cause you pain."

As if to seal the pact Forest bounced up, now sure that it was her master hiding within this suit of metal. This time he was ready, and the plate armour saved him from the usual cresting of her paws. Her voice made a rising bark that became a howl before finishing as a rumble deep in her chest.

"Ho girl, 'tis good to see you as well."

At which the leader of the knightly conroi dismounted and came forward, his visor raised. He was the man who had led the earlier charge from the castle and bore the bars of silver and blue across his tabard. Dismounted, he appeared nearly as tall as Jamie.

"I have the honour to introduce Sir Richard Grey," Jamie said. "I believe you have met Cristoforo Corio lately of Florence, and this Hercules is Mark of Cornwall."

"Well met one and all, and I'm right glad to make your acquaintance, Mark of Cornwall, for it has been a good day's work here that you have all played a vital part in, and one that will ensure the safety of the realm. My only displeasure is that we did not capture that whelp Glyndower. He has the luck of the Devil. Not for nought is he named the Magician. For once again he disappears seemingly in a puff of smoke. He will be a hunted man again, for his cause is lost forever and he will never find the following he once had. Forsooth we have his best captains below, captured and imprisoned and bound for London."

"Aye that is fair," Jamie agreed. "Scudamore, Tudor and of course Black Rhys, all for the Tower and trial, and as pretty a trio of scullions ever to grace the gallows or the block, I shouldn't wonder." Jamie looked down the slope to his vanquished foe, a slightly whimsical look upon his face. Black Rhys no longer looked the indomitable figure he once had. Instead he was a broken man, sacrificed upon the ambition of an aging self-styled prince.

Chapter Fifty-Six

London

"Have you heard any rumour as to the fate of Cristoforo?" Alice begged of Contessa Alessandria as they walked through the cloistered gardens within the palace grounds. The full heat of the August sun raised the temperature to stifling and unbearable levels within the court, yet a gentle breeze and shade from the veranda gave some relief to the Indian summer that was prevailing in London in early September.

Alessandria smiled at her companion: "And for that am I to read news of Jamie, perchance? My dear, you are an open page to be read at will," she chided her gently.

"Is it so obvious? Forsooth I will be undone, for I have missed him more than I supposed and I wear my heart upon my sleeve. Yet is there any news of our cause?"

"All that I have gleaned is that there was a battle of sorts involving the Welsh rebels and English forces led by Baron Sir Richard Grey. No more can I ascertain. As always, rumours fly faster than arrows yet none make their mark with any degree of accuracy. We must await the return of those they say have been captured and Sir Richard's meiny to court."

"Yet you are so calm. I fear for Jamie, and the charge of Lollardy that lies upon his head vexes me so. I cannot claim continued acquaintance or ask after him for fear of retribution against my name. Jamie warned me of such, yet 'tis a hard road to follow."

"Amen to that, and I fear too for Cristoforo, for he moves amongst shadows and fears the light that it should shine upon him too brightly and expose him so."

Alice frowned at this, for she did not know the whole of Cristoforo's story and was about to question further when a familiar visage made to pass them.

"My ladies," a courtly figure bowed as he passed through the cloisters, ambling slowly in the heat.

"Insufferable knave," Alessandria muttered when Jacques de Berry passed.

"You know something ill of him?" Alice asked. "For I hear he is most civil and charming, with a becoming manner."

"Him? I would as soon eat a rat than have him pay court to me. For he is a duplicitous toad, changing his colours and plumage to suit his needs."

"Verily? Pray, tell me," Alice beseeched Alessandria, to which the Contessa explained the whole story of his part in their adventures in France.

"I had not realised the whole story, for Jamie was as ever economical with his explanations. Now it all becomes clear, and the veil lifts for me," she answered, for the two ladies had become good friends since their introduction by the prince, and they had reached a mutual understanding and a shared love for the two men who sought the same quest: to quell any rebellion in Wales.

"Is there any news, father?" Jeanette asked, not for the first time, anxious of her brother's fate.

Thomas de Grispere sighed, looked up from his papers and then stood to obtain some respite from the heat and take advantage of the gentle breeze that blew in through the open casement. "My child, as I have told you one thousand times this past week," he gently chided, "you will be the first I notify of any intelligence. Rest easy, for the news I have heard is that the rebellion has been put down, and Sir Richard Grey was victorious in his efforts."

"Yes, but there is nought of Jamie, and the charge of Lollardy still hangs over him. Rumours fly abroad and I cannot sleep for my concern. You have declared yourself that it has caused you worry, that those within the guild are apt to scorn you by association."

"I am aware, my dear, yet once all has been explained Jamie – and we by association – shall be assoiled of all inference to that heinous belief. It was, as you are aware, a necessary instrument to keep him safe ere he ventured forth, and a fiat from the prince that could not be ignored. But by the same token it can be undone as easily in the prince's name. So be not afeard, all will be well," he assured her, patting her shoulder gently.

"Aye that it will, for the scoundrel is sure to be nothing but a sely dote," a voice floated in from the doorway in answer to their prayers.

Jeanette span around: "Jamie!" She ran towards him, ready to embrace her brother – yet halted a pace from his arms at the sight of the creature that appeared growling at his side.

"Down. Forest, 'tis alright. Sit girl, for she is my sister and is not a threat."

The faithful hound looked up at her master uncertainly, feeling admonished yet not understanding, waiting for further assurance.

"What fell creature is that?" Jeanette asked in horror, for Forest had grown and looked as wild and unkempt as the Welsh woodland from which she had emerged.

"Ah that is a long story, now come and embrace me for it has been too long ere I saw you last."

Tentatively, with a wary eye on the wolfhound she did as she was bidden, enveloping him in a fierce hug before breaking the embrace to look down into the wary eyes of the dog.

"Oh Jamie, you rogue. You must tell me all."

"My boy, it is good to see you, and it cheers my heart no end," Thomas moved forward to embrace his son. He saw a weariness in Jamie's face and fatigue from the long journey home and weeks of playing the role of traitor, aware at any time that his life could be forfeit for a tiny slip. These things took a toll on a man. "Come, sit and I'll arrange refreshment for you. Tell us all that you can, for we have heard fragments of news and gossip, yet none that would avail us of the whole story. I'll fetch John, for he would lief as not hear the whole and learn of all that has passed, and I'm sure you would not like to tell the story twice."

Thomas strode out, a smile on his face, delighted and relieved at his son's return. He almost bumped into Cristoforo, who was silently moving along the hall making his way to Thomas' private rooms to join Jamie.

"Cristoforo, you have returned too. I'm blessed, for it makes my heart glad to see you. Thank you for watching over James, as I'm sure that you will have ensured his safe deliverance."

"Not I, for he is a man grown and keeps his own counsel,

and he has proved himself a master of subterfuge. It is we who owe him, for he kept us alive."

"Well met, Cristoforo, yet I believe it not at all. We will judge when the story be told. Pray join us now."

"As you wish, Master Thomas."

"And the Cornish wrestler – Mark, I believe was his name. Is he safely returned among you?"

"Indeed he is. He has returned to the friary to make his peace with God and the abbot."

With the company assembled, the story of their adventures was told in full. John and his father had questions where Jamie glossed over certain details.

"You have served England well, lad. By God's grace you will be rewarded ere the prince hears all," John commented.

"I care not directly for reward, yet to be accounted one of the prince's men would be a long-held ambition. That and an England that is safe from traitors, by God's grace. On the morrow I needs must attend Sir Richard and give him my report of all that has occurred. Yet now I should like to wash, to sleep for a hundred years, dozing in the shade of the garden and know that I am home and safe, for I am weary and only now can I truly be at peace for the first time in many weeks."

With that he excused himself and went to attend to his ablutions and a hammock in which to doze.

Cristoforo too made his apologies. "Master Thomas, forgive me, yet I would be excused for I have to attend to a certain assignation..." he let the words hang.

Thomas hid a smile. "So soon? When did you make such arrangements, for you are just lately returned?"

"Forgive me, yet I made a long standing promise to a certain Contessa, where upon my return I should attend her forthwith." With that he bowed very graciously and slipped away to wash and change.

Chapter Fifty-Seven

The following morning Jamie attended Sir Richard Whittington in his offices and gave a full account of all that had occurred from leaving London weeks before.

"I'll not deny that we were concerned for your chances of success. You have given a fine account of yourself James, for I lost two *insidiores* afore you took that task. They were good men, yet probably lie rotting somewhere in shallow Welsh graves. The prince has received an account from Sir Richard Grey and considers your task most excellently performed by all accounts. Now, what reward would you have?" He asked, seeking the true measure of the young esquire.

"I am beholden to my companions, for without them I would not have been able to achieve the outcome that we did. Whatever reward is forthcoming, they too should share the spoils in some manner."

"Nobly said, James, yet what are your ambitions for yourself in this regard? Come man, speak freely, for the court and indeed the king are greatly in your debt."

Jamie did not flinch, and spoke his mind. "I should like

above all things to be part of the prince's household," he offered boldly.

"Fie, should you? Yet to achieve that aim you needs must be knighted. So 'tis fortunate that the prince has offered to bring you to a ceremony on the Friday next, assoiling you of all Lollardy implication and investing you into the knighthood by his own hand. This ceremony is to be held in the Great Hall of the Palace with all as witness. This will exonerate you in all respects and such an act will give credence of your status and esteem to the prince."

"By the rood, you do not jest with me?" Jamie exclaimed. "For above all to be knighted by the prince is indeed the greatest honour."

"Aye, and it makes my trials ten times harder, for 'tis a double-edged sword. More will know of your name and fame. I shall endeavour to keep your full part in this affair closer to me than others, for I doubt not that I shall have use for you again in other matters, and will have to choose with care what ventures I send you upon that you be not known abroad as my man, merely as a knight of the prince or a merchant in your father's employ. If my manner seems harsh, it is not meant to be so, for I wish you well and you have earned your reward. On the week hence you shall be Sir James de Grispere, a knight – and my spy," he finished softly.

Jamie's mind was in a whirl: *Sir James de Grispere, to be knighted by the future King of England.* Whittington broke in on his thoughts "What will you choose for your coat of arms? For you must give that thought and have it registered on the lists."

"Sir Richard, I am most indebted to you and I am lost for words."

"I doubt that be case, and indebted you are I and the realm shall have need of you again for sure. Now, go and attend the

Chamberlain of the Household, who will make arrangements for the investiture."

Jamie thanked Whittington again and left his chambers as excited as he had ever been. Sir Richard, for his part, gave a tight lipped grin and thought out loud; "Go with God, lad, for a knight you may be, yet you are my man now, to go as I bid."

In Prince Henry's private solar another audience was being held, with Sir Richard Grey in attendance upon his Royal Highness.

"Gentlemen, we are most grateful to you for attending us thus, and more so for the service that you have done us abroad and in Wales."

Mark and Cristoforo bowed their heads in acknowledgement of the praise.

"We know to our cost in earlier times what a complex and challenging place Wales can be. For this alone you have our sincerest gratitude, for the rebellion was thwarted ere it began and that whoreson Glyndower put to flight back to his forests with a much depleted force. Upon this we were vexed as to how to reward you both in recognition of your bravery. We cannot knight you as we shall for James – yes, your comrade in arms is to be raised to the knighthood. Yet keep our secret ere it be formally announced, we beg of you. For yourselves, a grateful prince must resort to the coin of his realm, and we trust that you will accept such in the manner of its granting. We would also ask, Mark, that you serve us as a personal member of my household under the good offices of Sir Richard who will instruct you thus. To you, Cristoforo, we can do no more, yet believe that you are employed by Thomas de Grispere in his household?"

"As your Royal Highness says, my prince," Cristoforo answered gracefully.

"Good. Most excellent. Well go to and serve me well, for we are sure that we will have need of you again as the kingdom has need of loyal and trusted men in these turbulent times."

At which Sir Richard Grey passed each man a full purse of coin as directed by the prince. The two men bowed three times and left the solar. Once the door had shut, they looked at each other in amazement, grins writ large upon their faces.

"I may not be the Earl of Cornwall, but I feel as rich as an earl. By God, Cristo, 'tis more money than our family ever saw."

"Aye Mark, and what shall you do with it? I shall send much back to my family by way of our Italian bankers."

"I know not, but t'would be right pleasing to buy my own house. Many are built now outside the walls in new areas and it would serve better than lodging with the other wrestlers in the friary. I shall think on't."

Chapter Fifty-Eight

As if in a trance, Jamie left the palace and clenched his fist as though in victory: *A knight, by the rood! I can now face Alice and court her as an equal*, was one of his first thoughts. He wondered if she might be in court at such an early hour, and thought it unlikely. She would still be at her father's house. He vowed to call there on his ride home.

Alice had mentioned a house in La Straunde that her father owned and where she and her family resided when they were in London. He recalled the bluff figure of Sir Andrew Bloor, Baron of Macclesfield, a strong knight of dark countenance and dour manner. Jamie had pondered upon how he had managed to sire such a fair and beautiful daughter as he rode through the crowded streets, weaving around carts, hawkers and ragamuffin children playing or begging, earning curses from those on foot.

He asked a well-dressed merchant leaving his front door if he might know the residence of Baron Macclesfield, and was pointed in the direction of a house a few dwellings along the street. Many of the properties were of only recent construction as the sprawling city of London had burst its walls to accommodate the newly rich, who sought residences within reach of the City and Westminster Palace. The properties here were of brickwork to lower elevations and the use of glass in the casement openings gave a good indication of the class of people who resided here.

The house was sturdily constructed and in many ways not dissimilar to his own father's home. Yet there we no rear quarters or places for industry, there was just a separate entrance through double doors that led to a stable block behind. Jamie dismounted and knocked loudly upon the large oaken door. He waited expectantly, although his nerves began to fray as the seconds ticked by. *I'd rather be facing a conroi of knights than this,* he thought, and almost turned and fled before the door was opened. He heard the bar latch being raised within and resolved to hold firm to his quest.

"Yes? Good morrow sir." A portly man addressed him. He had a discerning look about him that was intended to induce inferiority in the recipient of his stare. His gaze swept Jamie from head to foot, taking in the elegance of the clothes and the quality of horse held lightly in his hands. It was still too dangerous to the general public for Jamie to ride Richard through crowded streets, and Killarney stood patiently at his command.

"Good morrow to you also, sir," Jamie answered. "I come to enquire if I have the right house for Baron Macclesfield?"

"You do," was the stern answer, an eyebrow arched in a questioning manner.

"Verily then I am fortunate, for I seek the company of Lady Alice with whom I am acquainted. Is she within that I may attend upon her?"

"I shall see if she may be disposed to receive your addresses. What is your name?"

"I am James de Grispere of the Royal Court and St. Lawrence Lane in the Jewry."

At the mention of his name the steward took a sharp intake of breath and widened his eyes. "Wait here," he said, and with that the door was bolted against him once more.

Jamie was startled at the response and wondered what could have caused the steward's displeasure. Minutes later the door was once more un-barred and there on the threshold was Sir Andrew Bloor himself.

"You are James de Grispere? Am I rightly informed?"

"I am sir, at your service. I have of course seen you at court, yet we have never been formally introduced."

"Nor shall we be, you scoundrel. You, a follower of Lollardy, would call upon my daughter for your presumption? If you were a knight I would challenge you. Get you gone, impudent malapert, and do not have any further designs upon my daughter, for I will have no blasphemy associated with my estate or my name." With that the door was slammed shut and Jamie stood dumfounded upon the doorstep, his emotions a mixture of anger and sadness.

"By the rood," he muttered, "this must be remedied for I cannot be thought of thus."

With a heavy heart he remounted and rode back to his father's house, the news of his glad tidings dulled by his recent encounter. The journey was without incident and all thoughts were focused upon his state and how he might resolve his acquaintance with Lady Alice.

He paused as he dismounted in the courtyard behind his father's house, gathering his thoughts. No, he would not be defeated, and he had every reason to be hopeful that this would not darken his thoughts he resolved. With this he handed Killarney to a groom and marched into the house determined to be joyful.

"Father? Jeanette?" he called loudly, "Where are you all? For I have news of great import."

They emerged from Thomas's private solar, curious as to his enthusiastic summons. John too heard Jamie's call and came in from the hall.

"I am lately from the palace and in audience with Sir Richard Whittington who was very pleased with all that we had achieved in Wales. So much so that I am to be rewarded. Father, I am to be knighted by the prince himself on Friday, in recognition of my efforts both in Wales and in France," he enthused.

"By the good Lord," his father cried, embracing his son. "Sir James de Grispere. I am so very proud of you my boy."

"Well done lad," John cheered, "t'was richly deserved – and do not forget that they owe you a great deal."

"They owe me one thing above all else, father. Part of my disguise ere I joined the Welsh was, as you know, to be dismissed from the court and accused of Lollard sympathies. Rumour has spread its wings wide and I appear damaged with the taint of it. I have lately returned from the house of Baron Macclesfield, where my suit for his daughter was rudely rebuffed for just such a reason. I pray that the prince assoils me of all such charges when I receive the accolade, and I am mortally sorry if my activities have harmed your reputation, father."

"Think naught of it my son, for the Guild will tolerate me still as one of their aldermen, and Whittington as head of the Guild holds more sway than a tribe of gossips." Thomas declared.

Jeanette came up and hugged him, joyful for her brother, looking up to him: "Well Sir James – is that how I must address you now?" she teased, and for a fleeting moment a look of concern crossed her face for his plight and the words that had been said against him. It was gone in an instant and replaced with a smile. Thomas called for a bottle of his best wine to be opened in celebration of Jamie's new status.

"Where is Cristoforo, for I should like to be the first to inform him of my good fortune?"

Jeanette sported a saucy smile and declared coquettishly. "He is seeking rewards of his own and paying court to the Contessa, I believe." The comment earned her a rebuke from her father.

"Ah, that is well, for I understand from Sir Richard that both he and Mark have been rewarded in coin."

"That is good news, for their circumstances would prevent advancement to the knighthood," his father declared. "Tell me, you say that the accolade will take place on Friday next? Why, needs must that we provide a crest of arms to your design, Jamie. Have you given any thought to this?"

"I have father, I should like a *per saltire argent* and *gules* with a horse's head blazoned proper. For Richard saved me in the clash with Black Rhys and is worth his weight in gold," Jamie said.

Later that evening as the family made to retire, Jeanette caught up with Jamie as he made to enter his bedroom. "Jamie, pray spare me a moment ere you sleep."

"Yes sister – yet expect no sage counsel, for my head spins with wine," he warned with a grin.

"Fie on you, rogue, I need no counsel, and you cannot fool me for I believe it is you who needs such," she offered gently. "I know you too well, brother mine, what ails you? For you are happy, but I detect a cloud upon your visage."

Jamie sighed in resignation: "I cannot fool you, sister, for you speak the truth. Come, sit with me and I shall explain." He dropped to a settle on the landing by his door and clasped her hand in his calloused palm.

Jeanette listened in earnest, considering his problems with

regard to Lady Alice. When at last he finished, she comforted him and promised that all would be well. She continued, "I strongly believe that Alice was not made aware of your visit, knowing how jealous fathers may be of their daughter's virtue. Of Lollardy, father has suffered, as the seeds of insurrection were well sown for your protection. The guild and other merchants have become colder of late, and Whittington has remained unable to refute the rumours publicly until your safe return. Father is proud and will not admit such a thing as he knows it will sully the rightful pride you have taken in your achievements, yet the charge of Lollardy has damaged our reputation here, if not abroad. I pray that Prince Henry makes a strong public disavowal and removes all suspicion in that regard when he bestows on you the accolade."

Jamie picked up on their father's plight. "I am filled with remorse that Father has suffered, yet all will be well ere the prince assoils me publicly."

"The gossip is rife amongst the women as much as the men, brother," Jeanette said. "I have become friends with Cristoforo's Contessa and we will begin to counter any ill rumour as soon as we can – starting on the morrow."

They bade each other goodnight, brother and sister both set in their courses with renewed determination.

Chapter Fifty-Nine

"So, my peacock, you return with feathers un-plucked and a struthian gait. Have you been servicing the Welsh wenches whilst you were away? Fie on you for not attending to me yester eve."

"My lady Contessa Alessandria, I beg your forgiveness, but I did indeed call upon you yester eve. I was told that you were resting and not to be disturbed. My heart was broken at such news, and here I am today hoping to have it mended by your compassion. Yet I find more hostility here than I didst receive in Godforsaken *Galles.*"

"Verily? You did attend my uncle's house?"

"I did my lady, to no avail."

"Who turned you away?" she asked angrily.

"I believe it was your uncle's steward, a tall man of middle years who was overly superior in manner. I could of course have dealt with him in less than a moment, but I feared it would harm my suit."

Alessandria laughed at this, but then scowled. "By the rood I shall have words, for you must be made welcome there and your presence made known to me." She softened. "Yet you came, and stayed faithful to my suit. Cristoforo, in faith I'm right glad that you have returned," she replied switching to Italian.

"To have such a smile bestowed upon me is reward enough."

"Fie, for there he is once more – my peacock, his feathers bright and compliments silky upon his tongue. Now tell me all, for I would wish to know the whole of it." They faced each other, seated on a wooden bench within an arbour, their lips only inches apart, their eyes burning in intensity. Cristoforo whispered "*Amore,*" and stole a kiss from her lips.

What had been intended as a chaste kiss was enhanced by Alessandria, who pulled him close in a passionate embrace that heightened his senses and drove him wild. He felt unable to breathe, and concealed within the arbour of a rose garden they broke breathless, gazing aghast, locked in each other's arms, a fire ignited between them.

Chapter Sixty

Preparations over the next three days were rushed, and everyone in the de Grispere household was made aware of the great honour that was about to be bestowed upon Jamie – and by extension the whole family. New clothes were ordered and fitted for the occasion and the arms were registered in the lists.

The following Friday morning the great hall of the Royal Palace was filled with the full court in time for Jamie's investiture. Jamie had spent the night in prayer preparing for the occasion. Three esquires were also to be given the accolade that day, all of them in their twenties, a few years older than Jamie. The knighting ceremony always drew a large crowd of courtiers, keen to see who was in favour. Loyalty was as always, a question of perception – never more so than now, with the prince as heir apparent presiding over all in the name of the Council.

The de Grispere family and John were admitted for the ceremony, and stood proudly in the front on the left aisle as Jamie moved down towards the prince.

Fine tapestries and gilded hangings decorated the hall, with a huge azure embroidered damascene silk screen inlaid with gold fleurs de lys and lions rampant behind the carved chair in which the prince sat. Minstrels played softly as the ceremony progressed. Too nervous to look anywhere but forward, Jamie failed to notice the many friends who had come to support him, including Kit, Mark and Cristoforo, who stood with Sir Richard Whittington and Sir Richard Grey. Looking up he saw Prince Henry seated on the formal wooden settle before him. He was clad in white silk hose with pale blue shoes. A midnight blue tunic showed beneath the formal cowl of pale mauve, trimmed with ermine. Around his neck was his chain of office. He looked severe in repose, yet did Jamie imagine it, or did a smile tug at the corners of his mouth?

At length Jamie reached the knighting-stool, feeling as though he had run a mile in full armour. He bowed three times as custom dictated and then knelt on one knee before the prince.

Henry stood to his full height, dwarfing those around him, and moved forward down the three steps to the stone flagged floor. The company fell silent in expectation. The prince called out in a clear and resounding voice that all could hear. "My lords and ladies, today is a special day, and we owe James de Grispere a great debt for the service that he has rendered our court and our country. Against great odds and suffering, not least to his reputation that was falsely impugned, he delivered for us more than we could expect in extraordinary circumstances. In recognition of the debt owed by us, today we raise him to the ranks of knighthood by this accolade."

With that the prince drew his sword, tapping Jamie first on his right shoulder, then flipping the blade over to his left. "I name you Sir James de Grispere, may you serve us well. Here is your coat of arms, wear it well and honourably. My lords and ladies, the man you see before you, and his family by association, have been tainted by accusations of Lollardy. I refute those accusations in the name of the royal house, I demand in the king's name that they never be repeated, and to show my full and complete trust in my newest knight I invite you, Sir James, to join my household as one of my knights."

Jamie had not been privy to that final piece of information, and the blood coursed through his veins, thudding in his ears as though in the heat of battle. *A household knight, by the rood, and fully assoiled of any stain upon my character for Lollardy announced in front of the whole court.*

He rose, looking his prince in the eye. The prince returned Jamie's look with a small smile of gratitude. Jamie rose from the stool and bowed again before walking backwards from the royal presence before finally turning to face the court. There were smiles all around and he saw among the crowd a beautiful woman with cornflower blue eyes and golden hair. No smile was more radiant than that of Lady Alice.

By October of the year the heat had finally left the city and Autumn was starting to cast her golden spell. The sweet smell of dewy mornings and showers on warm earth pervaded the air, offering a welcome respite from the ripe heat of summer. For Jamie, the route he took drew him towards a most unwelcome odour – the rank smell of gaols. Close by the bank of the Thames, the Tower of London served as the city's main prison, and within its walls lay terror and torment. Hope was lost here in sentences to isolation and melancholy.

"Why do you venture here?" Cristoforo asked, uncertain as to why Jamie should make such a journey, yet determined to accompany his friend on what was obviously a disagreeable task.

"In truth I know not, yet it is something that must be done upon my honour."

Cristoforo had some inkling of the meaning behind Jamie's words, yet to him an enemy was just that: Someone who must be conquered in order to move forward in life. He surmised that the English were different.

The road sloped down to the Tower's entrance, where he was stopped by the castle guards, who beckoned him to dismount and leave his weapons with his companion. He passed his sword to Cristoforo and spoke to the sergeant-at-arms. "I have written to the Constable," he said, "and here is his reply, giving me a pass to visit a prisoner within."

The seal was broken by the sergeant and with a scowl Jamie was admitted in the company of a man-at-arms. The soldier offered no conversation, but beckoned Jamie to follow him through the grounds to a maze of passages that went deeper into the bowels of the Tower. As they dropped down into the lower areas of the prison, the stench became foul and rancid, reeking of old fish, rot and excrement. The air was fetid to breathe, and Jamie raised his cowl to his nose. Rats scuttled about his feet and pitiful cries came from the cells they passed. At last the guard stopped at a corner and produced a key to a heavy wooden door braced with iron belts.

"Prisoner, someone to see 'ee." The guard called.

Keys rattled and the lock squeaked open, then the door was pushed inwards on rusty hinges that protested at the movement. The stench inside was worse. The cell was gloomy, lit only by a narrow window set high up in the wall. Dirty straw lay on the floor, a wooden cot was set against one wall. A figure sat upon it, haggard in defeat. The black hair was matted and the once fierce beard was now unkempt and streaked with grey.

"Rhys? It is James de Grispere."

"What?" called a hoarse voice. "What do you do here, come

to gloat? For by God's legs you'll not find me accommodating there."

"Gloat? No, I came to see you with no other intention than to make peace, yet I know not why."

"Peace is it? Too late there, mun. Yet I hear that you profit from my early demise, for 'tis *Sir* James now, I'm bound." Rhys sneered.

"I do not profit from you, for we fought fairly in good honour and that is as it should be."

"You? You talk of honour? You sold your honour when you betrayed us on the field of battle. You came to us and we took you in good faith, yet you embraced our pride and honour and stole it from us like a thief in the night."

"You wouldst believe that? I came to you for sure, after the killing of my kinsmen and the robbing of English farms, as well as insurgence against my king and my realm. I faced you in chivalry and yet you talk of false honour. If any has betrayed your honour it is a false prince who misled you and sacrificed your honour on the anvil of his ambition. And to what end? To permit him to roam at will while you, his brave captain, will fall to the executioner's axe. Yet I come here to salute you as a brave and worthy knight in good grace."

Black Rhys was silent then spoke: "How old are you, lad?"

"Nine and ten years. Why?"

"You carry yourself well for such youth, both in skill at arms and in noble grace. You will do well in this world. Yet I caution you, beware those who would use you for their own means. Your one weakness is that you are too young to know these things, but nothing in power is as it seems. Now we're done, so leave, and say a prayer for me on the morrow ere I depart this world and meet my maker."

With that Black Rhys turned away, and Jamie left the foul

cell. Once the door was locked he followed the guard, eager to be back in daylight and fresh air.

"Did the traitor say aught?" asked the guard at the gate as he passed.

"No, nothing of import," Jamie replied, not wishing to be drawn. He found the lounging figure of Cristoforo waiting for him, concern on his face.

"Tis done, and my conscience and honour are clear."

"*Va bene.* Yet your conscience was ever thus, I believe. For Jamie, now you are a knight with chivalry and great honour."

"Am I? Aye I suppose I am that; a knight and a spy."

HISTORICAL NOTES

This is the first in a six book series that will take my characters through what Confucius would no doubt have referred to as interesting times to the year 1415. As with all my books, I have researched extensively before putting pen to paper – or fingers to keyboard, as the modern idiom dictates. This is my first historical novel, and I had to research not only the facts of the period, but also language, diet, arms and weaponry, medicine, horses, methods of fighting, towns, populations, and characters and how they interacted.

This was an extensive exercise and I am sure that I have made a mistake or two along the way which will no doubt be spotted by some keen eyed historian. For any such possible error I apologise in advance. However, I have tried to be as accurate as possible in all matters – especially regarding language and vocabulary. I checked every word to ensure that it was in existence and used in my time frame. I did allow a few words to filter back in time from the 16th century as it would have been difficult to manage otherwise. I have used the old spellings for certain words that would come into existence in their modern form – for example to parley, was then known as *parole,* so I have used the older form and spelling. Similarly, the word "connexion", which looks modern American, is in fact mediaeval English in its spelling.

Mediaeval foods and fashions are depicted here as they were used then, and I have also stayed true to courtly manners, attitudes and speech.

The Council that had just been formed in England at the time was as I describe it, with all the powers at its disposal and ruled by Prince Henry. He did fall out with his father and started to take control of everything as the king became sicker. The Royal finances and budget were of great concern to him, and there was a huge debate to this effect, with the wool revenues coming into dispute and much of the GDP of the time going to the defence of Calais.

The court was a nest of intrigue, with many spies cast in the role of everyday people. The spy network that was in place was indeed used by Sir Richard Whittington, who held the positions I have described – although I have had to invent and embellish certain aspects too, as there was not enough documented evidence to fill in the gaps. He was powerful figure, and time and again he played a pivotal role in all sorts of politics and financial dealings for both King Henry and Prince Henry.

Wrestling was a popular sport and played a significant role in courtly life. Prince Henry was a keen exponent and there was also a large wrestling contingent at court, so much so that the army that battled at Agincourt a few years later included the banner of a group of Cornish wrestlers who fought in its midst!

The French court was as I describe, dominated by an ever present battle between the Armagnac and the Burgundy dukedoms, with a council similar to that of England ruling as King Charles's grip on sanity became weaker. Coincidentally, both English and French kings were ailing, both countries had councils and both countries were ruled over by figureheads other than kings. In France, the Duke of Burgundy held sway at this point in time.

The incident at Saint-Omer cathedral actually happened, although no one knows for certain who started the fire that destroyed the cathedral and half the town – so why not Jamie and his friends? The siege engine did not become common knowledge for the simple reason that it was a secret. Its destruction was a pivotal point and did indeed prevent Calais falling to the French.

Cristoforo's character is imagined, yet there were Italian assassins at that time who were very good at what they did and put themselves up for hire. Their weapons of assassination included the miniature crossbow I describe.

The Scottish court is as I describe it, and was again ruled by someone other than the rightful king – strange days indeed. Talks were held between France and Scotland to start another uprising and emissaries were sent from the French court to co-ordinate a new war on three fronts: Scotland, Wales and France. Sir Jacques de Berry, however, is a fictional character.

Sir Robert de Umfraville was not fictional; he was a loyal friend of the king and Prince Henry and the Hammer of the Scots, who feared him and his name. He was based at Berwick-on-Tweed and led raids upon the Scots similar to the ambush at Peebles described at the beginning of the book. From there it was not too difficult a step to envisage him as a mentor to Jamie, with his Scottish ancestry.

The Prince of the Welsh, Owain ap Glyndower, was also a real figure and rebel to the English crown. Note that I have used the English spelling of his name in the text and where English people use his name. In the dialogue of Welsh characters I use his Welsh name, as would my characters. Glyndower really did meet with Scottish lords in the hope of bringing together Wales and Scotland in a final fight against the English, sponsored by the French. By 1410 his cause was all but lost and he was a hunted man. However, he wanted to reignite the flames of rebellion and made one last suicide raid on England in or around late August or early September of 1410 in the hope of reuniting his armies and bringing the Welsh back under his banner. I have researched everywhere but no one seems to know exactly where the raid took place other than it was on the border between Wales and England in the county of Shropshire. I chose Stokesay Castle for the site of this raid, which works well for a number of reasons. It is geographically correct, Jamie is likely to have visited there as it was owned by a famous wool merchant, it is not difficult to attack and it would form a good rallying point. Black Rhys, among others, was wounded and captured alive and sentenced to death for treason. He was hung, drawn and quartered along with Scudamore and Tudor.

Once again Glyndower, ever the magician, escaped. Little was heard of him again, although he did stay alive and will form part of a later story.

For the fight scenes, I have studied extensively the works of Fiore dei Liberi and Hans Talhoffer. I rehearsed all the scenes using my knowledge of fencing and martial arts. I also attended the School of Armoured Combat in Gloucester, where I fought with a real –though blunted – sword!

Finally, a note on horses. Killarney and Richard are real, although sadly Killarney is no longer with us. A picture of Richard can be seen on my website along with the coats of arms of the protagonists. Richard is an amazing High Goal polo pony who has played everywhere from USA to Spain and is exactly as I describe him. At 15' 3 he should have been too big to have played, and is now retired, but in his prime he could do everything I describe and was my son's best playing pony. He is a gelding now, but when he was a stallion he was fierce. Like his literary namesake he is afraid of blue off the polo field, and has also been clocked at over 44 mph! In all ways Richard is an awesome horse.

www.simonfairfax.com

A message from Simon:

I know that you have over a million choices of books to read. I can't tell you how much it means to me that you have made time to read one of my books.

I really hope that you enjoyed it and that you found it entertaining. If you did, I would appreciate a few more minutes of your time, if I may humbly ask for you to leave a review for other readers who may be trying to select their next reading material.

If for any reason you weren't satisfied with this book please do let me know by emailing me at simon@simonfairfax.com The satisfaction of my readers and feedback are important to me.

Best wishes,
Simon.

A Knight and a Spy 1411: Medieval series book 2

A PIRATE WAR, TRAITORS AT COURT, A SPY IN PERIL.

Sir James de Grispere and his two companions return in this second book, to fight courtly plots; pirates plundering the seas and a direct threat to the king's life. He has a choice to make and the wrong decision may well will cost him his life.

A Knight and a Spy 1411, is the second in the new 6 book medieval series by Simon Fairfax who is also author of the Deal series.

Acknowledgments

First of all my great thanks to my editor Perry Iles who helped so much in making my book come alive.

Unfortunately when researching a 15th century novel you can't just pop along and visit your local armourer or sword master. It requires extensive reading and research from better and more authoritative minds than mine. To this end and in an effort to fully understand the events and people of the period I read extensively, including Chris Given-Wilson's excellent book *HENRY IV* and Ian Mortimer's *THE FEARS OF HENRY IV.* Both give a brilliant insight to the events of the period. I would also recommend Ian Mortimer's *The time traveller's guide to medieval England* and I apologise if I have made any factual errors as a result. I would also mention Christopher Allmand's *HENRY V* which gave me such a fascinating view into this extraordinary King's life, events and personality.

I would also like to thank Professor Glen K. Johnson of Cardigan castle for help with Black Rhys and the Welsh history side.

I have studied martial arts for most of my life from teenage years onwards, including, Wing Chun, fencing and judo, all of which came into play for this novel as many of the throws and holds from judo are very similar to Cornish wrestling. Yet to add veracity, I attended the Armoured Combat Gloucester 'knight school' to wield a broad sword for real and see if everything I had written worked!

On sword fighting I also delved deeply into *The knightly art of battle by* Ken Mondeschien who explains the art as propounded by the brilliant Fiore dei Liberi. Also Hans Talhoffer's *Medieval combat in colour* and *Armourers* by Matthias Pfaffenbichler.

Finally my thanks to all the horses and particularly polo ponies- including Richard- who taught me so much.

Made in the USA
Las Vegas, NV
26 June 2022

50765679R00246